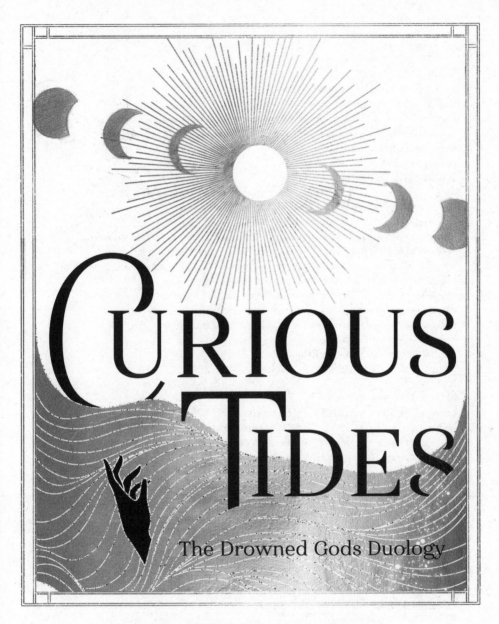

CURIOUS TIDES

The Drowned Gods Duology

PASCALE LACELLE

Margaret K. McElderry Books

New York London Toronto Sydney New Delhi

MARGARET K. McELDERRY BOOKS

An imprint of Simon & Schuster Children's Publishing Division

1230 Avenue of the Americas, New York, New York 10020

This book is a work of fiction. Any references to historical events, real people, or real places are used fictitiously. Other names, characters, places, and events are products of the author's imagination, and any resemblance to actual events or places or persons, living or dead, is entirely coincidental.

For information about special discounts for bulk purchases, please contact Simon & Schuster Special Sales at 1-866-506-1949 or business@simonandschuster.com.

The Simon & Schuster Speakers Bureau can bring authors to your live event. For more information or to book an event, contact the Simon & Schuster Speakers Bureau at 1-866-248-3049 or visit our website at www.simonspeakers.com.

Interior design by Irene Metaxatos

The text for this book was set in Haboro.

Manufactured in the United States of America

First Edition

10 9 8 7 6 5 4 3 2 1

Library of Congress Cataloging-in-Publication Data

Names: Lacelle, Pascale, author. Title: Curious tides / Pascale Lacelle. Description: First edition. | New York : Margaret K. McElderry Books, 2023. | Audience: Ages 14 up. | Audience: Grades 10-12. | Summary: Teen mage Emory must unravel the truth behind the secret society that may have been involved in her classmates' deaths. Identifiers: LCCN 2022061699 (print) | LCCN 2022061700 (ebook) | ISBN 9781665939270 (hardcover) | ISBN 9781665939294 (ebook) Subjects: CYAC: Ability–Fiction. | Magic–Fiction. | Secret societies–Fiction. | Drowning–Fiction. | Schools–Fiction. | Interpersonal relations–Fiction. | Fantasy. | BISAC: YOUNG ADULT FICTION / Fantasy / Dark Fantasy | YOUNG ADULT FICTION / Fantasy / Romance | LCGFT: Fantasy fiction. | Romance fiction. | Novels. Classification: LCC PZ7.1.L169 Cu 2023 (print) | LCC PZ7.1.L169 (ebook) | DDC [Fic]–dc23

LC record available at https://lccn.loc.gov/2022061699

LC ebook record available at https://lccn.loc.gov/2022061700

ISBN 9781665939270

ISBN 9781665939294 (ebook)

CONTENT WARNINGS: death, grief, branding/tattoos, body horror, mild panic attack, anxiety and depression, bloodletting, self-harm, alcohol, magical substance abuse, magical asylum/prison

THIS ONE, IF YOU'LL ALLOW ME A
MOMENT OF SELFISHNESS, IS FOR ME:

FOR THE TEENAGE ME WHO DARED
TO DREAM,

FOR THE TWENTY-YEAR-OLD ME
WHO ABANDONED HOPE,

FOR THE THIRTY-YEAR-OLD ME WHO
TRIED AGAIN–AND SOARED.

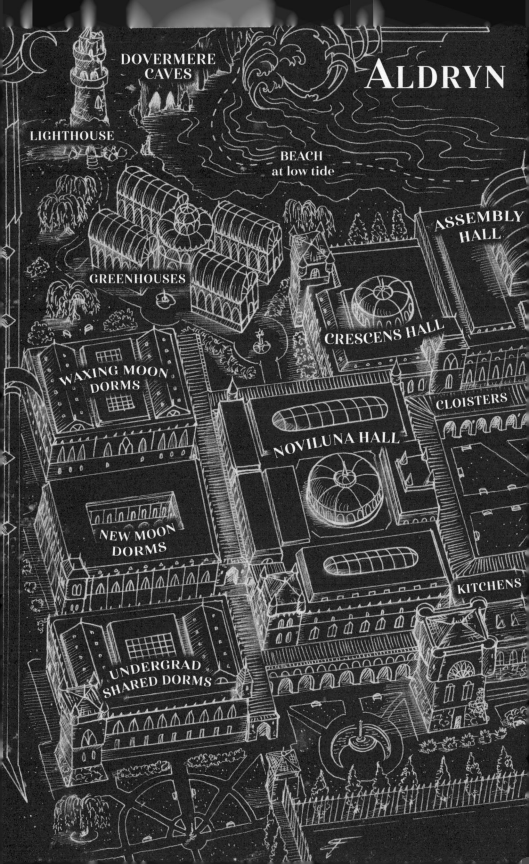

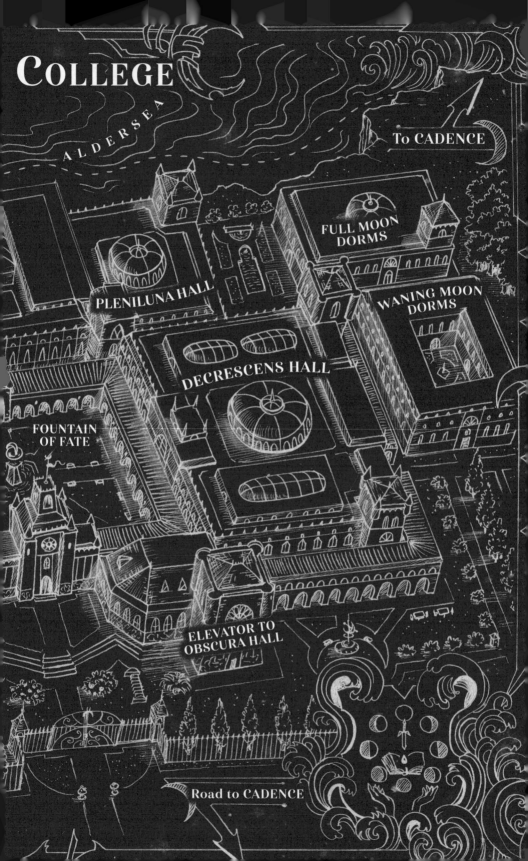

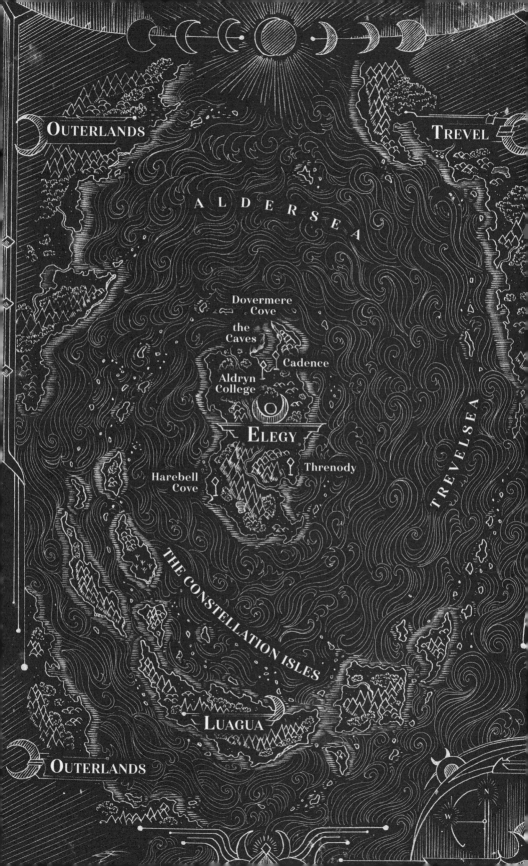

The Sacred Lunar Houses

& Their Tidal Alignments

HOUSE NEW MOON
Noviluna Hall

HEALERS (*Rising Tide*)
–ability to heal themselves and others

SEERS (*Ebbing Tide*)
–gift of prophecy and psychic visions

SHADOWGUIDES (*Rising Tide*)
–ability to see beyond the veil, commune with spirits

DARKBEARERS (*Ebbing Tide*)
–darkness manipulation

HOUSE WAXING MOON
Crescens Hall

—

SOWERS (*Rising Tide*)
−ability to grow and alter plants and other small organisms

GLAMOURS (*Ebbing Tide*)
−compulsion; charisma and influence over others

AMPLIFIERS (*Rising Tide*)
−ability to amplify the scope and range of other magics

WORDSMITHS (*Ebbing Tide*)
−ability to manifest things into being

HOUSE FULL MOON
Pleniluna Hall

SOULTENDERS (*Rising Tide*)
–emotion manipulation; empaths and aura-seers

WARDCRAFTERS (*Ebbing Tide*)
–ability to weave protection spells and ward magic

PURIFIERS (*Rising Tide*)
–ability to perform cleanses, balance energies

LIGHTKEEPERS (*Ebbing Tide*)
–light manipulation

HOUSE WANING MOON
Decrescens Hall

DREAMERS *(Rising Tide)*
–dream manipulation, dream walking; ability to induce sleep

UNRAVELERS *(Ebbing Tide)*
–ability to unveil secrets and decipher codes;
breaking through wards and spells

MEMORISTS *(Rising Tide)*
–ability to see and manipulate memories

REAPERS *(Ebbing Tide)*
–ability to reap life; death-touched

HOUSE ECLIPSE
Obscura Hall

Lunar eclipses produce variations
of other lunar magics

Solar eclipses produce rare new gifts
beyond other lunar magics

LAST SPRING

SHE WAS DROWNING IN A SEA OF STARS.

Emory knew this was how she would die, smothered by this strange tide. Selfishly, she hoped the thing brushing against her was Romie; she didn't want to die alone.

In the darkness between stars were memories she wished to forget: a cave like a womb, the students at its heart, the widening of Romie's eyes as the sea rushed in, swift and inevitable.

We are born of the moon and tides, and to them we return.

But Emory wasn't ready to go.

The thought was a flimsy lifeline she reached for, hands seeking purchase in wet sand until they found a clammy, solid weight to grasp.

Emory, Emory, the sea whispered, as if loath to let her go. It relinquished its hold as she hauled herself onto shore. The receding waves unveiled the shape of her anchor in the sand, and Emory jerked back, a scream lodged in her throat.

A body: limbs bent and broken and wrong.

Three other bodies were strewn around it, blue lips parted on silent screams, but all Emory could think as she searched their pallid faces and unseeing eyes was how none of them were Romie.

And if this was death, it was a cruel punishment to keep them apart at the end of all things.

Your fault, the stars above seemed to say.

Emory couldn't find it in herself to refute them.

SONG OF THE DROWNED GODS

PART I:

THE SCHOLAR
ON THE SHORES

There is a scholar on these shores who breathes stories. He inhales all manner of them, holds each one in his soul, and when his lungs are too full of words, he exhales at last, daring to breathe his own stories to life. Thus he breathes in words and breathes more out, in and out and in again like the measured rhythm of the sea, until one day he finds a peculiar book that sets even the tides off their fated course.

There is a world at the center of all things where drowned gods reign over a sea of ash, the book begins. *Theirs is an involuntary rule, for in this bleak world they have been marooned, forced to become dim echoes of their former glory while they await the heroes who might one day set them free. Can you hear their plea? It is a song that carries on the wind like ash as it flutters across worlds, and perhaps a piece of it lingers here on this very page. Look closer. Strain your ear. The drowned gods are calling; will you answer?*

The story it tells captivates the scholar, so much so that he finds himself beneath a colorless sky, alone in the stillness of a great expanse of ash. The book still hangs from his hand, the only tangible thing in this curious world, and before he can make sense of it, he is pulled back to his college by the sea, where the book turns to dust in his hand and the memory of the universe it contained already begins to fade. It would feel to him like a dream but for the taste of

ash left in his mouth, the fine coating of it on his clothes and hair, and this unshakable belief that now courses through his veins.

He has always viewed stories as a sailor might view their ship: vessels to carry their readers to other shores, other worlds. Portals on a page.

And here he has found such a portal. Not a figurative one at all, not a figment of his imagination, but real. He has glimpsed a world beyond these shores, hears an echo of it now between the stars. A symphony of drowned gods that beckon: *Come. Seek us as we seek you.*

The scholar heeds their call, and thus our story begins.

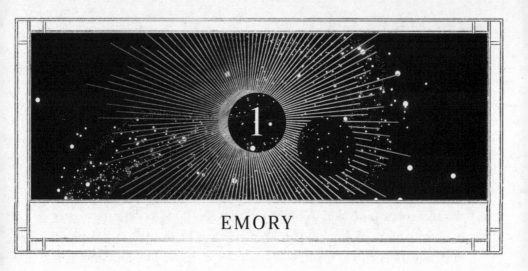

EMORY

TODAY WAS THE FIRST DAY OF A NEW MOON, AND ON the banks of the Aldersea, the tide was low.

There was a time when these facts meant nothing to Emory Ainsleif, but that was before the night her very life hinged on those details. Now the moon was no longer just a moon, the tide was something to fear, and though Emory was grateful for the sun still shining in the late-summer sky, unease gathered like stones in her stomach.

Aldryn College for Lunar Magics rose up ahead, ivy-clad buildings crowning the steep hill that plunged into the restless sea below. Emory dug her nails into her palm as the taste of salt water filled her mouth, a phantom impression she had yet to shake. Blood swelled from the wound. She closed her eyes, savoring the twinge of pain before the magic in her veins could heal it. It was an ordinary sort of pain. Comforting, almost. Nothing like the aching throb of images that surged in her mind—a blood-slick column of rock, a spiral burned in silver on her wrist, four bodies

splayed on the sand—as if coaxed free at the sight of Aldryn.

That particular pain she couldn't heal away, no matter how she tried to ease it.

"You're New Moon, then?"

Emory startled. The driver looked at her in the rearview mirror, motioning to her hand, where the sigil of her lunar house glistened darkly on her pale skin. A black circle wreathed in silver narcissus. It glared back at her as if taking offense at the trickle of blood marring its surface. Guiltily, she wiped at it, seeing only death in its delicate ink.

"What's your tidal alignment?"

"Healing."

The driver whistled an impressed note. His own hands gripping the wheel were bare. Everyone was born with the capacity for magic, a drop of it in their blood, but only those who proved proficient enough bore their house's sigil and studied at places like Aldryn.

"I've got a second cousin who's in House New Moon too," the driver said. "Shadowguide. Works at a morgue in Threnody." He repressed a visible shudder, grumbling something under his breath about how the dead should be left alone.

Emory could almost hear the pointed comment Romie might have made. *People fear what they don't understand,* she would say, nose tilted up in disdain at such small-mindedness. *But there's beauty in death, you know.*

Indeed, no one would ever dare frown upon a Healer, whose touch could prove more efficient than any modern medicine, but some magics, like a Shadowguide's ability to commune with spirits, or a Reaper's death touch, made most people uneasy—especially those with little to no magic. *They don't understand like we do that death is just as much a part of the sacred cycle as life,* Romie would say.

It didn't make losing her any easier.

"Here we are," the driver exclaimed as the cab crested the hill. "Aldryn College."

Everything in Emory seized as the heavy iron gates creaked their welcome, silver-wrought motto splitting down the middle as they opened: *Post tenebras lux; iterum atque iterum.*

After darkness, light; again and again.

Gravel crunched beneath the cab's wheels. Emory had the sudden urge to tell the driver to stop, turn back, but the gates closed behind them with a clang of finality. Nerves rattled on the heels of nausea as she took in the familiar stone steps up to the inner courtyard, flanked by towering elms. Here the driver stopped. Emory handed him a few coins, clutched the strap of her bag. No sooner had she stepped out of the cab than she wished she'd stayed in it forever, already missing the anonymity of that liminal space, the feeling of being nowhere and nowhen and no one for as long as she remained between the life she'd left at home this very morning and the one waiting for her at Aldryn. The person she would have to become here.

Her heart thundered in her chest as she climbed those eight steps, one for each of the moon's phases: a step for the new moon, three for the waxing, one for the full moon, and three for the waning.

She faltered at the top just as she had last year, though her nerves back then had been tinged with excitement, not dread. *This is it, college at last,* Romie had mused on their first day of freshman year, all starry-eyed as she took in the fabled campus. *We get to reinvent ourselves here, be whoever we please.* And though Emory had been eager to do just that, she never understood why someone like Romie would want to be anyone but herself, so effortlessly charming and unique in a way Emory had only ever dreamed of being.

For Emory, college was a chance to be known as more than what she'd been all her life: the girl who hailed from nowhere, who always came second-best, who'd been terrified of not getting into Aldryn because her magic was wholly unremarkable compared to her best friend's.

It offered a clean slate, the first page in a new notebook just waiting to be filled.

She ran a finger along the scar on the inside of her wrist, a silver spiral that started at the base of her thumb and stopped on the tangle of stark blue veins at her pulse point. Her gaze went to the fountain at the center of the lawn, where the Tides of Fate guarded the names of the drowned. It was too late now to erase what had been written in silver and blood, she thought. Too late to even ponder such things, it seemed: the quad was void of its usual hum of activity, and the few stragglers hurrying through the cloisters made Emory realize just how late her train had been as the dean's voice echoed from the assembly hall where she was giving her usual welcome speech.

Emory swore. As much as she dreaded this part—yearned to run to her dorm instead, shut herself in, and avoid everyone on campus for the rest of term—she had come back for a reason, equipped with a plan. And it all started here.

She tried to ease into the dark wood-paneled room unnoticed, but the heavy door slipped from her grasp and slammed shut behind her. Heads turned her way. Emory's cheeks burned, and for a split second, she caught herself searching the sea of faces for the one person who might have made this easier. She could almost picture it: Romie waving her over to the seat she would have saved for her. An anchor in the storm as she'd always been, before everything had changed and the girl Emory had known since childhood started slipping away, swept up by something more sinister than the tide that took her.

But Romie was not here. And neither, apparently, was Romie's brother. Relief and guilt churned in Emory's stomach at his absence. Before she could dwell on it, she tightened her fingers around her satchel and took the first empty seat she could find. Chin held high, she tried to adopt the devil-may-care attitude Romie might have had in her place, but still she felt the furtive glances thrown her way, heard the murmurs rising.

That's the girl who came back from the caves.

The student who survived the Beast.

The one the tide did not claim.

Dean Fulton called for silence. "I must insist once more that students stay clear of Dovermere Caves. After the tragic events of last spring, it begs repeating: Dovermere is unsafe, its tides unpredictable, and as such it remains strictly off-limits."

Her dark eyes flitted toward Emory as she continued. "I urge you to remember those who have fallen. Remember Quince Travers and Serena Velan of House New Moon, and Dania and Lia Azula of House Waxing Moon. Remember Daphné Dioré and Jordyn Briar Burke of House Full Moon, and Harlow Kerr and Romie Brysden of House Waning Moon. Remember their names. Honor them by ensuring no other ever knows the same horrible fate. There is no glory to be found in those caves. Only death."

Emory's nails dug into her skin again as students looked her way. Tears stung her eyes, but she refused to break. She'd spent months preparing for this moment, hoped the summer holiday might allow for things to settle—for the shock of tragedy to fade and the students of Aldryn College to forget, as she had tried so desperately to.

Eight of her classmates dead, and Emory the only one left standing.

She thought the images that burned behind her eyes might be visible for all to see. Nine freshmen standing in a circle around

a column of rock, their bloody wrists bearing a spiral mark that glowed silver in the dark. The sound of the tide rushing in earlier than it should have, death eager to have its fill. The sea and the stars and her name whispered in her ear.

Bodies on the sand.

Foolish of her, really, to think such a thing might be so easily forgotten.

The dean kept talking, but Emory didn't hear a word. Only when students stopped staring did she let out a breath, slowly uncurl her fists. Blood bloomed beneath her nails; her palms were a mess, but already the wounds were smoothing over, her healing magic surging with barely a thought from her to answer the pull of the new moon that governed it. She latched onto this small comfort as the pressure in her veins lessened. All summer she'd felt this inexplicable pressure, like an itch she couldn't scratch that grew to a painful throb unless she drew blood.

She eyed the row of windows behind the dean, wary of the breeze they let in. She swore she heard a whisper slithering in, the sea calling to her, looking to wrap around her limbs, desperate to pull her down, down, down toward the Deep–

Emory saw him out of the corner of her eye. He sat a few rows away, a barrier between her and the windows, the sea beyond. Dusty light fell on the side of his face as he peered at her over a shoulder, casting the rest of his features in shadows. His unflinching stare pulled her up to the surface, made everything go quiet. She recognized his boyish good looks, those thick-lashed eyes: they were the first living thing she'd seen after waking next to those broken and bloated bodies.

You're alive, she remembered him saying, his words nearly drowned out by the swelling tide. *You're all right.* And she'd clung to them so desperately, those words. A life raft keeping her afloat.

Keiran Dunhall Thornby was the perfect embodiment of his lunar

house, the bright light of a full moon bursting with promise, and his presence alone had chased away all the darkness from that moonless night. He looked at her now with such intensity, as if he needed to see that she was indeed still alive. Everyone around them seemed to disappear, and for a second it felt like they were back on that beach, shivering against the horrors strewn around them.

But then she blinked. He turned away. And just like that, the moment dissolved between them like sea-foam across the sand.

Emory stroked the spiral mark on her wrist, half expecting it to start glowing silver like it had when it first appeared through what-ever odd, ancient magic lived in Dovermere. She remembered the way Keiran had grabbed her wrist that night, the curious expres-sion on his face as he'd frowned at the mark that was mirrored on his own wrist—twin spirals a dull silver on their skin. It had haunted her all summer, how impossible it was that he should be marked with the same symbol, because he wasn't *in* the caves that night, hadn't been there for the ritual that marked each student fool-ish enough to have been. Still, he'd found her on the beach in the middle of the night. As if he'd been waiting for her—for *someone*—to make it out of those caves alive.

He knew something about what happened in Dovermere, she was certain of it. It was the only reason she'd bothered coming back to Aldryn—the one thing that managed to pull her out of this ocean of grief she'd been drowning in. She would stop at nothing now to get answers.

". . . and I wish each of you an enlightening term. Thank you."

The dean's parting words pulled Emory from her daze. Stu-dents were already out of their chairs, chattering excitedly as they exchanged handshakes and pats on the back and questions about each other's summers. She felt painfully disconnected from it all.

Gaze fixed on Keiran, she steeled herself for what she needed to do. Her thoughts raced in tandem with her heart as she mentally

listed all the questions she wanted to ask him. *Just walk up to him,* she told herself. *It's as simple as that.* None of it felt simple, though. Without Romie here to do all the talking for her, it was up to Emory now to be bold, something her quiet, timid self balked at.

Keiran's eyes found hers as she approached, and she was glad her steps didn't falter. She balled her clammy hands into fists at her side, pushed her trepidation down—and stopped short as a group of upperclassmen caught up to Keiran, stealing his attention away from her.

Emory watched, deflated, as a pretty redheaded girl kissed him on the cheek and a few boys clasped his hand enthusiastically, and through it all Keiran smiled a dimpled smile, such ease and charm emanating from him that it was hard to reconcile the image with the half-drenched boy in her mind.

She thought she heard her name spoken in the chaos of voices. Someone waved at her from halfway across the hall. Penelope West, one of the few friends Emory had made outside of Romie last year, and a fellow New Moon student she'd shared most of her classes with. She'd always liked Penelope, but with her too-bubbly nature and chattiness that could go on forever, the thought of facing her—of facing anyone, really—was suddenly unbearable.

Getting answers from Keiran would have to wait.

Before Penelope could reach her, Emory slipped quietly from the assembly hall, yearning for the solace of her room.

The noonday sun beat down on the quad, great curtains of it falling between the columns that lined the cloisters. Emory cut across the lawn toward the underclassmen dormitories. She slowed near the fountain, where the Tides of Fate—Bruma, Anima, Aestas, and Quies—cast long shadows on the ground. The four deities who ruled over the lunar houses stood in the middle of the basin with their backs to each other, forming a circle in the proper order of the cycle they represented: young Bruma of the

New Moon, beautiful Anima of the Waxing Moon, motherly Aestas of the Full Moon, and wise old Quies of the Waning Moon. Appropriately, the sunlight touched only Anima and Aestas, casting the other two in shadows.

Each Tide faced a different path to one of four academic halls: there was moody Noviluna Hall, its door painted black like the new moon sky that gave those of Emory's house their powers of cleansing darkness and divination; vibrant Crescens Hall, which saw to those born on a waxing moon, their magic tied to growth, amplification, and manifestation; stately Pleniluna Hall, which catered to those who bore the power of the full moon, tied to light, protection, purity, and mindfulness; and Decrescens Hall, as dark and mysterious as the waning moon students who dealt in secrets and dreams, memories and death—and who had been Romie's peers when she was alive.

There was a fifth hall, but no Tide watched over House Eclipse, and no path led to its door, a nondescript, nearly hidden thing.

Emory stopped by the fountain. Her fingers skimmed the surface of the sacred water, said to have been blessed by the Tides themselves. The water came from Dovermere, a network of caves as mythical as the Tides and in part what had attracted Aldryn's founders to build their college so close to it. Students were expressly forbidden to take water from the fountain, much less use it in their bloodletting practices—a way for those of the four main lunar houses to access their magic whenever their ruling moon phase wasn't in position, their power otherwise remaining dormant in their blood. Still, touching the water was meant to be grounding.

It wasn't.

Emory noticed the delicate flowers floating on the surface, two for each lunar house: black narcissus, indigo hollyhocks, white orchids, purple-black poppies. Eight flowers, one for each of the names she knew had been added to the silver plaques at the Tides'

feet, souls consigned to their care so they might watch over them in the Deep.

A name and a flower for each student claimed by the sea.

And suddenly the flowers weren't flowers at all, but bodies trapped in a cave with the deadly sea all around them. Emory turned from the fountain just as the door to House Eclipse opened.

The student who emerged made her stomach plummet.

Basil Brysden was tall and long-limbed, with a badly buttoned shirt and unruly brown curls that fell to his chin. He hugged a pile of books close to his chest, head bent low as if he were trying to make himself smaller, or perhaps invisible. Baz had long since succeeded at both: he was a ghost, a hermit, a curiosity only whispered about in the darkest corners of the college.

The Timespinner.

Such rare magic, even for one of the Eclipse-born.

Baz turned toward the fountain. Rich brown eyes met hers, and were it not for the thick-framed glasses they hid behind, Emory might have thought it was Romie staring back at her. They had the same pale, freckled skin, the same protruding ears. But Baz lacked his sister's sense of mischief, that dreamy, faraway look Romie would get that always infuriated her professors. The bright curiosity that had spread like wildfire until it consumed all she was and could have been.

Baz's eyes held none of Romie's bold fire, only timid uncertainty as he greeted her with an awkward, "Emory."

He looked like he might make a run for it to avoid this conversation altogether. She couldn't blame him.

"You missed the assembly," Emory said, if only just to say *something*. To fill the silence and drown out the guilt that threatened to choke her as Romie's face flashed in her mind—not as it had appeared in life, but as Emory last remembered seeing it: pale and stark in those fateful moments before the sea took her away.

How Baz must resent her, for surviving what his sister had not.

He blinked toward the assembly hall, where laughter sounded as students spilled into the quad. "I guess I did."

From his expression, Emory couldn't quite work out if he'd missed it on purpose or forgotten about the assembly entirely. She noted the tightness around his mouth and wondered when the last time he'd laughed was. She remembered how quick he'd been to smile as a boy, in what now felt like another lifetime entirely. When she and Romie and him had attended boarding school together, sneaking out to run barefoot in the wildflower fields behind it, as free and unburdened as the gulls they would chase down to the beach.

Baz adjusted the weight of the books in his arms. "How are you? How've you been?"

Emory swallowed past the lump in her throat, forcing a smile. "Fine."

Through the nearby cloisters, she spotted Keiran with his group of friends. Their talk of heading down to the beach for the start-of-term bonfires carried on the breeze, and though Keiran's attention was on them, Emory got the distinct impression he'd been looking at her only a moment before.

"We missed you at the funeral."

Her attention snapped back to Baz. There was no bitterness in his voice, no reproach. And that made it so much worse because if he knew the truth, if he knew what really happened in those caves, he wouldn't have wanted her there to begin with.

Emory's cheeks reddened as she tried to think of an excuse, but the truth of it was, she had none. She'd meant to go, had told him she would when he'd invited her right before they left for the summer. But the thought of facing Romie's mother, of lying to Baz about what happened, of saying goodbye to her best friend while Emory herself got to live . . . She couldn't do it. She couldn't stand the empathic way Baz looked at her now, couldn't bear this guilt

that clawed at her insides, knowing he must have so many questions, none of which she could answer.

"I'm sorry," she said quietly, averting her gaze. "I, uh . . . I have to get going. But I'll see you around?"

Baz hugged his books tighter, shoulders drooping in relief or disappointment, she couldn't tell.

Emory couldn't get away from him fast enough.

Reaching her old dorm room felt like crossing an ocean. The underclassmen dorms stood on the far side of campus, a plain stone building overrun with ivy where students of all houses were mixed in together, paired off into rooms no matter the sigil inked on their skin. It was only in their third year at Aldryn that they joined the housing facilities specific to their respective lunar houses.

Emory fumbled miserably with the key to her room until the lock gave way at last and she hurried inside, head falling back against the door. She blew a heavy sigh, grateful for the quiet.

Her breath caught painfully as she took in the room.

On one side was her narrow metal-frame bed just as she'd left it, with its dark linens and duvet perfectly tucked in. There was the tall mahogany armoire where her clothes lay forgotten and the small desk crammed in the corner, still covered with neatly stacked books and fountain pens. Everything appeared untouched by the passing of time, as though the past four months never happened, and Emory had never left, and everything was still the same as it once was.

Except it wasn't, because the other side of the room—Romie's side of the room—was bare.

The bed was still there, the armoire and the desk, but everything that had made it Romie's—the mismatched art and obscure books, the messy piles of clothes and rare, prickly plants, the forgotten cups of tea and plates riddled with crumbs . . . all those things were gone now, taken away like the tide took Romie herself.

There was not a trace of her left, but Emory's mind conjured her all the same, recalling the last time they'd been here together.

That day, Romie had been hunched over her desk, swathed in a shaft of dwindling sunlight that made her shoulder-length hair shine copper. When Emory came in, she startled, knocking over a teacup.

"Tides, are you *trying* to give me a heart attack?" Irritation laced her words as she righted the cup. Dusk, the stray cat she'd found on the school grounds their first week at Aldryn and taken in despite the rules against keeping pets in the dorms, jumped off her lap with an indignant meow to perch on the windowsill instead.

Emory dropped her books on her own desk. "Well, it *is* a new moon. Could be a good way to test my healing skills on a live subject."

Romie didn't seem in the mood for jokes. She furiously wiped the tea from the papers stacked haphazardly on her desk, angling her body as if to shield them from Emory.

"What's so interesting you couldn't be bothered to meet me for supper? I was stuck listening to Penelope talk about Darkbearer magic for what felt like hours."

Emory tried to keep her tone light, but it came out sharp-edged. Loaded. She couldn't help it: Romie had been acting all kinds of strange lately, constantly disregarding their plans, withdrawn and secretive in a way she'd never been before. In truth, Emory had noticed a change in her from the moment they'd arrived at Aldryn. She hadn't wanted to see it at first, blaming their heavy workload and differing schedules for the rift that had opened between them. They'd known each other since they were ten years old. They'd shared *everything*. But something had shifted, and Emory was too scared to ask why that was—too scared of losing her one true friend.

"Just research," Romie said distractedly as she gathered her tea-stained papers and stuffed them in her satchel.

Emory eyed the rumpled state of Romie's clothes, her unmade bed. "Have you been here sleeping all afternoon?"

"I was practicing. You know, Dreamer stuff."

Dreamer stuff. It was what she'd been saying for the past few months, brushing off every moment she spent in the sleepscape– the realm of dreams–like it was nothing. Like it wasn't hollowing her out, depleting her of the bright energy she used to glow with.

"You can't keep doing this, Ro. Missing class, spending all that time in dreams? It can't be healthy."

"I'm fine."

"The bags under your eyes beg to differ."

"You wouldn't understand."

Romie shouldered her bag and moved toward the door. Something gripped Emory at the sight of her hand on the knob, as though she knew that if Romie walked out then, the rift between them would become an unbridgeable chasm.

"Ro. I'm serious. Is everything all right with you?"

She watched the tension in her friend's shoulders ease, and when Romie turned to her, lips upturned in a signature smile, brown eyes molten in the golden hour light, she thought perhaps she might have imagined these past weeks, months–that everything might still be the same between them.

"Everything's fine, Em." She stood there for a moment, and though her smile never wavered, a shadow of doubt darkened her face. Emory thought she might come clean then, finally spill the secrets she'd been letting consume her, but Romie merely pulled the door open and said, "I'll see you later, all right?"

Once the door shut behind her, Emory looked at Romie's desk, too curious and concerned to let it go. Forgotten beneath a vial of salt water, half stained with tea, was a piece of parchment artfully burnt around the edges. The letters *S.O.* were stamped in the middle of the note. Emory flipped it over, where an inscription had

been written in sprawling silver script: *Dovermere Cove, 10 p.m.*

She put the note back where she found it, dread making her mouth taste like ash. Students tended to avoid Dovermere Cove because of the dark stain its infamous sea caves cast on it. Tales of all the drownings that took place there over the years were the first thing freshmen were told when starting at Aldryn. There were always a few foolhardy students who went into the caves looking to prove something to their peers, though Emory didn't think Romie would be reckless enough to do so. Yet when the clock neared ten and Romie still hadn't come back to their room, panic seized her. She looked at the note again, wondering what *S.O.* might stand for and if it had anything to do with Romie's change in behavior.

Unable to shake this sense of foreboding in her bones, Emory pocketed the note and went down to Dovermere Cove just in time to see Romie and seven other students slip into the caves where they would meet their end.

Emory shook the haunting image of that night from her mind. The room suddenly felt too stuffy. Too small. She rushed to the stained-glass window between the beds and threw it open wide, letting the breeze in to kiss her face. She took a deep breath, then another, and the panic that wanted to pull her under slowly receded.

Pressing her forehead against the window frame, she swore softly.

Maybe coming back to Aldryn had been a mistake. All summer, she had been able to pretend that dreadful night at the caves had never happened. She could look out at the Aldersea and not feel the weight of her guilt pressing down on her, because even though home and Aldryn bordered the same sea, they did not share the same shore, nor the same painful memories of darkness and drowning. But now Emory glanced at her friend's empty side of the room, and all she could see were the things she could have done differently.

If she'd said something to keep Romie from walking out that door. If she hadn't gone after her. If she hadn't been inside those caves. If she'd been quick enough, *powerful* enough, to save everyone, healed them as she'd healed herself . . .

If she had stayed home, she wouldn't have to wonder. She could shut everything out and not have to face this suffocating guilt.

But she had tried doing exactly that this summer. Sheltered up in her room, ignoring everything and everyone until the sight of that mark on her wrist and the spiraling nightmares of that night and this feeling of *wrongness* in her blood drove her out of her stupor at last, and she'd known that she had no choice but to go back. To seek answers as to why those students went into the caves and ensure no one else met the same fate.

It was what Romie would have done had their roles been reversed.

The hint of a voice slithered in through the still-open window, or maybe it was just the breeze. In the courtyard below, Emory glimpsed Keiran near the fountain. The ghost of his gaze on her lingered, the intensity of it raising the hairs on the back of her neck.

You're alive. You're all right.

She promptly shut the window, throwing the room into silence once more, and made her way to the armoire.

She had a bonfire to go to.

BAZ

I T WAS NOT UNUSUAL FOR BAZ BRYSDEN TO LOSE TRACK of time, which truly had to be the height of all irony, given the nature of his magic.

A book was all it ever took to hold him captive, make him forget to eat, to sleep, to exist in his own body. Naturally, nothing contented him more than libraries, and Aldryn College had plenty of those to indulge his fondness. Four, to be exact: a library for each of the main lunar houses, and a fifth if you counted the small collection amassed down in Obscura Hall, home of the Eclipse students. Though Baz firmly believed that a few shelves of dusty tomes in a severely underused classroom did not a library make, even if it did offer the quietest backdrop for studying–even quieter now, he supposed, with Kai gone.

And then there was the Vault. The heart of all knowledge, hidden in Aldryn's lower levels at the juncture between its four libraries. It housed some of the world's most precious and ancient texts, carefully warded against thieves and unwanted eyes and

the cruel passage of time. Only a select few professors and students were ever granted access, and only if the dean of students herself allowed it.

Three long years at Aldryn, and Baz had not once stepped foot in the Vault, despite all the research he helped Professor Selandyn with, which often required the perusal of such texts as those found in the Vault. But the aging Eclipse professor–who was an Omnilinguist, a play on Unraveler magic that allowed her to understand and speak any language she encountered, a rather benign ability as far as Eclipse magic went, yet one which brought her wide respect–was peculiar when it came to her books and her research.

She trusted Baz implicitly as her teaching assistant, yet she never let him do much more than run errands and transcribe her handwritten notes on his typewriter, a near-impossible task given the illegibility of her penmanship, but one he'd come to master all the same.

Today was different. Professor Selandyn needed a book for her new research topic–the mythology surrounding the disappearance of the Tides–and had sent him to retrieve it from the Vault in her place.

"It's your last year of undergrad," she'd told him this morning when he'd gone to see her instead of heading to the assembly hall. "It's time I start giving you more responsibilities if you're serious about becoming a professor."

He'd heard the unspoken words in the ensuing silence, seen the truth of them in the grief she wore like a shawl: that with Kai gone and Baz the only one left under her tutelage, her heart wasn't in it, the teaching. That he would likely be leading his studies himself this year while she remained in her office with her books and research and endless supply of tea.

The Vault's permissions desk was manned by a vaguely familiar

student. Her Waxing Moon tattoo, a muted silver crescent entwined with a creeping vine of blooming indigo hollyhocks, was stark against the tawny brown of her hand, which held up an all-too-familiar book: *Song of the Drowned Gods*. One of the newer editions, from the looks of it. A thrum of excitement ran through Baz. He wasn't one for small talk—or any social interaction, really, something Romie had constantly reminded him of, always trying to get him to engage in anything other than his books—but if he *must* speak to people, he didn't mind it being about this.

"Has the scholar found the other worlds yet?"

The girl's mouth quirked up as she set her book down. "Just the sea of ash, but I'm almost at the part where he finds the Wychwood."

"The rib cage that wraps around the heart of the world," Baz recited.

The girl dramatically pressed a hand over her heart. "My favorite." She gave him a rueful smile.

Baz palmed the back of his neck, incapable of thinking up more words. Behind the desk was an impressive silver door set into the crude stone wall, wrought with intricate motifs of frothy waves and the Tides of Fate themselves, fitting guardians for what lay beyond.

"You have your permission slip?" the girl asked.

He set his pile of books down on the counter and pulled the prized piece of paper from his bag, excitement tingling at his fingertips.

The clerk's gaze caught on his outstretched hand, and any warmth that had been in her eyes vanished as she made sense of the sigil inked on his skin.

Baz had always thought the Eclipse insignia was the most striking of the house sigils: a dark moon eclipsing a golden sunflower, the petals of which were rendered in the finest of details. Yet it was deceiving, that delicate beauty, for nothing about House Eclipse

was delicate, nor particularly beautiful. Especially not in the eyes of other students.

The girl's smile faltered. Recognition dawned, as it tended to do.

Baz fought to keep his own smile from slipping. "Dean Fulton signed off on it this morning," he said, still holding the slip aloft between them.

Every second the girl didn't grab for it left a dent in the armor around his heart. He was used to it by now, the unease that spread like wildfire whenever people realized who he was. *What* he was. It never stung any less, though, and after his encounter with Emory in the quad, the way she'd brushed him off as if scared to be in his presence for longer than was necessary, the sting went deeper than ever.

He still remembered a time when Emory had been enthralled by all things Eclipse. When she hadn't looked at him the way everyone else did, as if he were a ticking time bomb ready to go off. Back then, she'd made him feel like there was more to him than his magic. Tides, she'd gone so far as to make him *like* his magic, a sentiment that felt as foreign to him now as the budding friendship they'd once had, long since withered to dust.

At last, the clerk reached for his slip. She read it over carefully, scribbling things in the ledger in front of her. Silence roared around them. Were he any less careful, Baz might have turned back time, wound the minutes back to before he showed his hand and that Shadow-cursed sigil that always made people treat him differently. But time ticked painfully on until, finally, the girl rummaged through a drawer and handed him a delicate silver cuff.

"Special protocol for Eclipse students," she explained, sounding almost apologetic. "In case you . . ." She made a vague motion with her hand. "You know."

Her meaning was clear: in case his magic slipped, becoming so uncontrollable that it brought about his Collapsing, a gruesome

imploding of the self that awaited Eclipse-born who couldn't keep their magic in check.

"Right." Baz grabbed the magic damper, trying to fight the flush creeping up his neck.

The damper was more symbolic than anything, a mere show of good faith, given he could easily take it off himself. He didn't mind wearing it–he was a stickler for rules, after all–but on the rare occasions he was required to do so, all he could think of was how dampers were *made* of Eclipse magic, silver imbued with the power of Nullifiers, which was one of the more common gifts among Eclipse-born. Add to this the fact that this same magic was used on those who Collapsed–*branded* onto their skin to permanently seal off their magic–and the irony alone was enough to make him sick.

"Sorry," the girl mumbled. "Necessary precaution."

Baz wished he could disappear forever.

A part of him understood, though. Eclipse magic was erratic, unpredictable. Nothing like the structured, limited thing the other lunar houses practiced. And if he were to suffer his Collapsing while in the presence of such invaluable books . . .

A necessary precaution, indeed.

Baz dutifully snapped the damper around his wrist as the clerk mumbled another apology. "It's fine," he assured her.

Fine, Emory had said in the quad, even though she'd appeared anything but. It had been written all over her pallid face, how haunted and hollow she was. Baz couldn't reconcile that girl with the one who lived in his memory–blue eyes crinkled in laughter, hair whipping behind her like strands of gold as she ran ahead of him in the fields of their youth, trying to catch up to his sister. It was as if the most vibrant piece of her had drowned last spring, lain to rest with Romie in the depths of Dovermere.

The way she'd brushed off her absence at Romie's funeral as if she'd missed something as trivial as a study session or a coffee date . . .

Baz tried not to let it irk him. He could only imagine the sort of trauma she must be dealing with. If he'd been in her shoes, he likely wouldn't have had much strength for the funeral either. He'd already been holding on by a thread as it was, trying to organize everything on his own while his mother wallowed in her grief.

But it would have been nice to have Emory there. To not have to bear the burden of grief alone.

The clerk cleared her throat, tapping her pen against the ledger. "The rules are as follows: You're granted thirty minutes inside the Vault. In this allotted time, you're welcome to peruse the Vault's collection, but you may not take any other title than the one you've been approved for." She glanced at the permission slip and quirked a brow at the title inked at the top. "*The Tides of Fate and the Shadow of Ruin: A Theological Study into the History of Lunar Magics* by Hoyaken et al."

Baz mumbled something about it being for research, suddenly aware of how dull it must sound. The mythology surrounding the Tides and the Shadow was prevalent in their modern world, but it had long since stopped being something people truly believed in, as it once had been. Nowadays it was a fable they were told as children, an origin story for their magic—and the source of much of the deep-rooted contempt that House Eclipse was held in.

"You'll find your book in aisle *H*. There's another clerk inside if you need help finding your way. Lastly, magic is strictly prohibited while you're in the Vault." The girl gave him a sidelong glance. "Though I guess that won't be a problem."

The cuff seemed to burn against his skin.

"Any questions?"

Baz eyed the copy of *Song of the Drowned Gods* she'd set on the counter. Though it might be Professor Selandyn's research that got him into the Vault, the only title Baz longed to find was his favorite book's original manuscript. To touch the very pages that Cornus

Clover himself had written upon. For fans like Baz, it was already privilege enough to walk the halls of Aldryn knowing Clover had been a student here long ago, to sit in the same classrooms and haunt the same libraries late at night. Very few ever got the chance to set eyes on his actual *manuscript*.

Baz had hoped to be one of them, but the clerk's unease pressed against him, and all he could do was shake his head no.

He'd find his own way to the manuscript, if time permitted.

The girl proceeded to unlock the silver door behind her with an odd-looking key. The door pushed outward before sliding left, hissing across the stone floor as muted light spilled from within. She turned to Baz, blocking the way inside.

"You're Romie's brother, aren't you? The Timespinner?"

Baz blinked at the familiar way she said his sister's name, trying not to flinch at the sound of that Tides-damned title. *Timespinner*.

Spoken with a terrible sort of awe.

He nodded past the lump in his throat.

"She was quite the Dreamer," the girl said, and though her eyes were shaded so that Baz couldn't see the fondness in them, he heard it well enough in the soft lilt of her voice.

It didn't surprise him, really. Romie had been a bright light who effortlessly pulled people in. He'd always admired her carefree attitude, this ease with which she moved and talked and dreamed. A part of him might have even envied her for it.

Tides, he missed her.

The clerk stepped aside, and Baz promptly went through the door, the magic of old books beckoning him forward.

"Aisle *C*, by the way," the girl called after him. She looked at him over her copy of *Song of the Drowned Gods* as she settled back in her seat. "That's where you'll find the manuscript."

The silver door shut, seemingly of its own accord, and Baz stood alone in the Vault.

He wound his way down a narrow stone corridor lined with elaborate bronze sconces all alit with magicked everlight, a centuries-old invention the Lightkeepers of House Full Moon had perfected that stood the test of time even against the rise of electricity. The corridor seemed to go on forever until it spilled into a large, circular room around which were additional passages, these ones lined with books. It gave Baz the impression of standing at the center of a clockface, the aisles like the clock's minute marks. Up and up the rows of shelves climbed, all the way to the vaulted ceiling above, where a curtain of water fell from an opening in its middle.

Baz approached the marble rail in the center of the room. He could almost touch the delicate waterfall on the other side, felt its cold mist on his face. He knew the water came from the Fountain of Fate up in the quad, which must be directly overhead. It spilled into the darkness below his feet, too far down for him to discern the bottom, if there was one at all.

For once, Baz was all too aware of time slipping by, and so he promptly made his way to the *H* aisle, where *The Tides of Fate and the Shadow of Ruin* was easy enough to find. It was quite possibly one of the largest books he'd ever seen; his arms buckled under the weight of it as he heaved it off its shelf.

He knew better by now than to question Professor Selandyn's research, no matter how tired or innocuous or ludicrous her topics might seem at first. He'd once helped her compile a list of lesser-known swamps around the world and was awed at the brilliant paper she then produced on the varying effects of salt water and fresh water used in bloodletting practices. And last year, when she had researched the influence of blood moons over the mating tendencies of bloody-belly comb jellyfish, Baz thought she might have finally gone mad; the award she received for that paper proved him wrong.

Beatrix Selandyn's mind was praised in every academic circle there was. At Aldryn, at least, she didn't experience the kind of antagonism other Eclipse-born did, and was instead widely respected. Baz knew how lucky he was to be her assistant. Still, he couldn't help but wonder why she'd decided to research a myth that pinned their very own house as the villain.

Once, before the Tides vanished, as the myth went, magic was said to have been accessible to all, no matter the moon phase one was born to. People could divine the future and make plants grow and produce light and darkness and walk into dreams and reap lives all at once, so long as they made offerings to the Tides. But when the deities left their shores, they splintered magic into lunar houses and tidal alignments, making it so that those with magic could only practice the single ability they were born with.

And because the Tides were thought to have forsaken their world in order to defeat the Shadow of Ruin—the dark, unhallowed figure associated with House Eclipse—naturally, the Eclipse-born had shouldered the blame for centuries. People believed Eclipse magic was stolen from the Tides, something that should never have belonged to them. They were the outliers of magic wielders, a rarity not entirely belonging to the sacred lunar cycle the world revolved around, and as such, everything about them was made to be contrary:

Where others had their sigils tattooed on their right hand, the Eclipse-born had theirs on their left.

While each of the four main lunar houses was associated with one of the Tides, theirs was linked to the Shadow, the bringer of bad omens, the great eye in the sky that shadowed the world and gave those like Baz their odd, twisted powers.

And while the other houses' magics followed a careful cycle—a fully formed thing only during one's ruling lunar phase, thus only accessible for a few days every month unless called upon through

bloodletting–Eclipse magic could be accessed at all times, no matter the moon's position. No bloodletting needed.

That kind of relentless power . . . some people were envious of it, but it was a burden. A curse. It was why Baz kept to books and knowledge, choosing to hone his mind rather than testing the limits of his time-bending ability. He knew many would kill to have such a gift even if it belonged to House Eclipse, seeing it as power unmatched, a force to rival gods, a way to unmake the very fabric of life as they knew it. Baz himself had thought of using it to undo the things that haunted him most–his sister's death, his father's Collapsing–but he would never dare risk it. Time was of a slippery nature, and Eclipse magic was not to be trifled with. It was because of this that Baz wished to become a professor here at Aldryn, why he'd wanted to be Professor Selandyn's assistant. He'd seen one too many Eclipse-born consumed by their power, and maybe this way, he could help prevent more of them from Collapsing.

Baz lugged the heavy book back to the center of the Vault, where he glanced around for the other aisle the clerk had mentioned. It was only a couple of rows down, and there was no sign of her colleague, nor anyone else, for that matter.

He couldn't resist: he headed down the *C* aisle.

The *Song of the Drowned Gods* manuscript was displayed on a delicate easel inside a locked glass box. It was nothing but flimsily bound yellowing pages, but the sight of the fading title on its battered cover made Baz's soul stir. How he longed to feel it in his hands, to read the words as Clover had initially thought them.

He looked over a shoulder, then the other. Would it be so wrong of him to break the rules just this once? He might never get another chance to step foot in the Vault . . .

Without thinking, Baz set *The Tides of Fate and the Shadow of Ruin* next to the glass case and unclasped the silver cuff around

his wrist. Power thrummed in answer, deep in his veins. Before he could change his mind, he called his magic forward, ever so carefully. It was a small enough thing to reach for the threads of time linked to this particular lock, to seize the one that led to a time where it was *unlocked*.

With a click, the mechanism on the case gave way, the glass panel opened at his touch, and there was *Song of the Drowned Gods*, his for the taking.

Baz felt like the scholar in the story, reaching for a strange book that might carry him to other worlds. He put on a pair of white cotton gloves meant for handling old texts and took it reverentially between his hands, flipping to the first page.

"There is a world at the center of all things where drowned gods reign over a sea of ash," he read aloud. He held his breath and waited to find himself beneath the colorless skies he'd read so often about, a foolish, childish part of him daring to hope it might actually work.

But there were no such things as portals, no matter how transportive a piece of writing might be.

Baz laughed at himself. Curious, he flipped to the back of the book, where there was evidence of a single ripped-out page, all that was left of it now a torn fringe scarring the spine. He'd heard the rumors, of course, of an apparent epilogue discarded before the story ever made it to print. Kai had talked about it all the time, obsessed with theories on what Clover might have written.

"Maybe it ends with it all having been one big fucked-up dream," he'd joked. "Or maybe the scholar inhaled too much moldy old book fumes and went on some wild psychedelic trip."

Baz had rolled his eyes at him. "Like Clover would have stooped so low."

"Guess we'll never know, will we?"

Baz gently flipped through the rest of the pages, conscious of the

time slipping past. He thought of using his magic again to make the minutes stretch just a bit longer, but one bent rule was already too much. He was about to put the manuscript back in its glass box when a piece of paper fell from it, landing at his feet. For a delirious moment, Baz believed it might be the lost epilogue, but it was only a note scribbled in haste, ink bleeding on a torn bit of paper. And the penmanship . . .

He knew those curving letters, that needlessly elaborate question mark:

The call heard between the stars = DOVERMERE?
FIND EPILOGUE

The floor pitched beneath his feet. He read the note again and again, his throat constricting with the impossibility of what he was holding, something even more delicate and precious than the manuscript itself.

It was Romie's handwriting, no doubt about it.

She had underlined *DOVERMERE* multiple times, with such vigor Baz was shocked her pen hadn't pierced the paper. The note cut off abruptly, that final *E* in *EPILOGUE* trailing into a messy scribble that told Baz she'd been in a hurry.

He couldn't make sense of it. His sister had never cared for *Song of the Drowned Gods*, or at least had long since grown out of it, always teasing him about his obsession with what was essentially a children's book. So why the sudden interest in Clover's manuscript and its lost epilogue? How had she even gotten permission to come down here?

He ran a finger along that scribble, wondering if she might have been here *without* permission. If she'd been startled or caught while writing this note, leading her to leave it in the manuscript's pages.

His insides thrummed as he recalled a conversation he'd had with her a few months before the drowning–before everything between

them had soured. They'd gone home for the Winter Solstice, and Romie had been whistling a maddening tune under her breath the whole week they were there. When Baz finally snapped and asked her what in the Deep that gods-awful singing was, her eyes had sparked with that dreamy look she'd often get.

"It's this song I hear in my dreams sometimes." She'd grabbed his dog-eared copy of *Song of the Drowned Gods* from his hands, laughing at his indignation. "Just like in your precious story."

Baz had snorted at that. "So you're hearing the divine, now?"

"Or maybe," she'd whispered in a mock conspiratorial tone, "it's the guardian luring me to his gate."

"That's not—the guardian didn't *lure* anyone."

"He literally knew the drowned gods were tricksters and still thought it was a good idea to draw everyone a map to their door-step or whatever. I'd call that luring."

She wasn't *entirely* wrong. In the story, the young guardian in the fourth realm was the one to guide the story's heroes to the very gates of the sea of ash, where they would eventually free the drowned gods—only to be trapped there in their place. If the gods were the composers of this devious orchestra, the guardian was their favorite instrument with which to sing their trap. And he was all too willing to be bent and shaped to their will because he believed he could outwit them, defy the grim fate he knew awaited him and his companions. But the gods could not be vanquished, and in the end his naivety led the other heroes and himself to their doom.

Romie had hummed that maddening song again as she flipped through the illustrated pages of his book. "Tempting to follow it, isn't it?"

And what if that was exactly what she'd done?

A metallic sound made Baz jump. There was a scuttle of feet, a sharp voice in the distance. The sense that his time was up prickled against his skin.

He was no longer welcome here.

Baz stuffed the note in his pocket before locking the manuscript away, discarding the white gloves, and clasping the damper around his wrist once more. With his heavy book tucked under an arm, he hurried back to the center of the Vault, where he caught a silhouette disappearing down the *H* aisle, footsteps echoing in its wake. The clerk's colleague, no doubt, looking to tell him his thirty minutes were up.

Feeling like he was going to be sick, Baz slid down the narrow corridor out of the Vault. Behind the permissions desk, the clerk looked at him over her reading, oblivious to the way his heart was racing.

"Find everything all right?"

Baz gave a distracted nod as he handed her the cuff and the massive tome. She stamped the checkout card, and Baz muttered his thanks, carrying the weight of his newly acquired book and his old ones and all his unanswered questions back up to the quad.

She was quite the Dreamer, the clerk had said of his sister.

And she was. Had been. Not just in the way her tidal alignment made her—a Dreamer of House Waning Moon, able to slip into people's dreaming as easily as she might slip into their hearts—but a true dreamer in every sense of the word, bold and mercurial and more bright-eyed than any star in the sky.

Romie was the antithesis of Baz's own narrow existence. She never understood how content he was to sit alone with a book, nor why he desired to stay at Aldryn after finishing undergrad. She herself had rebelled against such small aspirations, wanting to experience everything she could while at Aldryn before leaving to see the world and find her place in it. She could never quite forgive him for not dreaming as big.

There's only so much of life you can experience through books, Baz, she would scoff at him.

But books allowed Baz to dream without fear of falling.

Because that was the thing about dreaming, wasn't it? Those who dreamed too big and reached too far were bound to fall, in the end. And if Romie had reached for something beyond her understanding, if her wild notions had led her to Dovermere and the death waiting for her in its depths . . .

There was one person who might have answers for him. One person who knew his sister better than he ever could.

Perhaps it was more than just grief that haunted Emory.

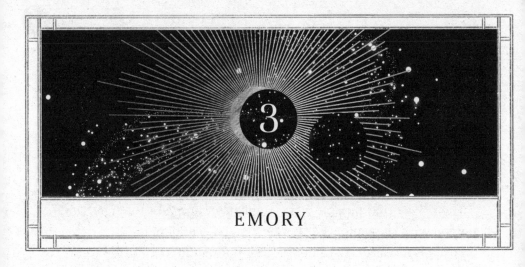

EMORY

THE SETTING SUN LINGERED ON THE HORIZON AS EMORY cut across town toward the beach. The college town of Cadence stood near the northernmost tip of Elegy, an island in the middle of the Aldersea flanked by the much larger Trevel in the east, the sprawling Constellation Isles in the south, and the vast Outerlands that curved around all of it. If the world was a spiral, Elegy marked the very center of it, and Cadence was by far its best feature. It was smaller than the port city of Threnody south of here, and much quainter, too, a postcard-perfect sight with stone cottages and tidy fenced-in gardens and weeping willows dancing in the breeze. And though it had lost some of its charm in Emory's eyes, tainted as it now was by the drownings, it certainly hadn't lost its appeal with other students.

Groups and pairs of them ambled down the cobblestone streets, filing in and out of cafés and taverns, leaving the busy corner store with handfuls of provisions Emory assumed were for the bonfires: cheap liquor bottles, packets of crisps, sausages for grilling,

bundles of firewood, and canisters of gasoline. Students would also be burning whatever notebooks or knickknacks from the previous year they didn't want to hold on to, as was tradition. A way to cleanse the past and start the cycle anew. Romie had loved it.

Emory took her shoes off once she reached the beach that stretched the length of town, white sand bordered by rippling tall grass. Idle chatter and carefree laughter pervaded the air, a dozen fires already crackling to life. She stuck to the shadows, trying to remain invisible, wary of the tide coming in. It was deceitfully beautiful, devouring the shore one gently cresting wave at a time. But the Aldersea remained quiet, no voice calling her name.

Still, the farther she walked, the more untamed the beach became, the sparser the fires and laughter. Emory braced for what awaited around the next bend. She thought briefly of turning back, finding the safety of her room, but the absence of Romie filled every empty corner of it with suffocating reproach.

She had to do this. For her.

Dovermere Cove greeted her like the revenant she was. Dark waves battered against the towering seaside cliffs, echoing the thundering in her chest. The cave mouth on the far side of the cove grinned at her wickedly.

There were more students here than Emory expected. Thrill-seekers who wanted to be close to Dovermere and its dark pull for whatever twisted reason. She saw a few of them passing around jars of moonbrew, a potent concoction meant to open one's senses to the moon and tides to better honor the dead. But there was no solemn remembrance in the gesture; they seemed to do it only for show, getting drunk on it the way they would on any cheap bottle of wine.

It sparked anger in her, bitter defensiveness. Had they even known the students who drowned? Surely their grief couldn't be more than an abstract thing, a pale shade of the monster clawing

at her own insides. She wanted to grab those bottles from their hands, smash them on the sand, wipe away their careless smiles.

His eyes met hers over one of the fires, as if called by the violence in her mind.

A chill ran through her as Keiran Dunhall Thornby stared at her for the second time that day. Flames danced golden on his skin and gilded his carefully styled-back hair, a few chestnut locks of which fell across his forehead. He was the picture of ease and nonchalance, sprawled as he was on the sand and leaning back against an impressive piece of driftwood. His pants were rolled up past his ankles, bare feet resting near the fire. A stark contrast to the last time she'd seen him here.

Beside him was a boy with umber skin, his throat bared to the moonless sky as he roared with laughter, and a girl with chin-length hair the color of flames, her painted lips curled up in amusement as she brought a bottle of sparkling wine to her mouth. Emory knew of them: Virgil Dade and Lizaveta Orlov. Along with Keiran, they were considered Aldryn's elite, upperclassmen who had *money* and *power* written all over them, from the clothes on their backs to the way they held themselves. A certain aura hung over the three of them, as if they stood a world apart from the rest of the students gathered on the beach.

Virgil nudged Lizaveta as he noticed Emory watching them. Recognition shone on both their faces. Other people on the beach were staring at her now too. *Look, it's the girl who survived the Beast,* someone said. *What in the Deep is she doing back here?*

Because that was all she was to them: a nameless curiosity, just the girl who'd made it out alive and was silly enough to come back.

She knew what Romie would have done in her place. She'd have spun this in her favor, held her head high and refused to be made a victim everyone tiptoed around and gossiped about. She would have walked right up to Keiran and his friends with that

bold confidence of hers, said some witty comment or another, and everyone would have laughed and moved on.

Emory wasn't Romie–something she'd been painfully aware of all her life–but she would need to be to get the answers she sought.

Keiran's voice reached her before her forced bravado could slip. "Care to join us, Ainsleif?"

Her stomach tied itself into knots at the sound of her last name on his lips. It felt both strangely personal and othering. Keiran was smiling at her with a lazy tilt of his mouth, as if the waterlogged corpses strewn on the banks of this very cove were a distant, forgotten memory.

Emory couldn't forget. The images were starkly imprinted on her mind: the loud clattering of her teeth, the echo of it running through her bones, the cold and the dread and the numbness in her soul. The odd way Serena Velan's and Dania Azula's limbs had been bent on the sand, Daphné Dioré's unseeing eyes, and the bluish tint of Harlow Kerr's lips. The spiral etched just below the palm of their upturned hands, the strange mark no longer a faint gleaming silver like her own but black–the lines of it smudging together like too much ink bleeding on paper.

She tried to push it all down. To *breathe* so she could get on with what she came here to do. She forced a bashful smile, kicking at the sand. "That's okay. I don't want to intrude."

"Nonsense, you *must* join us," Virgil said, earning a disbelieving stare from Lizaveta. He snatched the bottle from her hand. "Plenty of this to go around, and we'd love the company, truly. Isn't that right, Lizaveta?"

They exchanged a loaded look until Lizaveta turned to Emory with a tight-lipped smile. "If the boys insist."

"The more the merrier." Virgil grinned.

Keiran watched Emory with a feigned nonchalance that crawled under her skin. Like he was testing her, waiting to see if she'd be

dumb enough to say something about that night—about the mark they both had—in front of his friends.

Two could play this game, Emory thought. And if she had to drink and exchange pleasantries to get her answers, so be it.

She sat next to him on the sand, wiping her clammy hands on her corduroy pants. The bottle was passed around until her fingers curled around the neck of it, brushing Keiran's as they did. His Full Moon tattoo reflected the firelight, a silvery disk with a stalk of white orchids curved around it, the opposite of the dark sigil on her own hand. Emory felt his eyes on her as she took a sip, acutely aware of the quiet intensity in them.

"I'm surprised to see you out here," Keiran said conversationally. The words *After what happened last spring* hung unspoken in the air.

"I'm not," Virgil chirped with a lopsided grin, giving Emory an appreciative once-over. "There's a certain undeniably attractive quality to death and tragedy." He swept a hand to the students on the beach, a few of which were still glancing at Emory. "We simply can't keep away from it."

Lizaveta rolled her eyes. "I think that's just the Reaper in you talking, Virgil."

Emory peered at the back of Virgil's hand, where the sigil of House Waning Moon shone, a thin crescent curved around a deep purple poppy. Those who specialized in death magic had the most closely regulated tidal alignment outside of House Eclipse. But despite the grim nature of their power, it was far better regarded than any Eclipse magic ever was. Death, after all, was part of the holy cycle of life, something to be respected, revered—whereas Eclipse magics were deemed unnatural, something born beyond the perpetual cycle of the moon and tides.

Emory knew Reaper magic was rarely ever about death itself, but rather bringing an end to things. She supposed there *was* a certain

beauty in that. Still, she couldn't help the gooseflesh rising on her arms as Virgil's dark eyes met hers from across the fire, and he said, "She's a Healer. She gets it, this pull death has on us. I bet it's why you came here, isn't it?"

Behind him, Dovermere loomed like some ominous death god, thrumming a sinister heartbeat. He was right, in a sense. She'd needed to see it, this place that haunted her nightmares. It didn't seem as threatening as she'd imagined it would, with the Aldersea sighing beneath a muted sky as sparks from the bonfires danced upward like homebound stars.

She swallowed past the lump in her throat and gave Virgil a sad smile. "I figured I'd need to face it eventually."

Was that a glimmer of sympathy she caught in Keiran's gaze? She could use that to her advantage, make him see her as this lost, broken thing he might take pity on if that got him talking.

She took another sip and handed Lizaveta the bottle, noting the crescent-and-hollyhock sigil of House Waxing Moon on the back of her hand. Emory couldn't recall what her tidal alignment was.

"The girl who bested Dovermere," Lizaveta mused. There was something almost grudging in her eyes as she sized Emory up. "You must be some Healer to have survived the Beast."

Emory's nails dug into her palms. *The Belly of the Beast.* It was what students called the very deepest cave within Dovermere, the point of no return. Its name was an apt one, for like any starved beast, it had jagged teeth and a habit of swallowing whole those who got too close; those who believed they could best it.

Virgil took the bottle from Lizaveta and tipped it toward Emory with a wink. "Ah, but what is death to a Healer, hmm?"

"Healers aren't impervious to death, Virgil." Lizaveta scowled. "No one is. Not even you Reapers."

She was right, and no one was impervious to the dangers of Dovermere, either. To slip into the Beast and out before the sea

could rise to trap them inside was no small feat. Tides were fickle things, and time itself tended to lose all meaning in the damp and gloom of Dovermere. It could slip away at a moment's notice, and once the sea came rushing in, there was no way out but through. No way to vanquish the Beast but with magic and luck.

Emory was blessed to have had both on her side that night. With the new moon reigning the sky, her magic had been at its peak, same as it had been for Quince Travers and Serena Velan, the other two House New Moon students who'd been in the caves—one a Healer, the other a Darkbearer. The rest of them would have had to resort to bloodletting to access their abilities, given that their magic lay dormant in their blood until their own moon phase came around.

But the tide had not given them a chance to even try, death sweeping in too fast for any of them to react. Even Emory couldn't remember reaching for her healing magic.

"One of the drowned students was a Healer too. Quince Travers." Lizaveta's gaze pierced Emory. "Did you know him?"

A shock of ginger hair, big eyes gawking at her as the tide came crashing in.

Emory shifted uncomfortably. "A little."

They'd had nearly all their classes together, both being freshmen in the same lunar house, with the same tidal alignment. She'd never gotten to know him much outside of that, though. He'd been rather haughty, preferring to spend his time alone or with equally elitist upperclassmen.

"He was top of your class. Brilliant, I'm told." Lizaveta tilted her head to the side, studying Emory like a cat assessing her prey. "Yet you survived and he did not."

The silence hung heavy around them, as if the crackling fires and crashing waves and bouts of conversation were suddenly muffled, distant things.

"What's your point?" Emory asked tightly.

"I just find it odd that most students who drowned were all top of their class. The best at the magic they specialized in. The Azula twins were in some of my advanced Waxing Moon classes despite being first-years. Romie Brysden was said to be the most prolific Dreamer of our generation. That Dioré girl was a fucking Ward-crafter; her protective magic alone should've been strong enough to save everyone, even through bloodletting. And then there's Emory Ainsleif, a decent enough Healer, but nothing special, if rumors are to be believed. Mediocre at best. Yet the only one who made it out alive."

Emory's cheeks burned furiously.

Mediocre.

The word stung more than she cared to admit. All her life, she'd felt lacking where magic was concerned. She *was* mediocre, had never been the best at healing. She'd fought tooth and nail to earn her place at Aldryn, kept her head buried in books all through prep school because if she was doomed to be average at mastering the practical side of her magic, at least acing the theory behind it might give her a leg up.

Romie had been the complete opposite; everything seemed so innate for her. Emory had envied the effortless ease with which she mastered her own magic. In truth, she'd envied a lot of things about Romie. Call it the result of years standing in her shadow, of being an unnamed entity, wholly unremarkable compared to the bold and magnetic Rosemarie Brysden. While Romie was the life of any party, Emory usually stayed quiet and withdrawn in groups, intimidated by the way everyone around her had such smart opinions, witty retorts, and well-informed worldviews. It made her feel inadequate, like she had nothing of note to contribute. Of course, she wasn't like that when she was alone with Romie, who would always try to coax that chattier, more self-assured version of her

out when they were in larger groups. A social crutch Emory had gladly depended on.

Romie had the sort of effect on people that Emory always wanted for herself, like a dream that washed over them and wouldn't let go. Always the most interesting person in a room, the funniest and liveliest and loudest in the best possible way, Romie knew exactly what to say and how to act, no matter who she was with. Being her best friend was enough to make Emory feel important. After all, she got to see a side of Romie no one else ever did, was privy to all her secrets and most sacred thoughts. *She* was the one Romie depended on to talk some sense into her when she was being too impulsive, the one Romie shared her deepest fears with when the rest of the world believed her to be fearless.

No one would ever dare call Romie *mediocre*.

Before Emory could say anything, Lizaveta waved a hand in the air. "Oh, but don't mind me. Why anyone would risk their life going in those Tides-damned caves is beyond me, that's all. Honestly, what's the point?"

Virgil coughed on the sip he was taking, bubbles sprouting from his nose. Lizaveta took the bottle from him with a sly smile.

What's the point?

It was exactly what Emory had asked herself every day since Dovermere. She dared to look at Keiran now, hoping to find some sort of answer on his face. It betrayed nothing as he looked between Virgil and Lizaveta with a faint smile of his own.

Virgil mastered himself enough to say, "There's no point, Liza. Just foolish freshmen with their silly little initiations, same as every other year."

"We've heard of the odd drowning over the years, sure, but this? *Eight* students at once? That's no coincidence." Lizaveta brought the bottle to her lips and looked at Emory. "So why *did* you go into those caves?"

Emory still wasn't entirely sure. She told herself it was worry that had prompted her to follow Romie, concern for her friend and the odd way she'd been acting. Curiosity, too, for why would Romie be summoned to Dovermere, of all places? She never did figure out who or what *S.O.* stood for, nor why Romie had kept all of this from her in the first place.

And perhaps that had been the biggest factor of all: this underlying bitterness at the fact that her supposed best friend was keeping all these secrets from her. Resentment at not being included. Jealousy, this ugly, vicious beast that weighed shamefully on her now.

All she knew was that she'd gone after her in those caves despite every bone in her body protesting at the rashness of it all.

Emory remembered her labored breathing and erratic heartbeat as she wound deeper through the network of caverns, remembered standing transfixed at the mouth of the Belly of the Beast, watching as Romie and the others stepped onto the natural platform at the center of the vast grotto. There, a giant stalactite and an equally large stalagmite reached toward each other, linked by a fragile thread, like an hourglass that had withstood the tides' whims since the beginning of time. Water trickled down the length of it, the wet rock striated with veins of silver, and at the base of the stalagmite was a great spiral carved in the stone, the ancient symbol resembling a conch, or a wave curling in on itself. Silver flowed toward it, hugging its curve like the deliberate brushstroke of some long-forgotten drowned god.

Lia Azula, a Waxing Moon student, had walked up to it as if in a trance. "I can't believe it's actually real," she'd muttered, reverentially stroking the stone.

Her twin, Dania, had huffed. "I don't think it was ever a question of whether the Hourglass was real or not but whether it can actually do what it's supposed to."

"So let's get on with it." This from Quince Travers, who'd been glancing impatiently at his watch, a greenish tint to his pale face. "Who knows how long we have left."

"Relax, there's like *six hours* between low and high tides," Jordyn had laughed, hitting Travers hard on the back. "We're swimming in time, Travy."

"The only thing we'll be swimming in is the tide that's going to kill us all when it comes in quicker than expected," Travers bit back. "This place messes with time. And don't call me *Travy*, jerk."

"Ass."

"*Boys,*" Romie had warned loudly, extending her arms between the two of them. "If you're quite finished, we have a ritual to perform. You can keep bickering like an old married couple once we're out of here and everyone's drunk enough to tolerate you. Got it?"

Romie's tone had caught Emory off guard. Here was the Romie she knew and loved, with the snark and take-charge attitude that had disappeared the more secretive she'd grown. Still, Emory knew her well enough to notice the underlying tension in her words, the set of her jaw.

Romie was *nervous*—which could only mean something far more sinister was at work here.

The eight of them formed a circle around the rock, a perfectly unbroken cycle of the moon's phases: Travers and Serena of House New Moon, Dania and Lia of House Waxing Moon, Daphné and Jordyn of House Full Moon, and Harlow and Romie of House Waning Moon. Each of them had produced a knife and sliced across their right palm, and there was nothing Emory could do but watch, biting down hard on her lip, as blood dripped down their hands. In unison, the students stepped forward and brought their bloodied hands flush against the rock, intoning what sounded like a prayer.

"To Bruma, who sprang from the darkness. To Anima, whose voice breathed life into the world. To Aestas, whose bountiful

warmth and light protect us all. To Quies and the sleeping dark-ness she guides us through at the end of all things."

For a second, or perhaps a minute or an hour, nothing happened.

Then something changed in the air, as if all the dampness in the grotto ceased to exist. The metallic hues lining the rock came to life. They pulsated with bright light, running up and down the length of the formation like rippling sand, the reflection of moonlight over water. Droplets of silver detached from the rock and hovered just above its surface like raindrops frozen in time.

In the dead silence, a faint whisper rose, making the hairs on the back of Emory's neck stand. It beckoned her forward, as if the rock *called* to her. The others didn't see her as she stepped onto the platform and picked up a discarded knife to slash her own palm, nor as she wedged herself between Romie and Travers and pressed her hand against the rock.

A tendril of silver mixed with the blood that pooled from her wound. It wrapped around her wrist, tethering her to the rock, and it was the cold of a thousand stars and the deepest of oceans, flaring like a brand so painful it brought tears to her eyes, tore a soundless scream from her throat.

Something prickled against her magic, and bright silver light flooded the Belly of the Beast.

Someone screamed.

Emory tried to wrench her hand from the rock but was rooted to it, to that burning cold liquid searing her skin.

Then all at once the light vanished, and Emory brought her trem-bling hand up to her face, blinking at the silver spiral inked on her blood-streaked wrist, a mirror image of the glyph on the rock, still aglow with its strange light.

Romie stood before her, eyes wide with terror, an identical spiral on her own wrist. "Em," she breathed, voice raw, "what the fuck are you doing here?"

Everyone stared at her, and for a moment the cave was deathly quiet.

"She shouldn't be here," Travers said at last, a look of horror on his face. "What if it messed up the ritual?"

An echo of that earlier whisper was the only warning before another sound rose in the depths: a great, deafening roar as the rising tide rushed in.

Time had slipped away from them, and the tide seized its opportunity. Hysteria crested over them before the water did. Someone swore, another burst into tears, and a few had the good sense to scramble to the nearest puddle to try to call on their magic through bloodletting. Romie simply looked at Emory, mouth open on words that were drowned by the roaring of the tide.

And then:

Darkness. A sea of swirling stars. Emory's name whispered in the night, and those spirals bleeding black on the corpses on the sand.

And Keiran. Keiran, who was the first to find her on the beach in the dead of night. Keiran, who had the same mark they'd gotten in the caves. Keiran, who looked at her now with brows slightly furrowed, as if he could see the memories running through her mind. Beside him, Virgil and Lizaveta watched her intently, waiting for her answer.

Why had she gone into those caves? How had she survived what others more magically gifted than her had not?

Even if she *could* explain it—if she remembered what happened once the sea rushed in, how she'd ended up on the beach with four corpses strewn around her, the other four lost to the churning depths of Dovermere—it wouldn't matter. The only thing anyone wanted from her, the reason all these students kept stealing glances her way, was a good story. A way to build up the myth and mystery surrounding Dovermere.

Emory knew what Romie would do in her place: if people

suspected there was more to the story, she would gladly let them make their assumptions, would feast on their curiosity and let it mold her into an enigma everyone wanted to solve. Perhaps that was exactly what Emory needed to do. Let them believe what they would. The truth remained a mystery even to her, and she owed no one the slivers of knowledge she did have. Those fragments were her only bargaining chip to be used when it counted.

She gave a coy smile and what she hoped was a nonchalant shrug. "You know us first-years. Must have been all that foolishness got to our heads." She peered at Keiran and asked, in the most innocent of tones, "Surely you must have done the same during your freshman year?"

Tension crackled in the air like sparks from the fire.

There was a challenge in Keiran's eyes. "Now, what makes you say that?"

She was spared from answering when a girl suddenly plopped down in the sand next to Virgil. "Sorry we're late!" She handed him an unopened bottle of wine. "Brought gifts."

Virgil beamed. "Ife, you magnificent creature!"

Ife shoved him off with a laugh when he kissed her cheek. She swept her mass of long, tight braids over a shoulder and said something to another girl who sat beside her, whom Emory recognized all too well.

Her heart dropped as their gazes met.

"Emory, hey," Nisha Zenara said with a tentative smile, a note of surprise in her voice. "How've you been?"

Keiran raised a brow. "You two know each other?"

Nisha looked as uncomfortable as Emory felt. "We met once or twice through a mutual friend."

Her blood boiled. *Mutual friend.* More like the friend Nisha had all but stolen away from her.

Emory had been there when Nisha and Romie first met. It was

their first week at Aldryn, and Romie had been dragging Emory all over campus, so eager to see everything their new life had to offer. Her excitement had been infectious, and when they'd stumbled upon Nisha in the Crescens Hall greenhouses where Sowers practiced their botanical skills, Romie being Romie had walked right up to her, and the two of them had instantly bonded over their love of plants–all while Emory stood back, feeling entirely out of place. She'd heard nothing but *Nisha this* and *Nisha that* for the better part of the following weeks, before Romie grew so secretive and distant that she barely spoke to Emory at all.

And if Nisha was friends with Keiran . . .

Was she a part of it too, whatever Romie had been involved in?

Her throat closed. She couldn't handle this. Facing Keiran was one thing, but Nisha she hadn't accounted for. She suddenly felt terribly out of place. Coming here was a mistake; she would have better luck confronting Keiran when he was alone anyway.

"I'd better go." Emory grabbed her shoes and shot to her feet, wiping the sand from her trousers. She read the question in Keiran's expression, felt the awkward silence hanging over the others. "Thanks for the wine," she said lamely.

How pathetic.

She headed for the water's edge without a backward glance. The waves lapped at her ankles, the squishy sand between her toes making her feel unsteady. She took a deep breath in, berating herself for not being able to go through with her plan.

"Ainsleif, wait up."

Keiran was heading her way. Maybe she hadn't so completely messed up after all. He caught up to her just as a wave slammed into her shins, knocking her off-balance. She yelped in pain as she stepped onto something wickedly sharp. His hand shot out to steady her.

"Are you all right?"

"I– Oh."

Blood trickled down her foot where a piece of broken shell had pierced it, still lodged in the soft pad near her toes. Balancing on one foot, with Keiran's hand around her elbow, she made to pull the piece out, swearing in anticipation of the pain.

Keiran's hand closed over hers. "I've got it."

He was standing so close, she could smell the subtle notes of his aftershave, see the warm greens and golds of his irises. At Emory's nod, he tugged the shell clean out. She winced, but half a thought had the wound already closing.

A decent enough Healer, but nothing special.

Keiran flipped her hand over to rest the jagged, bloodied conch in her palm, the spiral shape echoing the mark on her skin, the matching symbol on his own wrist.

She regarded him squarely. "That mark you have. How did you get it?"

Another wave hit them then, stronger than before. They gripped each other's arms as they lurched at the impact. She dropped the shell in the water.

The wind picked up, and Emory swore she heard a voice carried by the breeze, dark and teasing and lovely.

Emory, Emory.

It was just a memory, she tried to tell herself. It wasn't real.

Come find us, Emory.

A shiver up her spine. "Did you hear that?"

Keiran frowned, still gripping her wrist. "Hear what?"

Before she could answer, someone screamed–a high-pitched thing in the night that rose and broke like waves yielding against rock.

She turned toward the sound. A student stood a little farther down the beach, pointing at something in the water: a dark, floating mass pulled in by the tide.

No, not something, Emory realized.

Some*one*.

The world went still.

For a beat, no one moved, and even the sea seemed to pause. Emory stood rooted at the edge of the water, her breath coming in fast and shallow, blood pounding in her ears. She watched numbly as Keiran sloshed into the water and a few other students followed closely behind him. They reached the body, dragged it back to shore. From where she stood, it looked like a young man, and though Emory was here and now, she was suddenly transported back to last spring, when she was the one dragging herself from the sea, fingers clasped around another's body.

Someone swore loudly. "It's Quince Travers!"

Emory blinked. The words were so impossible she thought she must have dreamed them. They meant someone else, *had* to mean someone else. Or maybe this was indeed a dream—a nightmare.

Her feet started moving without her telling them to, and then she was standing with the others, looking over Keiran's shoulder at the body sprawled on the sand.

His face came into view, and Emory stumbled back.

It was indeed Quince Travers, with his constellation of freckles, his unmistakable shock of red hair and wiry frame. Quince Travers, still dressed in the clothes he'd worn that night four months ago when the sea claimed him.

His body didn't have a scratch on it, only a few stray weeds and barnacles tangled in his clothes, slick algae clinging to his hair. His skin wasn't bloated from staying so long in the water, nor wrecked from being battered against the cliffside. He looked . . . *alive*, his cheeks still rosy with the faint glow of life.

Keiran lowered his ear to Travers's chest—and jerked back with a swear as the boy's eyes shot open.

Travers did not spew water, nor even draw breath. He merely sat

up, empty eyes searching the faces around him until, impossibly, they landed on Emory. His mouth opened, and the words that came out were an indistinct gargle as water trickled down the sides of his mouth.

Emory, Emory, the sea whispered.

And suddenly Travers convulsed, collapsing on the ground. He seized and frothed at the mouth, his eyes so wide the whites around his pupils showed.

Keiran looked up at Emory, yelled something about healing him—because of course she could heal him. She was a Healer of House New Moon. Her magic could save him, just as it had saved her that night.

But Emory couldn't tear her eyes away from Travers, couldn't get her feet to move or even remember how to breathe. It made no sense. They were all supposed to be dead. It didn't matter that there had only been four bodies accounted for that night, the other four lost at sea. It wasn't unheard of that those who ventured inside Dovermere lay trapped there, the currents entombing them in the confines of the caves, their bones bound to turn up eventually in some fisherman's net.

But here was Travers. Whole. *Alive*—though perhaps not for much longer if she didn't do something.

In his seizing, his eyes met hers again, and she could plainly read the accusation there.

Your fault.

She caught sight of the inside of his wrist, where the spiral on his skin had begun to bleed black. As if death were readying its final blow.

Someone pushed past her and knelt beside Travers. Another Healer, an upperclassman she recognized as a teacher's assistant in one of her classes.

"Emory," Keiran snapped. *"Help him."*

His voice pushed her to action. She moved past the fear and dropped to her knees across from the other Healer. Louis, she thought his name was. He looked bleary-eyed, unsteady, his labored breathing smelling of alcohol. If he was inebriated past the point of having any sort of grasp on his magic . . .

Heaving a shaky sigh, Emory laid a hand on Travers's chest and tugged on her magic. It answered willingly under the new moon sky, the pressure in her veins instantly lessening.

She felt the magic start to work. Travers's convulsions slowed, then came to a stop. Someone behind her breathed a sigh of relief, thanking the Tides. But now his skin was horridly pallid. Gone was the rosy flush that had been there before. Gone, too, was the light in his eyes; they were milky white, the skin around them all shriveled up. His cheeks were caving in, the skin on his face growing sallow and tight, as if he were aging faster than he should be, deteriorating before their very eyes.

"What the fuck is happening to him?" someone cried out.

Louis pulled away from Travers with a defeated look. "I don't think my magic's helping," he mumbled before doubling over and retching on the sand.

Keiran caught her eye. "Have you got this on your own?"

"I . . . I don't know," Emory admitted, on the verge of tears. "I don't understand what's happening to him."

"Liza," Keiran called, producing a switchblade he shoved in the redhead's hand. "Help her."

Emory watched incomprehensibly as Lizaveta slashed her palm before dunking her hand into the sea, head tilted back, lips moving in what looked like a silent prayer to the night sky. It dawned on Emory that she was bloodletting to call upon her dormant waxing moon magic—though how it might help heal Travers was beyond her.

She frowned as Lizaveta came to stand beside her and rested her

wet, bloodied hand on her shoulder. "What are you doing?"

Lizaveta's ice-chip eyes were steady and sure. "Don't fight it."

It was like the doors to Emory's magic were thrown wide open, and everything around her became too sharp. The pressure in her veins inexplicably returned, so intense she bit back a sob. She could practically taste the magic in the air, the surge of power that trickled down to her fingertips at Lizaveta's touch.

An *Amplifier's* touch.

"Try healing him now," Lizaveta urged. *"Hurry."*

Emory turned back to Travers, but it wasn't really Travers anymore. It was a hulking shell of a person withering before her, emaciated skin stretched too thin over bones. She could almost see his heart through his rib cage, beating fainter by the second.

Emory couldn't let him die.

The power in her veins was all too eager to answer Lizaveta's touch. Her amplified healing magic surged into Travers's body, but it still wasn't enough, still didn't slow down the deterioration.

"It's not working," she cried.

She needed more. Without warning, Lizaveta flung everything she had into Emory, fingers digging painfully into her shoulder. Where before, her amplifying magic had been a mere trickle of power, it became a riptide, pulling Emory under. She buckled under the weight of it, fighting for control as hollow echoes of *mediocre* rang in her mind. Her magic plunged to depths unknown, and as she reached the bottom of her well of power, something twisted and *wrong* rose to greet her, the very same something she'd felt all summer. The magic in her blood ebbed and flowed, answering a tide she couldn't see, didn't know. With it, that pressure in her veins mounted until it hurt, and she wanted to scream. It was as if Lizaveta's amplifying magic had thrown open a floodgate she'd been trying desperately to hold shut until now.

She gasped as power not entirely her own flooded her—as she unwittingly unleashed it.

Tendrils of light slithered from the palm of her hand, still resting atop Travers's frail chest. Ribbons of darkness weaved through the light to wrap around his body, where the algae and weeds and barnacles that clung to his clothes began to pulse, coming alive at whatever strange magic she wielded. Emory could do nothing to stop it, only gape at the impossibility of what poured out of her. It was the light of the full moon and darkness of the new moon and growth of the waxing crescent, none of which were her own, none of which were *possible*.

She was a Healer of House New Moon—but these were other magics coursing through her veins, as if she were siphoning them off those around her. Lightkeeper, Darkbearer, Sower . . .

Reaper.

Emory tried to pull away, to sever the connection to all these magics that were not hers, alignments she should have never been able to use, to *this* one in particular that she did not want, could not possibly wield. But the Reaper magic rushed through her as if it were her own, the antithesis to the healing magic she'd always known.

It was the lush darkness of a waning moon sky, the quiet of sleep, the peace of eternal rest.

She was powerless to stop the death magic that blasted from her hands, looking to silence the heart beneath them.

BAZ

THE ECLIPSE COMMONS WERE ALDRYN'S BEST-KEPT SECRET. Every year, it seemed there was a new rumor surrounding them. During Baz's freshman year, students believed they were located in an old dungeon deep below the school, and at some point, the tale running rampant had Eclipse students living in the damp caves of Dovermere, in the Belly of the Beast itself.

They'd at least gotten one thing right: Obscura Hall was indeed built below the school, and the only way to reach it was by riding the singular elevator down to the very bottom, a thing so old and rickety it was a marvel it still worked at all. Hazing rituals always had a couple first-years heading down to try to crack the mysteries of Obscura Hall, but once the elevator gates opened at the bottom, the wards would always kick in, manifesting as some barrier or other: a brick wall, an impenetrable tangle of thorny vines, a bottomless precipice.

And because no student outside of House Eclipse knew what lay beyond those wards, naturally, everyone imagined the worst.

Whatever the whispers, they always seemed to paint it as a cold, wicked place to match the wicked souls within.

The reality was much sunnier. Fading wallpaper with dainty sun-flower motifs and old patterned carpets over pale wooden floors. Well-loved chairs and sofas in shades of burgundy and rust and what must have once been gold. The smell of coffee and brine and the warmth of amber light as it poured from the open window, the sound of crashing waves and screeching gulls a near-constant melody in the backdrop.

Sure, the furniture was rickety and the armchairs were sunken and the gauzy curtains that blew in the breeze were horribly moth-eaten, but that was all part of the charm, Baz thought. The place held history. Old trinkets from students past lay in every nook and cranny. Initials were carved on the walls, with no one to remember them by. Books whose owners were long dead were crammed in the tiny bookshelf by the fireplace, one large tome away from top-pling over.

Baz thought it was the most wonderful place in the world. Then again, he never did mind the broken and forgotten things. But it was an empty place, lonely since Kai had left, and that Baz could not quite stand.

Once, he would have given anything to be here alone, with no other Eclipse student to disrupt his peace. His first year at Aldryn, Obscura Hall had housed three students: himself and two upper-classmen on their last year of undergrad, one of whom had been so *impossibly* chatty, Baz could never step out of his room with-out having his ear talked clean off, and the other so completely immersed in her studies, she wanted nothing to do with either of them except to yell at them to shut up—even though Baz was rarely ever the one doing the talking. Suffice to say he'd looked forward to his sophomore year without them, hoping there wouldn't be any new Eclipse students to take their place.

Nothing could have prepared him for Kai Salonga.

It had been apparent from the very beginning they were as different as night and day. Where Baz was soft light in a dusty library, made up of a muted assortment of cozy old sweaters and shirts that fit awkwardly on his lanky frame, Kai was piercing starlight, with the kind of presence that commanded attention even when he said nothing at all, the way the night sky drew such fascination from poets and artists. With supple black hair he kept in a low bun, a broad nose and high cheekbones and angular eyes that were coldly calculating, Kai was handsome in a way that made Baz all too aware of his own awkward appearance—ears that stuck out and messy hair that wouldn't cooperate and a freckled, pink-tinged complexion that always betrayed how flustered he was.

More than that, Baz had never been so conscious of his own sheltered existence. While he'd never strayed far from home, preferring to discover new worlds through books rather than any real experiences, Kai had lived all over, from his native Luagua, the largest island within the Constellation Isles in the south, all the way to Trevel in the east. He spoke several languages he'd picked up while traveling with his parents, wealthy merchants who dealt in the trade of precious metals, and had attended one of the world's finest magical prep schools in Trevel—where he'd been an insufferable menace, apparently, testing the limits of every magical rule there was just for the fun of it.

And therein lay the starkest difference between them: Baz had long abstained from using any real sort of magic, feeling uneasy about being Eclipse-born, but Kai . . . Kai was completely at ease in his identity. As if the Eclipse sigil on his hand wasn't enough, it also adorned his neck, where a delicate sunflower-and-moon-in-eclipse pendant hung from one of the fine golden chains he always wore, complementing his tawny beige skin. Even the tattoos on his collarbone, which Kai had once told him were traditional to his

Luaguan culture, referred to the eclipse and the Shadow.

Unlike Baz, Kai was not one to shy away from his magic.

He was a Nightmare Weaver, his particular strand of Eclipse magic a dark variation of what Dreamers could do. It let him walk into people's nightmares, conjure their worst fears, and make them real—or at least, make them *feel* real, even if they were mere illusions. One time, he'd produced a horde of furious bees pulled from Baz's subconscious as he napped in the commons. Baz had had to use his own magic to make them disappear, winding the clock back to a time where they did not exist, all while Kai laughed darkly in a corner.

"I'd love to see *you* have your nightmares come to life like that," Baz had mumbled furiously.

"That's the thing about dealing in fears and nightmares: I'm immune to it all."

"Please. Everyone fears something."

Kai had tracked the motion of a stray bee as it landed on the windowsill. "This didn't even scratch the surface of what you truly fear, Brysden. Most people suppress their worst ones. Bad memories, traumas, childhood wounds. They bury them so deep they aren't even aware of them anymore." His dark eyes had slid to Baz. "It's always the quietest minds that hide the worst sort of violence."

Something about the way he'd said it—almost fondly, his voice a midnight breeze—had made Baz shift uncomfortably in his seat. He remembered the dwindling light gilding the side of Kai's handsome face, the supple strands of jet-black hair that fell from his bun to kiss his jawline. Baz had hoped Kai wouldn't notice the flush creeping up his neck, mortified at the thought of him seeing the horrors that lived in his mind. It wasn't the first time the Nightmare Weaver had found himself in Baz's nightmares—something about their proximity, he'd explained, that called to his mind more than most. The thought was horrifying in its intimacy.

Kai's cologne lingered now in the commons, a scent at once upsetting and oddly comforting. Baz could almost picture him coming into the room and draping himself over the chaise longue by the fireplace, imagined him unscrewing the lid of his trusty flask with that sardonic smile of his.

It felt like only yesterday he was here, but now Kai was gone and never coming back.

Baz knew more than most how unpredictable and dangerous those of their house were when their powers went unchecked. Unlike those of other lunar houses, whose magic lay dormant in their blood, slowly building until their moon phase came around again, their own magic didn't follow such a cycle. It flowed freely in their veins at all times, power that seemed to *want* to be used, building to dangerous levels in their blood until they released it.

The danger was in letting it consume them.

One slip was all it took to take that power away from Kai. One feat of magic that pushed him too far past that precarious line between small magic and big magic, a line Baz himself was always keenly aware of.

There was a difference, he knew. Small magic was innocuous, safe. It went unnoticed by the world. It was the time he slowed by a fraction of a second, all so that a minute could turn into a minute and a half, allowing him to get a bit more reading done in a night. It was the seconds he sped up to brew a pot of coffee in half the time it usually took, all so he could hit the Decrescens library before anyone was even awake. It was the thread he pulled to see a lock unlocked so he could hold the fabled manuscript of his favorite book in his hands.

Small things that took the edge off. Inoffensive bursts of magical release. That was all Baz would allow himself.

Big magic, on the other hand, was the sort he dared not touch— the kind he wasn't entirely sure he could wield, even if he tried. At

least not without deadly consequences. Not without Collapsing.

"Magic sustains us like air," his father had taught him long ago. "Go without it and you suffocate. Keep too much in your lungs and you'll burst. The key," he'd said, "is taking carefully measured breaths."

The lesson was deeply ingrained in Baz. It sounded easy enough, but even his father, Eclipse-born like him, had ended up slipping. Baz remembered all too well how Theodore Brysden's face had been plastered in every newspaper and shop window around the city of Threnody after his Collapsing. How the other children Baz's age had stopped wanting to play with him because of it, seeing all Eclipse magic as dangerous, perverse. Evil.

The sins of the Shadow, theirs to carry on.

Even then, Baz couldn't fault those kids for how they'd acted. He couldn't blame Romie for distancing herself from him either; his sister wasn't Eclipse-born and therefore didn't need to shoulder the weight of what their father had done as Baz did. The other kids still wanted to include *her* so long as Baz kept his distance. And he understood, truly. No one was as shaken as he was by the deaths his father's Collapsing had left in its wake, because all he kept thinking was how that might happen to him one day. So he retreated into himself, doing everything he could not to be contrary.

The world is as it is, he would think, *and who am I to challenge it?*

That had never been Kai Salonga's way of thinking. A challenger through and through, so much so that he'd risked his life to dispute everything people thought of Eclipse-born and Collapsings.

Much good it had done him in the end.

Kai had Collapsed right on the heels of Romie's death, two painful blows that left Baz utterly unmoored. He'd come back from Romie's funeral having decided to spend the summer at Aldryn, the thought of staying home without her there too unbearable. Kai, too, was staying at Aldryn over summer break, as he always did, claiming to

have no interest in following his parents around the way he'd done his entire childhood, moving from country to country, boarding school to boarding school.

Baz had looked forward to it. A full summer with almost the entire campus to themselves and a near-abandoned Cadence to explore, the quiet evenings they would spend reading in the commons, the debates they'd have as they reread *Song of the Drowned Gods* for the umpteenth time.

Instead, he'd come back to find Kai gone, taken to the Institute to have his magic sealed.

With a sigh, Baz reached for a cup of lemon ginger tea long since gone cold. He should go up to Kai's room and start packing up his belongings as Professor Selandyn had requested. She wanted everything ready for when Kai's parents arrived; apparently, they were traveling to Cadence to pay their son a visit at the Institute. But Baz couldn't bring himself to do it because all he kept thinking of was the last conversation he'd had with Kai before Kai Collapsed and how, if he hadn't gone home, if he'd taken Kai more seriously, Kai might not be rotting away at the Institute, the Nightmare Weaver no more.

Instead, he reached for *The Tides of Fate and the Shadow of Ruin.*

The heavy book began with illustrations he remembered poring over as a child, included in every piece of literature on the Tides. He would stare at the detailed renderings of the deities for hours on end, even tracing them on blank sheets of paper he would then gift to his mother. He'd always loved drawing, had devoured picture book after picture book as a child, but had eventually come to focus on the words more than the illustrations themselves. That was what he was truly interested in, the stories they told.

Baz let himself look at those images now, mesmerized once more. According to the oldest myth, the Tides had once been a single

person, a girl born of the sea who had lived an entire lifespan in the space of one moon cycle. It started with the one who was now known as Bruma, depicted here as a child standing on the frozen banks of a sea amid a fierce winter storm. Above her was a dark, moonless sky dappled with stars. Black narcissus flowers bloomed behind her, impossibly sprung from the cracks in the ice.

The Tides were first birthed in darkness, the text below the image read, *when the seas were still ungoverned by the moon, and from the chaos of their motions emerged a child whom both life and death called their own. She understood the seas, predicted their moods so that sailors could safely make port, and the moon marveled at the child's cunning.*

Then came a slightly older version of the girl, known now as Anima: rosy-cheeked with eyes a deep indigo like the stalks of hollyhock around her that bent toward a sparkling sea. Her hands reached for the heavens, where three moons shone among the constellations: the waxing crescent, the first quarter moon, the waxing gibbous.

As the moon grew to a sliver that ate the darkness around it, so did the child grow into a maiden burning bright, so lovely and full of laughter that the seas calmed at her feet, a triumph not even the moon could boast of.

Aestas followed, her naked body heavy with child, waves lapping gently at her ankles. Her eyes were the same shade as the pale orchids that adorned her flowing silver hair, reflecting the milky light of a full moon.

When the moon became full, the maiden, too, made new life bloom in her womb, and the sea sighed as it welcomed this blessing, content to bask in the mother's light.

And finally, Quies, a crone as beautiful as the decaying autumn life around her. Her dark gray hair rippled down to the frothy waves that seemed intent on dragging her into the sea, death or

sleep or dreams waiting to claim her at long last. She held a single poppy in her bony hands, and her violet eyes were turned toward the sky, where three dark moons reigned among a dizzying array of stars: the waning gibbous, the last quarter moon, the balsamic moon.

With the last remnants of light before the inevitable dark, the mother-turned-crone looked at the last whisper of moon and shared with it all the secrets of the seas. "Now I am ready for death to claim me." But the moon did not wish them to part. "I will govern the seas through your capable hands, my tides," it decreed. And as it once more went dark and its cycle started anew, the child and the maiden and the mother and the crone rose together and remained, watching over the seas that had birthed them as one.

Baz ran a reverential hand over that starlit sky above Quies.

"She's my favorite," Romie had declared once when they were children.

They'd been perched in the branches of the willow tree that grew behind their house. Baz couldn't remember how old they were, only that it was before their father Collapsed. He had laughed, the sound almost foreign to him now. "You only say that because you're Waning Moon."

"So?" Romie had shot back, eyes sparkling as she'd glanced at the illustration of Quies again. "She's like in my dreams. So many stars."

His heart twisting in his chest, he flipped to the next illustration.

The Shadow was a stark contrast to the other sacred figures. The patron deity of House Eclipse was depicted as a man with cruel and imperious features, his fathomless black eyes ringed with silver and gold. The moon and sun in eclipse hung above him, and in the darkness that threatened to engulf the page were things of nightmare, bodiless creatures made of shadow and bone and blood that reached skeletal hands toward him.

"Sometimes I see those in my dreams too," Romie had said that day. "The bad ones."

The umbrae. Monsters that dwelled in the sleepscape–the realm of dreams and nightmares those like Romie and Kai could walk into. The umbrae feasted on dreams, warping harmless reveries into something more than nightmare, like black holes of despair. Dreamers were trained early on to recognize the signs. If they found themselves in a dream the umbrae decided to feast on, they needed to pull themselves back to the waking world before their own consciousness was devoured–before their soul could be trapped in the sleepscape forever, leaving behind bodies in a state of permanent slumber.

Kai had power over the umbrae that Dreamers did not. To wield nightmare magic was to master fear, in a sense; he could draw the darkness away from dreams, cloaking himself in it until it built and built around his heart. It risked consuming him in a different way, but Kai had come to realize that pulling nightmares into the waking world helped. As if, once they manifested in the real world, they lost any sort of power.

Baz read the two lines below the image: *The Shadow was born in the imbalance between sun and moon, rendering the seas so restless that the Tides themselves knew not how to govern them. He was ruination, and with his cunning brought the Tides to their doom.*

The words had always left a sour taste in his mouth. As the myth would have it, the Shadow stole the Tides' sacred magic to give to those born on eclipses, with whom the Tides refused to share their own power. After the Tides vanished, trapping the Shadow with them in the Deep–the realm of death beneath the sea–their worshippers, once able to call upon all the Tides, found themselves limited in their use of magic. A fate the Shadow's disciples escaped.

Tidecallers, people would call them begrudgingly. *Tidethieves.* Unworthy of the stolen magic in their blood, a version of which Eclipse-born today still carried.

"See, this is why I hate this version of the myth," Kai had said to him once. "It's bullshit. In the Constellation Isles, we tell a different story, where neither the Tides nor the Shadow are portrayed as evil."

Baz had come to know the story quite well. It was one of love and sacrifice, in which the Shadow, cast aside by the sun god he had sprung from, found sanctuary with the moon-blessed Tides. They shared with him the power of their loving moon goddess, and when the vengeful sun found out, he twisted the Shadow's power, turning it against those he had come to love. The Shadow begged the Tides to send him to the Deep, willing to sacrifice himself to keep this power in check. They decided to leave these shores with him, thus appeasing the moon and sun gods and saving the world together.

It had been Kai's favorite story to tell.

Something pressed against Baz's leg. He looked down to find a gray-and-black tabby nuzzling against him.

"Hey, Dusk," he crooned, scratching behind the cat's ear.

His sister's cat—a stray that Romie had found on school grounds one day and adopted as her own, which Baz had taken under his wing after her death, meowed at him before darting off to the windowsill, where he sat looking back at Baz with piercing green eyes. Baz joined him at the window that overlooked the cove, giving Dusk a little scratch on the chin. Outside, *actual* dusk painted the sky in various shades of purple mirrored on the Aldersea's surface.

The Eclipse commons offered the best vantage point at Aldryn, built as they were in the cliffside the college stood upon. When the tide was particularly high and the waves especially strong, Baz could poke his head out the window and feel the spray of salt water

on his face as the sea broke loudly against the rock below. He did so now and noticed the bonfires littering the beach, the students amassed around them.

"Guess I won't be going there tonight," he grumbled to the cat.

Since Romie's drowning, he'd made it a habit to go down to Dovermere Cove on every first day of the new moon, a way to sit with his grief, his regrets.

You just like torturing yourself, he imagined Kai would sneer at him if he'd still been here. And maybe he'd be right, but Baz found it strangely cathartic, despite the horrors of that place.

He reached for the note in his pocket, reading his sister's hand-writing for what felt like the thousandth time today. He'd spent all day debating if he should find Emory, show her the note, get her to talk. She had to know something, and perhaps that was why she'd acted so shifty around him earlier. But he never did find the courage to go knock on her door, and not because he didn't know where it was–he remembered the way easily enough, hav-ing been there once at the beginning of last year when he helped Romie move her things in, and again at the end of last spring, when he packed up all her possessions to bring home to their mother.

No, it was fear that kept him from seeking Emory out. Irrational, stifling fear.

This was something he was all too familiar with: to become so overwhelmed when confronted with a difficult situation, he sim-ply shut down, fear keeping him confined to the prison of his own mind. Time would slip past him mockingly in those instances, as if to say, *You have the key, idiot. Let yourself out.*

Time sounded a lot like Kai, he thought. A trigger switch to bring Baz back to himself. But Kai wasn't here to push him to action, and Baz didn't know how to do it alone. He'd been trying to snap out of this stagnant state all day without success, and thus he was here,

hiding away in the Eclipse commons instead of looking for Emory on campus.

Below, Dovermere Cove was dotted with the light of a dozen fires or so. Baz remembered how much Romie had loved the bonfires when she'd gone with Emory last year, how she'd teased him for not going himself.

He thought he heard a bawdy tune being sung, and the revelries suddenly angered him, so out of place in such a site as Dovermere, with the recent casualties hanging over it. It was like death attracted students to it like flies to a corpse.

He paused his scratching of Dusk's chin. Surely Emory wouldn't have gone back . . . would she? She hadn't even come to Romie's funeral, for Tides' sake. But if this was her own weird way to grieve . . . to face the horrors she'd lived through that night . . .

Shadow burn him.

Baz stuffed the note back in his pocket. "I'll be back later," he told the cat, unable to explain this urgency tugging at him. He didn't *want* to go with all those students there, would probably be better off waiting to track down Emory tomorrow. But he had to know what brought Romie to Dovermere. What made his sister march so carelessly to her death.

He took the secret passage down to the beach, a steep stairwell etched in the rocky cliffside, so worn and overwhelmed with weeds and hanging vines, moss and grass, that no one except for the Eclipse students—namely himself—knew of its existence. His feet thudded quietly on the sand as he emerged from the tangle of vines. He was far enough away from the light of the fires that he knew no one saw him, but still he snuck toward the path that emerged from the tall grasses to make it seem like he was coming from town.

It was too dark for Baz to see the cave entrance from here, but he could feel the presence of the odd magic within, like static crawling along his skin.

He spotted the body a fraction of a second before someone screamed.

It floated in the water near the shore, unmistakably person-shaped.

And then a name was spoken against the wind, sparking a burst of horrid light in the hopeless pit of Baz's heart. His ears rang, all the blood in his body rushing to his head as he followed the rest of the students congregating around the body of Quince Travers. Except it wasn't a body at all, because Travers was alive. He was *alive*, and then he was not, all the life nearly drained out of him so that he was mere skin and bones.

Emory was at his side, trying to heal him through tears, and Baz knew enough of fear to recognize it plainly on her face. He saw the moment she lost her grip on her magic—felt her unraveling before he could spot the signs that something was very wrong indeed, because it was no longer her healing magic she was wielding, but the dark of the new moon and growth of the waxing moon and light of the full moon all at once, in a feat so impossible Baz wondered if he'd fallen down the steep stairs and hit his head, or slipped into one of Kai's living nightmares.

But the horror twisting Emory's features couldn't be imagined. She wrenched away from Travers, away from the Amplifier's grip, as death exploded from her hands.

Reaper magic. Emory—a Tides-damned *Healer*—was using *Reaper* magic.

Baz acted without thinking.

Instinct kicked in, snuffing out his better judgment. The fabric of time itself appeared to shift as he reached for its threads the way he'd done earlier today. The tendrils of light and ribbons of darkness and tangle of weeds around Travers's unmoving form receded at his command, flowing back into Emory. It was like winding back a figurative clock to a time when these impossible powers had not

yet manifested. The death magic was trickier, an intangible thing made to outwit time, to elude it, but Baz pushed against it with everything he had, all too conscious of that line between small magic and big magic, of how dangerously close he was to it, closer than he ever allowed himself to be.

He thought of his father and Kai, of how scared he was to meet the same fate. He nearly let go of his magic then, but at last, the cogs fell into place and death bent to time's will, fading back to inexistence, to a moment when Emory had yet to wield it.

At once, Baz let go of the threads of time, heart beating a rapid pulse in his throat. Around him, no one seemed to have noticed what Emory had done, her strange powers there and gone in what would have felt to them like the blink of an eye, thanks to Baz's magic.

It made little difference, in the end. Travers still sighed his last breath, face turned unseeing toward the sea as whatever degenerative process plaguing him dealt its final blow.

Silence hung over the beach like a shroud, unbroken but by the roar of waves. Emory's wide-eyed gaze found Baz at the edge of the crowd. Her hands shook at her side, the New Moon sigil like a farce on her skin.

Impossibility filled the space between them. She was a *Healer*— he'd seen it firsthand as a child, how she would heal her own scrapes and bruises like it was nothing. She'd healed him once too. He still remembered how she had found him cowering from bullies shortly after his father's Collapsing, how she'd healed the cut on his brow, not caring who saw, not afraid of him like the others were, a kindness he'd carried with him since.

But a Healer couldn't also bend light and darkness or make things grow. A Healer couldn't wield death at her fingertips. Power like that was impossible. It was the stuff of myth, echoing back to a time when people could call upon all magics, no matter their lunar

house or tidal alignment. No one could use other magics than the singular one they were born with, not even those of House Eclipse—not since the Shadow and the first Eclipse-borns.

Unless Emory was exactly that.

Not a Healer, not from House New Moon at all, but something so rare it was only ever mentioned in books—something Baz had read about not even an hour ago.

She was a Tidecaller.

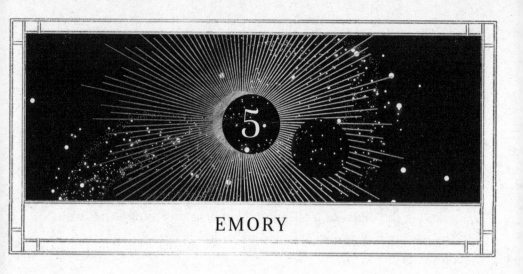

EMORY

VIRGIL WAS RIGHT IN SAYING DEATH HELD A CERTAIN allure.

It had them all transfixed as the authorities came to examine the body–Healers and Shadowguides alike who assessed the nature of the wounds, confirmed the death. Students who had witnessed the horror recounted the event with morbid fascination, and every story remained the same: Quince Travers washed ashore and was revived for a moment before suffering a twisted, gruesome fate, which could only be attributed to the caves he'd drowned in and the unexplained magic that dwelled there.

Emory's name was mentioned only to say she'd tried to heal him. No one spoke of what she'd done, of how she'd revealed herself to be not only a Healer, but somehow also a Lightkeeper and a Darkbearer, a Sower and a Reaper.

It was impossible. People could only wield the specific magic they were born with, and only during their ruling moon phase. Even bloodletting couldn't grant them access to other magics,

only their own. And yet . . . that night in the caves . . .

The blood rite and silver light, the whispers and the strange movement of time as the tide came unexpectedly quick, taking them all by surprise. Everything going black and loud and disorienting, a nightmare of a world trapped and churning in the confines of the Beast.

And in the midst of it all, *something* brushing against her magic. The resulting pressure in her veins, as if that something yearned to be set free.

Hadn't she been on edge all summer, hearing her name in the sea breeze, seeing Dovermere in her dreams? She'd chalked it up to grief, the aftermath of such a traumatic experience, but now she recalled the overwhelming feeling of all those foreign magics rushing through her, the dark caress of death yearning to silence the frail heart below Travers's rib cage, and she wasn't so sure.

In the end, it wasn't the Reaper magic that dealt the final blow, but death found Travers all the same. Yet no one spoke of it now because none of them had *seen* it. And it seemed Emory had Baz Brysden to thank for that.

It had been the oddest thing. One second she could feel death bursting from her fingertips, weaving itself between the ribbons of light and dark, the algae that pulsed to life around Travers's body. She'd tried to wrench free of Lizaveta's amplifying touch, to put distance between her and Travers, incapable of stopping these inexplicable, impossible magics coursing through her veins.

Then time paused, held its breath, wound backward. These powers she'd unwittingly unleashed flooded into her like a tide called back to the ocean, a wave in reverse smoothing into the calm waters it had emerged from.

When time resumed, those around Emory kept looking at Travers

as if nothing had happened, because nothing *had*. Baz had prevented it. Baz, whom she hadn't seen use his Timespinner magic since prep school.

He'd stopped time for her, saved her from herself.

His gaze had not left her since. It burned through her, followed her every movement as if he thought she were a ticking clock set to unleash death upon the beach after all. She avoided him, avoided Keiran and his friends, too, who were as quiet and grim and unsuspecting as everyone else.

Students started to leave only when the authorities took Travers's body away. Emory couldn't help but look when it was carried past her on its stretcher. She caught a glimpse of his lifeless upturned hand, where that Tides-damned spiral had bled black on his pale wrist. His eyes were closed, but she could still see how they had looked at her as he convulsed on the sand.

Your fault.

She turned from his sallow form, cheeks burning with the weight of that lingering accusation and the phantom feel of Reaper magic bursting from her fingertips. A horrible conclusion pressed against her mind as she gripped her wrist, pressing a thumb to the spiral mark, but the thought was so unbearable she shut it out, cast a glance about for anything that might keep her from unraveling. There was a slight crease between Keiran's brows as he watched Travers's body be carried away. Nisha's face was tearstained, her head resting against Ife's shoulder. Lizaveta stood with her arms wrapped around her middle like it was all that was keeping her from falling apart.

And Virgil . . . Gone was that bright smile, the amusement in his eyes. There was such profound sorrow on his face, as if everything he'd said earlier about the allure of death was a lie he told himself, as perhaps all Reapers did. He caught Emory's gaze, and the look of understanding he gave her made her wonder if he *had* seen

what she'd done, or almost done. But then Lizaveta touched his arm, drawing his attention to her.

"Come on," she said quietly. "Let's get out of here."

Keiran hung back as his friends retreated down the beach, watching Emory carefully. "Are you all right?"

She wasn't, but all she could say was, "I will be." She nodded toward Keiran's friends. "You go ahead. I'm fine, really."

His attention caught on a spot behind her where she knew Baz was burning holes in her skull. He hesitated like he might say something, decide to stay with her. But at last, he murmured a quiet *See you around, Ainsleif,* and left.

Emory turned to Baz, knowing she would have to face him eventually. But he was no longer there. She frowned, searching the few faces left on the beach until she spotted him striding farther down, shoulders hunched against the wind, feet furiously kicking up sand.

She moved without thinking. "Baz, wait!"

He did no such thing, his pace quickening at her voice.

"Baz." She caught up to him, watched his stern profile, but he refused to look at her, only kept walking in those infuriatingly long strides.

Emory huffed a disbelieving laugh. "That's it? You're not even going to ask me what that was back there?"

"I know what I saw."

"Then enlighten me, please."

He scoffed. "Like you don't know."

"I don't." She tried to block his path, to make him stop and *look* at her, but he brushed her off, yanking away from her touch as if burned. She flinched, hurt and angry and on the verge of breaking like the waves did against the shore. "Would you please just *stop* for a–"

Baz whipped around, nearly colliding with her. "Come on,

Emory." He looked at her like he'd never seen her before. Like he didn't know her at all, and all those years of him pining over her at prep school were a nightmare he was just now emerging from. "You're a Tidecaller."

She took a step back. "What?"

"It makes no damn sense, and it was so *stupid* of me to help you hide it, but somehow, you're a Tidecaller."

Her ears rang. The night seemed to pause around them, its curiosity piqued at that mythical word. Because that was all Tidecallers were—a thing of myth, the fabled first followers of the Shadow who could still call on all the Tides' magics when the rest of the world no longer could.

All of it a myth, so why did the skin on the back of her neck prickle? She cast a look around to see if any students were in earshot, but they were the only ones left on the beach.

"Tidecallers aren't real, Baz."

He laughed, a bitter, half-crazed sound. "Trust me, I know that. But how else would you be able to call on all those magics? On *Reaper* magic, for Tides' sake? There's only one house that could produce a Tidecaller." His next words cut through her like a brand, a curse. "You're Eclipse-born."

Emory shook her head. "No. No, I'm a *Healer*."

"Not if you weren't actually born on a new moon."

"What are you saying?"

"I'm saying maybe your mother lied about when you were born."

Emory flinched. She had told him of her mother only once, right after Baz's father Collapsed. *At least your dad's still here.* She'd given him a sad smile as she healed the wounds a particularly vile senior had inflicted on him. *I never even got to know my mother.*

She was surprised he remembered at all, and though what he was insinuating was impossible, she couldn't help but wonder . . . Was there any way to know for certain, if the woman who'd brought

her into the world–the only person who'd actually been there at her birth–had left Emory on her father's doorstep when she was a baby, then disappeared forever?

All Emory knew of Luce Meraude was what little informa- tion her father had of her: she was a sailor who'd made harbor near Henry Ainsleif's lighthouse when her boat nearly capsized during a violent storm. She'd stayed with him while working on repairs, and because the lighthouse was in such a desolate place and Henry such a gentle, lonely soul, they took a liking to each other.

It didn't last. Once her boat was mended, Luce returned to the open seas, only to find herself at Henry's doorstep again nearly a year later to leave their child in his care–a child Luce said was born under a new moon, and even had the birth certificate to prove it.

Emory was House New Moon; it was the incontestable truth.

And even if her birth certificate *were* falsified, everything else proved she was a Healer. Like every young child, she'd had her blood tested, had undergone all the Regulation Tests to confirm her tidal alignment, had met every criterion needed to warrant a formal education–a requirement for those who were deemed magically gifted enough for such schooling, a way to ensure no one abused their power or lost control of it. Her lunar tattoo had been given to her when she graduated prep school, like all the others who'd go on to Aldryn College and similar establishments around the world. It was a mark of one's potential, a way to keep each of them accountable for the power they wielded. A clear indi- cator that said, *This is the magic I have, and these are the rules that govern it.*

Emory had worn it like a badge of honor, but now the sigil seemed to burn on the back of her hand, as if willing her to see past this damnable lie inked on her skin.

Eclipse-born.

She couldn't be. Her blood would have marked her as Eclipse-born. And surely Emory would have *known*, would have pieced it together at some point during her training. These other powers would have manifested. She would never have had to resort to bloodletting to use healing magic outside of the new moon, because the Eclipse-born could call on their power at will, no matter the moon phase.

But that had never been the case. She'd had no inkling of these magics until . . .

Emory looked at the dark stain of Dovermere in the distance. She pressed a thumb against the spiral scar on her wrist, the same symbol that was burned black on Travers's corpse. The same one gleaming silver on Keiran's skin.

If the ritual had done something to her that night, burned this symbol on her . . . could it be the source of all this strangeness?

"Is that what happened in the caves?" Baz asked as if he could read her thoughts. "Romie . . . All those students who drowned . . . It was you, wasn't it? Your magic."

You killed them.

He didn't say the words aloud, but the look on his face conveyed them all the same. Tears sprang to Emory's eyes. She couldn't blame him for thinking it, not after what he'd just witnessed her doing—what she would have done had he not stepped in. Not when she herself was wondering the same thing.

Your fault, Travers's eyes had screamed.

Was it her fault, what happened in Dovermere? Had she called upon Reaper magic then, too?

She couldn't bear the thought. She already felt guilty enough as it was, wondering how things would have been different had she not gone into those caves.

"It was the tide," Emory professed, words nearly drowned out by the Aldersea. "Nothing more."

Perhaps saying it would make it true.

Baz tore his gaze from her, shaking his head. "You need to tell Dean Fulton about this."

It took a beat for his words to register. The threat beneath them. Emory blanched. "She'll send me to the Regulators."

"Better that than you losing control."

Fear bloomed in Emory's chest. If the dean found out, if people learned she'd used magic outside of her lunar house—that she might, in fact, be in the *wrong* lunar house . . .

They would brand her with the Unhallowed Seal.

To receive the seal—to have one's magic, their *lifeblood*, permanently sealed off—was a fate most often reserved for Eclipse-born who Collapsed, a steep price to pay for losing control. But others could receive it too. Reapers who used their death touch to murder innocent people. Glamours who made others do terrible things against their will, thanks to their gifts of compulsion. She'd heard of Shadowguides whose necromantic practices were too sickening to speak of, Memorists who wiped people's entire minds until they were left with nothing, not even their own names.

The Unhallowed Seal was the ultimate penalty for misusing magic. And to lie about one's tidal alignment was among the very worst offenses.

Once, the Eclipse-born had been so wildly feared that it wasn't uncommon for parents to forge birth certificates in the hopes of protecting their children from persecution. And though that was a long time ago, and lying about one's alignment had since become damn near impossible to do, what with the appearance of intricate machines that tested their blood to verify their lunar house and tidal alignment, Emory was fairly certain *this* had never happened. That no one had ever suddenly *become* Eclipse-born, much less anything as unheard of as a Tidecaller.

She curled her hands into fists at her sides. This was the

spiral mark's doing, it had to be—she refused to believe she was Eclipse-born.

"You can't tell anyone. This has to stay between us."

Baz's eyes bored into hers. The wind tore at his tangled curls, the only sound in the silence that stretched between them. He was the one person who knew, and if he turned from her now . . .

Fear and desperation seized her. "Please, Baz. I didn't want this. These powers aren't . . . I'm still the same as before." She took a tentative step forward and Baz *recoiled*, as if he feared death still clung to her. "You have to believe me." She hated how her voice broke.

Baz ran a hand over his tired face, pushing his glasses up to pinch the bridge of his nose before letting out an angry sigh. "Don't you have any idea how dangerous Eclipse magic can be? It isn't something you can keep secret. Even to the most well-trained of us, it's unstable and unsafe. It has to be controlled, and from what I just saw, you have no control over it whatsoever. You would've likely Collapsed if I hadn't intervened."

Realization dawned on Emory. He was right. Whether or not these magics were the mark's doing—that it somehow *gave* her Eclipse magic, made her into a Tidecaller through whatever twisted ritual she'd interrupted in the caves—she'd had no control tonight, had nearly killed someone because of it.

She couldn't let that happen again.

"You could train me," she said quietly.

A nervous laugh bubbled from Baz's mouth before he saw how serious she was.

"Absolutely not."

"You could." Her heart thudded in her chest at how perfect this was. The answer to her problem, staring right at her. "You could show me how to control it, how to— *Where are you going?*" she yelled at Baz's back as he stormed off again.

"Did you not hear a single word I just said?"

Emory hurried to catch up to him. "I get it, it's dangerous. So teach me how to control it so I don't hurt anyone before I can even make sense of it."

"There's no way in the Deep I'm training you. I don't know the first thing about Tidecaller magic."

"At the very least, you know more than I do about Eclipse magic."

"Exactly, which means I know that if you slip up, there's *nothing* I can do about it."

"That little display of power you did back there begs to differ. You wound back time, kept my magic from slipping further. You said it yourself, you probably stopped me from Collapsing." His pace quickened, but she matched it stride for stride. "If Eclipse magic is so dangerous, then having you train me is the best solution for everyone."

"No, it isn't. It's stupid and irresponsible and I don't want any part of it."

"Please, Baz."

"You're on your own."

"You know I'll get branded if I go to the dean!" Emory shouted as he kept walking away from her. Her desperation sharpened. "She'll send me straight to the Institute, and they'll seal my magic off without question because when's the last time anyone's heard of a fucking *Tidethief* existing?"

Before she could think twice, the words Emory knew might finally reach him tore angrily from her throat: "Do you really resent me so much you'd let them brand me like they did your father?"

His back went straight as a rod. Emory's face flushed as he ever so slowly turned to her. She almost wished she had his ability so she could swallow the words back, knowing how sore a subject his father's Collapsing was. It was the moment that changed everything for Baz—that changed everything between them, too, squashing

the budding friendship they'd had as he became a recluse and she let him, finding it easier to keep him at a distance like everyone else did because the alternative would have been social suicide.

She wasn't exactly proud of herself for it, nor for bringing the subject up now. But she wouldn't back down from this. She needed him. Needed someone to help her control this magic while she figured out why–*how*–she had it at all.

"I can't do this on my own," Emory whispered against the chaos of the wind and the sea, on the verge of tears at the veracity of those horrible words. She'd never been alone. Romie had been by her side since their first day at Threnody's prep school for gifted children, a steady presence to count on at every turn. But not here now when Emory needed someone most.

And whose fault was that, in the end?

Baz pressed his lips together, glancing around uneasily.

"You don't have to decide tonight," Emory suggested at his hesitation. "We can meet up tomorrow before class, figure out how to go about this. I just . . . Please don't go to the dean. I don't want to be sent to the Institute."

His gaze found hers and held it this time. She could see the wheels turning behind his eyes, the conflicted emotions churning in them at her plea. She saw the moment his decision skewed in her favor by the way his shoulders drooped. He gave a resigned sigh. "Fine. Tomorrow morning at seven. I'll keep this between us until then."

Before she could say anything, Baz took a step back, holding up a hand as if to ward her off. "Right now, I need to think. Just . . . let me think this through."

"Of course," Emory breathed. "Thank you, Baz." The words felt entirely inadequate.

Baz turned from her, and she was left to watch his figure recede down the path that cut toward town. She was alone, yet she got the impression someone was watching her again. Dovermere's looming

presence, perhaps, or the lingering blame in Travers's eyes.

Emory tipped her head back to the sky, wondering at the moonless expanse she'd once regarded so fondly. It held no kinship now, only questions and cold, distant stars that looked down on her as accusingly as they had last spring. She still couldn't refute them, not with the memory of death on her fingertips.

Dovermere calls to her in a dream.

She enters a world of foreboding darkness where the only marker of time is the strange, slow dripping of water. The breathing silence of Dovermere walks beside her, unsettlingly alive.

She finds them in a ring around a great silver hourglass. Fine black sand falls from one elongated bulb to the other. She watches as they bring their hands against the glass. Flowers bloom in the top bulb, narcissus and hollyhock, orchid and poppy, shifting with the sand slowly swirling down.

And now blood mars the surface of the hourglass where eight red hands claw at it, desperate to break it, but the glass does not shatter. Flowers drop in the bottom bulb and bodies drop in answer. Their time is up, and Emory tries to move, to help, to speak, but she is here and not here, and she thinks they do not see her until a boy with red hair turns to her.

"Emory," says Travers. Water spills from his open mouth, black and oozing like blood. "Help us."

Black narcissus blooms sprout from his ears and lips and skin like fungi on a cadaver, because that is what he is becoming, bone and shadow and lifeless eyes, death personified.

"This is your fault."

Travers crumbles. Buds sprout from his corpse. They spread on the algae-slick rock and feed into the pools of salt water

until nothing remains but a mound of narcissus in the deep.

Emory looks at her hands, where the ink of a new moon runs like blackened blood. A diamondlike narcissus appears in her palm, delicate, ethereal, damning. It slips from her fingers and shatters on the cave floor like glass as a monstrous screech echoes, out of place and out of time. A shiver runs up her spine. There is a wrongness to the shadows lengthening around her and those that claw at the inside of the hourglass, looking to shatter it from within.

The

glass

breaks

and black sand and wilted flowers that turn to ash and fearsome beasts forged in the Deep burst forth, a tidal wave of nightmares–

Emory woke with a gasp.

The clothes she'd fallen asleep in were damp from sweat. She didn't remember dozing off, had merely lain here on top of her bed, staring at the ceiling as images of Travers plagued her. All summer she'd had these dreams of Dovermere, perhaps more memory than dream, fragments of reality trapped in amber, though nothing ever as clear or as chilling as this. Nothing that ever felt so real.

She looked at Romie's empty bed, wishing she were here to make sense of it.

Your fault.

Emory sprang up and sat at her desk, retrieving the birth certificate she kept stashed in a drawer. It clearly stated the lunar phase she was born on–new moon–as well as the location of her birth, some small port town on the western coast of Trevel, where the Aldersea met the Trevelsea.

She was adamant there was no way she was Eclipse-born, but for good measure, she scribbled two hasty lines on a piece of paper:

Could Luce have lied about my birth? Weird magic—need answers.

She slipped the letter inside an envelope she addressed to her father. There was no other way to reach him in the remote area where he lived—the lighthouse at the edge of the world, he liked to call it—since the telephone lines that had become all the rage across Elegy and beyond had yet to make their way to the tiny hovel that was Harebell Cove. Emory affixed a sepia-toned postage stamp depicting a familiar coastline, her heart lurching at the image of smooth rocks lapped by frothy waves; all it was missing to be a perfect picture of home were the fields of harebells sighing toward the sea, her father's white clapboard lighthouse standing firm against the wind.

Outside, the sky was graying with the approaching dawn, thick mist clinging to the school grounds. Emory changed, hopped on an old school-issued bicycle, and cycled down to the post office at the edge of town. She liked Cadence this way, cloaked in fog, quiet save for the peal of a bell down at the harbor and the answering call of seagulls. It reminded her of home.

She slipped her letter in the box attached to the front of the post office, a squat stone building with ivy-clad walls and a tattered shingle roof. She could only hope her father had the answers she sought.

The way Henry spoke of Luce had always enticed Emory as a child. Luce was a Dreamer who'd left her home to see the world, and to a girl growing up in the middle of nowhere, having a sailor for a mother was quite the romantic concept. Emory had dreamed of having both parents at her side, one half at sea and the other on land. How often she'd imagined her mother coming back for her. The two of them would sail toward the horizon together, and that lighthouse would always be there to guide them home.

Even as her childish wonder gave way to anger and resentment

at being abandoned, Emory still found ways to romanticize the idea of her mother. Luce roamed the world unburdened by the concepts of home and duty, free to carve her own path wherever the currents led her. It was probably why Emory had been so drawn to Romie when she first met her at Threnody Prep, another Dreamer with wild notions who could never stand still for very long, always looking toward the next irresistible thing.

Romie herself had been quite taken by the idea of Emory's mother. "I want to be like her," she'd stated.

At first the comment had baffled Emory. "Why?"

"Everyone I know, it's like they're here but not really *living*, you know? They're stuck in their comfortable routines and boring old lives, and I want more than that. I want to sail away like your mom, go on a new adventure every day, meet new people, fall in love, try everything the world has to offer. Now, *that's* living."

Emory had told herself she'd wanted all that too, though in reality her ambitions were much more practical, starting with *Get into Aldryn College so you don't become a magical reject*. It was easy to be swept up in Romie's grand ideas, this hunger she had for *more*. But just like Luce, that drive only seemed to push Romie to keep secrets, leaving those she loved behind to put the pieces together in her absence.

There was the sound of a bicycle bell, and out of the mist a boy appeared, rushing past Emory as he threw a stack of newspapers at her feet.

The headline made her stomach turn.

BODY OF DECEASED ALDRYN STUDENT RESURFACES MONTHS AFTER DROWNING IN DOVERMERE CAVES.

A shiver licked up the back of her neck. She imagined Travers's emaciated form emerging from the mist, nightmarish claws and elongated limbs reaching for her.

Your fault.

She hurried up the hill. Aldryn's ghostly outline loomed at the top, barely discernable through the fog. Everything was still. Emory got off her bicycle and squeezed through the creaking gates. Her steps faltered. Someone knelt by the bicycle racks. She recognized Keiran's chestnut head, the profile of his face. The sleeves of his shirt were rolled up around his elbows, a jacket slung over his shoulder–the same clothes he'd been wearing last night. From the way he was doubled over, it looked like he might have kept the party going after the bonfires.

Good, Emory thought bitterly as she marched up to him. This way she could catch him unawares, finish what she'd started on the beach.

He must not have heard the soft rhythm of her bicycle's wheels or her footsteps on the gravel. His hand hovered over a dark form at his feet. A crow, she saw, its wing bent at an odd angle. Like the limbs of those broken bodies on the beach.

Keiran's fingers brushed the twitching bird's wing, bluish black against his skin. Emory blinked incomprehensibly as the wing mended itself at his touch. The crow cawed, got to its feet, and flew away with a great flap of two perfect wings.

Keiran drew himself up just as the campus clock at the top of the stairs struck seven, a small, satisfied smile playing on his lips. He froze when he saw her. The impossibility of what he'd done filled the space between them, chilling her to the bone. Keiran wiped his hands on his slacks, affecting an air of nonchalance. "Morning, Ainsleif."

"How did you do that?"

"Do what?"

Somewhere above them, a crow cawed.

"*That.* You healed its wing. You used New Moon magic."

For a moment, she thought he'd deny it. But a sheepish grin lifted

the corner of his mouth. "Ah." He ran a hand through his already mussed-up hair. He looked so boyish, with that smile and those thick-lashed eyes, that sleepy look on his face. "You weren't supposed to see that."

"It's that spiral mark, isn't it?"

Keiran's smile faltered, and it was all the answer she needed. All the tension of last night came crashing down around her like a wave breaking against the cliffside. Baz was wrong–she wasn't Eclipse-*born*. These strange powers were hers only because of this mark, the same way they were Keiran's.

She wasn't alone in this.

It struck her how badly she'd needed this one thing to be true. It was ironic, really: all her life she'd wanted to be singular, unique in the way she always viewed Romie to be. But not if it meant being Eclipse-born–and a *Tidethief* at that. Not if it disconnected her from everything she'd ever known about herself, made her into something others would fear and loathe because it made no sense, went against everything they knew.

But if Keiran was like her . . . if their impossible magic could be blamed on this Tides-damned mark . . .

Emory thought of the other students who'd been in the caves, how their spirals had turned black when they died, and wondered if death would come for her, too. If this was Dovermere's way of claiming those who'd escaped it.

She looked Keiran over carefully. One thing still didn't make sense. "You weren't there last spring. In the caves, I mean."

"No."

"But you've been before, if you have the mark. You know about the Hourglass and the ritual that burned the spiral on our wrists. It's what the others died for, isn't it?"

Why they'd risked Dovermere at all–a chance at wielding magics outside of their respective lunar houses.

It was absurd, and yet . . . not. Romie had always been fascinated with magic in all its forms. She'd been furious when Aldryn wouldn't let her take electives from other lunar houses. *Just because I can't actually practice other magics doesn't mean I'm not interested in learning the theory behind them,* she'd fumed. *Isn't the acquirement of knowledge the whole point of college?*

It had to be the reason she'd gone to Dovermere: to acquire knowledge in the form of magic like the kind that Emory could now wield. Like the kind that Keiran had just used.

Keiran's eyes glimmered knowingly. He took a step closer, his fingers brushing hers as he casually gripped the bicycle handle wedged between them. "Why are you so sure the mark is what let me heal that bird?" His face was inches from her own, so close she could see the flecks of gold in his irises. "Has it let *you* use other magics?"

It felt like he was trying to pierce through to her very soul.

Emory's hands went clammy. "It might have."

Surely there was no danger in admitting to what Keiran himself had just done. If the truth convinced him to tell her what he knew, she had to accept the risk.

"I wasn't supposed to be there that night. I found a note in my friend Romie's things that said to go to Dovermere, I followed her there, and now I just . . . I don't know what's happening to me." She narrowed her eyes at him. "But you do."

A slanted smile, a cocked brow. "Do I, now?"

"It was you who wrote Romie that note. You had to know she and the others were heading to Dovermere, and that's why you were on the beach. You were waiting for them."

"Seems you have it all figured out."

The way he smiled at her—so completely unaffected by it all— was *infuriating*. She opened her mouth to protest, but just then, shuffling steps sounded down the stairs, students no doubt hurrying to day jobs or internships in Cadence.

"As much as I've enjoyed your little interrogation," Keiran said, "I need to get to class." He gently tugged the bicycle from her grasp and wheeled it backward onto the rack, leaving her dumbfounded. He winked at her. "See you around, Ainsleif."

"No no no, you are *not* leaving without telling me what all this is," she huffed after him as he started up the stairs.

"And what is *all this*, exactly?"

"The illicit magic, the secret ritual, whatever the letters *S.O.* stand for. Don't pretend you don't know what I'm talking about."

"I didn't say a thing."

"You know I could go to the dean, tell her what I saw you doing."

"With all the proof you have, I'm sure she'll send me straight to the Regulators."

They reached the fountain at the center of the quad, and as Keiran cut toward Pleniluna Hall, Emory's hand shot out to stop him.

"Please. My best friend died, and I need to know why."

She hated the desperate note in her voice. Keiran must have heard it too. Something softened in his eyes, more golden than hazel in the sunlight that pierced the fog. Emory realized she still had her hand on his arm, could feel the warmth of him beneath it, all too aware of how close they stood. She was transported back to that night on the beach, hanging on to Keiran for dear life as the sea she'd narrowly escaped battered the shore. He tracked the movement of her hand as she took it away, and she thought maybe he, too, might be thinking of that night.

His lips parted on an answer that never came as he spotted something behind her. A shadow fell over him, a muscle feathered in his jaw. "Your friend's waiting," he said tightly.

"Wait–"

But he was already walking away. Emory turned on her heels to find Baz standing there, staring at Keiran's retreating form like he'd seen a ghost.

BAZ

BAZ WAS UP BEFORE THE SUN.

In truth, he hadn't gotten any sleep at all, his head too full of angry seas, emaciated bodies, and the phantom threads of time pulling on his wrists. When he could take the restless tossing and turning no longer, he descended into the common room and put on a pot of the strongest coffee he could find, yearning for the rich aroma to fill the room and clear his mind.

The first sip anchored him to his body, a miracle in liquid form.

Outside, the tide was receding just as the sun began to rise, though it did little to chase away the darkness of the night.

Baz took his mug back up the stairs. He'd put off packing Kai's belongings for too long and desperately needed something to distract himself with now. He headed straight to the room at the end of the small corridor, the door to which had been kept shut since Kai left. Baz opened it now, steeling himself for the other boy's scent to engulf him.

The narrow bed in the corner was still messily unmade, the gauzy

curtains not even pulled open. Dusty light filtered in, a dull shimmer that touched all the lingering traces of Kai with something close to reverence: various souvenirs from his travels adorning the walls, tapestries and garlands and postcards that had seen the world with him; incense sticks and candles and golden Luaguan relics sitting orderly atop the otherwise messy desk, where unopened and likely untouched schoolbooks were strewn across it; an old chessboard on the floor, all its pieces missing save for the white queen and a chipped black rook. Sad remnants of someone gone.

With a pang, Baz realized he had never once been in here. It was much like his own room, the tapestry faded and fraying around the same exposed wooden beams, but the ceiling, he noticed, was painted with stars. Muted gold and silver winked down at him, forming a constellation he did not know. Among them were words crudely carved into the wood:

HEAR THE BLOOD AND HEAR THE BONES AND HEAR THE FIERCELY BEATING HEART.

Baz's own heart gave a painful squeeze at the line Kai had loved best from *Song of the Drowned Gods*. Their obsessive interest in Cornus Clover's book was perhaps the only thing they'd ever had in common, a shared language to bridge the gap between opposites. He remembered the first time he'd seen Kai reading it in the commons, and all his unease about having to share this space with someone new had faded away to nothing.

On the bench below the window was a stack of multiple editions of *Song of the Drowned Gods*, all of them in different languages Kai had spoken fluently. Baz picked up the only copy in the one language he knew, an illustrated first edition. Something had been nagging at him since seeing Quince Travers's body last night, a feeling he couldn't pinpoint until just now. He flipped through the well-loved pages to the part he was looking for. "The

Guardian at the Gate" had been Kai's favorite section in the book, where the scholar and the witch and the warrior made their way to the fourth realm, wherein they found the guardian. The final member of their band of heroes, the missing piece of their grand puzzle.

He'd never been surprised at Kai's fascination for the guardian. It was fitting, really, that he should so ardently defend the most widely criticized character. The guardian was just a boy at first, one who sought to be a hero, with grand dreams of one day guarding the mighty gate that separated his world from the sea of ash. Only those who could tame the winged horses that ruled this world's stormy skies could become guardians, and so the boy journeyed to the icy gate atop the highest mountain peak, where an aging guardian stood, a god in his own right.

The old guardian laughed at the youth before him, certain he would never have the skill to tame the fabled beasts when so many had died trying. But the boy was undeterred, for he had purpose and something else others before him did not: he had skill with the lyre, an instrument said to make the winged horses amenable.

The guardian of the gate asked him to play a song to judge his talent for himself. And so the boy played, the guardian wept, and the gate itself sighed at the melody that echoed around the mountain. The winged horses descended from the skies and blessed the boy, marking him as the newest guardian of the gate.

Baz looked at the illustration beneath the part header. It depicted the boy sitting by the great gate as he plucked the chords of his lyre. Frost lined his lashes, and on his brow was the silver marking the winged horses had blessed him with.

The symbol went by many names: the Sacred Spiral of Rebirth, the Lunar Conch, the Selenic Mark, the Shadow's Seal. Always associated with the Tides or the Shadow in some way or another, meant to depict the descent from the physical world, which was

on the outermost ring of the spiral, into the Deep, which lay at the center. He'd never thought much of it before, why such an archaic symbol would be used in *Song of the Drowned Gods*. Clover was indeed known to include religious symbology in his story; after all, the drowned gods were a thinly veiled metaphor for the Tides, believed to have forsaken their shores long ago, sinking to the bottom of the ocean—the Deep they ruled over—just as the drowned gods in the story ruled their sea of ash.

But here it was, plainly drawn on the guardian's brow. A symbol of divine connection, though *which* divinity it was attributed to was highly debated. Tides or Shadow. Or mythical flying horses, in the story's case.

Baz's insides thrummed as he thought of Romie's note. His fingers skimmed the text below the illustration—the epigraph that preceded each part in the book, giving readers a glimpse into the new world they'd be entering—and quickly found the lines he knew so well:

He sings himself a role in their story, wills the chords of his lyre to draw them a map among the stars. Come, he beckons the scholar and the witch and the warrior, whose souls are an echo of his own. Seek me as I seek you.

He couldn't make sense of why Romie would have thought this song—the call heard across worlds, a rallying cry for all the heroes spread across the stars—might be associated with Dovermere, or why she'd suddenly been so interested in anything having to do with *Song of the Drowned Gods*. But one thing he knew for certain:

That symbol was the same one he'd glimpsed on Quince Travers's wrist, dark as dried blood, as his body was carried from the beach.

It could be nothing. Probably was. Yet he couldn't shake the sense it was all connected.

He wished Kai was here. With how obsessed he'd been with the guardian and the missing epilogue, he might have been able

to shed some light on all of this. But Kai wasn't here, and so Baz would have to make do with who *was*, the only one who might have answers, even if the thought of seeing Emory now made him want to hide down here forever.

A Tidecaller. He still couldn't believe it, thought it all might have been a fever dream.

Last night, between the howling wind and crashing waves, the pleading in her voice and the image of Travers's withered body, it had been too much to bear, too loud and grating against his senses. A nightmare he couldn't escape, like Kai's Tides-damned bees. Baz had agreed to consider helping her out of a sense of duty, sympathizing with her fear of the Unhallowed Seal, but he'd done so against his better judgment. By the time he'd come back to the Eclipse commons, he'd all but decided to tell her no. A part of him realized he should have been jumping at the opportunity. If he so badly wanted to become an Aldryn professor, help keep other Eclipse-born from Collapsing, why not start with her?

But Emory wasn't just any other Eclipse student. If she'd believed herself a Healer until now, she would need to start training from scratch, learn all the intricacies of Eclipse magic the way any Eclipse-born child did, with next to no real knowledge of the threat of Collapsing. It made her dangerous. Her magic, her very *existence*, bent every rule there was, and Baz couldn't fathom where to even begin. He was scared of using his *own* magic, for Tides' sake. How in the Deep was he supposed to help her use hers when he had no understanding of it whatsoever because it wasn't supposed to be *real*?

This was not what he had in mind when dreaming of becoming a professor. After everything that had happened with his father and then again with Kai, he didn't want anything to do with yet more unchecked Eclipse magic. Emory was unpredictable, unstable, untested, and what he'd seen her do last night—what *he*

had done to stop her from barreling toward something even more dangerous—had shaken him to his core.

She was a *Tidecaller*. That kind of power was wrong, even by Eclipse standards; a thing of myth that painted them as scapegoats for the other lunar houses' restricted magic. And if she were to Collapse with power like that . . .

No. Keeping this a secret put her and the entire student body at risk, and Baz couldn't live with himself if something happened.

And yet.

Romie's note burned in his pocket. He needed answers. Maybe he could get Emory to tell him what she knew about Romie and Travers and Dovermere before trying to convince her to go to the dean. He'd make her see it was the only option, and if she wouldn't listen . . . he wasn't above telling the dean himself.

It was still too early to go meet her, so Baz set down the book and got to work packing Kai's belongings. It struck him how much there actually was, despite how often Kai had moved around growing up. In the end, he managed to throw all of Kai's clothes in a bag and fit the rest in a box. When he was done, the rising sun pierced the dense morning fog. His coffee had gone cold, and he yearned for a second cup, but a quick look at his watch told him he didn't have time. Coffee, regrettably, would have to wait. He tucked the box under his arm and heaved the bag over his shoulder, meaning to drop them off at Selandyn's office after meeting with Emory.

As Baz waited in the quad, part of him hoped Emory wouldn't show, that she'd have come to her senses last night and gone to the dean after all. He began to think she'd done exactly that as the minutes slipped by and she was still nowhere in sight. The campus clock struck seven, seven fifteen. And just as Baz was about to give up and head to Professor Selandyn's office, he spotted her at last next to the Fountain of Fate.

With Keiran Dunhall Thornby at her side.

The floor pitched under him. In his mind, he heard Kai's disdain. *Dungshit Fuckby*, he'd called Keiran once. *He can shove his holier-than-thou attitude where the sun doesn't shine.*

Baz had never liked Keiran either–but he'd arched a brow at Kai, shocked to find out that he knew him at all.

"We went to Trevelyan Prep together," Kai had explained. "I used to date his best friend."

"Used to?" Baz had echoed, face warming slightly at the idea of Kai dating someone. He himself had never dated *anyone*. He'd had the briefest of infatuations with a girl in his grade back at Threnody Prep after she'd kissed him out of the blue one day when they were thirteen. He'd spent a week trying to get the courage to talk to her after that, romanticizing the idea of her until he realized that she'd only kissed him as part of a stupid card game that people liked to play called Kiss the Moon, where you had to kiss someone with the tidal alignment of whichever card you drew.

"He broke things off with me because of his friends. Because people like Dungshit Fuckby despise Eclipse-born so much that they can't ever see past our alignment. They'll always choose each other over us, Brysden." Kai's eyes had darkened to something fierce then, sending Baz's stomach into complicated knots. "And we deserve someone whose loyalties aren't so torn. Someone who understands what it's like to be us."

Time seemed to shift again, and suddenly it was last spring in Baz's mind, and it was Romie he was catching in Keiran's company, not Emory. He still remembered the shock of finding them together in the Decrescens library.

"What in the Deep were you doing with *him*?"

"We were just studying."

Baz knew her well enough to know she was lying. "Does he know who you are? Who–"

"Yes, he knows. It's fine."

But how could it be fine?

"You know how he feels about me. About all Eclipse-born."

He'd seen the guilt plainly on her face before she tossed her head as if to shake it away. "Everything's not always about you, Baz. He certainly doesn't have a problem with me, so just butt out."

Baz had flinched at those words. It was the first time his sister had ever said something so vicious to him. He'd thought she would take it back, but she simply stormed off, and the next thing Baz knew, she was gone. Drowned.

He watched Keiran now and felt sick. He was everything Baz was not: confident where he was shy, admired where he was feared, destined for something more while he remained stagnant. Students looked at Keiran Dunhall Thornby with nothing but awe, seeing him as this paragon of perfection: he was attractive, mild-mannered, well-connected, top of his class, and already had offers trickling in from the world's most elite post-graduate programs. In fact, he was apparently developing a way to use his Lightkeeper magic to restore old, nearly unsalvageable photographs, which had drawn the attention of several museums across the world.

Keiran was a success story; he'd pulled himself out of tragedy and was now on a path anyone might envy him for, full of bright promise.

His gaze flickered to Baz, and beneath that perfect mask, Baz saw the simmering hatred, felt it from a distance. It rooted him in place well after Keiran turned to leave.

Emory swore under her breath, marching up to him with an apologetic look. "Sorry. Something came up, I didn't mean to be so late."

The shadows beneath her storm-colored eyes told him she'd gotten as little sleep as he did, though the rest of her was perfectly composed: mousy blond hair pulled back in a thick ponytail, the sleeves of her crisp white shirt rolled up as if she meant business.

"It's fine," he said reflexively. But it wasn't. How could it be? He watched Keiran's form disappear into Pleniluna Hall. "I didn't know you two were friends."

"Oh. No, we just–" She adjusted the strap of her satchel, clearly flustered. "We bumped into each other, that's all."

We were just studying, Romie had said.

"Be careful around him," Baz warned.

"Why?"

"What do you think would happen if someone like him–if *anyone*–finds out what you are? People already have every reason to be wary of Eclipse magic. If you slip up around them . . ."

"I know. I won't." She looked at him with hopeful expectation, biting her lip nervously. "Not with a bit of help, at least."

Baz shied from the question in her tone. He wished he could disappear rather than face the disappointment in her eyes, the slump of her shoulders as she understood his silence for what it was.

"I see," Emory breathed after a moment. "You're not going to help me."

"I'm sorry. I don't know what I was thinking last night. Keeping this secret . . . it's too dangerous."

"So you'd have me go to the dean, then."

Baz shifted beneath the weight of the box in his arms and that of her gaze. He thought of Romie, of Kai. Of how, if he'd done something more, been more involved, he might have stopped them both from doing these reckless things that led them to their ends. He wouldn't let that happen again. "It's the only sensible thing to do."

Tides, were those tears on her cheeks? He couldn't bear to have her look at him this way.

Emory wiped angrily at her face. "I don't know why I asked for your help in the first place. Who was I kidding, right? Baz Brysden would never dare go against the rules."

"You nearly *killed* someone." Anger suddenly rose in his throat,

and all the pent-up tension from last night came tumbling out. "For all I know, Romie died because of you. Do you even care that she's gone?"

The words took them both by surprise.

Emory inhaled sharply and stepped back, hurt blooming in her eyes. Baz regretted it instantly. "I didn't mean that," he mumbled. Shame made the top of his ears redden. "It's just . . . Tides, Emory, you didn't even bother coming to her funeral. I know we're not exactly friends, but I thought . . ."

He bit back the words, shook his head. He had no delusions about where the two of them stood. They weren't close, not anymore. Perhaps they'd never been. They'd met at Threnody Prep when she was ten and he was twelve, and the only time they ever really spent together was when Romie was there, the glue holding together all their disparate parts. Even when they grew older and he'd thought—*hoped*—there might be a chance of something between the two of them, that Emory might reciprocate the feelings that had started taking root in his heart, his father had Collapsed and everyone around him had pulled away. Even her. And he'd accepted it because it was easier that way. He wouldn't risk hurting them if he kept to himself.

He'd thought, at the very least, that Emory would have come to the funeral. If not for him, then for Romie. But she hadn't. It had been him and his mother and a handful of family members who didn't know Romie, not like he and Emory did. And it had been unbearable.

"She would have wanted you to be there," he said finally.

Emory's face was a hardened mask. "Yeah, well. Romie wanted a lot of things. And look where that got her." A group of students walked past. She lowered her voice, gripping her satchel so tightly her knuckles were white around the strap. "I appreciate what you did for me last night, I do. But I'm not telling the dean."

"Emory–"

She stormed off toward Noviluna Hall. "You're off the hook. I'll manage on my own."

Baz realized Romie's note was still in his pocket, and he was no closer to getting any answers.

Professor Selandyn's office was a tiny room on the upper floor of Decrescens Hall, with a single large window that overlooked the old lighthouse and the sea below. The aging woman claimed the view up here rivaled that of Obscura Hall, but Baz always thought it was the proximity to the Decrescens library that made her choose this particular office space–her favorite of Aldryn's libraries, just like his. She spent most of her time here rather than in the small lecture hall she sparsely taught in; she'd always trusted her students to lead much of their studies on their own, encouraging them to practice their magic together within the safety of Obscura Hall.

As Selandyn set a steaming cup for him on the table, Baz toyed with the idea of telling her about Emory. He didn't feel right keeping such a thing from her, and after their conversation in the quad . . .

If Emory wasn't going to do the sensible thing, he would have to do it for her. It was for her own good, he told himself.

Besides, the Eclipse professor might be able to help her far more than he ever could–that is, if she could convince Dean Fulton and the Regulators to hold off on branding Emory with the Unhallowed Seal. To at least give her a chance to learn to control her newfound magic. Surely it was rare enough that they'd want to study it in depth before blindly sealing off her access to it.

Selandyn tightened a frayed-edged shawl over her tiny frame, smoothed the dark, gray-streaked braid that hung over her shoulder. Baz was suddenly gripped with how burdened she looked. Sunlight danced on the deep bronze of her skin, lined with years of

laughter and knowledge, but there was something else lining her face now, a profound grief in her countenance.

She reminded Baz of his mother then—of the pit of sadness she'd fallen into after his father Collapsed, and again after Romie drowned.

"Is everything all right?" Baz asked quietly.

Professor Selandyn gave him a wan smile. "One day, when you're the one sitting in this chair wondering what more you could have done for your students, you'll understand this sorrow."

Baz's heart constricted as he thought of Kai. How she must feel like she'd failed him, despite all her careful teachings. Was this what he was signing up for? A lifetime of hurt and loss and guilt?

His eyes settled on the box of Kai's things, at the top of which sat his trusty flask, an ornate silver thing with his initials wrought on the embossed surface. The memory came unbidden. They'd been studying quietly in the commons late at night—or at least Baz had been, desperately cramming for a selenography exam while Kai was sprawled in a chair across from him, long legs hooked over the armrest. Baz had been hunched over the coffee table, sitting on the floor with Dusk, who often found himself in the Eclipse commons even before Romie died. How the cat managed to get down there at all was a mystery to everyone.

Baz remembered nodding off when a ball of crumpled-up paper hit him in the face.

Kai had smiled at him wickedly, taking a long sip of his flask before offering it to Baz. "Need some research fuel?"

Baz had taken his glasses off, running a hand over his tired eyes. "That's not exactly how research works."

"Speak for yourself."

"Oh? And what are you researching, exactly? How fast you can get to the bottom of whatever poison that is?"

He'd waited for Kai to flip him off, cheeks burning at the boldness

of his retort. But the other boy's lips had merely quirked up.

"Hilarious, Brysden. If you must know, asshole, it's medicinal."

"Whatever you need to tell yourself."

"I'm serious. I bribed some Dreamer kid for this experimental thing that's supposed to prevent you from sleeping."

"So now you're trying to drug me? Great."

"I'm trying to help you study."

Baz had turned his nose up at the smell.

"And this *experimental thing* just so happens to smell like gin?"

"I may have added a gin component to it, yes. For safe measure." Kai had screwed the cap back on and put the flask in his pocket. Dusk, that traitorous bastard, left Baz's feet to jump onto Kai's stomach with a loud purr. "You try sleeping like a normal person when you're constantly getting pulled into people's nightmares. I doubt you'd last a single night."

The hair on the back of Baz's neck had lifted. He forgot, sometimes, how different the Nightmare Weaver's abilities were to those of Dreamers like Romie. From what Baz understood of it, Kai could slip into the sleepscape just as any Dreamer could, but the darker nature of his power made it harder to navigate. To control. As if fear called to him in the night and pulled him unwittingly into the most terrible of dreams, the darkest corners of this strange realm where the umbrae lay in wait, nightmare given form.

Kai's gaze bored into him. "You had the nightmare again last night."

Baz knew exactly which one he meant. Images flashed before his eyes: his father at the center of a blast like that of a dying star, silver veins of power running along his skin. The crumbling building around them and the blood and the screams. The ticking clock through it all that Baz could never stop.

The nightmarish sequence was a recurring one he'd had since his father's Collapsing. It'd often left him screaming in his sleep, the

primal fear he'd felt that day unwilling to leave him after all these years, making his bones heavy and his throat raw. The first time Kai appeared in this nightmare, he'd managed to ease Baz through the worst of it.

It's not real, Brysden, Kai had said as the blast of power wrought destruction around them, leaving them both untouched. *It's not real.*

They'd never discussed it afterward. But every time Baz had that same nightmare, Kai managed to find him in it, his quiet presence acting like a balm. Making everything a little less painful.

"The strangest thing happened after," Kai had said with a frown, scratching Dusk's chin. "I think I ended up in another Eclipse-born's nightmare. Someone who's Collapsed."

Baz had gone cold all over, his father's face in his mind.

"And you know what I realized? It's the first time I was in the mind of someone who's had their magic sealed. I've never seen anything more terrifying." Kai's voice had been low, his eyes not quite meeting Baz's, as if that made the admission easier. "Their nightmare wasn't full of the normal fears and dreads I'm used to seeing. It was just . . . hollow. An infinite, empty sort of darkness."

"I guess it's a good thing you have that flask, then," Baz had said uneasily.

Dusk had jumped from Kai's chest, scurrying over to the window. Kai's eyes had slid to him. "Don't you think it's strange? It's like having their access to magic cut off makes them *soulless.* I don't care how destructive Collapsings can be or that people think we become these irredeemable, demonic echoes of the Shadow or whatever when we Collapse." He'd snickered, full of disdain. "I refuse to believe that one slipup equates eternal damnation for us."

Baz had said nothing at that. He was torn on the matter: on one hand, what Kai described sounded awful, and imagining his father leading that kind of soulless existence at the Institute weighed on

him heavily. But on the other hand, his father's Collapsing had *killed* people. If he hadn't had his magic sealed, that raw, uncontrollable power in his veins would have done even more irreparable damage, both to him and to others.

How often they'd heard the stories, meant to warn Eclipse children of the dangers of using too much magic. *Slip up, fall into darkness. Evil awaits the careless.* They were told Eclipse-born who Collapsed became wrong and twisted and unhallowed. Wholly irredeemable. As if that silver blast of power erased the people they once were, leaving this darkness inside that sought only to destroy.

Kai thought it was bullshit. He never failed to remind Baz that in the Constellation Isles, people didn't demonize Eclipse-born the way they did here. But even they knew the Collapsing was dangerous, something to avoid at all costs. The tattoos on Kai's chest were said to be a way to ward off such evil.

"During an eclipse," Kai had said, "the moon moves in front of the sun and plunges everything into darkness, but it passes. The world goes back to normal. What if it's the same for those who Collapse? If this great evil that supposedly overcomes them is its own eclipse—fleeting and temporary?"

"Then how do you explain those who escape the seal?" Baz had tried to reason with him. Few who Collapsed managed to escape the Institute's clutches. That blast of power was too destructive, garnered too much attention for anyone to pretend it never happened. And though the blast itself faded quickly enough, making it possible for the Regulators to approach them and take them into the Institute to administer the seal, their blood remained silver, a clear indicator they'd Collapsed.

The Unhallowed Seal was their only salvation, the only thing that kept the madness at bay. By severing their ties to magic, they stood a fighting chance at a normal life.

"Whatever you need to tell yourself, Brysden. I for one think we're trading one curse for another. Maybe I'll push myself to Collapse for the heck of it, just to prove everyone wrong."

Baz had gawked at him, shocked he would say such a thing. Kai knew how badly his father's Collapsing haunted him, must have known what such a suggestion did to him, even if it was said jokingly. The shadow that had fallen over Kai's features told Baz he'd realized his blunder.

"Relax, Brysden. I'm not stupid enough to try it."

Baz had believed him. They hadn't spoken of it again. A few weeks later, Romie drowned, Baz headed home for her funeral, and when he came back, it was to find the commons empty.

"Kai's at the Institute now," Professor Selandyn had told him. "He's been given the seal."

Trading one curse for another.

Baz wanted to tell Professor Selandyn that Kai's Collapsing wasn't her fault, that he'd had a mind of his own and would have done what he'd done regardless. That, if anything, it was Baz's own fault for not taking Kai seriously then.

I refuse to believe that one slipup equates eternal damnation for us, Kai had said—and had become so obsessed with the idea that it had led to his downfall.

Baz couldn't bring himself to say anything. Call it a twisted sense of loyalty to Kai, but he couldn't betray him like that.

Professor Selandyn brought her teacup to her lips and asked, "Was there anything else, Basil?"

He cleared his throat, righted himself in his seat. "There is, actually."

This was the part where he told her of Emory. *There's a Tide-caller in our midst. Another student for you to train. Someone else to worry yourself sick over and mourn when they inevitably Collapse and end up at the Institute.*

He couldn't do it—couldn't burden her further.

Instead, he eyed *The Tides of Fate and the Shadow of Ruin* lying open on the table between them. "I was wondering about your new research topic. It got me thinking . . . What do you make of the parallels between the deities from the myth and the gods in Cornus Clover's story?"

Selandyn laughed, and the sound warmed Baz's heart. "You and that book," she said fondly, patting his hand as she leaned over to put her cup on its saucer. "It's no secret Clover's manuscript draws heavily on the myth of the Tides and the Shadow, though I'm certainly no expert on the matter. You should ask Jae about it. They've just arrived in town."

Baz's ear perked up at that. Jae Ahn was an old family friend, and if anyone knew anything about *Song of the Drowned Gods*, especially the missing epilogue, it was them. "I'll give them a call," he said, wondering with a pang of disappointment why Jae hadn't told him they were coming to Cadence. "But I'd still love to hear your thoughts on the matter. Do you think it might be something worth exploring in your research?"

She seemed to consider it. "Perhaps. It's evident to me that, if Clover *did* intend to write his story as a sort of retelling of the fall of the Tides, he drew inspiration from the most common of the myth interpretations. But it might be interesting to see if he was influenced by some of the lesser-known, more obscure interpretations too."

The professor settled back onto her divan, and Baz recognized the look on her face, that of a storyteller settling into a tale.

"Most interpretations start the same. Bruma, Anima, Aestas, and Quies ruling together for centuries, sisters in all things, mistresses of fate. Each one ruled over a different moon phase, as we know, yet the people they bestowed their magic upon back then could touch all magics, so long as they honored the Tides. Until the Shadow of

Ruin came along, of course." She laced her fingers together. "Now, this is where the different interpretations start. Some believe the Shadow was a monstrous entity who rose from the Deep when the first eclipse occurred, others that it was the sun itself, a rival to the moon the Tides served. The most common belief, though, is that the Shadow was only a man, once. Phoebus was his name. Born on the first eclipse to ever shadow the world. The bringer of bad omens, they called him, for strange things would always happen in his presence. He was shunned by his own family because of it, his entire community. The Tides took pity on him. He was a pious man, after all, who swore he only sought to do good and be worthy of the Tides. And so they blessed him with magic of his own.

"But this magic became odd and twisted once it touched him, warping into a dark variation of the Tides' sacred gifts. Phoebus took that power and molded it into something other and wrong. He became greedy with it. Took vengeance upon those who had wronged him by ripping their magic from them and adding it to his own reservoir of power. The Tides, for all their wisdom, hadn't foreseen this. They didn't know what to do, how to intervene and fix this mistake they'd made in trusting Phoebus with magic." She rolled her eyes. "Again, up for interpretation–this certainly wasn't told by an Eclipse-born, since this way of framing the Shadow has long painted us in a bad light.

"Alas, when the next eclipse shadowed the world and birthed others who bore an echo of the same strange power as his, Phoebus the Shadow called them all to his ranks, and soon enough, he had an army at his command with which to face the Tides and wrest their own godly magic from them. The Tides knew they had to stop him. It was Quies, the Withering Crone, who came up with the solution: they would trap the Shadow in the Deep. The Realm of Death, the very one she ruled over.

"But Quies was not strong enough to keep him there on her own,

so she called upon her sisters. Together, the four Tides trapped the Shadow in the Deep. They made a prison from their own blood and bones to contain him, to ensure he could never be freed."

Baz's mind raced with the clear similarities to *Song of the Drowned Gods*, where blood and bones and heart and soul–the four heroes of the story–were bound together to hold the great beast of shadow at the center of the sea of ash and free the drowned gods from their fate.

"Does the myth ever make mention of Dovermere?"

He couldn't shake it, this dread that crawled along his skin at the thought of that place. A cave that had swallowed nine souls and spat two of them out wholly changed: a Healer withering away to bones, and another reborn with the power of the Eclipse in her veins.

Professor Selandyn was slow to answer. "Some believe Dovermere was both the birthplace of the Tides and the place where they trapped the Shadow. But I wouldn't put too much stock in that theory. Every coastal place of significance around the world lays claim to the origin of the myth. It's why all the best magical colleges are built near the sea, because their founders thought they could benefit from being near that source of power, the traces the Tides might have left behind."

She regarded him carefully, as if she saw exactly what was going through his head. "What is this really about, Basil?"

"Just curious, is all."

"Can I tell you what I think? I think you're looking for an explanation to your sister's drowning, searching for meaning and magnitude where there is likely none. She was a force of nature, and for her to meet such a senseless end is inconceivable."

Selandyn leaned closer, eyes soft. "You know the magics at play in Dovermere are beyond anything we can understand. It cannot be tamed or unraveled or vanquished, not by you or I or anyone else. It's best to leave it alone. There are no answers there to find.

Sometimes death is just that, and accepting it is the best we can hope for."

Baz swallowed a great scalding sip of tea, the note burning a hole in his pocket.

A sudden knock at the door startled him. Selandyn drew herself up with a smile.

"Ah, that must be them."

It didn't register who she might be talking about until she'd opened the door and Baz was staring at two faces that were near mirrors of Kai's.

Professor Selandyn greeted his parents in their native tongue and proceeded to introduce Baz. It was a punch to the gut as their sorrowful faces took him in, as they shook his hand and asked him polite questions about how he knew Kai, if he'd been with him the day he Collapsed.

I wish I would have been, Baz thought, his throat locking up. *I wish I could have convinced him not to do it.*

Baz couldn't bear the thought of hurting his parents any further by telling them what he knew. He couldn't stand there any longer and made some excuse about being late for class. Only as he walked out of Selandyn's office, leaving all of Kai's belongings in his parents' hands, did it hit him fully:

Kai was truly gone.

There might be a slight chance of him eventually being let out of the Institute if he was deemed stable enough to leave, because unlike Baz's father, his Collapsing hadn't hurt anyone, had caused no casualties. But Kai as he knew him was gone. Whoever might walk out of there would no longer fully be Kai. Not the Nightmare Weaver, but a hollowed-out shell of who he used to be.

Later, he stood on the wet sand of Dovermere Cove, the Aldersea's blue-gray waters glistening in the afternoon sun. In the distance,

the entrance to the caves was a half-hidden scar below the rising tide.

Baz listened intently to the wind that pulled at his hair, to the waves crashing against the cliffside. In these sounds, he searched for a melody, the call of the drowned gods or the plea of the guardian pulling on his soul. But all he felt was the dark thrum of Dovermere, which pulsed in time with his own heartbeat.

Death masquerading as mystery, seeking to lure him to his watery end just as it had his sister.

Perhaps Romie, intrepid dreamer that she was, had not been able to tell the difference—had been duped by her grand notions and constant need for something *more*.

And maybe Selandyn was right. Death was just death, a cave was just a cave, and the best thing Baz could do was accept that his sister was never coming back.

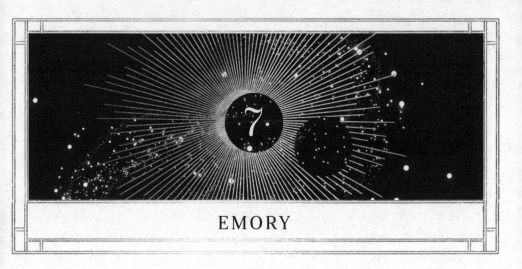

EMORY

SHE WAS LATE FOR HER SELENOGRAPHY LEVEL II CLASS, where her professor was already rambling on about moon placement degrees and calculations and nodes, things that generally tended to go over Emory's head. It was one of those mandatory subjects everyone had been studying since prep school, an exploration into the science that governed their magic and bored most people to death.

When Emory walked into the familiar classroom—the same dark lecture hall last year's class had been held in, tucked away in the lower levels of Noviluna Hall—she was met with a fresh pang of grief, her eyes instantly going to the top row where she and Romie would always sit together, trying not to fall asleep as the professor droned about all the ways silver, water, and blood were connected to magic. Above her, an impressive tableau of waves that went from frothy pastel seafoam to churning black depths was painted on the sloped ceiling, where dainty globes of everlight hung from silver chains like shimmering water drops. She hurried to the

first empty seat she could find, Baz's words grating against her skull.

Do you even care that she's gone?

The fact that he would ask such a thing stung more than his questioning her role in Romie's death. Because *of course* she cared. It was why she'd gone after her to Dovermere in the first place, why she'd come back to Aldryn now. It was why she hadn't given up on their friendship last term, even when Romie seemed so adamant to push her away.

Emory had cared enough to notice everything: all the late nights Romie spent Tides knew where, the parties she came back from with a glazed look in her eye, the classes she missed in favor of sleeping, the way her grades started slipping and the plants in their room died from neglect, and the students Emory occasionally saw her with on campus, huddled together in dark corners with this impenetrable air of secrecy hanging over them. Travers, Lia, Dania. Other students who'd drowned in the caves. Nisha Zenara most of all, who'd seemed to have all but replaced Emory at Romie's side.

Emory had cared even despite how isolating it had felt. While she'd been spending the better part of her time studying in the Noviluna library, fighting for her place at Aldryn because getting in was just the first step and now she had to earn that place by keeping her grades up, Romie had been off chasing the next best thing, the next best friend.

We get to reinvent ourselves here, be whoever we please.

Never had Emory thought this new life Romie imagined for herself might not include her at all.

She barely registered Professor Cezerna dismissing them at the end of class. She was merely going through the motions, grabbing her books only because everyone else around her did, her thoughts so full of Romie she almost didn't hear her name being called through the hum of chatter.

"Emory!"

Penelope West stood a few steps down the creaking wooden staircase, peering up at her with large doe eyes and a friendly smile. "I'm so glad I caught you."

Emory gripped her satchel strap tight as she descended toward her, forcing a smile of her own. "Hey, Nel."

"I tried to catch you at the assembly yesterday, but I don't think you saw me. How are you holding up?"

A question Emory would rather never hear again in her lifetime. "All right, I guess."

Penelope cast a wary glance around them. "Did you hear what happened last night? They're saying Travers's body washed up. That he was still *alive*." She shook her head in disbelief. "I'm sure it's just a rumor, though. He drowned; there's no way he could still be alive."

Emory's throat constricted. She looked away. Penelope gripped her arm. "Wait–were you *there* when it happened?" At Emory's telling silence, her eyes widened to saucers. "And it's all true?"

"Yeah, it's true." She couldn't stand the images that swam in her mind.

"Impossible," Penelope breathed. Her brows knit together. She squeezed Emory's hand. "You poor thing. I can't imagine . . . all those memories it must have dredged up . . ."

The pity in her expression was suffocating. Emory wanted desperately to be anywhere but here. She knew Penelope was only being nice, knew she should be grateful to still have a friend who cared while everyone else only whispered and stared. But Penelope was a reminder of the friendship she'd lost, the one that had meant the world to her. And Romie, she knew, was wholly irreplaceable.

"Ms. Ainsleif, a word, if I may?"

Never had she been so glad to hear a professor calling her name.

"Meet me for supper later?" Penelope asked eagerly as they

climbed down the rest of the steps to Professor Cezerna's desk.

"Yeah, sure."

She touched Emory's arm again. "I'm here if you need anything, Em."

The kindness in her voice made Emory feel bad for being so standoffish. Shaking the thought, she turned to Professor Cezerna. He looked at her sternly from under his bushy brows. "I'm letting you take this class as a courtesy so that you don't fall behind, but since you missed your Level I exam last spring, you'll have to retake it to pursue my class."

Emory dug her nails into her palm. It sounded so painfully normal, given everything going on. But the selenography classes were requirements for all students to graduate; she needed those credits.

"I'll give you time to go over what we covered last year before giving you the exam. How does two weeks sound?"

"That's fine," she said with a polite smile, though inside she wondered how, exactly, she would pull off studying for it on top of doing the work for all her other classes *and* dealing with this new magic she found herself saddled with, all while seeking answers about Dovermere. She'd been keeping on top of her coursework by a single, flimsy thread last year; the chances of her managing it now seemed all but inexistent, though for some reason, she felt entirely disconnected from it all, knowing there were more important things to focus on. "Thank you, professor."

She left the lecture hall feeling unmoored. The rest of her morning was free. She tried to spot Keiran on campus, determined to press him further, but he was nowhere to be found. She was on her way to the library when she passed the Fountain of Fate and halted, an idea springing to mind.

Those sacred lunar flowers still floated on the water's surface, one for each of the students who drowned last spring, the blooms

perfectly preserved by some magic or other despite the early September chill. Emory forced herself to look at the silver plaques fitted below the Tides' marble feet and read the names that had been added to an already long list, all of them dated on the same spring day:

QUINCE TRAVERS–NEW MOON, HEALER
SERENA VELAN–NEW MOON, DARKBEARER
DANIA AZULA–WAXING MOON, WORDSMITH
LIA AZULA–WAXING MOON, WORDSMITH
DAPHNÉ DIORÉ–FULL MOON, WARDCRAFTER
JORDYN BRIAR BURKE–FULL MOON, SOULTENDER
HARLOW KERR–WANING MOON, UNRAVELER
ROSEMARIE BRYSDEN–WANING MOON, DREAMER

She fought down the nauseating images those names conjured. Her eyes traveled up the list. There had been a single drowning victim three springs ago, two more a few years before that. The list of drownings wound back fifty years, a hundred, a hundred and fifty, all the way back to Aldryn's inception nearly four hundred years ago. Never more than a name or two here and there, nothing like the absolute carnage of last term.

But nearly all the drownings, Emory realized, had one thing in common: they happened in May, within the last few weeks of school.

It might be coincidence. If these names proved anything, it was that Dovermere had always been the dangerous beast that it was. But Emory couldn't get her pulse to slow as she rifled through her satchel for a piece of paper to write on. She scribbled names and dates in a hurry, purpose keeping her hand steady.

She would scour the campus archives for every tiny morsel of information she could find on these drownings if it meant

getting any insight into the circumstances that led Romie to Dovermere.

You see? she wanted to yell at the thought of Baz's earlier words. *I do care.*

She didn't find much in the archives, which were located right next to the library in Noviluna Hall. A few newspaper articles about the drowning victims from the last couple decades or so—mostly freshmen, it seemed—and interviews with deans of years past in response to public outcry on the dangers of the caves. She did stumble upon a rather lengthy article on the most recent drowning dated two and a half years ago, which again had taken place in May, but all it told her was that Farran Caine was a Reaper who'd had excellent grades for the entirety of his short-lived time at Aldryn and was sorely missed by all who knew him. He looked dapper in the faded color photograph the newspaper had used, with pale blond curls and a strong jaw, a crinkle around his eyes as he smiled brilliantly at someone who'd been mostly cropped out. It hurt to look at that smile. All Emory saw in it was Romie and the others who'd had their futures ripped away by Dovermere.

What Lizaveta said at the bonfire came back to her. How the eight students who'd drowned were all top of their freshmen class, the best at what they did—same as Farran and some of the others mentioned in these articles, it seemed. But none of it explained what they'd been involved in, why they'd gone to Dovermere at all.

Fury suddenly swept through her. If this was something that had happened for years and kept happening still, why had no one thought to stop it? To barricade the way into the caves to prevent others from dying, or *something*. Whatever it was, Emory couldn't let it happen again, couldn't let anyone else meet their end in the Belly of the Beast.

A familiar voice made her head snap up as she thumbed through the microfilm catalogue in search of older articles that might be pertinent. Keiran was standing near the entrance of the archives, leaning casually against a shelf. He'd changed out of his rumpled clothes and now wore a navy sweater vest over a crisp shirt rolled around his elbows. She couldn't see who he was speaking with, but she didn't care. Determination thrummed in her veins. She slammed the metal drawer shut and strode toward him—only to stop short as Dean Fulton came into view, a grim expression on her face at whatever Keiran was saying.

Emory's ears rang, her vision blurred, as if all the blood in her body suddenly rushed to her head. The gall of him—was he telling on her to the dean, when he'd mocked her just this morning for threatening to do the same to him?

No. No, he couldn't be. He hadn't seen *her* using other magics, not like she had him. She hadn't even properly admitted to being able to do such a thing. *She* had the upper hand here—not him.

Dean Fulton handed him a small object Emory couldn't see, though the way it caught the light had her thinking it was something metallic. The dean met her eye then, making Emory's stomach drop. She muttered something to Keiran before coming her way, and Emory could only think that someone else knew her secret— someone who was very much a stickler for rules and could have very well decided to go to the dean.

Baz.

"Emory," Fulton said, looking as put together as ever in a tweed suit, her salt-and-pepper hair trimmed close to her head. "I've been meaning to catch you."

Here it was, Emory thought. She'd be taken away to the Institute to be interrogated by the Regulators, those in charge of policing the entirety of the magic world, enforcing its rules and meting out punishments. She'd receive the Unhallowed Seal before she

could explain her twisted magic, because who in their right mind would believe this was all Dovermere's fault? They would think, like Baz did, that she'd lied about her birth, hidden what she truly was.

Tidecaller. Tidethief. Eclipse.

"How are you holding up?" Fulton asked.

Emory shifted awkwardly. "Fine, thank you." She braced for what was to come.

"I do hope this time away from Aldryn helped you recover from everything that happened last May. I admit I was worried you might not return at all after the summer holiday. It would have been a shame to lose such a hard-working student." The dean eyed her over her thick glasses. "I'm told you tried to help Quince Travers last night."

She was going to be sick.

But Fulton only placed a gentle hand on her shoulder. "It was admirable, what you did, trying to heal him like that. I hope you know his passing wasn't your fault."

Understanding was slow to settle on her mind. And then, all at once, she realized neither Keiran nor Baz had said anything at all.

Her secret was safe.

Relief flooded through her, instantly followed by a twinge of guilt at the phantom memory of the death she nearly gave Travers. She swallowed with difficulty to ask, "Do they know what caused his death?"

"The Institute's Shadowguides and Unravelers are still looking into it, but it seems there was no stopping whatever strange magic afflicted him. You did everything a Healer could, Emory, especially in such a situation."

"Thank you," Emory said, too relieved to think of anything else, even as Lizaveta's words rang in her head: *A decent enough Healer,*

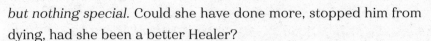

but nothing special. Could she have done more, stopped him from dying, had she been a better Healer?

The dean gave her a sad smile. "If you need anything, my door is always open."

As she left, Emory looked at the spot where Keiran had been, but he was no longer there. She went back to her table. Atop the pile of newspapers she'd left chaotically spread out was a reel of micro-film that hadn't been there before.

Emory frowned. She deftly picked it up and looked around at the now-empty archives. Keiran must have left it there while she spoke with Fulton. She didn't question it as she went to the closest microfiche reader, fumbling around with the slots and wheels and film. She'd never had reason to use these things before, a fairly new invention that had been introduced at Trevelyan University, the most prestigious non-magic school in the world. She got the hang of it at last and pressed the buttons to move through the film.

It was an old *Cadence Gazette* issue dated eighty-some years ago. Emory quickly scanned articles about a brutal winter storm, food shortages due to a ship that capsized off the coast, a new store open-ing down the main road that she was fairly certain still stood today, and some kind of Solstice event the townsfolk had thrown together. She was beginning to think there was nothing here of interest when she came upon a column on Aldryn College's clubs and organiza-tions and, most interestingly, its elusive secret societies.

One name jumped out at her amid the rest, a name that perfectly matched the *S.O.* initials she'd been puzzling over.

The Selenic Order.

Her pulse quickened. The passage read:

> *Among the societies mentioned, the Selenic*
> *Order is perhaps the oldest and by far the most*

*secretive. Little is known of it other than its name,
whispered of between Aldryn's students as being
a sinister cult with a hand in peculiar magics
and arcane rites. Indeed, the recent Dovermere
drownings of students Giles Caine and Hellie
de Vruyes, both of affluent families with a long
history at Aldryn, have led some to believe they
were recruited by the Selenic Order and killed in
what might have been a ritual sacrifice or a failed
initiation. The Dean of Students has denied such
allegations, stating he is unaware of any such
cult or otherwise illegal activities among Aldryn's
student organizations.*

Certainty swelled in Emory's chest. A secret society dealing in odd magics and rituals? This had to be what Romie and the others had died for. And that name . . . Giles Caine. Like Farran Caine. She wondered if other students had been asked to join this secret cult because of their family name rather than the merit of their grades.

Above all, though, she wondered why Keiran, who'd seemed so tight-lipped this morning, had left this out for her to find.

If it was a small kindness on his part, or a trap.

She went about the rest of her day pretending not to hear the broken pieces of conversation about Travers, but it seemed last night's morbid scene was all anybody could talk about. And though none of them had seen Emory's strange magic, thanks to Baz, and it would seem neither Baz nor Keiran had yet to spill her secret, she couldn't help but feel terribly on edge.

That evening, as she pushed food around on her plate while the dining hall filled with students who kept glancing her way, Penelope approached her, food tray in hand.

"Mind if I join you?"

Emory motioned for her to sit, feeling strangely grateful for the girl's presence. She figured people might not stare so much if she wasn't alone. And she was right; they seemed to lose interest in her as Penelope chatted away about her summer vacationing on the southern coast. But when the subject turned to their classes and Penelope offered to lend Emory her old selenography notes and help her study for her makeup exam, Emory thought, somewhat irritably, that her pity might be worse than the whispers and the looks. Still, she smiled and said, "Thanks, Nel."

As Penelope went on and Emory only half listened, her ears pricked up at a nearby voice saying, ". . . why no one's talking about the Eclipse-born who Collapsed over the summer."

Her gaze swept the busy dining hall, landing on a table not too far from theirs where four people sat: Lizaveta, her perfectly coiffed hair curling around her chin; Virgil, with his arm draped across the back of a chair occupied by Louis, the Healer who'd tried to help her with Travers; and Nisha, who seemed entirely engrossed in the book she held in one hand, the other holding aloft a bite of salad that remained untouched.

Louis leaned toward Virgil, his lowered voice making the hair on Emory's arms stand: "I heard he's at the Institute now, got branded and everything."

"Which one was that?" Virgil asked. "The Timespinner?"

"Not him," Nisha said without looking up from her book. "I saw him just yesterday down in the Vault."

Louis shook his head. "It was the other one. The freaky nightmare guy."

"The Nightmare Weaver," Lizaveta said matter-of-factly as she studied her nails.

"Yes, him."

Emory's heart dropped. If Baz had seen his classmate Collapse

after everything that had happened with his father and so soon after Romie's death . . .

No wonder he was so reticent to help her.

Louis leaned forward on his elbows. "Apparently, it happened right here on campus, in the middle of the quad."

Lizaveta rolled her eyes. "You really need to stop believing everything you hear, Louis. It happened at Dovermere Cove."

"How do you know?"

"Because I was the one who found him."

"*What?*"

"I was with Artem down the beach when we saw the blast. Thankfully, Artem had damper cuffs on him. He put them on the Eclipseborn as soon as it was safe to do so and brought him straight to the Institute." She shrugged. "Perks of having a Regulator brother, I guess."

"Well. You know what this means, don't you? With the Nightmare Weaver gone and no new Eclipse students enrolled this year, the Timespinner's the only one left at Aldryn."

"Can you imagine being the only one in your hall?" Virgil sneered. "The parties must be a total bore."

"Their numbers are dwindling, I'm telling you," Louis said.

"Not this again," Nisha grumbled, going back to her book.

"I'm *serious*. Some scholars have been writing about it. There are fewer and fewer ecliptic events, so naturally there's less of them, too."

Emory didn't hear what Lizaveta muttered in response to that, though it looked an awful lot like *Good.*

"Tides, I hate them," Penelope muttered. She watched the group's table with a seething look. "They act like they're above everyone else at this school. I heard they throw these exclusive parties where they do all sorts of weird magic they're not supposed to."

Gooseflesh rose on Emory's arms. Exclusive parties with weird

magic, the kind of thing a certain secret society would do. If Keiran was part of this Selenic Order, it would stand to reason his group of friends might be too. Anger rose in her throat. She glared at Nisha, who looked so innocent reading her book. She'd likely been the one to introduce Romie to the Selenic Order, and Romie, so infatuated with her new friend, had wanted nothing more than to join up.

"Like what kind of weird magic?" she asked Penelope.

"No idea. But whatever it is . . . I know for a fact Lia and Dania started acting weird last year after they started going to the same parties as them. I'm sure you noticed the same happening with Romie, right?"

Emory blinked at Penelope. It hit her then that while she had lost a best friend in Romie, Penelope had lost the same in Lia and Dania, the Wordsmith twins. The three of them had been inseparable, just like Emory had been with Romie. At least, before they'd all gotten involved with the Selenic Order.

Tides, no wonder Penelope was so eager for Emory's companionship—it wasn't out of pity at all, she realized, but a sense of understanding. A shared pain.

Shame roiled in her stomach. She'd been so caught up in her own grief, the thought hadn't even crossed her mind that others had lost friends last spring too.

"Yeah, I did notice." Emory pushed her plate away, feeling nauseous. She'd never seen Romie with anyone from that group other than Nisha, but it would track.

Penelope worried her lip. "Can I ask . . . Why were you all at the caves that night? Was it really just some drunken dare?"

Lying to her left a sour taste in her mouth, but she did all the same. "It was." She hated this. "I went along with it and I shouldn't have, but . . . I was worried. About Romie. And I figured if I went with her . . ."

Penelope's hand reached across the table to grab hers. "Hey.

I get it. I wasn't suggesting–this wasn't your fault, Em. I'm glad you're here."

The food she'd managed to swallow suddenly turned to lead in her stomach. She didn't deserve Penelope's kindness.

Penelope gave her hand a squeeze and drew herself up. "So. Selenography makeup exam study session. How about it?"

Emory had no choice but to indulge her. And it felt . . . *nice*, to do something so normal. To forget for an hour about the horrors that followed her like a shadow. By the time she was heading back to her own room a floor below Penelope's, she felt lighter than she had in months. But when she opened her door, the pit inside her yawned open again.

Nothing was normal, nothing would ever be normal again, because Romie was no longer here.

Emory darted out of the dorms and sought the only place that might ease this ache inside her.

The Waxing Moon library took up the entire first and second floors of Crescens Hall, with a few classrooms down in the lower level of the building. It looked like a giant greenhouse more than anything, bright and airy and full of plants and flowers growing among the books and sprouting from the pale-wood floorboards. Amber light came in through the domed glass ceiling and enormous windows, hitting the vine-covered shelves just so.

Emory always thought that Crescens Hall didn't take itself as seriously as the other ones. Students gathered on long wooden tables in the open-concept space, chatting and debating while the Aldersea glimmered in the distance, the sun setting on its horizon. There was always music playing, delicate strings and notes that spilled from the plants themselves and changed depending on the weather–some kind of Wordsmith magic woven into the fabric of the place.

Romie had loved it. She'd always had an inexplicable fascination

for all things House Waxing Moon, the opposite of her own lunar house in every way: where waxing moon magics were all about growth and amplification, manifestation and influence, waning moon magics were darker, more mysterious. Dreams and memories and secrets and death, things coming to an inevitable end.

Emory imagined that in another life, Romie might have been born under a waxing moon instead of a waning moon. A Sower instead of a Dreamer, since she loved plants so much. But maybe it was just part of Romie's nature to want to dabble in everything, understand how every small facet of life worked.

Emory slipped out the back door that led to the courtyard beyond the hall. The path to the greenhouses was lined with lampposts all aglow with magicked everlight as the sun set, making the hundreds of windows gleam gold. She wound her way through the cluster of glass buildings until she found the small, ramshackle greenhouse Romie used to always disappear to. She still knew her way around the rickety doorknob, the wooden door with its chipped paint, unsteady on its hinges as she pushed it open. An earthy smell wrapped around her, so familiar it nearly brought her to tears.

The feeling was short-lived, for underneath the familiar smell was that of decay and rot. Emory paused, taking in the dreary sight. Though Romie's greenhouse had always stood in a state of neglect—too small and old and weathered for the Waxing Moon Sowers to bother with, with its broken windowpanes and crooked door that let in too much of a draft—it had always been teeming with lush life, kept that way by Romie's careful tending.

Everywhere Emory looked were dead things, once-lush plants and vines now riddled with wilted leaves, clay pots carelessly tipped over and void of life. Empty husks and withered ghosts.

But in a corner of the greenhouse was a pile of objects Emory recognized, curiously untouched by the neglect the rest of the place

had fallen prey to. There was Romie's favorite school sweater, the blanket and pillows she'd arranged on the floor, a pile of books she'd likely borrowed from the library and never had the chance to return.

Behind her, the door creaked loudly on its hinges. Emory whirled to find Baz standing on the threshold, looking as surprised as she felt.

"Sorry," he muttered. "I didn't think anyone would be here."

They stood staring at each other from across the wilted space. Emory noted Baz's disheveled appearance, the glasses that sat crookedly on his nose. He looked tired, as if the events of last night and their encounter this morning had taken everything out of him.

He palmed the back of his neck. "I can go if you . . ."

"It's fine."

"I'll go."

He shuffled awkwardly, hesitating by the door. Like her, he seemed unsure of what to say to fill the silence, to mend what was broken. The space felt at once too big and too small for just the two of them. It needed Romie. Not her ghost, but the real her, the easy way she struck up conversations and made everyone feel instantly at ease. They needed the girl who'd coaxed them out of class at Threnody Prep to run through the wildflower fields down to the beach—something neither of them would have done on their own, but who could ever resist Romie? They needed the girl who'd kicked up sand behind her as she ran barefoot with her arms thrown out wide on either side of her, pretending to be one of the gulls.

That girl had made them laugh. Had made them feel free.

"What are you doing here, anyway?" Baz asked.

Emory glanced at the sorry collection of dead plants. "I don't know." What had she hoped to find here? Romie was gone, and

even the things of hers that remained would not bring her back. "I guess I needed to see this place again."

Baz ran a hand along a beam of whitewashed wood, the paint flaking away. "I came here at the end of last spring to pack up her belongings, but I couldn't bring myself to do it." He cleared his throat, looked away from the pile of blankets and books. "I didn't come back after that. Too many dead things taking root."

Emory brushed a withered plant. "I'd give anything to see it back the way it was."

The leaf beneath her finger was a crisp brown. She wondered what it would be like, to have Sower magic flowing through her like it had on the beach, to grab hold of it and return the plant to a healthy, waxy green. Her eyes flitted over to Baz, who seemed to know exactly what she was thinking.

She let her hand fall.

Baz stuffed his own hands in his pockets. "I'm sorry about what I said earlier. That wasn't fair of me."

Emory ducked her head, picking at her nails. "No, you were right. The funeral . . . It's not that I didn't want to go. I tried, I really did. But after the memorial they held at school . . . I just couldn't go through it again."

"I get it." He looked like he meant it—like he wished to take back everything that happened this morning. "I'm sorry I implied otherwise."

"I'm the one who should apologize for pressuring you into helping me." She thought of what she'd overheard in the dining hall, about his classmate Collapsing. "I get it, you know. The dangers of this type of magic. And as much as I don't want to hurt anyone, I don't want to have them take away my magic either. So I need to figure this thing out before either one happens."

Emory studied him. She could tell it was eating away at him, this conflict between following the rules and helping an old friend in

need. She saw in that hesitation the soft spot he'd always had for her, wondered if it might swing his decision in her favor. If she might use it to her advantage.

She needed him to keep what she could do secret. More than that, she needed his help controlling this magic she knew nothing about, and no one had as much control over their own peculiar power as Baz did. If he could master his Timespinner abilities without ever coming close to Collapsing, surely he could help her master these strange powers the mark had given her. She might not be Eclipse-born like he believed her to be, but it wouldn't hurt to learn everything she could, all the while keeping him close enough to ensure he kept her secret.

Emory ignored the tightness in her chest. Her reluctance was nothing next to the growing desperation she felt. She had to do this, but needed to approach the matter delicately, didn't want to appear too forceful. "I understand if you don't want to help me," she said with a sad, wobbly smile she hoped might tug at his heartstrings. "If you could just point me in the right direction. A book that might help me understand Tidecaller magic, *something* to help me make sense of this . . ."

Baz dug his hands deeper into his pockets, as if rummaging for something in them. He worried his lip, and then the words spilled out of him in a jumbled mess: "Why did you go to Dovermere that night?"

Emory's hands curled inward, nails biting into her palms. *Anything but that,* she thought. It had been one thing to lie to Penelope, but him . . .

Baz let out a sigh and closed his eyes. "The truth. That's all I ask for."

There was such anguish on his face, in his voice, it dislodged something in her. She owed him, yet she couldn't bear to tell him the truth of what little she remembered, see his expression once he

realized he was right to be wary of her magic. That it might very well be to blame for all of this.

Her gaze darted past him as she finally said, "We were drunk and foolish and thought we could best Dovermere. We got to the Belly of the Beast, and then the tide came and I . . . I don't remember much else after that. I woke up on the beach surrounded by bodies, and Romie was gone."

Lying to him—at least in part—was ten times worse than doing it to Penelope. She blinked past the tears forming in her eyes, wholly aware of Baz looking at her. "I'm so sorry. I wish I could go back and stop us from ever going."

Surely, he had to know just how much she cared that Romie was gone. She felt like all these plants around them, left to wither away in Romie's absence. And though the rot had started to set in the moment they'd arrived at Aldryn, with Romie pulling away from her so inexplicably, Emory had still felt like there'd been something salvageable between them then. Now it was too late.

She couldn't save what had been lost, but she could find the reason behind it, at least.

"I would do anything to not have to miss her like this," she breathed.

Baz stared quietly at his feet. "Thank you," he said after a beat, taking his hands from his pockets. "For the truth."

Emory swallowed past the guilt. "It's the least I can do."

Her shoulders dropped as he took a step back toward the rickety door, thinking that was the end of it, that she hadn't been able to sway him. But then he stopped, heaving a sigh. "If you agree to take this seriously and do the work, then I'll do it. I'll help you."

She blinked at him. "You're serious?"

"No using your magic until we figure this out. And if I decide it's too dangerous—if your magic becomes too much of a threat to you and me and everyone around us—you go to the dean."

"All right."

"I mean it, Emory. If I say we stop, we stop."

"We stop."

He studied her face. The dwindling light was reflected in his glasses in a way that she couldn't quite make out the look in his eyes. Finally, he said, "We start tomorrow. Decrescens library, seven a.m. sharp."

"I swear I won't be late this time," Emory said, trying to lighten the mood.

Baz pushed the door open with his shoulder. "Please don't make me regret this."

Alone in the greenhouse, Emory looked at the decay around her and thought perhaps it wasn't too late to mend things after all.

SONG
OF THE
DROWNED
GODS

PART II:

THE WITCH
IN THE WOODS

There is a world not far from our own where things grow wild and plenty.

The soil is rich from decaying flesh and bones and another sort of magic entirely. Trees have roots planted firmly in the underworld and hands that graze the heavens. Everything is tinged in greens and browns and smells of earth and moss as the skies rain down their blessings and marvel at how the world below awakens, stretching its limbs to bask in its own luxuriance.

At the center of this world lies the Wychwood, a forest older and wilder than any other. It is the source of all growth and greenery. Veins run from it, pump magic and other nutrients into the land, and at its helm is the singular witch tasked with protecting it. She is the rib cage that wraps around the heart of the world, her very skin and bones made to keep the Wychwood safe. To ensure each cog in the wheel of life works as intended.

This is not her story, at least not entirely. She is a part of a whole, for where there are flesh and bones surely there must also be a beating heart and flowing blood and a soul to fill the spaces between. The witch knows this, and so she waits for one of these crucial parts to find her, alone in her fortress of roots and rot.

Patience, the trees whisper. *Take heart.*

The first to find her is the scholar from our shores, with the stories he inhales and the words he exhales, as much sustenance to him as air. (Perhaps it would have been a more fitting metaphor to call him the lungs, but in truth he is much more like a bloodstream, for magic runs in his

veins as he runs through worlds like rivers to the sea and blood through arteries.) He knows now that to return to his sea of ash, he must first sail to other shores, other worlds, seek the stories there that might carry him farther than any sailor has gone before.

And here is the first.

Have you come to seek the drowned gods? the witch in the woods asks him, for she, too, has heard their call.

The moon and sun and stars collectively sigh.

They know the story has only just begun.

BAZ

"FIRST LESSON IS: TRY NOT TO KILL ANYONE."

Emory glared at him from across the table, clearly not amused by his lame attempt at a very bad joke. Baz could almost hear Kai snickering at him over his shoulder. *Smooth, Brysden.*

They sat in an alcove between the Dreamer and Memorist sections of the Decrescens library, a wide variety of books strewn open between them on the table. Rain pattered against the small stained-glass window above, creating an illusion of dew on the deep purple poppies it portrayed.

Emory toyed with her disposable coffee cup, picking apart the rim piece by flimsy piece. "You know, in the papers they're saying Travers's death was from natural causes. *Mysterious drowning incident at Dovermere*, they called it."

Baz snorted. He'd read the newspapers. An inquiry had been made into Travers's death, and expert Shadowguides, Healers, Reapers, and Unravelers alike had deemed it mysterious, sure enough, but natural all the same, ruling out any kind of foul

play. "As if there's anything natural about Dovermere."

Emory remained quiet at that. She took a sip of coffee, giving a pointed look at the untouched cup she'd brought him. An offering, even if a tasteless one. "Are you going to drink that?"

"Oh. I, uh, don't drink coffee, actually." At least not that sorry excuse for it the campus coffee carts sold.

"There's a stain of it on your shirt," Emory pointed out.

Baz eyed the telltale brown patch on his favorite cream-colored sweater and palmed the back of his neck. "I just . . . prefer to brew my own."

Tides, did that really sound as pretentious as it felt saying it?

Emory's mouth thinned. She glanced around the empty library, still picking away at her poor cup.

"So why here and not Obscura Hall?" she asked.

"People might ask questions if they saw you coming and going in Obscura Hall all the time." His face heated as Emory lifted a brow. "That's not—I meant they might suspect you're Eclipse-born, not that . . ." Why was he so nervous around her? "Never mind."

The ghost of a smile touched her lips. She drew her legs beneath her, looking at ease in her slacks and fine-knit sweater. "I always liked it here."

Me too, Baz thought. Decrescens Hall was his favorite of Aldryn's four libraries, with its old creaking wood and mazelike aisles, the mismatched tables and chairs strewn about under a ceiling of stars. Golden trinkets and elaborate clocks that told everything but time hid in every corner like plundered treasures, their uses long forgotten. It was a place where dreams slumbered, full of the same dark whimsy that permeated everything House Waning Moon touched.

Mostly he loved it because it was said to be the library Cornus Clover frequented the most when he was a student at Aldryn, possibly even where he wrote his book.

And it was usually quiet enough that Baz could remain unnoticed and unperturbed. Perhaps not as secretive a place as the Eclipse commons themselves, but it would have to do for their purposes; he'd be damned if he let Emory into his one sacred space. It felt odd enough as it was to be in such close quarters with her, breathe the same air, refamiliarize himself with all her mannerisms. It didn't feel real, somehow, and yet it also felt *right*. Like all those years of not really talking to each other melted away and they were just two teens, bonding over magic the way they had before his father Collapsed.

Baz tracked the shimmer of gold in the strand of hair she tucked behind her ear, images of that golden-hued era stark in his mind. He cleared his throat. "Right. So, the Collapsing." He pointed to the book in front of him.

Emory leaned over it. "*The eclipsing of one's self,*" she read.

They both stared at the horrifying sketch below those words, a young man screaming to the heavens, his face distorted in pain as he erupted in an incendiary blast of power. Silver veins bulged on his arms, his neck, his temples.

Baz tapped the illustration. "This is what happens when Eclipse-born aren't careful. We slip into something wild and untamable, a state of power so vast it seeks to erase us entirely. Our magic acts as a sort of eclipse of its own then, burning bright and destructive and consuming us from the inside. Then it goes dark. Makes us . . . evil. It's known as the Shadow's curse. The only way to save us from that curse is for Regulators to brand us with the Unhallowed Seal that puts our magic to sleep."

Emory gave him a sidelong glance. The words she spoke were soft, hesitant. "Like what they did to your dad?"

A tightness in his chest. Silver veins rippling in his memory. A blinding blast of power.

The key is taking carefully measured breaths.

"Yeah," Baz said. "Like that."

He could tell by the way she looked at him that she remembered it too, how it had been back then. The kindness she'd shown him while everyone else shunned him—at least for those first few days after the incident, before even she pulled away, no doubt realizing the other students were right to keep their distance. To fear his magic lest he Collapse.

"I heard another Eclipse student Collapsed over the summer," Emory said slowly. "Were you two friends?"

Baz swallowed with difficulty, trying not to think of Kai's sharp smile and midnight voice. *Had* they been friends? Their relationship could be chalked up to circumstance, two people forced to occupy the same space and confront all the ways in which they were different and alike. They were cognitive dissonance. Night and day. By all logic they shouldn't have worked, yet they'd been *something* enough for Baz to miss him, to feel his absence every time he read in the commons or walked past Kai's shuttered room or brewed too much coffee before remembering it was only him now.

They'd been something enough for him to be furious with Kai for what he'd done, to feel such crushing guilt that he hadn't taken him seriously enough to try to stop him.

The last time Kai had slipped into Baz's dreaming was right after Romie's funeral. Something about sleeping in his childhood bed had made his recurring nightmare more unbearable than usual—until the Nightmare Weaver showed up, making the darkness ebb away. He'd sat beside Baz in the rubble of the printing press until the chaos around them calmed and Baz's dreaming self could breathe easy again.

Are you that bored at Aldryn without me that you find me in sleep even here? Baz had asked.

Clearly you're the one who can't handle being away from me. The

teasing in Kai's tone hadn't quite reached his eyes. *Are you going to be all right?*

I will. I have to be.

Just remember to breathe, Brysden. Don't let the nightmare control you.

I know. Easier said than done.

Kai had drawn himself up, the darkness of Baz's nightmare rippling behind him like a cloak. *It's over now.* A hint of that sharp smile, though it lacked some of its usual mischief, weighted by an uncharacteristic sadness. *Night, Brysden.*

Baz hadn't realized it then—that it had been Kai's way of saying goodbye. The last moment they'd shared before he Collapsed.

"Yes, we were friends," Baz said at last, even though *friends* sounded entirely too reductive.

Emory arched a brow at whatever she heard in his tone. He focused on the book in front of him, clearing his throat. "This is why knowing our limits is so important. Control is crucial, because our magic isn't like the other lunar houses. It's not exactly something you call on. *It* calls to *you*, and you have to learn how to resist that pull while at the same time succumbing to it just enough that the pressure doesn't become too much."

He flipped to the next page, where blood was shown dripping from a hand. "Bloodletting helps relieve some of that pressure, if needed. The other lunar houses use bloodletting to access their magic when it's not their moon phase, essentially leeching from their power's growth cycle so that when their lunar phase comes around again, the scope of their power depends on how often they tapped into it through bloodletting. But it's different for us. Eclipse magic doesn't go through this regeneration cycle. It's just always there beneath the surface."

One of the many reasons people loathed the Eclipse-born so much: they resented the fact they had to live with all these limitations on

their magic—the phasal nature of it and how bloodletting, while practical, came at the price of weakening their magic once their moon phase came around—while the Eclipse-born did not.

"When we use bloodletting," Baz continued, "it actually *weakens* our ties to our magic, lessening that pressure, at least for a little while. Using magic in small doses has the same effect."

Emory glanced at her palms, brows furrowed slightly, as if she could see the power growing in her veins. There was a glimmer of a scar on her wrist, there and gone as she curled her hands into fists and set them in her lap.

Storm clouds gathered in the depths of her blue-gray eyes. "You keep saying *us* and *our*," she said tightly, "but I'm not convinced I'm Eclipse-born at all. I mean . . . Yes, I felt the sort of pressure you're describing this summer, and it did seem to lessen whenever I drew blood or used my healing magic. But all my life, bloodletting has worked the way it should for me, letting me call on my magic outside of the new moon like anyone else."

"Then how would you explain it?"

"I don't know. Maybe it's just a weird coincidence. Something about Dovermere warping my magic. Look what it did to Travers—I wouldn't put it past it to be at the root of this, too."

Baz shifted in his seat, pondering the possibility. The newspapers could spin it however they liked; he knew there was no way Travers's death was natural. It was strange enough that he'd still been alive after all this time—though that might be attributed to his Healing abilities—but the way he died, combined with the sudden appearance of Emory's impossible magic . . .

Maybe Dovermere *did* do something to them.

Baz reached for the note in his pocket, the paper worn completely smooth by now. Again, he thought of showing it to Emory. He wanted to believe what she'd told him in the greenhouse, about why she'd gone to Dovermere and what had happened there. He

wanted to give her the benefit of the doubt, that if she *could* make sense of Romie's note, she'd give him a straight answer.

But after seeing her with Keiran yesterday . . . he had to wonder if she was hiding something. If she, like Romie, was part of something bigger, a larger piece of the puzzle he wasn't being allowed to see.

He left the note in his pocket, feeling somewhat protective of it now, this last piece of Romie he had. Besides, he was meeting Jae Ahn tomorrow, and if anyone knew anything about the missing epilogue and might be able to shed some light on this, it was Jae.

"You're certain the Regulators tested your blood when you were a child?" Baz asked. He couldn't work it out, how it seemed her Tidecaller magic had somehow been locked inside her until now—until Dovermere.

Her voice was honed to something sharp. "I can show you everything—birthing chart, selenograph results, they all say I'm New Moon. A Healer. I know how impossible it sounds, trust me. But I have no more explanation for it than you do because, as you pointed out, the only person who *might* know something left me on my father's doorstep when I was a baby and disappeared forever."

Baz remembered her telling him about her mother, how vulnerable she'd been. *I want to learn how to sail,* she'd said, *and maybe I'll find her out there, still traveling the seas.* He didn't know what to say to her now as she toyed with the ripped-up pieces of her disposable cup, frowning at them as if they were the sad remnants of that childhood dream.

He pushed his glasses up, glancing around the empty library as an idea suddenly struck him. "We should test your blood."

Emory's face blanched. "What?"

"That way we'll know for sure whether you're Eclipse-born or not." He pushed out of his chair. "I know there's a selenograph here somewhere . . ."

The Decrescens library was full of things there was no apparent

use for, from those intricate, mysterious clocks to things as mundane as selenographs, the metal contraptions the Regulators used to test magic in children and confirm the lunar house and tidal alignment that comprised their birth chart.

Baz liked to imagine this was the library the scholar in *Song of the Drowned Gods* had inhabited, full of treasures he might have brought back from other worlds: the marble busts flanking the arch that led down to the Vault, the gold war helmet wrought with motifs of delicate flowers, the wooden effigies depicting gods and goddesses their own world held no recollection of. The selenograph was certainly not from other worlds, but he was certain he'd seen it in here.

They found it in the Memorist section, so high up on the shelves that Baz had to climb up the rolling ladder to tug the machine out from between two thick, cobwebbed tomes. He set it atop the pile of open books on their table and blew on the layer of dust coating it, Emory watching nervously at his side. The selenograph was made up of various cogs, knobs, and needles, an older model than what Baz remembered being used when he was younger. Three vials sat atop it like a crown, one filled with liquid silver, another containing salt water, and the last one empty, meant to be filled with the person's blood. It was the three elements thought to govern their magic: silver for moonlight, salt water for tides, and the blood they both flowed through.

A rusty, antique-looking syringe came with the selenograph. Emory's mouth twisted in disgust as Baz gingerly picked it up.

"I am *not* stabbing myself with that," she warned.

After a moment's hesitation, Baz pulled back the threads of time so that the selenograph and the syringe looked new—still old by all accounts, antiquities, really, but shiny and unmarred, at least.

Emory quirked a brow. "Thought you didn't like using your magic."

"Small bursts of magical release, remember?"

He tried to hand her the syringe, but she shook her head, looking slightly queasy. "I can't do it on myself. I'm bad enough as it is with needles to think about finding my own vein. You'll have to do it." At his horrified look, she put her hands on her hips and said, "This was your idea, not mine. It's easy, you'll see." She sat down and pushed her left sleeve up around her bicep. "I'll walk you through it."

Baz pushed his chair close to hers. He was suddenly all too aware of his body, the awkwardness of his limbs, the blood pumping in his ears. Emory instructed him on how to search for a vein in the crook of her arm. She rested her free hand atop his, guiding it to place the tip of the needle on her skin. He tried to concentrate on her words as she explained how to insert the needle and draw the blood, but the feel of her fingers around his own consumed him.

Tides, when was the last time he'd sat this close to someone? He could see all the delicate strands of gold in her hair, the way the messy fringe that swept her brow curled slightly at her temples.

Get a grip, Brysden.

He swallowed hard and focused on the task at hand. He did exactly as she'd instructed. Emory winced as the needle pierced her skin.

"Are you okay? Am I doing it wrong?"

"I'm fine." She looked up at the ceiling. "Just tell me something."

"What?"

She breathed loudly through her mouth. "Anything, please."

Her unease somehow made him feel more assured, and with her blood slowly filling the syringe in his hand, he felt bold enough to ask, "Do you remember *Song of the Drowned Gods*?"

Emory's grimace twisted into a smile. "Of course. You always had your nose buried in it. You were so obsessed, I remember you drawing the characters in that old sketchbook of yours."

Baz was grateful she wasn't looking at him as a flush crept up his neck. Better she didn't know how obsessed he still was—or that he occasionally still made art inspired by it, in the rare moments he could find the time. "Did Romie ever say something to you about it?"

"Like what?"

"I don't know." His hand almost twitched with how badly it wanted to reach for the note in his pocket. "You know she used to love that book as much as I did when we were kids? We'd play-act scenes together, pretend we were going off on these wild adventures across worlds." He thought of those memories fondly, how he would always play the scholar or the guardian, and she the witch or the warrior. "She grew out of it, but me . . . Romie always teased me for it, but then I found out she was reading it last spring, just before . . ." He stopped himself. "I guess I just thought it was odd."

He took the syringe out, full of Emory's blood. There was a stark look of relief on her pallid face as she pressed a finger to the red pinprick on her arm.

"Maybe she felt nostalgic," she said distractedly, eyes closed and head tilted up to the ceiling.

Baz studied her openly, trying to discern any hints of deceit. He'd never noticed the small freckle on her neck, the particular curve of her mouth, the way it parted as she heaved a grounding sigh. His cheeks burned as he heard again what sounded an awful lot like Kai's sneering voice in his mind, telling him to pull himself together. Before she could catch him staring, he turned to the selenograph, pouring her blood sample into one of the vials.

The three vital liquids—silver, water, blood—dripped slowly into a fourth compartment, a slender horizontal glass tube where they blended to form a murky substance. Beneath it all was what resembled a clock, divvied up in nine sectors: one for each of the

moon's eight phases, and the last for the eclipse. Each sector was quartered off into four tidal alignments, except for the eclipse one, which was cleaved in two—one half for the lunar eclipse, the other for the solar eclipse.

New Moon and Full Moon students, Baz knew, were rarer than their Waxing and Waning counterparts, given that their respective phases lasted no more than three days, while the waxing and waning moons lasted three times as long as that, each one composed of secondary phases—crescent, quarter, gibbous. Without bloodletting, adepts of House Waxing Moon and House Waning Moon could only wield their magic on the specific secondary phase they were born to, which leveled the playing field between lunar houses, everyone having access to their magic for roughly the same amount of time.

If Emory's blood had once made the hand on that clock stop in the New Moon sector, in the first quarter that confirmed her as a Healer, it did no such thing now. It stood firmly in the solar eclipse sector.

"There you have it," Baz said. "Eclipse."

Emory's mouth twisted downward, as if the result displeased her—as if she'd expected something else. But these tests never lied. There was no denying it: she didn't belong to House New Moon. She was Eclipse-born, or perhaps Eclipse-*formed* was more accurate, if her powers had unlocked in Dovermere rather than manifesting in her early childhood.

They locked eyes, and Baz could tell she was thinking the same thing. Wondering if whatever happened in those caves *made* her this way, changed the very fabric of her blood somehow.

Emory rubbed at her wrist. "What are the chances of others having this kind of magic?"

"I think we would have heard of other Tidecallers by now if it was a common gift. Besides, Eclipse-born are rare enough as it is,

so the chances of there being others with the exact same ability as you are slim to none."

"Surely I can't be the only one."

"You might very well be. No two ecliptic events are ever truly the same, which is why Eclipse magics are always so different from one another. There's no real pattern, and that makes it hard to pin down what dictates our abilities." He pointed to the Eclipse sector on the selenograph's clock, marked by a painted yellow sunflower. "It's why we don't have tidal alignments like the other houses do. At least not beyond the distinction between lunar and solar eclipses."

The tide's influence on ecliptic events and vice versa was too curious a phenomenon for even the most brilliant minds to make sense of. Professor Selandyn herself had abandoned her research on the subject a few years ago, dejected by the lack of reasoning behind it. It was part of why House Eclipse had been so misunderstood in the course of history. There was a clear science behind the other lunar houses' magics. They each had four tidal alignments dictated by the tide's position at the time of one's birth—two low tides and two high tides a day, each one birthing a different magic depending on the moon cycle.

But there was no such rhyme or reason behind Eclipse magics other than what scholars had deemed different between lunar and solar eclipses. Lunar eclipses, which occurred during full moons, brought out different variations and offshoots of other lunar magics: nightmares instead of dreams, nullification instead of amplification, festering instead of healing, curses instead of protective spells, and so on.

Solar eclipses, which only occurred on new moons, were even harder to pin down. There were trends, sure enough. Repeating abilities catalogued over time. Illusion magic was the most common among them. It seemed to borrow heavily from Wordsmith magic; indeed, the subtle differences between the two had become

a favorite subject of analysis among scholars. Illusions ranged from small parlor tricks to elaborate ones like the kind that made the wards around Obscura Hall manifest as ever-changing barriers, each more ludicrous than the last. (The wards themselves were Wardcrafter magic, of course, but the shape they took on to scare non-Eclipse students off was Illusion work at its finest.)

Then there was the rare and inexplicable, like Timespinners such as himself and Poisoners who rendered any liquid toxic and Reanimators who could quite literally wake the dead. And if *they* were oddities, then a Tidecaller was an even bigger mystery.

Emory sank deeper into her seat, looking dejected. Baz tried not to take her obvious disdain at the idea of being Eclipse-born too personally. He remembered a time when she'd been intrigued by all things House Eclipse. The awe she'd viewed his magic with . . . She'd thought it made him special, unique, something he'd clung to well after his father's Collapsing forced him to bottle everything up.

Clearly, she didn't feel that same sort of awe now that *she* had Eclipse magic.

She heaved a frustrated sigh. "So what's it going to be, then: Are you going to teach me how to use these powers, or are you going to have me bleed myself dry so that I don't accidentally implode?"

Baz shifted in his seat. Why in the Deep had he thought he could do this when he didn't know the first thing about teaching magic— much less Tidecaller magic?

"What did it feel like, exactly, when you used those powers?"

Emory pondered the question. "Like I was mirroring the abilities of those around me." She frowned. "But I can still feel them inside me. It's like I absorbed them and they're a part of me now, and if I just reach for them, they'll bend to my will because they're mine, not anyone else's."

Baz pushed up his glasses, considering her. "And the other night on the beach. Did one ability feel easier to call on than the others? Apart from healing, of course."

"Why?"

"Well, since you specialized in healing all these years, I think it would make sense for you to have more of an aptness for New Moon magics than the others. Especially with the new moon in position right now, those magics might be easier to wield. Like when you used Darkbearer magic. Was that easier than, say, the Lightkeeper magic?"

Emory looked at her hands, as if picturing the tendrils of darkness and light she'd called upon. "I'm not sure. It all happened too fast."

"I might be wrong, but I think if you were to reach for it again, you might notice it comes easier than the other lunar magics. And then tomorrow, once the moon starts waxing, you'd have a better affinity for *those* magics. Clearly you can use all of them regardless of the moon phase, but it's something to consider."

Emory turned her palms up in front of her and stared at them as though they held all the answers she was looking for. Her brow scrunched in concentration.

The shadows around them shifted.

Baz froze. "What are you doing?"

"I'm trying to reach for the darkness."

"Are you mad–*stop!*"

Darkness gathered between them, shadowing the window. The soft glow of poppies on the stained glass made purple hues dance in the dark nebula. Baz reached instinctively for his magic. Time paused, and for a second, so did the pattering of rain against the window. He plucked the thread that would unmake the darkness, winding back the clock on its existence. It rushed back into Emory, a thing undone.

"What in the Deep was that?" he snapped. "Someone could have seen, or worse, you could have spun out of control."

"Oh, come on, it was harmless."

"There's no such thing as harmless when it comes to Eclipse magic. Haven't you been listening to a word I've said?" Baz sighed, pinching the bridge of his nose. "You can't just start flaunting these powers you know nothing about. You need to learn the theory behind them first."

Emory set her hands in her lap. "I wanted to see if I could do it, make sure the other night wasn't a one-time thing."

"Well, it works. Don't do it again."

Her eyes flitted to the book and its gruesome illustrations on Collapsing. "You're right. I'm sorry."

Mindlessly, Baz took a gulping sip of the coffee she'd brought him, trying to calm his nerves. He winced at the watered-down, almost cardboard-like taste of it before pushing it aside.

Emory watched him carefully. "You know, I've never seen anyone exert so much control over their magic as you do. It's like using it is as easy as breathing for you."

"Trust me, it's not."

"Downplay it all you want, but I've seen what you can do. It's a shame you keep it so bottled up all the time. You could do anything you want with such power."

The words echoed Romie's own questioning of his small aspirations. But where Romie's criticism of him was always dipped in disdain because *she* wanted more for herself and couldn't stand the idea of anyone not wanting the same for themselves, Emory's comment felt different. Flattering. He saw in it that same curiosity and awe she had back at Threnody Prep, reminding him of what his magic could be if he let himself use it without so much fear.

But Baz was no longer the naive boy he'd been back then. In his mind's eye, he saw Professor Selandyn, the grief she carried

at losing her student. Nothing good came from thinking oneself invincible.

"Control is more important than power," he told Emory.

She looked like she wanted to say more on the matter, but instead she asked, "Where should I start, then?"

Baz rifled through the pile of books between them and handed her *An Introduction to Alignments*.

She raised a brow. "I read it last term."

"You studied it through a Healer's eyes and probably didn't pay much attention to all the intricacies of the other tidal alignments. If you're going to use Darkbearer and Lightkeeper magics–*Reaper* magic, for Tides' sake–you need to understand how they work just as much as anyone who specializes in those magics."

Emory thumbed through the thick volume, looking dejected. "There are four alignments for each house. That's–"

"Sixteen alignments to study."

"I'll be reading this until my senior year."

"Best get started, then."

Emory made a show of turning to the first page, righting herself on her chair. Baz grabbed for his own book and noticed her looking at her hands again.

A small smile tugged at her lips. "You have to admit, that darkness was kind of . . . beautiful, wasn't it?"

Baz was too wary of Eclipse magic to ever call it beautiful, but he thought of the darkness reflected in her eyes, of the way her lips had parted in awe as she wielded this small wonder, and his chest tightened.

"Just read the book."

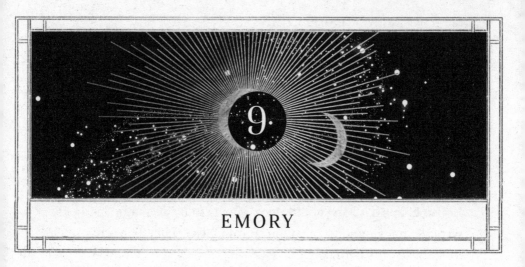

EMORY

EMORY KEPT DOING BAZ'S IMPOSSIBLE READING ASSIGN-ment well into the next day. She read about Seers on her way to her first class and was seized by how strangely accurate their psychic sense could be. She read *in* class, too engrossed in the intricacies of Glamour magic—the compulsive power those with this alignment could wield to bend people's will to their own or influence others' decisions—to care about her selenography notes or the makeup exam she would have to take soon. She read between bites at lunchtime, her razor focus on the way Soultenders could manipulate emotions drowning out the bits of conversation in the dining hall—which, from what little she gleaned, still revolved around Travers's grim demise.

She was still reading later that afternoon on a sunlit bench beneath a cloister window, so captivated by a chapter on Memorist magic that she completely forgot about her next class. A thought occurred to her as she read: If Memorists could see people's memories, could one potentially bring to light the bits and pieces

she couldn't remember from that night in Dovermere?

It would be too much of a risk to ask one—too intrusive and damning to have someone poking around in her head. But if she was a Tidecaller, she might in time learn to do it herself.

The thought was at once thrilling and unbearable, because all Emory saw was the selenograph saying she now belonged to House Eclipse. All she could think of was that this magic made her *wrong*. She wanted to burn the spiral mark off her skin and pray it took these gifts with it.

And yet, even as all those feelings churned inside her, she felt a small glimmer of excitement, too. This sense of *rightness* that had started when she'd reached for the Darkbearer magic in the library—a risk she'd taken only because Baz was there, and she trusted him to turn back time if she got out of control, like he did at the bonfires. That sense of rightness only kept growing the more she read about each alignment. She couldn't deny the curiosity that vibrated through her now, this itch to try all of it, to reach for these magics that could be hers if she wanted.

She did stop reading long enough to meet Penelope in Noviluna Hall for a late-night selenography study session. The library there was as somber as a new moon sky, with two stories of polished dark wooden shelves lined with narrow ladders, a domed ceiling accentuated with silver filigree, and gleaming black marble floors.

It was beautiful in an austere way, calling to mind a winter's night; in fact, a permanent chill permeated the library, as if the dead themselves lingered, out of sight for all but the Shadowguides who might commune with them. The long tables in the middle of the main alley were dotted with frosted everlight lamps and lanterns of varying shapes and sizes, their suffused light casting the place in a silvery blue glow. It would have been an unpopular place among students if it weren't for the thick, luxurious furs that covered the benches, the baskets of woolly blankets found at each table, and,

perhaps above all, the coffee and hot cocoa cart at the entrance of the library that made the whole place smell divine.

Emory stifled a yawn as she looked up, bleary-eyed, from her selenography textbook. She and Penelope were among the last few students here. The other girl was engrossed in an old leatherbound journal from a long-ago Darkbearer, content to sit here with Emory while she studied for her selenography exam. She had even indulged Emory's questions earlier about all things Darkbearer magic, without so much as batting an eye as to her sudden curiosity. It was as if they'd picked up where they'd left off last term, going back to their old routines, and Emory was grateful for this small slice of normalcy.

She'd had quite enough of selenography for one evening, though, and longed to get back to her room so she could keep reading *An Introduction to Alignments* in private.

"I think I'm calling it a night."

Penelope blinked up at her. "Want me to walk with you?"

"It's fine. I wouldn't want to tear you away from your book."

"It *is* rather riveting. This Darkbearer could manipulate her own shadow to do her bidding and used it to spy on people at her queen's request. Can you imagine?" She shook her head in awe. "I'm barely able to fully cloak myself in darkness."

Emory knew Penelope, like herself, grappled with feelings of mediocrity when it came to her magic. Darkbearers had a less practical alignment than most—much like Purifiers and their balancing of energies, which didn't always translate well into the real world. There was a certain unspoken hierarchy to the alignments, magics viewed as elite and those that were less so. Students whose abilities garnered enough attention from talent scouts usually pursued postgraduate studies with full scholarships to the best magic universities and obtained the highest-ranking magically inclined jobs on the market. Meanwhile, students with less desirable

alignments might end up going to regular university after Aldryn to pursue careers outside of their magic, much like those who didn't have enough magic to warrant collegiate studies to begin with.

With a wistful sigh, Penelope turned back to her book. "I think I'll stay here a while to finish reading. See you tomorrow?"

"See you tomorrow," Emory echoed, shouldering her bag. "Good night, Nel."

The hallway outside the library was just as dark and empty, illuminated by a few silver sconces of dim everlight. Her steps were muffled by the thick navy rug that ran the length of the main corridor, so it came as a shock to hear the sudden clink of keys hitting the floor just around the corner. Someone swore softly. Emory slowed as the intersecting corridor came into view.

She recognized Keiran even with his back turned to her. She'd kept her eyes peeled for him these past couple of days, intent on confronting him about the microfilm he'd left her, without any luck. And here he now was, standing before the door to the archives—which the archivists kept locked at this hour.

Odd, she thought, that Keiran should have a key.

He inserted it into the antique-looking knob in the center of the door and disappeared inside without a backward glance.

Emory slipped in after him, careful not to make a sound. He'd turned only a few of the lights on and was making his way to the back of the archives, looking all too at ease in a place he should not have been. Emory watched him rifle through a cupboard and take out a pile of thin, flat wooden cases, which he then gently set on a nearby table. He opened one and bent over its contents with a magnifying glass.

"Keeping tabs on me, Ainsleif?"

She froze. Keiran looked at her over his shoulder, eyes glimmering with amusement. Trying to keep her cool, she stepped out of

the shadows like she'd meant for him to see her all along.

"Just seeing what other illicit tricks you have up your sleeve. More birds that need healing, maybe?"

"I'm afraid last time was all the avian generosity I had in me."

"A shame for the birds."

His mouth lifted in that boyish grin of his, making it difficult to remember why she was here. She came to stand beside the table and looked at what was inside the suede-lined wooden case: a silver plaque that looked like an antique mirror, its surface so tarnished it resembled a mottled, overcast sky.

Emory raised a brow. "You snuck in here like a fiend to look at dirty mirrors?"

"Not mirrors, photographs. And it isn't sneaking if you have a key."

"Which you oh so conveniently have on you."

A dimple deepened in his cheek. "I might have convinced the dean to let me come in here after hours." He gave her a teasing look. "I usually work best undisturbed."

"And what exactly is it you're working on?"

Keiran leaned back in his chair, pointing to the photograph. "Somewhere beneath all that tarnish is a picture. It's one of the oldest forms of photography, where pictures were captured on these silver-plated sheets of copper and revealed when exposed to mercury vapors. The technique is a fascinating one, but as you can see, it hasn't held up well over time. Art conservators and restorers have been racking their brains trying to figure out ways to restore them, but even wiping gently at the surface damages the image particles." He gave her a sheepish smile. "So I'm putting my Lightkeeper skills to the test and developing a method of restoration through concentrated light exposure."

Emory lifted a brow. She couldn't help but be impressed—*this* was the kind of magic that garnered attention and accolades. Keiran

seemed so . . . knowledgeable. Meanwhile, she was struggling to catch up on basic selenography concepts.

With his elbows on the table, he bent toward her. "You see," he said, "no illicit tricks here."

Her cheeks warmed at his sudden closeness, the way his eyes caught on her lips. She was sure he was only trying to disarm her, to keep her from asking questions he didn't want to answer. Two could play this game, though. She fluttered her lashes at him, ran a hand along one of the wooden cases. The way he tracked the movement made her pulse race, giving her the confidence to say, "The Selenic Order must be proud to have you in its ranks."

A slow smile. "You did your research."

Her stomach made a pleasant flip at his appreciative tone. "I had help." She leaned back against the table. "Someone left a rather telling microfilm for me to find."

He arched a brow. "Did they now?"

"Strange, for someone so tight-lipped to suddenly be so forthcoming."

"Maybe this someone was simply trying to be kind."

"Why?" She searched his face for a trace of something real. "You don't owe me anything. You're clearly part of this secret society and either don't want to or can't tell me anything about it since you keep answering my questions in circles. So why help?"

Keiran's smile turned wistful then as he said, "Let's just say I know what it's like to lose a friend to Dovermere. To want answers so badly you risk losing yourself."

Emory blinked back her surprise. She saw in him the haunted look of someone who was well acquainted with grief. A raw sort of understanding passed between them. She had the sudden urge to reach for his hand.

"Farran Kaine," she murmured, thinking of the photograph she'd seen in the paper, the cropped-out person standing next to Farran.

Now that Keiran was in front of her, it was painfully obvious it had been him. "Is that who you lost?"

His throat bobbed almost imperceptibly at the name, but it was all Emory needed to know she was right.

"He was the closest thing I had to a brother," Keiran said quietly. "We grew up together in Trevel, went to the same prep school, came to Aldryn hoping to achieve greatness together. We were nearing the end of our freshman year when he . . ."

"When you went to Dovermere together, trying to get into the Selenic Order?" Emory finished for him. "And he drowned just like the others did last spring."

Keiran didn't deny it.

Anger suddenly sparked in her—anger at the Selenic Order, at anyone who thought risking their lives in such a way was a worthy cause. Still, she couldn't help but feel for him. They'd both lost a friend in Dovermere, had survived what Romie and Farran had not. The difference was, Keiran knew *why*. He was privy to that information while she was kept in the dark, wondering why anyone would let the same deadly ritual happen year after year, evidenced by the long list of names at the Tides' feet.

"So why do it? Why risk your lives for this?" She clutched her marked wrist to her chest, nails digging into that blasted spiral. "Having these other magics running through our veins . . . It's wrong."

He contemplated her before saying, "Some might say we should be allowed to know more than just a fraction of the moon's might, the way it was before magic was splintered into lunar houses and tidal alignments. It certainly wasn't wrong then. Why should it be now?"

Emory thought back to the Darkbearer magic she'd wielded in the library and couldn't deny the appeal. This power—having all magics at her fingertips—she would give it all up in a second if it

meant getting Romie back. But maybe embracing it was the only way forward, the only way to get the answers she so desperately needed to understand *what*, exactly, Romie and the others had died for. To know why she'd been spared too.

And the only way to do that was from within.

"If that's what the Selenic Order believes, then I want in." At Keiran's cocked brow, she pressed, "I survived whatever fucked-up initiation Dovermere was. I did the ritual just like the others and have the mark to prove it. Haven't I earned my way in by now?"

She thought he would deny everything, tell her she'd gotten it all wrong, spin some lie or other to keep the secrecy going. But he seemed to genuinely be thinking her question over. At last, he said, "You being marked is a moot point because the Order didn't invite you. You weren't an official candidate, weren't supposed to be in the caves that night, so it doesn't count."

"Seriously? They'd deny me on some technicality? I was there and I survived, that should be enough."

"Not to the Order. Its leaders are old and set in their ways. Rules are sacred to them."

"Then how else do I prove myself worthy of their oh so sacred ranks? Whatever it is, I'll do it."

"You don't know what you're asking," he said darkly. "What you'd be getting yourself into."

"I don't care. I'm sure I've survived much worse already." She looked at him pleadingly. "You said you know what it's like to lose someone to Dovermere? Try looking for answers and coming up short at every turn. It's killing me, being kept in the dark. I need to know what they died for. Please. It's the only thing that will make this grief bearable."

Understanding rippled between them again. Finally, Keiran leaned back with a resigned sigh. "You heard of the meteor shower happening tomorrow night? The Order's hosting an exclusive

soiree for the occasion. They'll let you in if you show your mark, and I can introduce you to those you need to convince, but . . . the rest will be up to you."

He dropped his gaze to her marked wrist. His fingers alighted on the spiral scar, making her breath hitch. "If you want answers, if you really want in on this . . . you'll need to earn your place. Make them see what you can offer."

She would have to convince them with magic, she realized. Show them the kind of power the mark had given her.

Keiran leaned closer. "Just be sure you want to do this, Ainsleif. Once they let you in, there's no turning back."

A shiver ran up her spine at the underlying danger in his words. It hit her fully then, that people had *died* to join this Order—and here she was, contemplating diving headfirst anyway.

She swallowed past the dryness in her mouth and asked, more confidently than she felt, "Where's this soiree, then?"

Something sparked in his hazel eyes. "The old lighthouse."

BAZ

ASIL BRYSDEN'S LIFE WAS SPLIT INTO TWO DISTINCT
categories: everything that came before his father's Collapsing, and all that came after. In the library of his mind, they were
catalogued under sections aptly labeled *The Peace Years* and *The
Aftermath*. The former held a collection of colorful books stacked
haphazardly among happy memorabilia both material and not: his
favorite *Song of the Drowned Gods* figurines and artwork; the pre-
ciously bottled scent of his mother's baking; an old pocket watch
he and Romie had spent hours tinkering with when they were
younger; the sound of machinery in his father's printing press; the
smell of ink; the warmth of sunlight and the sway of wild grasses
in the breeze and the fervent cries of gulls joining the melody of a
young girl's laugh.

The Peace Years were gold-hued and joyful. Void of fear and hurt.

The Aftermath was a more austere section, every scar archived
in neatly displayed tomes that each looked drabber than the last.
His father receiving the Unhallowed Seal. His mother's subsequent

depression. Baz's own isolation from the world as he realized what it truly meant to be Eclipse-born. Romie's drowning and Kai's Collapsing.

Moments of joy were few and far between here, and most of them could be attributed to a single book. Indeed, there was a copy of *Song of the Drowned Gods* wedged on every shelf, in between every other dreadful volume of his life after the incident. It was Baz's only constant, this book. The one bit of solace that carried him through both peace and aftermath.

His father's old business partner had been the one to introduce him to Cornus Clover's book. Baz remembered very clearly sitting in the Brysden & Ahn printing press when it was still a budding enterprise, his father a frazzled mess with ink stains on his hands and his shirtsleeves bunched up around his elbows, while Jae Ahn sat unperturbed as ever, feet kicked up on a bit of machinery, absentmindedly humming to themself as they looked over the quality of the printers' work.

Young Baz had been enraptured by Jae. They always had a story for him, about the voyages they'd made or of the home in the Outerlands they'd left long ago or of the beasts and dragons and heroes they'd read about in all the fantastical tales they consumed. Jae had been the most fascinating person to Baz, who was already so in love with stories that he couldn't help but delight in Jae's knack for telling them. Jae was also the first adult to not treat him like a child. They fostered his interests, showed him how everything at the printing press worked, thus getting him to appreciate the labor that went into the making of every single book.

When Baz first saw Jae with a copy of *Song of the Drowned Gods*–a beautifully illustrated special edition–he'd been mesmerized by an illustration of the scholar meeting the witch in the woods. And though Baz had been too shy to ask, Jae had noticed his interest and handed him his own brand-new copy the very next day.

"This here is the best book you'll ever read," they'd said. "Do you know why?"

Baz had shaken his head, overwhelmed with wonder.

"Because this book is magic. It's like a portal, you see. It lets you step into other worlds and exist there for a time."

"What kind of worlds?"

Jae had winked at him. "Open it and see."

Baz had done just that and fallen irrevocably in love. The rest was history.

Jae was easy to spot now in the shabby tearoom Baz entered; in fact, they were the only person there, other than the plump woman behind the glass display full of whimsical sweets, and Baz himself, whose presence was announced by the chime over the door.

It was a strange little shop, an oddity in the middle of Cadence. Baz knew of it only because Professor Selandyn had once sent him to purchase not tea, as one might think, but a rare sample of rainwater the shop was known to collect and sell for bloodletting practices. Faint sunlight filtered in through the slender windows, falling on the back shelves burdened with multiple vials and recipients of water—an impressive collection, Baz had to admit.

Once, magical adepts who wished to use their abilities when it was not their ruling moon phase bled into a particular body of water, like the sea or a lake or a stream, where they would wash their blood as an offering to the Tides. Nowadays, most people simply kept a small collection of water samples on hand. Bloodletting only worked when one's blood came into contact with water, after all, and different water sources were believed to yield different magical results. Professor Selandyn was a tad obsessed with the study of water properties and bloodletting, if only to debunk baseless myths—like the shop's rainwater, rumored to make one's power never wane, which turned out to be nonsense, as she'd suspected.

Baz just came here for the tea.

Thin, narrow eyes swept over him as he approached Jae Ahn's table at the back of the room. "By the Shadow," they swore as they jumped from their seat, "you look more like him with each passing year."

Baz smiled shyly as they drew him in for a bone-crushing hug, then held him at arm's length, peering at him over tiny half-moon glasses to assess all the ways in which he resembled Theodore Brysden. Jae hadn't changed one bit: they were on the small and slender side, with jet-black hair kept in the same short style Baz remembered, though it was now streaked with faint strands of silver. They had never ascribed to the gender binary, preferring to use neutral pronouns, and their style could be described as androgynous: today they wore a charcoal knit vest over their ample-sleeved white shirt, layered silver chains visible around their neck.

"Thanks for meeting me." Baz sat on a plush lavender upholstered chair. In the background, a jaunty tune blared from a gramophone. "How've you been?"

Jae swept an impatient hand in the air. "Never mind little old me. What about you, Basil? How are you?"

Baz shrugged; Jae hummed as if he'd said quite a lot indeed, and leaned forward in their chair. "I'm so sorry to hear about Rosemarie—sorrier still I couldn't make it to the funeral."

"That's all right." Unlike Emory, Jae had at least notified Baz of their absence—they'd been away on a research trip to the Constellation Isles and couldn't make it back in time.

"How's your mother been dealing with everything?" Jae asked. "I called her last time I was in Threnody, but she must have been out. I'll have to try her again next time I'm there."

"She'd love that, I'm sure."

Jae gave him a knowing smile tinged with sadness. They both

knew she likely wouldn't answer next time either. It hadn't been easy on his mother for a long time now. Anise Brysden had begun to shut down after her husband Collapsed, distancing herself from the warm, lively woman she used to be. A part of Baz always felt guilty at being here at Aldryn, leaving her alone in that big empty house. Whenever he asked, she always swore she was fine. He knew she wasn't, but Baz didn't know how to help her because he'd often felt much the same, as if he were simply going through the motions of existing. He knew Jae had tried many times to coax his mother back to her former self, inviting her to gallery openings and tea outings every time their work brought them to Threnody. But Anise always gently shut them down, staying sheltered in the safety of her home. Alone with her ghosts.

Baz's eyes drifted to the Eclipse sigil on the back of Jae's sun-kissed hand as they poured him a cup of steaming tea. Jae dealt in illusions, the most common magic among the Eclipse-born. Professor Selandyn still talked fondly of the illustrious Jae Ahn, the best student she'd ever taught in her long career.

"How is everything at Aldryn?" Jae asked, wrapping their ring-adorned hands around their own gold-rimmed cup.

They didn't need to elaborate for Baz to know they meant specifically with the Eclipse students. He took a sip of his tea. Jasmine, with notes of vanilla. It scalded the roof of his mouth.

"I'm the only one left."

Jae's mouth thinned. "I heard about the Salonga boy Collapsing. Did you know he'd contacted me sometime before, asking about my research on the matter?"

Baz went very still. "I wasn't aware of it, no."

He'd once told Kai of Jae's vested interest in all things House Eclipse, but he never thought Kai would go so far as to reach out to them.

"By the time I tried getting back to him, I'd learned he'd Collapsed.

It's partly why I'm in town, actually. He's at the same Institute as your father, so I mean to go pay him a visit." Jae regarded Baz over the rim of their glasses. "Have you been to see him recently?"

Whether they meant Theodore or Kai didn't matter, because the answer remained the same.

Baz fiddled with his teacup. "You know how particular the Institute is about visitors."

It wasn't the real reason—though the Regulators *did* make it especially difficult for Eclipse-born visitors to step into the Institute—but Baz felt ashamed enough as it was; he couldn't admit to Jae that facing his father and Kai was too difficult. That the thought of the Institute still gave him nightmares.

The Institute was multipurpose: There was the administrative side where magical laws were written and enforced, and the correctional and rehabilitation side where magic gone wrong all but went to die. There was, of course, the Collapsing wing where Eclipse-born who'd received the Unhallowed Seal could adjust to their new magicless existence before being sent out into the world again. There was even a Dreamer wing, where those who'd lost their minds to the sleepscape, leaving behind comatose bodies, were watched over and taken care of by Healers. And then there was the prison wing, where anyone who misused their magic was sent, like Reapers who took lives or Glamours who coerced people into doing unspeakable things or Eclipse-born like Baz's father whose Collapsing had killed those trapped in the blast.

At the center of it all were the Regulators. Both legislators and law enforcers where magic was concerned, they governed the entirety of the magical population, answering to their own hierarchy within their ranks.

Self-serving bastards, Kai would sneer, rightfully hating the power they wielded.

Baz had visited his father at the Institute only a handful of times shortly after the incident. It never sat right with him, being inside those walls. It was suffocating, and whenever his mother had wanted him to go with her, his answer would always be the same: *I can't.* At least Romie had been there to step in, hold their mother's hand through the pain those visits caused her.

Jae grumbled into their tea. "Last time I went, the Regulators almost didn't let me through. I had to . . . *persuade* them, if you know what I mean." They winked at Baz. "A little harmless illusion work to get me through the door."

The corner of Baz's mouth lifted at that.

"Your dad would love to see you, I'm sure."

His throat constricted. He suddenly remembered what Kai had said about the nightmares of those who'd Collapsed: an infinite, hollow darkness. If that was the state of their dreaming, Baz could only image what cruel sort of torture their waking hours must consist of.

He tried not to think of how, somewhere in the middle of the city of Threnody, only two hours from here by train, the printing press his father and Jae had worked so hard to build from the ground up was now a pile of rubble. The skeleton of a building no one had bothered tearing down years after the incident that destroyed it. Baz had made the mistake of walking past it once during a Solstice holiday. Vines grew along the solitary piece of brick wall still standing. Snow had blanketed the rest like ash, all that was left of the destruction his father's Collapsing had wrought.

Memories of that day were frayed. Baz couldn't recall how his father's Collapsing came about, only that it did. Only that it *killed*. None of the employees who worked for him and Jae, but the three clients who'd been in the building at the time. All had been caught in the blast of Theodore's uncontrollable power.

Jae and Baz had been inexplicably spared. It was nothing short of a miracle they were both still alive–especially Baz, who'd been standing at his father's side when it happened. He remembered how Theodore's arms had curved around his small frame, sheltering him from the crumbling building, from the outward blast of his power itself.

Silver veins and light and blood and screams.

"You could come with me if you'd like," Jae suggested, dark brown eyes roving over Baz's face. "If it's too difficult to face alone."

Baz took a sip of tea. "Maybe. I don't know."

At the prolonged silence, Jae set their empty teacup on its saucer and draped an arm over the back of their chair. "So. You called me here because of our mutual love of Clover's masterpiece."

Baz was thankful for the change of subject. "Yes. I'm wondering what you can tell me about the missing epilogue."

Jae vibrated with excitement. "I was wondering if you'd ever come around to asking me about that." They'd written many papers on Cornus Clover over the years, and were widely considered to be one of the leading experts on all things *Song of the Drowned Gods*. Their main area of expertise was the epilogue, with all the intrigue and theories surrounding it. "You always seemed so content with how the story ended, never asked yourself what might have been Clover's intended ending."

Baz shrugged. "It's a good ending as it is. Bittersweet, sure, but I can't see how else it could have gone."

"Really? It's all I ever think about."

"Kai too."

Jae made a low humming sound. "He did mention something about it when he wrote me, asking me all these questions about the epilogue."

"What kind of questions?"

"Oh, the usual. Where did it disappear to? Was it lost, stolen,

destroyed? What do I think the epilogue might have been about? That sort of thing."

Baz himself had never wanted to speculate on the matter. If he couldn't know for certain what Clover had truly intended, then he would content himself with the book's current ending. And he genuinely *liked* the bittersweet way it ended. In the last chapter, the four heroes of the story finally made it to the sea of ash to free the drowned gods, only to end up trapped there themselves. Lured by the gods—a thinly veiled analogy for the Tides—to their prison of ash so they could take the gods' place, free them from their sentence in that bleak world.

Once freed, the gods disappeared, leaving the heroes trapped, alone in the dark. They heard a great rumbling at the center of the sea of ash, a beast unleashed with the gods' leaving—the Shadow, as some speculated. And now the beast was theirs to watch over, their duty to keep it contained in the sea of ash.

The scholar, the witch, the warrior, and the guardian *became* the drowned gods, joining forces to face this darkness at the center of all things, as the gods before them had done for centuries. A life for a life. The cycle starting anew. The sea of ash needed its keepers to guard the deadly beast within. Blood and bones and heart and soul, combined to keep chaos and death from spilling across all worlds.

Baz looked at Jae and asked, "What *do* you think Clover wrote in that epilogue?"

"I think the possibilities are endless." Jae's fingers danced against their teacup. "The story we know is a cautionary tale because of how it ends. But it might have been something else entirely with that epilogue. Did the heroes defeat the monster slumbering below the ash? Did they find a way to leave their new prison like the drowned gods before them and return to their respective home worlds? Or did they find contentment in the sea of ash, because

these people they'd crossed worlds to find had, in a sense, *become* their home?"

Many believed the heroes of the story were metaphors for the four lunar houses: the scholar was House New Moon, the witch was Waxing Moon, the warrior, Full Moon, and the guardian, Waning. They imagined the fate reserved for the heroes was Clover's way of likening the four houses to divinity–to show that, even with the Tides gone, they were mighty enough to rise to the challenge without them.

Jae scoffed at such theories, arguing the ending was proof that Clover, a known Healer, was a fervent criticizer of religious zealots back in his day, a time when the myth of the Tides still held weight, and distrust of the Eclipse-born ran much deeper than it did today. Which Baz had to admit made sense, given the trickery the drowned gods resorted to in order to betray the heroes in the book–those who'd believed in the good of these gods so much, they'd traveled across worlds to find them, only to meet their doom.

Jae took a sip of tea. "Why the sudden interest in the epilogue?"

Baz let the heat from his cup seep through his hands. "Romie, actually. Did she ever ask you about it?"

"*Romie?* No, never. Didn't even know she was interested in the book."

"Me neither. Until just recently."

Baz told Jae about the manuscript in the Vault, of Romie's note inside it. He shared his suspicions about the Sacred Spiral, how it represented the descent from the physical world to the Deep–or, as Clover put it, the descent from one world to the next, all the way to the sea of ash at its center.

Jae arched a dark brow. "What are you asking me, exactly?"

Baz shifted uncomfortably, conscious of how he must sound. "I guess I'm wondering if there could be some elements of truth to Clover's story. If these things could all be linked to Dovermere and

the epilogue somehow." He fidgeted with his cup. "There's something strange about the drownings there, Jae."

Baz proceeded to tell them about Travers, how it was not a corpse that washed ashore the other night, but someone who was still very much alive before he suffered such a horrid end.

Jae rubbed pensively at their chin. "And you think the same might be true of Romie? That she might be . . . not quite dead?"

"I don't know what to think anymore."

Jae watched him carefully, the music from the gramophone and the strident whistling of a boiling kettle the only sounds around them.

"Don't take this the wrong way," they said at last, "but have you considered going to a Shadowguide? Might be worth the trouble asking one to seek Romie's soul beyond the veil, if it can bring you a sense of closure."

Baz stared at his near-empty cup. The thought had crossed his mind, but he couldn't bring himself to do it. Couldn't let himself hope she *wasn't* dead, only to have those hopes crushed and face the full weight of his grief once more if she *was*. There was something of Selandyn's words in Jae's suggestion, and though normally Baz would be the first to jump at any chance to get closure, to put all these difficult thoughts to rest and return to the ease of his routine, he couldn't let this go.

Jae blew out a sigh and wrote something down on the back of a lavender-trimmed napkin. "If you're adamant about going down this path, I know people here who might know something about the epilogue." They held the napkin between them, but snatched it back before Baz could take it, hesitation lining their features. "The missing epilogue has always been a source of fascination among Clover fans, and something that's become an unhealthy obsession for many. Don't let it consume you, too."

They handed Baz the napkin, where a name had been scribbled

over an address in Cadence. "*The Veiled Atlas*?" Baz read.

Jae rolled their eyes. "It's what this group calls themselves. That, or *Clover's Inner Circle*, which really is just laughable."

"Who are they?"

"One might call them a cult. They believe everything Clover wrote about in *Song of the Drowned Gods* was true and that Clover him-self went through all these other worlds." They snorted. "Specu-lations bordering on fanaticism, if you ask me. I would take what they say with a heavy pinch of salt. None of them have any sort of credentials to back up their claims. But if hearing what they have to say gives you closure . . . Ask for Alya Kazan. She's usually quite secretive about all this, but if you tell her I sent you, she might be willing to help."

They considered him closely. "She's a Shadowguide, and a damn good one at that. Do with that what you will."

Baz folded up the napkin and stuffed it in his pocket. "Thank you, Jae."

Jae reached across the table to pat his hand. "You know you can come to me with anything. We're family, you and I. We stick together until the bitter end."

Emotion threatened to choke Baz. He knew Jae meant well, but their words only conjured his father's face, Kai's too, and more guilt than Baz could bear.

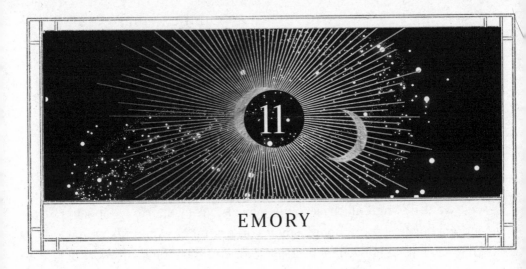

EMORY

EMORY'S STOMACH WAS IN KNOTS ALL DAY AS SHE THOUGHT of tonight's Selenic Order soiree.

She'd barely gotten any sleep after her encounter with Keiran in the archives. Instead, she'd stayed up all night reading *An Introduction to Alignments*, determined to learn all she could in the short time she had. She refused to walk into that soiree ill-prepared; having at least some grasp on this new power of hers would put her mind at ease, but for that, she needed *practice*.

It was how she found herself in Romie's greenhouse before the sun had even begun to rise, hoping to make something happen before her study session with Baz. It was a risk without him here to stop time for her, she knew, but one she was willing to take. No help was needed, in the end, because try as she did, she couldn't quite grasp the Sower magic she'd used on the beach the other night, despite it now being a waxing moon. And when she aimed for Darkbearer magic instead, thinking of the cloud of shimmering

blackness she'd called upon in the library the other day, it was like the rising sun that filtered through the dirty glass panes chased away the flimsy shadows she tried to pull on. By the time she reached for Lightkeeper magic, head pounding and ears ringing with Lizaveta's voice chanting *mediocre* over and over, she was late meeting Baz.

She left the greenhouse with a frustrated sigh, feeling like a failure. It felt like she was back at prep school, ten years old and trying to achieve the simplest magic that every other Healer in her class had already mastered. She had been ridiculed; told she'd never wear House New Moon's sigil. *Go back to being a nobody in your nowhere town*, a particularly nasty girl called Mildred had jeered at her. And Emory had been ready to do just that because everyone was right. She didn't belong at Threnody Prep, wasn't like most kids there who were either brilliant or came from families with money. She was the motherless daughter of a humble light-house keeper, whose own magic was never enough to send him to Aldryn College.

Her father had scraped for every penny to send her to Thren-ody, knowing how badly she wanted to go to Aldryn and make something of herself. *My place was always here*, he'd told her, *but there are wider horizons calling you, just like they did your mother.*

She'd wanted so desperately to be like Luce, had entertained all these grand notions about herself, which all got reduced to dust when she got to Threnody and realized how insignificant she and her magic were compared to others. If it weren't for Romie, she might have run out of there crying and never left her father's light-house again.

Emory remembered the morning everyone in their dorm room woke to find a crying, embarrassed Mildred had wet her bed. Romie had looked innocently at her and said, "You shouldn't drink

so much water before bed, Mildred, if you're going to dream about running streams and waterfalls all night."

Fury had swept over Mildred's face. "You *bitch–*"

"It's pronounced *Dreamer*, actually," Romie had said, looping her arm through Emory's. "You'd do well to remember it next time you want to come at my friend."

The two of them had become inseparable right then and there. Emory had been enthralled by Romie, had tried to emulate everything she was–bold and magnetic and uncaring of what others thought of her. Emory had eventually found her stride at school, thanks to her, and without the pressure of bullies, she'd come to realize she wasn't bad at all, was even better than some. Never as good as Romie, of course, but that had always been fine because *Romie* thought she was good, and special, and funny, and deserving of her friendship. And that was all that ever mattered to Emory.

But without her here, she couldn't see it, her own worth.

She had everything she'd once wished for–something that made her unique, the ability to pull on all alignments the way Romie had always wanted–yet she seemed doomed to be just as mediocre a Tidecaller as she'd been a Healer.

Emory was in a foul mood by the time she got to the Decrescens library, itching to get something done more than reading. She slumped into the chair across from Baz and dropped the book he'd given her onto the table. "All done."

Baz eyed her over the rim of his glasses. "All of it?"

"Front to back." She smiled sweetly, fluttering her lashes at him. "So can we start practicing some magic now?"

His mouth quirked up like he thought she was joking. "You can start *A Deeper Look into Alignments* next. I think there's a copy lying around here somewhere. Dreamer section, maybe."

Emory picked at the coffee cup she'd stopped to get on her

way–her second by this point already. "How long will you have me studying all these books before I get to practice? Until I know all the ins and outs of every tidal alignment?"

"If that's what it takes, yes."

She rolled her eyes. "No one even knows that much about their *own* tidal alignment. You can't expect me to know every single thing about every single one of them. It's impossible."

"A few days ago, I'd have said Tidecallers are impossible." He cocked a brow at her. "Yet here you are."

Something in his teasing tone–in the way he held her gaze more steadily than he normally would–took Emory aback. Was he trying to *flirt* with her? She took a scalding gulp of coffee, breaking his stare. Her leg bounced nervously beneath the table, and she couldn't tell if it was from the caffeine or Baz or the creeping restlessness she felt, this same pressure in her veins that had been there all summer.

"Maybe I should go grab my bloodletting instruments," she mused. At Baz's puzzled expression, she added, "If I'm not going to use magic anytime soon, I'll have to resort to bloodletting, won't I? You said the pressure would become unbearable and I'll likely Collapse unless I use magic or bleed myself of it."

She couldn't keep sitting idly by in this library; she needed to *do* something.

"I'm losing my mind, Baz. All this studying won't get me anywhere if I don't start practicing. And I know you have this weird thing about using your own magic, but–"

"*Shh.*"

Baz's eyes widened on a spot behind her, his face leeched of color. Emory turned to see a student in a nearby aisle, looking right at them.

Shit.

If he'd heard her . . .

But as the student neared, Emory noticed his glazed, distant look, the slow, methodical shuffle of his feet. He passed by without so much as a second glance their way, blood dripping from his palm. The poppy-and-crescent sigil of House Waning Moon on his hand had her breathing a sigh of relief. It was only a sleepwalking Dreamer, caught in the throes of whatever magic he'd accessed through bloodletting.

The color still hadn't come back to Baz's cheeks when he muttered, "Maybe we should find another place to study."

"He didn't hear anything."

"He *could* have."

"And you could have wound back time to make it so that he never did." She took a sip of coffee, looking at him pointedly. "Because *you're* allowed to use magic."

He gave her a wry look and was about to say something when they heard, "Oh, Basil, there you are," and nearly jumped out of their skin.

Someone else was here, almost completely hidden behind a lop-sided pile of precariously stacked books. "Help me with these, will you?"

All tension left Baz's shoulders. He leapt from his chair to grab the books from the person's hands, and Emory instantly recognized the Eclipse professor. The Omnilinguist. Her eyes found Emory's, and it was like the professor could pierce through her soul and sense the Eclipse magic in her veins.

"Who's your lovely friend?" Professor Selandyn asked Baz with a familiarity that reminded Emory just how small House Eclipse was, how close-knit those within it must be. Her heart ached at the thought in a way she didn't quite understand.

"Emory Ainsleif," Baz said for her, and she couldn't help but notice the way his ears went red. "She's . . . She was Romie's friend."

"Oh." The professor looked between the two of them and hummed,

nodding her head sagely. "Good. Grief is too heavy to carry alone." She gave Emory a sad smile, then patted Baz on the arm. "Could you help me bring these up to my office? I want to get an early start this morning. I'm feeling inspired."

Professor Selandyn disappeared with a wink at Emory.

Baz shifted beneath the weight of all those books. "Sorry," he said. "Maybe we can meet in Romie's greenhouse later tonight?"

Emory wanted to grumble at the thought of the greenhouse full of dead plants, a reminder of what she still could not do. But she was adamant to try again before appearing in front of the Selenic Order.

She looked Baz over, a thought occurring to her.

The Eclipse professor had a point: grief was a heavy burden, and maybe she could use it to her advantage, leverage it to convince Baz to help her practice.

"All right," she agreed, smiling despite the guilt that threatened to consume her. "See you tonight."

Emory found a note had been slipped under her door after class, stating simply: *Dress to the nines, Ains.–K*

She stormed her closet in a panic, pulling every piece she had until, at last, she found a cream-colored satin dress she'd never gotten to wear, purchased in town with Romie at the start of their first term. An overlay of gauzy, bluish-gray material started at the waistline, giving it the impression of sea-foam kissing the shore, the delicate hues of a conch shell under the sun.

"You look like one of the Tides just emerged from the sea," Romie had said to her in the shop, eyes wide with envy.

It *was* gorgeous—something she was starkly aware of as she entered the greenhouse. Baz was already there. He looked up from the book in his lap, gaze catching on her dress the way a few students had on her way here. Emory hadn't felt out of place out there, though: with the meteor shower tonight, party preparations were

already well under way across campus, the student body abuzz with anticipation, and more than a few people dressed just as fancy as she. But here, alone with Baz . . .

He made no comment, but as his eyes quickly slid back to his book, Emory saw the faint blush creeping over his neck and wondered if the torch he'd carried for her all those years ago still burned. If their working together might have rekindled it.

Her mind drew back to that time, to the boyish infatuation he'd had with her. It had flattered her, made her feel seen and wanted and important. He'd never acted on it, of course, but she'd always known. Might have even felt the same for the briefest moment. But everything had changed after the Collapsing incident. Not at first—she hadn't cared then, not as she healed Baz's wounds and thought how very cruel the students of Threnody could be.

It's nice of you to stick by his side like that, Romie had said when she'd found out about Emory healing him. *I always thought the two of you were meant for each other.*

Emory felt ashamed of it now, how much that comment had bothered her. She didn't think she was anything like Baz, so how could Romie suggest they were meant for each other? Baz had always been a bit quiet and reserved, but after his father's Collapsing, he became a complete recluse, reminding her of everything she'd been trying so very hard not to be: someone who led the kind of unassuming life on the sidelines that her own father had settled for, that she never wanted for herself.

What Emory wanted was to be like Romie and Luce, not this nobody girl she'd been when she first got to Threnody Prep. She couldn't go back to that sheltered life, didn't want Romie thinking she wanted that either. So she pulled away from Baz after that. Started to seek the attention and approval of boys who weren't such outsiders, the kind Romie had no trouble getting. Her first kiss was with one such boy, a student a grade above them who

was always getting in trouble with the principal. *I guess I had you figured out all wrong,* Romie had laughed after that. She'd never mentioned Baz to her in that way again.

And now . . . Baz was still that recluse, but one Emory needed.

She sat next to him on the arrangement of blankets on the floor and cleared her throat. "I'm heading to some party later for the meteor shower," she said by way of explanation, smoothing the folds of her dress. A half-truth, at least. "It's supposed to be quite a show." She gave him a sidelong glance. "Are you going?"

Baz snorted. "To a party? No. Besides, I can watch it here just fine." He motioned to the ceiling, where some of the windowpanes were broken, unveiling the skies above.

Emory watched him for a beat. She was used to seeing him tense and on edge, a tightly wound bundle of nerves held up by a single thread, but here among the decaying leaves, he seemed different. More at ease. And she liked this version of him: it called to mind a younger Baz, the one from before his father's Collapsing, whom she had seen then as an extension of her and Romie's friendship.

She wasn't sure if it made it easier to use that to her advantage— or tougher on her conscience. Ignoring that nagging pang of guilt, she rested her head back against the glass pane and looked up at the sky.

"Looks like it's already started."

A white line darted across the dark expanse, another right on its heels. They looked on in silence as stars winked in and out of existence. It was a comfortable sort of silence, a sacred silence, and Emory thought Romie might have smiled to see them like this.

"Remember the time Romie snuck us out of our dorms in the middle of the night to look at the stars?"

The corner of his mouth lifted at the memory. "She nearly got us in trouble."

"Wasn't she always? You didn't mind that sort of rule-breaking so much back then."

"Trust me, I did. I just wanted to . . ." He trailed off, ducking his head like he'd said too much.

"Wanted to what?"

He palmed the back of his neck. "To keep an eye on her. On both of you. So you didn't do something *too* reckless."

Emory couldn't help but think he'd started to say something entirely different. That the sole reason he tagged along on all of Romie's reckless ideas was for *her*.

"She told us stars and dreams are the same," Baz murmured. "That when she walked in the sleepscape, all she had to do was reach for a star, and that's how she'd end up in someone's dream."

Another streak of white shot across the sky. Emory suddenly yearned for the clear skies of Harebell Cove, where she and her father would trace constellations in the stars and she would wonder if her mother was out there somewhere navigating by the same ones. If those same stars might lead her back to Harebell Cove one day.

"My dad always said they're lost souls trying to find their way back."

"Back to where?"

Emory shrugged. "Home, I suppose."

Baz looked at her for a second longer than he normally would, making her blink, caught off guard again at the effect she seemed to have on him. She let her eyes flicker to his mouth. He looked away then, staring blankly at the book in his lap. Emory hugged her knees close to her chest and reached for the dead trailing vine at her feet, running a delicate finger on a crisp leaf. She watched it disintegrate at her touch, something breaking inside her.

"You know, I think I could revive these plants if I tried."

Baz sighed and closed his book. "I knew this was coming."

"I have to start somewhere, right? Why not here, with this?" She pointed at the sky through the broken window. "Tonight's a waxing moon, so if your theory's right, it should be easier to call on Sower magic. And more importantly, there's no one around."

"You're not ready."

"How will I know if I don't try? The more I read about Sower magic, the more I think it's a lot like Healing. When I heal some-one, I feel what's wrong in their system, what it needs from me. And I just . . . mend it. Sower magic follows a similar principle. The whole point of it is to make things grow and bloom. To heal them, in a sense." Certainty thrummed in her veins as she swept a hand through the bits of crumbled leaf. "It got me thinking . . . What if I could restore this place so it doesn't feel so much like a grave?"

She waited for him to come up with yet another excuse for why she shouldn't access this power in her veins. He remained quiet, which she took as encouragement.

"Just *one* plant, Baz. That's all I ask."

He looked up with a sigh, muttering something under his breath that sounded like *For Tides' sake, what did I get myself into.* "A single leaf," he consented. "And we'll see how it goes."

Emory beamed at him. "A single leaf. I'll take it."

She stepped up to the nearest plant, a once majestically trail-ing philodendron, and ran a hand over it hesitantly, unsure how to begin. She opened her senses to the thin waxing crescent above, recalling the feel of Sower magic rushing through her on the beach that night, the way the algae and barnacles clinging to Travers's body had pulsed with life. The magic was still there inside her, as if it'd always been a part of her. Emory pulled tentatively on it, direct-ing it to the vine between her fingers. The faintest sheen of brown-ish green appeared on it, but it was there and gone again as her grip on the magic faltered.

She gave Baz a withering look. "See, this is what happens when you won't let me practice. I lose my touch."

"It's been all of ten seconds. Try again."

Emory did, but again she couldn't quite seem to grasp it. She heaved a frustrated sigh. "All I see is *dead plant*, and I have no idea how to restore it. It's like I have the magic, but I can't visualize it. I don't know how to direct it."

Baz's arm brushed against hers as he reached for another one of the philodendron's vines. "It starts at the root, not the leaf."

She watched, mesmerized, as he wound back the time. The sand-like soil in the clay pot turned a deep brown, and the smell of damp earth filled her nostrils. The stem emerging from the fresh soil became green, color traveling up and up until it reached the tip of the first leaf, then the second.

Baz looked at her. "Like that."

This close, she could see the spatter of freckles on his nose. And suddenly she was a younger version of herself, the one who'd been endlessly fascinated by Baz and all things Eclipse. She could still recall all the times she'd pestered him with questions, much to Romie's annoyance, and the handful of occasions she'd seen Baz use his magic—a falling pebble he'd stopped before it reached the ground, the old coin they'd found in the field that he'd restored to its shining state—small things that seemed inconsequential now, but had held all her attention back then.

Emory wondered again if he saw it, this power he held. Despite all his reservations, the ease with which he used it, the control he exercised over it . . . it was nothing short of incredible.

She realized she was staring at him. Realized just how close they stood as his throat bobbed and his gaze wandered to her lips. Emory stood frozen with the sudden understanding that she'd been right—there was still something here, at least on his part. And here she was using it to get what she wanted.

Baz cleared his throat, becoming a flustered mess once more as he pulled away. "I, uh . . . Here." He held up the vine for her and stepped aside. "Try it again."

Emory swallowed past the sudden tightness in her throat. She focused her attention on the philodendron, trying to banish the lingering feeling of Baz's closeness. It took her quite a few more tries before the forward motion of growth and transformation flowed through her fingers. The philodendron came to life under her touch, first at the roots, then up the stem and down to the very tip of each heart-shaped leaf. A delighted sound escaped her.

"There," Baz said quietly. "Now it feels a bit like Romie's again."

Emory beamed at the fruit of her efforts, clinging to the earthy scent of this one live plant. But as she watched it, the leaves began to wither again, as though the magic had only been temporary. Her smile waned. *Mediocre.* "It's not enough."

"It's a start," Baz countered softly.

Again, something seemed to pass between them. Before she could make sense of the fluttering in her stomach, they heard a sound: footsteps outside, laughter in the night.

Baz ducked to the floor, swearing as he tugged on Emory's sleeve. "Get *down.*"

She plopped down beside him, heart in her throat at the urgency in his voice. They pressed close to the wall, hidden below the windowpane as the doorknob turned and the door slowly pushed inward, creaking on its hinges.

"Nisha, come on!" someone outside yelled, their voice muffled. "We're going to be late."

There was a pause. Faint moonlight filtered in through the door standing ajar. It clicked shut after a tense moment, and the footsteps outside receded. In the distance, a light flickered on. Emory peered through the window. Four outlines were visible behind the

clear glass panes of the adjacent greenhouse, cast in shadows by the soft light within.

She settled back against the wall and noticed Baz clutching his hand. "What's wrong?"

"There's glass on the floor," he mumbled, holding up his hand. Bits of broken glass cut into his palm, blood welling from the wounds.

Emory grabbed his hand to study the damage. She managed to brush off most of the glass that had crumbled to dust, leaving several small bits and two bigger pieces wedged in his skin. As she took out the glass piece by piece, she let out a breathless laugh. "I can't believe the *one* time you agree to let me use my magic, we almost get caught."

Baz shot her an unamused look over the rim of his glasses. "It's not funny. They could have seen us."

"And? Look at the poor plant. It's already wilted. No one would ever know I did any sort of magic to it."

"Doesn't mean we should be reckless about it." Baz winced as she took out a longer shard. "Next time, we're meeting in Obscura Hall."

Emory arched a brow. "Next time?"

"Yeah, I mean . . . You're right. It's time you start properly training. And at least in the Eclipse commons, we can do so without getting caught."

She blinked at him, still holding his hand between them, her fingers slick with his blood. The trust he was putting in her by agreeing to this . . . She knew how much that took from him.

She didn't ask and he didn't stop her as she reached for the Healing magic that had been hers all her life. It was still there, still familiar, and it answered her now despite the waxing moon in the sky. The puncture wounds on his palm closed over, and Emory gently squeezed his hand.

"Thank you," she whispered, hoping the words conveyed everything she felt.

The moonlight danced in the reflection of his glasses. Emory made to pull away, but Baz's hand suddenly wrapped around her elbow, fingers digging into her skin. For a wild, unfathomable second, she thought he might kiss her. Wondered what might happen if she let him, just to see what it was like. But he only stared at her wrist—at the spiral scar gleaming faint silver in the moonlight.

"That mark. Where did you get it?"

Emory pulled her arm out of his grip, hugging it to her chest. She willed her pulse to slow, tried to give him a bashful smile. "It's just a silly tattoo."

The suspicion in his eyes told her she wasn't very convincing.

"I saw it on Travers's hand," Baz said. He swore. "Did Romie have one too?"

"I . . ." Her mouth opened and closed, stuck on that one word as she scrambled for what to say. She swallowed, looked away, knowing full well her silence spoke volumes.

"Are you in that cult?"

Emory went very still. "What cult?"

"The Veiled Atlas. Clover's Inner Circle?"

A knot of tension uncoiled in her stomach. He didn't mean the Selenic Order. "I have no idea what that is."

"The *Song of the Drowned Gods* fanatics."

She stared at him blankly, wondering if he'd lost so much blood from the glass that he'd gone delusional. "What does that book have to do with anything?"

"The Tides-damned song in the story!" he said impatiently. "The reason—you know what, here." Baz rifled through his pocket and shoved a piece of paper at her. "See for yourself."

Emory unfolded the note.

The call heard between the stars = DOVERMERE?
FIND EPILOGUE

"This is why Romie went to Dovermere, isn't it?"

The words barely registered over the loud beating of her heart; the only thing she saw was that handwriting she knew so well. Maybe this *did* have something to do with the Selenic Order, if Romie wrote it. She couldn't imagine Romie would have risked her life going to Dovermere for some Tides-damned children's book unless there was more to it than that.

"You were her best friend," Baz pressed. "You went with her. Clearly you know something about all this."

"I don't." Emory handed him the note back, adding, "Romie and I weren't exactly the closest last term. You know how secretive she'd become. I don't know why any of them went to Dovermere. I only followed her there because I found out she was going, and–"

She realized her mistake a beat too late as a shadow fell on Baz's face.

"You told me you all went to Dovermere together on some drunken dare."

Fuck. "That's what I meant," she tried smoothly. Anger swelled in her at her own blunder. It was clear he didn't believe a word. "They were drunk, and I didn't want to leave her alone, so I followed them in. Then the tide came and none of it matters in the end because they're all dead and there's nothing we can do about it. Just let it go, Baz."

"*Let it go?* Do you hear yourself? My sister–*your best friend*–is dead. Her dreams, her aspirations, all of it is gone. That's not something I can just let go of. All that's left of her is what little she left behind, and none of it makes sense, and you're not exactly helping matters. So don't tell me to let it go."

Emory couldn't do this right now. She drew herself up, smoothing her dress. "If we're done here, I have a party to get to."

There was a sudden weariness to him that made him look older, breaking the illusion that they'd been the same kids they were at Threnody, before everything went to shit. Emory didn't give him the chance to say anything before she made her way out.

She looked over at the other greenhouse. From this angle, she recognized the students inside immediately: Lizaveta with her perfect hair and sardonic smile, Virgil with his dark, mischievous eyes, Nisha with her head bent low over Lizaveta's outstretched arm, holding something Emory couldn't see . . . and Keiran, leaning casually against a windowpane. He looked dapper in a dark gray suit and tie, his chestnut hair effortlessly styled back. She could have sworn she saw rosebuds blooming around him–around all of them, pulsing open and closed, the rhythm like that of a heartbeat.

A cult. Was this truly what this was, then? It had all the makings of one. Rituals in a cave. Dead students. Impossible magics–all of them remade into Tidecallers.

She stomped her way toward them, Baz's words ringing in her ears like a battle cry.

The larger greenhouse was nothing like Romie's. Moisture and warmth and green earthy smells embraced her. Virgil was the first to spot her, amusement sparking in his eyes. The smooth dark panes of his chest peeked out of the shimmering white satin shirt he'd only buttoned halfway, a bright indigo tie draped lazily across his shoulders.

"Lo and behold, the Healer has arrived."

Did she imagine the slight edge to his tone as he said *Healer*?

Everyone looked up at her. A startled Nisha, dressed in a low-cut suit of crushed mauve velvet, swept something silvery out of sight with a low swear. Keiran pushed off the wall, the slight narrowing of his eyes the only sign of his surprise. Lizaveta's ice-chip eyes bored into her as she snatched back her arm from whatever Nisha

had been doing. She wore a green satin gown that clung to her in all the right ways, accentuating her auburn hair.

"What are you doing here?" she asked in that haughty voice of hers.

Emory forced lightness in her tone, a smile on her lips. "Keiran invited me to the lighthouse. I'm sorry I'm a little early, though. I guess we all had the same idea to come here before the main event, huh?"

Lizaveta's icy gaze swept from her to Keiran. "What is she talking about?"

"Did he not tell you?" Emory asked, feigning innocence. "I'm sorry. I thought you would have . . ."

Keiran cut across to Emory, face guarded. "I told you to meet me at ten."

She eyed the expensive-looking bottle in Virgil's hand. "Looks to me like the party's already started."

Virgil handed her the bottle with a mischievous smile. "Darling, the party never stops when I'm around."

Emory took a long sip, willing the bubbles to ease her into this role she'd have to play. Her eyes never left Keiran's. Was that fear she saw in them? Annoyance? She felt no small amount of satisfaction at that, certain she'd unwittingly wrested the upper hand from him by showing up here just now.

"Well? Are you going to tell us why you invited her?" Lizaveta asked Keiran, arms crossed in displeasure.

Before he could answer, Emory held her wrist up. "It seems I'm going to be part of the Selenic Order too."

There was a tense silence as they took in her spiral mark, the implication of her words. Virgil gently pried the bottle from her grasp, muttering something about not being drunk enough for this.

Emory met Keiran's gaze squarely. She had to wonder why he hadn't told them about her. She didn't trust him, wouldn't let herself

be played by him. And she was so very tired of being kept in the dark.

Secret society, cult, it didn't matter. Either way, she would do her damned best to infiltrate the Selenic Order—and find a way to stop them from ever holding another one of their initiations at Dovermere. She would have justice for Romie and Travers and all the others.

No more senseless deaths. It ended here.

Baz thinking she was so quick to move on from Romie's death had set her aflame. She felt like one of those stars racing across the sky. She wouldn't stop now even if she was doomed to burn out entirely by the end.

BAZ

THOUGHTS OF THE GREENHOUSE—OF EMORY'S UNGUARD-
edness, the way the moonlight had limned her face as they
watched the stars—warred with the bitter sting of everything that
followed.

She had that Tides-damned mark just like Travers and the Guardian at the Gate and probably Romie, too.

Baz knew she had to be lying to him, had to know *something* she
didn't want him finding out. And yet . . . she was right about this, at
least: Romie had been hiding things from both of them, it seemed.
He knew firsthand how different his sister had been acting during
those months leading up to her death. Standoffish and scattered.
Secretive about everything and everyone she was suddenly spending time with, like Keiran Dunhall Thornby—whom Emory was now
apparently hanging around with too.

Baz caught a glimpse of them in the adjacent building as he left
the ramshackle greenhouse. Emory had her head ducked to hide a
smile as Virgil Dade whispered something in her ear. There were

others there too: Lizaveta Orlov, Nisha Zenara–whom he recognized now as the clerk who'd manned the desk in the Vault–and Keiran. The same group, no doubt, that Romie had fallen in with before her death.

Baz walked away before he could make sense of the tightness in his chest.

Music and laughter and conversation flitted over to him from all around campus, and his heart ached at the lightness of the sounds, the ease and camaraderie that felt so foreign to him. He had never truly realized how disconnected he was until now, in this very moment, when he understood that everyone had a life outside of the classroom, events like the meteor shower they were excited about and people to make plans with, to share things with. They were part of something. A mainland of activity and connection bound by a desire to belong, to experience, to *live* in all the messy senses of the word.

He was an island that stood wholly apart.

Kai had been there with him for a time, but even then, it'd been as if they both stood on opposite ends, an invisible line drawn between them that they dared not cross, or perhaps didn't know how.

It was a predicament of his own making, really. Baz had crafted this perfect bubble of solitude, a narrow existence that could be contained between the shelves of the library, the tapestried walls of the Eclipse commons, the pages of a story. For as long as he could remember, he'd only ever needed his books and studies for company, but suddenly the idea of returning to the empty common room felt unbearably lonely.

He paused by the Fountain of Fate. From his pocket he pulled both Romie's note and the napkin from the tearoom with the address for the Veiled Atlas. Maybe Selandyn and Jae were right about accepting Romie's death, that he was looking for meaning where there was none. But he knew if the roles were reversed, Romie would

have hunted down answers to the ends of the earth–probably had done exactly that, driven to Dovermere by this strange idea that, like a mad dream, would not let her go.

Romie, Kai, even Emory–they were people who acted without fear, and Baz envied their fearlessness. Maybe he could try to be like them.

He cut across the lawn, turning his back on Obscura Hall and the hollowness carved within. For one night, he would do something, and damn the consequences.

The Veiled Atlas was a private taproom in the poshest part of Cadence. The lighting was brassy, the furnishings dark and moody, and if it weren't for all the *Song of the Drowned Gods*-themed baubles and antiques strewn around–a life-size statue of a winged horse, a solid gold heart run through with an equally golden sword, sepia-toned portraits of Cornus Clover smiling attractively in every one, a rusting typewriter said to have belonged to him, and so many framed paintings on the wall that it was a wonder it didn't collapse–Baz would have felt entirely out of place.

A long claw-footed table sat in the middle of the room he'd been brought to, finely set with silver cutlery and crystal glasses and the remnants of a feast. At the head of the table was an elegant middle-aged woman swathed in gossamer fabrics and pearls, her white-blond hair falling in perfect curls down to her middle.

"I wasn't aware Jae was back in town," Alya Kazan said tightly, her wine-red lips downturned in a sour expression.

"I think they're just passing through."

A scoff from Alya. "Figures. Always so swift to move on to bigger and brighter things."

Baz palmed the back of his neck. When he'd mentioned Jae's name at the door, Alya had laughed and nearly shut the door in his

face. "If Jae thinks I'll do them any favors after they left without so much as a goodbye last time . . ."

She'd agreed to speak with him only because another girl who'd poked her head in the door convinced her to let him in. Baz had followed them both into this private room upstairs, mortified at the thought that Jae might have sent him to someone they had unresolved history with.

"I don't think our guest is here to talk about your failed relationships, Alya."

This came from the other girl, who was closer to Baz in age. She was short and plump, with green eyes, dark hair buzzed close to her head, and a smattering of freckles on her golden-beige skin. Where Alya was all poise and elegance, primly sitting at the head of the table with what looked like a martini in hand, this girl had her feet up on the chair beside her and picked at a cheese platter, dressed in an ensemble of dark slacks, lavender suspenders, and a buttoned-up blouse with a floral-print bow tie.

She winked at Baz. "I'm Vera, by the way," she said in a lilting accent. "Vera Ingers."

"You'll have to excuse my niece's lack of manners." Alya swirled her martini around with an olive pick. On her hand glistened the sigil of House New Moon. "I don't know what exactly they teach over at Trevelyan University, but apparently it's not that." A scoff. "And they have the nerve to stare down their noses at schools like Aldryn."

Vera rolled her eyes, and suddenly her accent made sense, as did the lack of any house sigil on her hand. Trevelyan University was on the continent to the east of the great island of Elegy and was one of the most elite non-magic schools in the world.

Baz had often imagined what his life might have been like had he been born without magic. He always pictured himself walking the grand sandstone halls of Trevelyan University, free to study art,

history, languages, his mind flourishing without the burdens and fears and limitations that came with being Eclipse-born. He envied Vera for this freedom to explore her interests outside of whatever drop of magic she'd been born with.

He looked between her and Alya. "You two are related?"

"On my mother's side," Vera said around a bite of cheese. "Dearest Aunt Alya and the rest of the Kazans claim we're all related to Cornus Clover."

Alya gave Vera a death stare. "Clover, yes. The reason we're here, is he not? So tell us, Baz. What is it you want to know about him?"

"Jae told me you believe what Clover wrote was true, in a way? And I guess I'm just wondering . . . how, exactly, that is." His eyes flicked to the gold-framed paintings on the wall, one of which depicted an all-too-familiar cove with towering cliffs and a cave mouth cut into its side, unveiled by the low tide. "And more specifically, if it has anything to do with the missing epilogue or Dovermere."

"Funny how you Aldryn students suddenly seem so interested in all of this," Vera drawled. "There was another Eclipse fella who came by not long ago with the exact same questions, and a girl before him." She tilted her head, studying him. "She kind of looked like you, come to think of it. Romie, was it?"

Baz's heart skipped a beat. "She was my sister."

"Was?"

"She drowned at Dovermere last spring."

Vera swore and fell back against her chair.

"I'm sorry," Alya said. Her face softened to something almost motherly. "I heard about that but didn't realize that was her. All those students . . . Such senseless loss."

"It's why I'm here. My sister, she . . . had some interesting ideas about *Song of the Drowned Gods* and Dovermere. And I'm wondering if it's part of why she went there in the first place."

Alya set her glass down on the table. "I don't know how Dover-mere might factor into this, but as for the rest, yes, we believe there's truth to what Clover wrote in *Song of the Drowned Gods*. That there are other worlds and ways to travel between them. Or at least, there used to be."

"Used to be?"

Vera toyed with a piece of cheese. "Anyone with a brain can tell Clover clearly wrote himself in as the scholar. A college student writing stories by the sea, just like Clover himself, who was a student at Aldryn? Obvious enough. Naturally, the next conclusion to draw is that, just like the scholar in his story, Clover himself found a portal to other worlds. Be it through a book or an actual door or something else entirely, that's up for interpretation."

"You believe he *actually* went to all those other worlds?" Baz said dubiously. "The Wychwood, the Wastes, the snowy mountains with the gate, the sea of ash . . . You think they're all real?"

Vera shrugged. "Why not? You can't tell me you've never wondered if it was all real when reading the book. That you never uttered those words to yourself . . . *There is a world at the center of all things where drowned gods reign over a sea of ash. . . .* wishing so hard that a portal on a page would magically appear."

Goose bumps rose on Baz's arms. Of course he'd thought it. He'd wished it were real with every fiber of his being, held his breath every time he picked up an old, odd-looking book in Aldryn's libraries, wondering if it might be the same one the scholar had found, or a book Clover might have picked up himself and used as inspiration for his novel. But to actually *believe* in the existence of those fictional worlds when no rational thing pointed to the plausibility of it . . .

"So what then, Clover went to other worlds, came back here, and wrote down all his adventures in *Song of the Drowned Gods*?"

Alya tipped her martini glass his way. "Precisely. A thinly veiled

atlas pointing to other worlds, hidden in a children's book. Genius, really."

Baz understood now why Jae had warned him about these people and their beliefs.

"This is where the epilogue comes into play," Vera added, leaning in close with her elbows on the table. "From everything experts and scholars and fanatics have pieced together, we believe that elusive sixth part of the book tells us exactly how to travel between worlds. That it might in fact be the portal itself, the key to everything. A way to find the sea of ash at the center of it all."

"Why would Clover take the epilogue out of his manuscript, then?" Baz asked.

Vera raised a brow. "Who says he's the one who did it?"

"Clover's manuscript was published posthumously," Alya added. "His death coincides with the disappearance of the epilogue. It wouldn't be a stretch to say he died at the hands of whoever ripped those pages from his manuscript. We believe the epilogue was hidden by those who wish to see the doors to other worlds forever closed. Those who fear travel between worlds might wake the evil that lies at the center of all things."

Her gaze flicked to the back of Baz's hand—to the sunflower and moon in eclipse inked on his skin.

"The Shadow of Ruin," Baz murmured.

Alya nodded with a wry smile. "The monster in the sea of ash."

Baz pulled back his hand, folded it in his lap. "Some say the real monster was always the drowned gods themselves."

Alya seemed delighted by this. "I see you're familiar with Jae's thesis on the matter. That's how I met them, you know. I've always admired their insight into the kind of person Clover might have been, a critic of the Tides and defender of the Shadow, a fervent ally of the Eclipse-born." She chuckled. "That ruffled a lot of feathers among the purists of the literary world."

"Point is, we think the missing epilogue is out there somewhere," Vera continued, "calling to those who might be able to travel between worlds. Those who hear the song woven between the stars."

It's this song I hear in my dreams sometimes, Romie had said. *Tempting to follow it, isn't it?*

Baz wouldn't put it past her to try something as reckless as going into those Tides-damned caves for such a nonsensical reason. To answer the call of something inexplicable and unseen, an echo she'd heard in a dream, in the imagined space between stars. Just like the song the characters in the book followed to their doom.

She had sought the epilogue because she'd thought—hoped—that it might lead her to these other worlds.

Baz glanced at the painting behind Vera. Dovermere, dark and mysterious. It had an odd pull on him even now, here, in painted form. And though Alya and Vera might not think it was pertinent, Baz knew, with the utmost certainty, that it was the key to unraveling all of it.

Eight students taken by the tide. Quince Travers's not-quite corpse resurfacing, enduring that horrible death. Emory's impossible magic and the marks on both their hands, all birthed in the depths of Dovermere.

FIND EPILOGUE, Romie had written.

If she'd been led to believe the answer lay in the Belly of the Beast . . .

"What did you tell my sister about the epilogue? Did you maybe give her a hint as to where it might be?"

A beat—then Vera burst out laughing. "I'm sorry, I have to ask—do you think we handed her a map like this is some kind of treasure hunt? *First one to find the epilogue gets a pot of gold?*"

Baz shifted in his seat, thinking, *Well, your name is the Veiled Atlas.* He pushed his glasses up the bridge of his nose. "Surely you must have some theory or other."

"The epilogue is said to be lost for a reason." Alya set her glass on the table with a clang of finality. "No one knows where it is, not even the likes of us who've devoted our lives to searching for it. People have scoured the world to find it without an ounce of success. It's as much of a myth now as the Tides themselves."

At his crestfallen look, Vera added, "Although . . . there was a Trevelyan woman years ago who was rumored to have cracked the mystery."

"Vera." Alya's voice was sharp with warning.

Vera ignored her. "She traveled here to find the epilogue and never came home. Disappeared from the world without so much as a whisper."

"Who was she?"

There was a tense silence as a look passed between the two women. Alya lifted her chin in what seemed like steely defiance at the grief in her eyes. "She was my sister."

Baz looked to Vera. "Your mother?"

"Aunt," she corrected. "Adriana, the youngest of the four Kazan sisters." She tilted her head at him. "I told your sister the same story. She thought she might be able to find Adriana in dreams."

"And did she?"

"She couldn't have." Alya had a faraway, haunted look. "My sister's dead."

"You don't know that," Vera muttered.

Baz eyed the New Moon sigil on Alya's hand, reminded that she was a Shadowguide, able to commune with the dead. The vehement look she shot Vera told him they'd likely had this conversation before.

"I can't feel her spirit beyond the veil. That means she's either still alive, in which case my magic is useless and we'll likely never find her, or she's dead and her spirit has left this plane, moving too far beyond the veil for me to reach."

Left this plane. Something tingled on the back of Baz's neck. "What does that mean?"

"Spirits who aren't tethered to this plane sometimes seek horizons even us Shadowguides can't reach. The dead move on, and so must we." Alya caught his gaze on her hand and added, "If your sister sought the epilogue, she wouldn't be the first to perish in search of it."

His throat worked for air. "Could you . . . look for her? Beyond the veil?"

He thought she would say no, that he'd already asked too much of them. Alya only regarded him with a strange sort of softness.

"Jae used to talk about you and your sister all the time," she murmured. "They showed me a picture of the three of you together once, from when you were kids and that printing press was still standing. They love you a great deal. I can only imagine how crushed they were at your sister's passing."

Emotion churned in Baz. Jae had always been part of their family, more than just his dad's business partner but his oldest friend, too. Jae had stayed with them for months after Theodore's Collapsing, helping them through that tragedy. They'd even stayed to take care of Anise once Baz and Romie returned to school. Only once everything was in order and the destroyed printing press was taken care of did Jae leave. They had another business opportunity lined up in the Outerlands, they explained to Baz and Romie, a research gig they couldn't pass up. But they would come back. All of them would always be a family.

A small part of Baz had resented them for leaving then, even as he saw how broken up about it Jae had been. But Jae had made good on their promise: they'd come back for important holidays and events, as often as they could. And they kept in touch regularly with Baz, asking him about his studies and how he was doing with his Eclipse magic. Reminding him that if it ever got to be too

much, if he ever felt he needed help, Jae would come to him in a flash.

Alya stood and went over to a large cabinet. From it she took out elaborately carved silver bloodletting instruments and set them on the table. She poured water into the shallow bowl and sliced the knife across her palm. Baz watched with growing anticipation as she submerged the wound, calling on the magic slumbering in her veins now that the moon was no longer new but waxing.

A suffocating silence settled over them as Alya closed her eyes. They flew wildly behind their lids. Baz sat very still, finding it hard to breathe. Slow, careful breaths, just like his father had taught him. In, hold, out, and repeat. Like the rhythm of the sea.

At last, Alya's eyes shot open. She blinked rapidly, appearing disoriented, as if she were slow to reacclimatize to this plane of existence. When she finally looked at Baz, the sad lines of her mouth told him everything he needed to know.

"It's the same as with Adriana. There's nothing there for me to find, I'm afraid. If your sister drowned in Dovermere, her spirit must have moved on."

The words settled like lead in Baz's stomach. He wasn't sure why it came as a surprise, didn't know what he'd expected. Of course Romie was dead. She was dead a week ago, a month ago. She died last spring, and she was still dead now. Nothing had changed. It was just like Emory said: there was nothing they could do about it.

"I'm sorry I couldn't offer you more," Alya lamented.

Baz was sorry too, because even though he *knew*, deep down, that Romie must be dead, all signs pointing to this one great, terrible truth, a minuscule part of him had started to wonder—to hope, against all sense and logic, that she might simply be *gone*. That she'd followed the song not to her death, but to someplace else.

Seeing Alya's haunted expression, however, he understood now

why Professor Selandyn and Jae and even Emory were so adamant he let this go.

The dead move on and so must we.

So why couldn't he?

Baz lingered outside the Veiled Atlas, feeling utterly dejected. He threw his head back against the stone wall and let the cool night air wrap around him. In the distance, the Aldersea was a dark, impenetrable mass, its faint whispering drowned out by sounds of laughter and music coming from busy taprooms and restaurants.

He'd never felt so alone.

Vera emerged from a side door. She wore a tweed coat that was two sizes too big and had a cigarette hanging from her mouth. Baz watched her take a drag and tilt her head up to the sky, mesmerized by the cloud of smoke that blew past her lips. He didn't think she'd seen him, but then she cracked an eye open, looking straight at him.

"The other Eclipse-born who came by," she said casually. "He a friend of yours?"

"Why?"

Vera shrugged, flicking her cigarette. "Figured you must be classmates, at least." She took another drag. "He seemed to have a pretty vested interest in your sister's plan."

"What do you mean?"

"The dream thing. When I told him what Romie said about trying to find Adriana, he got this wild look in his eye. He stood up so fast Alya spilled her martini and cursed up a storm after him." She crushed her cigarette under a booted foot. "He hurried out of here like a man possessed."

If Kai had known Romie was trying to find Adriana and the epilogue in dreams, he might have attempted the same. Might have found something in the sleepscape that would explain everything.

Baz suddenly recalled a moment between Kai and Romie he'd never been able to explain. He and Kai had bumped into Romie outside Obscura Hall, and she'd frozen up at the sight of Kai.

"Dreamling," he'd said in that chilling voice of his, blocking her path. A single, innocent word, yet nothing had ever sounded quite so loaded.

Romie had narrowed her eyes at him. "Out of my way, nightmare boy."

Baz remembered Kai's dangerous smile, Romie's defiant glare. Kai had finally stepped aside so she could stomp away from them without another glance, and that was the end of that—but there had been something so odd about the exchange, Baz had never dared to ask Kai about it.

Always too afraid to speak his mind, to ask questions whose answers might upset the delicate balance he strove for.

He was so Tides-damned *tired* of it all.

Baz pushed off the wall. "I need to see him."

"Didn't he Collapse this summer?" At the quizzical look Baz shot her, Vera shrugged. "I keep tabs on everyone who comes inquiring after the epilogue. If he's at the Institute, you won't have much luck getting in this late."

Baz wasn't sure a cab driver would be willing to drive him all the way out there at this hour either. He swore. This inexplicable sense of urgency had him thinking this couldn't wait, but it would have to. At least until the morning. He could find Jae then and take them up on their offer to go to the Institute together, trust that they could get them in past the Regulators.

"I can help get you in. Tonight, if you want."

He stared at Vera. "How?"

She smiled at him like a cat as she shuffled toward a clunky motorbike leaning against the side of the building. "Let's just say I know my way around wards and magical trip wires." A wink as she

hopped on. "I might not have enough Unraveler magic to bear my house's sigil, but I always thought the drop of it I do have made me into a bit of an engineering genius."

The engine sputtered to life beneath her, so loud Baz thought he misheard her next words. "It doesn't hurt that I studied Institute buildings back at Trevelyan University. I can get you in and out without anyone ever knowing you were there."

He barely caught the helmet she threw at him, too shocked to form thoughts. Vera looked at him expectantly.

"So do you want my help or not?"

For once in his life, Baz didn't question it. He hopped on behind her.

EMORY

THE OLD LIGHTHOUSE STOOD AT THE VERY TOP OF THE cliff that overlooked the Aldersea, half crumbled and ridden with vines of ivy. Warm, golden light flickered in the small glassless windows that dotted the tower, and though Emory saw shadows moving inside, the only sound that permeated the night was the deafening crash of waves below, as loud as the pounding in her ears. She felt like she was going to be sick, her skin flushed despite the cool bite of the wind.

She regretted having that wine.

Virgil must have sensed her apprehension. He nudged her gently, saying, "You'll be fine."

Emory was glad for his presence. Things had been tense since the greenhouse, with Lizaveta glaring at Keiran so intensely that it was a miracle she didn't burn a hole in his skull, Nisha throwing Emory sidelong glances that felt loaded in a way she didn't understand, and Keiran . . . Well. Keiran had quickly recovered and affected his usual cool demeanor, as if her presence didn't bother him in the

slightest and this was all part of his plan. Which irked her to no end. Virgil, at least, seemed wholly unbothered by it all. He'd stuck by her side and made pleasant conversation as they both sipped wine, and though it might have been a diversion to keep her from eavesdropping on the others' hushed conversation, Emory was grateful for it all the same.

"What are these grand soirees usually like?" she'd asked him.

"Now, now," Virgil had crooned, "that would spoil all the fun."

As they stood in front of the lighthouse door, staring at the wrought-iron details of carved moons that formed a ring in its middle, Emory thought they must have very different ideas of what *fun* entailed.

With a grating sound, the full moon on the door suddenly slid upward, revealing a bright green eye peering at them through the opening.

"Marks," came a honeyed voice.

The others lifted their wrists so the person could see their spirals. Emory followed suit. The eye blinked at them, and the full moon shutter closed over it once more.

A beat, and the door opened to reveal a woman in an elegantly flowing sage dress. The top half of her face was covered with a porcelain mask of Anima, Tide of the Waxing Moon. A mass of luscious dark curls fell down her back, studded with pearls that looked like stars. She grabbed each of their right hands in turn and ran a manicured finger along the slightly raised ridge of their spiral marks, as if to attest they were real. She then word-lessly handed each of them a porcelain mask of the Tide corre-sponding to their respective lunar house: a cherub-faced Bruma for Emory, a pair of rosy-cheeked Animas for Nisha and Liza-veta, motherly Aestas for Keiran, and the ever wise, wrinkled Quies for Virgil.

No Shadow masks, Emory noted with a hint of relief. They must

all still honor their original lunar houses despite the Eclipse powers the spiral mark gave them.

Once they'd donned their masks, the woman ushered them inside and pointed to a narrow staircase. Nisha and Lizaveta went up first. Keiran looked at Emory expectantly. She couldn't bring herself to move, suddenly feeling hot despite the cold porcelain on her skin.

Virgil appeared by her side, an easy smile on his lips. "Shall we?"

She took his proffered arm, glad to have something solid to hold on to. She wondered if that was a hint of jealousy she saw on Keiran's face, but he turned and started up the stairs before she could make sense of it.

"Just be glad these masks leave our mouths uncovered," Virgil commented. "All the better to drown your nerves in wine, my dear."

She smiled, the knot of nerves in her stomach loosening ever so slightly.

On each floor up, classical music played from sets of enchanted instruments, no doubt bewitched with Wordsmith magic like the kind used in the Crescens library. White sheets covered the remnants of what used to be Lightkeeper classrooms, for the lighthouse had once been an extension of Pleniluna Hall before it started to crumble, pieces of it falling to the restless sea below. The tower was no longer in use now, bordered up and abandoned as it was—the perfect spot, it seemed, for such an exclusive party.

"Behold the Selenic Order," Virgil said grandly once they reached the top. "Aldryn College's most distinguished minds."

There were about thirty people, so elegantly dressed they should have looked ridiculous standing in such a decrepit place. But the lighthouse had been transformed from bare-bones ruins to the height of opulence: tables groaned under an array of expensive bottles and carefully arranged platters of duck and foie gras,

aged cheeses and oysters, with lit candles carelessly dripping wax between them; gauzy curtains hung in the windowless arches, dancing gracefully in the breeze; strings of tiny everlight bulbs were woven with the vines of ivy that crept through the windows and engulfed the walls and parts of the floor; and thick, richly patterned rugs covered the rickety floorboards, where people lounged against leather poufs and velvet cushions like ancient gods, all languid smiles and sensuous laughs as they clinked together crystal flutes and glasses. The thin crescent and its court of stars hung above them like a grand chandelier, visible through an opening where the roof had caved in.

Emory couldn't help it: she was utterly seduced by the clothes and the drinks, the glamour and mystery of it all.

"Is it everything you expected it to be?" Virgil asked.

"I don't know what I expected. Scholars in a dark room with whiskey and cigars, maybe? Animal sacrifices to the moon. Ritual drownings."

"Ah, well. The night's still young." At the perplexed look she gave him, his mouth slanted upward. "Tides, I'm only joking. This is a time for celebrations, Healer. Lighten up."

"What are they celebrating, anyway?"

Virgil swept two sparkling flutes from a nearby table and handed her one. "This is usually the night we introduce our selected initiates for the year. The eight freshmen who show the most potential." He bent his head toward her and added in a conspiratorial whisper, "Or whose families have the deepest pockets or longest histories within the Order."

Romie must have come to this same event last year. It didn't come as a surprise that she'd been noticed by the Order so soon after starting at Aldryn. Emory wondered how many parties like this Romie had gone to over that first term. All those nights she would sneak out of their room without a word. All those lies she'd tell

whenever Emory asked where she'd been. It had all been for this.

She couldn't help feeling envious. This was the kind of world she'd always dreamed of having access to, the kind Romie effortlessly fit into. Back at Threnody, Romie had always made sure Emory was included in everything she was. *We're a package deal,* she would say. *Where I go, she goes.* No one ever denied her. And while Emory was glad to be included, she knew people only did so to please Romie. They made polite conversation with her out of respect or duty, but it was Romie they fawned over, Romie who dazzled them. Emory was an afterthought, a wallflower easily overlooked.

Now she was in the thick of it. Still not as a first choice, but here of her own choosing, at least.

"Are the new candidates here, then?" she asked, blood boiling at the thought of Dovermere's next potential victims.

Virgil took a big gulp of his drink. With a trace of uncharacteristic melancholy, he said, "After the last fiasco at the caves, we decided to withhold initiations this year, lie low for a while."

Thank the Tides. One less thing to worry about tonight. "So they decided to throw this soiree anyway because . . . ?"

"The Tidal Council—they're the heads of our order—were adamant we select new candidates regardless of what happened last year. Tradition and all. But Keiran managed to convince them otherwise. This was their way of compromising. And to honor those who've passed."

The Tidal Council was likely whose opinion she needed to sway tonight, she realized. As if reading her thoughts, Virgil winked at her and said, "They'll go feral over you. Their unexpected newest addition."

"Careful what you say, Virgil," Lizaveta seethed, suddenly at their side along with Keiran and Nisha. "She might bear our mark, but she's not one of us yet."

"You're certainly in a mood tonight, Liza," Virgil quipped. He

knocked back his drink. "I think more of these are in order, yes?"

He winked at Emory again before looping his arms through both Lizaveta's and Nisha's, whisking them away to one of the tables laden with food and drinks.

Left alone with Keiran, she felt her nerves come back. She was acutely aware of his eyes on her but couldn't make herself meet them, taking a closer look at the people around her instead. They seemed to range widely in age, older than the average student, though it was hard to tell with all of them donning masks. Alumni, no doubt; members of the Selenic Order from years and decades past. There was an air of importance to them, a thrum of power; they looked for all the world like they were the Tides themselves.

Keiran moved closer to her—much too close. With a glass of amber liquor in his hand, he pointed subtly to a stout man wearing Bruma's face, whispering in her ear, "That there is Raine Avis, the most sought-after Seer among politicians from all over the world."

The man laughed loudly with a statuesque woman who wore a Quies mask. "And that's Vivianne Delaune," Keiran said, his breath making the fine hairs on her neck lift, "a prolific Memorist who's developed ways to sense memories in objects. She works with the highest-ranking Regulators and crime units in Trevel."

With a hand on her elbow, he turned her gently to the other side of the room, where an older woman sat on a divan, her cloud of silver hair perfectly framing her Anima mask.

"Leonie Thornby," Keiran murmured. "A Wordsmith artist of the highest caliber."

"Thornby?"

Emory twisted to look at him, all too aware of how close they stood.

A corner of his mouth lifted. "A great-aunt of mine. I'm afraid I'm what you might call a legacy within the Order." He directed her attention back to Leonie. "I've always been in awe of her. Her work

is divine; she's composed songs that have brought upon storms and made rivers run to her rhythms like the universe is her own orchestra. In fact, the instruments you hear playing tonight are her doing. She's the one who came up with the idea to have these play in Crescens library."

Emory looked at the woman with fresh awe. Magic like that was the kind she'd only ever dreamed to aspire to. It reminded her of Romie, who'd always been in a league of her own, even at Threnody Prep. The Dreamers there had a long-standing tradition of making a sport out of who could go furthest in the sleepscape—which, according to Romie, appeared endless and became harder to navigate the further that Dreamers traveled. Romie had made it further than Dreamers older and more experienced than her when she was only thirteen. By sixteen, she had found she could take things out of dreams—shimmering illusions that disintegrated to dust soon after she woke, but an achievement nonetheless, for few Dreamers could do such a thing.

Romie would have fit right in here, Emory thought. It was no wonder she'd been selected as an initiate. Her gaze traveled to where Virgil, Nisha, and Lizaveta stood at a table, joined by a girl wearing a Bruma mask who had to be Ife Nuru. She wore a long-sleeved dress of shimmering black material, her braids arranged in a crown atop her head.

"Are all of you legacies?" Emory asked.

Keiran followed her line of sight. "Lizaveta and Virgil are. Javier, too—you haven't met him yet, he's probably hiding here somewhere with Louis. They can't seem to get their hands off each other."

She didn't miss the way his own hand brushed hers as he lifted his glass to his lips, his eyes intent on her as he drank. She fought her blush and asked, "Louis–Clairmont?"

Keiran nodded. "He, Ife, and Nisha were selected based off merit alone. Ife's a brilliant Seer, Nisha is more skilled than any Sower I've

ever met, and Louis is a much better Healer than what his drunken skills at the bonfires might suggest, I assure you."

Emory threw him a sidelong glance. "And Farran? What was he?"

"Farran was everything," he said quietly. "Both a legacy and a total force to be reckoned with. His Reaper skills were unrivaled. Much like Romie with her Dreaming."

"Was she a legacy too?"

"No. I don't know how she found out about the Order in the first place." A private smile touched his lips. "She wasn't even on my radar until she barged into my dreams one night and practically held me hostage there until I agreed to give her a shot at initiation."

Emory laughed. It sounded so very much like Romie—when she wanted something, she went after it, even if it meant harassing people in their dreams to get it.

Keiran's hazel eyes fell on her laughing mouth, looking for all the world like he might want to bottle the sound. She didn't miss the way he tracked a shaft of her unbound hair as it fell forward on her bare shoulder, shimmering golden in the candlelight. His hand twitched as if he yearned to run his fingers through it.

She swallowed. Hard.

"I'm glad you decided to come, Ains," Keiran said.

Emory was grateful for the mask hiding her blush. She was here for a reason; she wouldn't let herself be seduced by him and his charm and his silly nicknames.

"You didn't seem so glad earlier."

"You just caught me by surprise. I hadn't told the others about you yet."

"Clearly."

She caught Lizaveta glaring at them from across the room. She quickly turned back to the group she was speaking with, red painted mouth widening into a sultry laugh at something one of

them said. She looked like a queen holding court, like Anima herself with her ever-waxing magnetism and youth.

"Some of you aren't too keen to have me here," Emory said sullenly.

"Liza's very particular about who she lets in."

"Cult members only, huh?" Around them, the music swelled in a familiar melody, something Romie used to hum constantly in their dorm. She frowned, thinking of Baz. "Does the Selenic Order have anything to do with *Song of the Drowned Gods*, by any chance?"

"The children's book?" Keiran arched a brow. "Why would you think that?"

It suddenly felt silly; of course, Romie's death had nothing to do with a book. She was letting Baz's obsession cloud her own judgment. "That's the thing: I don't know *what* to think," she said. "You invited me here with the promise of answers, remember?"

Keiran leaned ever so closer, making her stomach flip. "Didn't I say you would have to earn them?"

His breath was warm and smelled of whiskey. Her eyes dropped to his lips, that maddening smile full of ease and confidence and sensuality. The world narrowed to the two of them, until a loud voice ripped them apart.

"Keiran! There you are."

A man with auburn hair and faint reddish stubble clasped Keiran on the shoulder. He couldn't be much older than them, yet he carried himself with authority.

Keiran smiled widely as they embraced. "Good to see you, Artie."

Artie turned to Emory. Blue irises so pale they were almost white peered at her from the eye holes of his Anima mask. "And who is this stunning creature?"

Something in his tone made her skin crawl.

Keiran brushed her arm. "Emory Ainsleif, this is Artem Orlov. He was a few years older than me when I got initiated."

"Taught him everything he knows," Artem said with a wink. "You probably know my younger sister, Lizaveta."

Of course. The resemblance was uncanny, even with the mask. Especially the eyes.

"I know her, all right," Emory said sweetly. *And she hates me for no apparent reason.*

Artem's smile never wavered as he took in her Bruma mask and the New Moon sigil on her hand. "Emory Ainsleif. The girl who bested Dovermere, I'm told." He extended a hand. "A pleasure."

Emory shook his hand, only for him to flip her wrist over and peer at her spiral mark. He looked at Keiran with narrowed eyes. "You mean to present her to the Tidal Council."

Keiran knocked back the last dregs of his drink. "She wants to plead her case."

Artem dropped her hand with a hum. "Well. Seems we might get a new initiate this year after all." He didn't appear too pleased at the prospect. "I think the last of the Council should have arrived by now. I'll let them know you're here."

He clasped Keiran on the shoulder again, nodding at Emory with a hint of disdain. Some of the tightness in her shoulders eased as he strode away.

"Is *he* part of this Tidal Council I need to impress?" she asked Keiran.

"No. The Council is made up of the four oldest Selenics, one of each lunar house. The title can only go to those who were leaders of their cohort when they were at Aldryn. Artem was his cohort's leader, so he will be on the Council one day, just not yet."

"Who's the leader of the cohort now?" At Keiran's smile, she arched a brow. "You?"

"You sound surprised."

"No, I just . . . didn't know."

All of it made sense. Why Romie had walked into his dreams and

not Nisha's, who she was already close with and had better access to. Why Keiran was at Dovermere Cove waiting for the initiates—*his* initiates—to come out of the caves. Emory suddenly noticed the way people kept stealing glances his way, as if he were as beloved as Aestas herself. She recalled the night he found her on the beach, how anchoring he'd been—a light in the dark—and thought she understood what they saw in him.

Just then, Virgil came up to them holding a small pouch with the sigil of House Waxing Moon stitched on the indigo velvet. "Who wants a party favor?"

Nisha was right behind him, arms crossed and looking at Virgil with her nose upturned in mild disdain. Emory watched him dig out a tiny flake of something silvery from the pouch and set it on his tongue. It dissolved before her eyes. Virgil turned his face to the ceiling-less sky and intoned in a voice laced with theater, "Youthful Anima, bestow upon me the powers of your tides."

Her heart pounded in her chest. "What is it?"

A booming laugh. "*What is it*, she asks. Oh, to be so innocent."

Emory felt her cheeks burn so hot she wished to disappear.

"It's just a party trick, really," Nisha said.

"An expensive and *illicit* party trick," Virgil amended, "so best you keep quiet about what you see here, Healer, yeah?"

What Penelope had said about exclusive parties and weird magics came back to her. "What does it do?"

"It's a way to bend the rules of magic so we can know what other alignments feel like," Nisha explained. She jerked her chin at a group of Selenics who were sampling the food with such elation, they seemed to be having a religious experience. "This one uses Amplifier magic to sharpen the senses."

Emory frowned at the Selenics around her. Most of them had the same air of mindless wonder about them, like they were seeing the world in color for the first time. Whatever this thing was

bent the rules of magic, sure enough, but it was a far cry from what she could do, from what she'd seen Keiran doing too. Healing the bird, making roses bloom–that kind of magic had been purposeful. Deliberate. Whatever *this* was felt exactly like Nisha said: a mere party trick for those who couldn't do the real thing.

Keiran was watching her carefully, his features hidden beneath the mask, but the meaning in his eyes was plain enough: this wasn't the same thing she'd seen him do. And if Virgil was resorting to such measures, perhaps the Sower magic she'd glimpsed in the greenhouse had only been Keiran's doing, no one else's.

Could it be that only she and Keiran could do such magic at will?

She contemplated the bag still in Virgil's hand. "So it lets anyone use Amplifier magic?"

"You can't actually manipulate the magic," Nisha supplied. "It's more just an impression of it. A small taste of magic without any real sustenance."

"And what a glorious, painfully fleeting taste it is," Virgil mused. "Nothing like the s–"

"The Tidal Council has all arrived," Lizaveta interrupted, showing up at their side. She gave Emory and Keiran a cold once-over. "They're waiting for you."

Time to prove herself, Emory thought. Keiran gave her a small nod of encouragement and guided her in the right direction, his hand hovering at the small of her back. It felt oddly grounding.

Four people sat on high-backed chairs fit for kings in front of a large archway, watching Emory like a council of regal owls. Their heads were crowned with their house's lunar flowers, making them look like ancient deities against the backdrop of the night sky, with the curtains billowing softly around them and a carpet of ivy at their feet.

The first was a tall, reedy man in an emerald three-piece suit wearing Bruma's face and a crown of black narcissus; the second

was Keiran's great-aunt Leonie, an arrangement of indigo holly-hocks now sitting atop her silver hair; the third was a smiling man wearing Aestas's face, a brilliant wreath of white orchids resting on his dark curls; and the fourth was Vivianne, the Memorist that Keiran had pointed out to her, towering over the rest of them with a bouquet of purple-black poppies crowning her head.

Keiran led Emory to stand before the Council. The rest of the Order members threw curious looks their way. As if sensing some-thing noteworthy was about to happen, they moved closer, fanning out into a semicircle around them. Their murmurs were unsettling, and Emory was glad for her mask again as some thirty porcelain faces stared at her.

A hush settled over the lighthouse.

"Whatever happens," Keiran breathed at her side, "I've got your back."

His words were more comforting than she cared to admit. Still, Emory had never been this nervous. This was it. Her fate to be decided by the Tides themselves, or their likeness, at least. She felt like a wave rushing inevitably toward the shore, unsure if she'd shatter against a barrier of rock or sigh gently across welcom-ing sands, unnerved as she was by the four porcelain faces staring blankly at her.

Keiran folded his hands behind his back and intoned, "Illustrious Tidal Council, I bring forth Emory Ainsleif, Healer of House New Moon."

There was a momentous quality to his voice, to the air around them, as though the walls of the lighthouse themselves were wait-ing with bated breath to hear what would be said next.

"Four lunar cycles past, she faced the depths of Dovermere with the rest of our initiates and lived to tell the tale," he continued, addressing the room at large. "The sea took eight of our brightest that night, the best the Tides had to offer, yet it spared her. A ninth

soul there by happenstance, whom fate chose to return to us with the sigil of our Order on her skin. Marking her, for all intents and purposes, as one of our own." He turned to Emory and gently lifted her arm so that the Tidal Council could glimpse her spiral mark. "She appears now before you to seek acceptance in our ranks."

There was a resounding silence, more deafening than the waves outside or the whispers Emory thought would have risen at the revelation. But she felt the tension in the air, the hostility, all the same. This, she knew, was something that had never happened before. That went against the Order's precious rules.

The man wearing Bruma's face spoke first: "You're saying she was never tapped for initiation, yet passed our initiation rites all the same?"

"Correct."

"Then she's an intruder," the man with Aestas's face seethed. "Why was she at Dovermere to begin with? Trying to weasel her way into our Order, perhaps?"

Emory stood frozen, unsure what to do. If it had been Romie standing here before the Tidal Council, she would have brazenly told them all to shove it, would have proved her worth with one clever trick. If there was ever a time to be more like Romie, it was now.

Emory took a grounding breath and slid off her Bruma mask. "I knew nothing of your Order at the time, sir," she said loudly. "I simply went after a friend whose well-being I was worried about and ended up in the wrong place at the wrong time."

"And now?" This from Vivianne, the Memorist. "Surely you must know enough about our Order to end up here tonight." She threw Keiran a suspicious glance. "Unless someone told you about us?"

"She pieced most of it together on her own after discovering an initiation invitation in her roommate's things," Keiran said smoothly. "Romie Brysden, one of last year's initiates. It was only

when she approached me with this information that I invited her here to appear before you."

Emory was grateful for his quick intervention. The Tidal Council looked at her expectantly, and she seized her chance. "I did the ritual, same as the others. I survived the tide filling the Belly of the Beast. I escaped Dovermere, and though I wish I could say I wasn't the only one who did, I was. I already bear your mark. Why not your title, too?" She swallowed hard, Romie's face flashing before her eyes. "Please, let me join your ranks so I can honor those who've fallen."

"I admire your mettle, Ms. Ainsleif," Leonie said with a kind smile. "Unfortunately, surviving Dovermere alone is not enough. There are traditions to follow, preliminary trials to pass, all of which last year's initiates went through to be deemed worthy of becoming Selenics."

"So let me do those trials," Emory pleaded. "Let me prove to you that I deserve my place here too."

"I don't know how to put this gently, girl," the man with Bruma's face said gruffly, "but the Selenic Order accepts only those of the highest quality into its ranks. Nothing but the best and brightest. As I recall, your name was never even on our list of potential candidates."

Anger rose in her at that. "With all due respect, sir, I survived what eight of your apparent best and brightest could not. I might not be from one of your legacy families or have the highest grades, but surely that must mean something."

"It means you were lucky," Vivianne said. She looked to her companions with bored annoyance. "I say we wipe our name from her memory and be done with this nonsense."

Emory's thoughts raced. She would be damned if she let them take her memories. She stepped forward, holding out her wrist. "Your initiates died for this mark, for a chance to wield all lunar

magics as their own. When the mark engraved itself on me, it gave *me* that chance too. It made me into something more than just a Healer. Allowed me to wield magics outside of my own tidal alignment."

She reached for the Sower magic first, just as she had earlier tonight. She tried not to think of the fact that, even under Baz's careful tutelage, she hadn't been able to wield the magic for much more than a few seconds, or how the philodendron she'd tried to revive was just as dead now as it had been before.

Instead, she thought of Romie, a memory rising unbidden to the surface. It was Emory's sixteenth birthday, and the only time Romie had ever gifted her a plant. "String of hearts," she'd announced proudly. "I propagated it myself from some cuttings I collected. Pretty, isn't it?"

It hadn't survived the week. When Romie found out, she'd laughed herself to tears and teased Emory for her lack of a green thumb.

"I'm a Healer, Ro, not a Sower!"

Romie had gotten that dreamy look in her eyes. "Don't you wish you could be everything all at once?"

Now Emory had what Romie wished for: access to every magic, something Romie would have never struggled to master had their roles been reversed. But Romie was dead. She was gone and Emory was still here, and the only thing she could do to honor her friend now was to seek justice from within.

She gritted her teeth, imploring the waxing crescent to unlock its mysteries for her, to share its secrets until they became as known to her as the Healing magic she'd been born with.

And it did.

The ivy at the Tidal Council's feet moved at her command, leaves rustling in an imagined breeze. A vine crept toward her, slithering up her dress to wrap around her wrist. She heard the faint hum of awe in the crowd but did not let it distract her, reaching instead for

more. Light and dark answered, as they had the night of the bonfires, but this time, she was in control. The candles flared dramatically, then burned out all at once, plunging the room into darkness
except for the everlights strung on the walls. Emory called those
lights toward her. They moved slowly, made to look like floating stars, and came to rest in her outstretched hand where they
formed a single bright light.

Pride swelled in her as she beamed at it, this impossible magic
she wielded. Not the shade of magic that Virgil had imbibed, not
a mere taste or impression of it as Nisha described, but the real
thing, here at her fingertips. Hers to command.

She let the light extinguish, the vine of ivy fall at her feet. A few
bulbs of everlight had remained untouched on the walls, now the
only source of light that remained.

In the semidarkness, Emory held her head high as she looked
at the Council. "You see? I, too, have the mark and the Tidecaller
magic it gave me. The same as Keiran, who can heal birds and
make roses bloom. Should that not be enough to earn my place in
your Order?"

Something crackled in the air, a tension she couldn't understand.
Scathing remarks of *Tidethief* and *Eclipse-born* slithered along her
skin. Her heart sank to the pit of her stomach.

This was a horrible mistake.

Emory rounded on Keiran, searched his face for answers; the
half of it she could see beneath his mask gave nothing away, but his
eyes . . . His eyes glittered with what looked like triumph.

"I'm not a Tidecaller, Ainsleif," he said quietly.

His words pounded in her head, utterly incomprehensible. "But
I *saw* you . . ."

"What you saw me using was synthetic magic. A stronger version
of the amplification synths being passed around tonight, but a fabrication all the same."

He'd played her. He'd let her believe they were the same, that the spiral mark had given them both this impossible power. And she'd been foolish enough to believe it. She should have dug deeper, pressed him harder for the full truth instead of the veiled admissions he'd given her. There was no way out of this now; she'd walked into his trap and revealed her hand, proclaiming herself a Tidecaller in front of all these people.

Tidethief, she heard someone seethe.

False Healer.

Eclipse scum.

Emory threw a furtive glance at the stairs. If she could slip past them, make a run for it . . .

"Where's Artem?" a woman asked. "He's a Regulator, let him deal with her!"

Some of the Selenics echoed their agreement. Emory's veins filled with ice, her breath coming in shallow bursts. She took a step back, blinking furiously as black spots gathered at the edge of her vision. She needed to get out of here, needed to–

Keiran's fingers wrapped around her wrist. "Wait. Trust me."

Artem stepped up to the front of the crowd, slipping his mask off. There was a look of complete authority about him–a *Regulator,* here to bring her to the Institute where she'd be branded with the Unhallowed Seal.

Emory wrenched free from Keiran's grasp. She wouldn't be so naive as to trust him again. She headed for the stairs.

"Don't go anywhere."

Artem's words were laced with such command that Emory froze. Slowly, she turned to him. Power thrummed from him–Glamour magic, she realized, the power of compulsion he wielded under the waxing crescent's might.

He was compelling her with it.

"Artie," Keiran said tightly. "Let's not be rash about this."

"Rules are rules, Keir," Artem spat. "And Eclipse-born who lie about their alignment is one of the biggest offenses there is."

"I didn't lie," Emory said weakly.

"If she were to Collapse, the havoc it would wreak—"

Then, more forcefully, "I *didn't lie.*" Artem gave her a scathing look that she returned in kind. "I was born a Healer and have all the documents to prove it. These powers only started manifesting after Dovermere." She looked pleadingly at the Tidal Council, at Keiran. "You have to believe me."

Artem stepped toward her. *"Tell the truth."*

Again, his words were laced with power, bending her will to his, and Emory couldn't have lied even if she wanted to. "That is the truth," she said. "I swear it."

Artem seemed inflamed by her response. "I don't care when your powers manifested, Tidethief. I'm bringing you to the Institute."

He came at her with burning hate. Emory scrambled backward in fear, but Keiran stepped in front of her, hand outstretched to stop Artem.

"Wait."

"She's Eclipse-born, Keiran, and no doubt untrained at that."

"I know."

"If she Collapses . . ." Artem swore, angry veins stark on his neck. "I'm not going through that again. I *can't.*"

Keiran clasped him on the neck, trying to calm him down. "I know. But we're safe, Artie. Everyone's safe. Just hear me out for a minute. That's all I ask."

Artem stepped back with a furious grunt. Keiran turned to Emory, taking his mask off. There was a fiercely protective gleam in his eyes. "Are you all right?"

She didn't know how to answer that, stood frozen with fear as if Artem's compulsion were keeping her here against her better judgment.

Keiran slowly swept his gaze over the room, commanding every-one's attention. "We're in uncharted territory here," he said loudly. "What we decide next could change the fate of our Order forever."

He stepped closer to the Tidal Council, spun around to make sure all eyes were on him. "The Selenic Order has long believed magic shouldn't be quartered off into lunar houses or splintered further into tidal alignments. We believe it should be as it once was, when magic was a thing earned, not born. That's why we resort to these synthetic half-measures we've kept to ourselves for centuries, all to get a modicum of the kind of power the Tides once blessed us with. My parents, whom all of you held in the highest esteem, believed we could go further than that. Wield all the moon's powers as our own."

His eyes settled on his great-aunt. "You know I have constantly sought to carry out their legacy, make them proud from the Deep their souls now rest in. Tonight, I meant to appear before you all to say I've finally succeeded in doing what they only dreamed of. I've found a way to *use* other lunar magics instead of merely tasting them."

At a jerk of his chin, six people stepped to the front of the crowd: Lizaveta, Virgil, Nisha, Ife, and Louis, as well as a boy with supple long hair wearing an Aestas mask who had to be Javier. Each of them held a wilted flower in their hand. Keiran pulled one of his own from his jacket pocket. In unison, the seven of them held up the dead flowers and, mirroring what Emory had done in the green-house with Baz, breathed life into them once more, so that each of them now held the brilliant, blooming flower of their respective lunar houses.

Awed murmurs rose around them. Leonie leaned forward on her chair. "How?"

Keiran dug a small silver vial from his pocket. "It's the same sub-stance we've always used, a bit of silver and salt water and blood,

but more potent." He nodded to where Artem stood next to his sister, still quietly seething. "Together with Artem, we've found a way to develop this new form of synthetic that we ink directly on our skin, right on top of our Selenic Marks. It lets us wield whatever magic the person whose blood we use has. Tonight, we used Nisha's blood to access her Sower magic. And the results, as you just witnessed, are like nothing we've ever done before."

Keiran turned to Emory. "That's how I was able to use the magics you saw. Healing the bird, making roses bloom—it was a fabrication, a lie dressed in silver and salt water and blood. This is the Selenic Order's legacy. We hold the key to all magics in these synthetics. It's a false key, a shade of what *you* can do as a Tidecaller, but the closest we have to the real thing. You, on the other hand . . . Wielding all magics at will? It defies everything," he said with a breathless sort of awe.

He turned to the Council. "The Tides put her in our path for a reason. She bears our mark, completed our initiation ritual, survived what the eight candidates we'd chosen could not. With what we showed you tonight, the progress we've already made to synthetics . . . What Emory demonstrated she can do . . . Imagine what more we could accomplish with her at our side."

"Absolutely not," Artem spat viciously. "Are you out of your mind? This is not what I signed up for. She's *Eclipse*, Keiran. We've never allowed them in our ranks, and for good reason."

Behind him, Lizaveta and some of the other Selenics seemed just as incensed.

Keiran extended a hand between them as if to appease him. "You know better than anyone I don't take lightly to unchecked Eclipse magic. But you can't deny the potential here. The Order prides itself on seeking the rarest talents to lay claim to. And here she is, a Tidecaller with magic the likes of which we have only ever *dreamed* of. A rarity like no other."

They wanted power to match her own, Emory realized. Not the fabricated version they imbibed or inked themselves with, but magic like hers, free-flowing in her veins. Unease lined her stomach, coated her mouth, as she wondered how, exactly, they planned to attain it. She took an involuntary step back.

"Come now, you're scaring the girl." Virgil drawled from where he stood at the front of the crowd, twirling the restored poppy in his hand. "Will someone please tell her we don't mean to sacrifice her to the Tides and bleed her dry of her power?"

Keiran shot him a dry look, as if to say, *Don't be absurd.* "I believe she was meant to be a Selenic. To share with us the secrets of her magic." His eyes met hers. "If she wishes to."

Emory read the promise behind his words: If she agreed to it, they would keep her magic a secret. If she didn't . . . Artem glared at her in a way that made it clear he would be all too happy to bring her straight to the Institute.

The Tidal Council seemed to consider it, exchanging a few hushed words. At last, Vivianne said, "Should anyone outside the Order ever find out what she is, we won't be able to protect her without dragging our name through the mud. As leader of the current cohort, do you agree to take full responsibility for Ms. Ainsleif and bear the consequence if anything goes wrong?"

"I do," Keiran said without hesitation.

Surely, Emory thought, he must have an ulterior motive, a reason to want her so badly to join the Order he would put his neck on the line like this.

"Then it's settled," Leonie declared. "You'll have her take her oath tonight, like any other candidate does when first tapped for initiation, and officially induct her into our ranks. Do you accept this, Ms. Ainsleif?"

It was exactly what she had set out to do, but Emory couldn't shake the feeling she'd gotten more than she could handle. It hit

her fully then that everything she'd so desperately believed about her Tidecaller magic was false. It had nothing to do with the spiral mark, so why then did her blood now run with Eclipse magic?

Eclipse-born, Eclipse-*formed*.

Whatever her title, she was alone to bear it.

Keiran gave her a near-imperceptible nod, as if to say it'd be all right, that this was the right move to make.

Whatever happens, I've got your back.

She didn't trust him for a second, not after he'd gotten her to reveal her magic in such a chaotic mess of a way. And yet . . . she couldn't refuse the Order. Not when she was so close, and certainly not if the alternative was having her memory stripped or being escorted to the Institute.

She could do this—could be brave like Romie always was. Once she was in, she could finally find out the truth behind the drownings, ensure no one else suffered such a fate.

And perhaps there were answers about her own magic to be found here too.

Emory lifted her chin. "I do."

14

BAZ

THIS WAS MADNESS.

It was the only thought Baz had as he gripped on to Vera for dear life. The wind tore at him as they sped their way out of Cadence, making his eyes water. His heart bounced up and down between his throat and the pit of his stomach, and every sharp turn and rushing descent had him thinking he would die. He had never felt more reckless in his entire sheltered existence and wondered if this was what it felt like to be truly alive.

He wasn't sure if he hated it or loved it.

The rush of adrenaline left him on trembling knees when they arrived, leaving the motorbike down the road to avoid detection. The dark wood and stone of the Institute stuck out like a sore thumb against the quaint thatch-roofed cottages and sprawling estates on the outskirts of Cadence. The Regulator crest glittered silver above an imposing door, the sight of it enough to make Baz sick.

He looked at Vera and silently berated himself for his unchar-acteristic spontaneity. He was trusting someone he didn't know,

about to break into the last place he ever wanted to step foot in.

Vera smirked at his expression as she worked to unlock a side door with a hair pin.

"So when you said *engineering genius*," Baz muttered, "you meant *picklock*?"

"Picking locks is a bonus," Vera said with a fiendish smile. The door pushed open. "What you need a genius for is *this*."

Inside was a sort of engine room–full of electrical wires and machinery with knobs and lights that emitted soft sounds. It reminded Baz of his father's printing press, but with much more modern equipment. Vera wasted no time: she quickly assessed the machines, pulling knobs and levers and pressing buttons here and there.

She jerked her chin to another door at the back of the room. "Should be good. Let's go."

Baz didn't like her use of *should*, but he followed her all the same. Whatever she did had apparently deactivated all security around them, magical and otherwise, and they quickly wound through the empty corridors without so much as a hiccup.

He'd forgotten how bare and white and clinical everything was.

He would have gotten lost without Vera there to guide them. Soon enough he stood in front of a door labeled *Kai Salonga*, which Vera worked on unlocking again with her hairpin. Faint light shone through the small window on the door. Baz could just make out Kai's outline inside. He lay on a narrow bed, one arm casually draped behind his head, the other occupied with twining what looked like a chess piece between his fingers.

Nerves gripped Baz. This really was the most senseless thing he'd ever done, but he was here now, just a step away from the one person who might hold all the answers. He looked at Vera and hesitated.

"Go," she said knowingly. "I'll be your lookout."

Baz gave her a grateful nod and stepped inside.

Thin, dark eyes slid to him, full of cold fury that dissipated as soon as Kai recognized him. He sat up slowly, his hand engulfing the chess piece–a white pawn, Baz saw–and stared at Baz as if trying to work out if he was real.

Baz himself grappled with reality. He almost didn't recognize Kai against such a bleak backdrop, a stark contrast to the shabby coziness of the Eclipse commons. Kai wore a simple white undershirt, the intricate geometrical tattoos on his collarbone peeking out at the top. He'd been allowed to keep his fine gold chains, Baz noticed–surely a small comfort to him, as he never took them off.

Mind racing with something clever to say, Baz palmed the back of his neck. His throat worked for air. Words would not come.

Kai's mouth thinned to a knife-edged smile. "Nice of you to finally visit, asshole."

His voice was conjured night. It was a dark wood at midnight, the chilling howl of a beast; it was the quiet of dreams and the pull of nightmares, lovely and frightening all at once.

And Baz had sorely missed it.

"You know how they get about Eclipse visitors," he offered weakly.

Kai wasn't fooled. "I'd hoped it might be you the other day when my parents came to visit. From halfway across the world, might I add. Even your friend Jae had the decency to stop by earlier." The teasing note in his accusation didn't quite reach his eyes. "Honestly, I'm surprised to see you here at all, given your aversion to this place."

Kai knew better than anyone how Baz feared the threat of Collapsing so much he refused to visit his own father. Such was the Nightmare Weaver's plight, to be burdened with the fears and nightmares of those around him.

Or at least, it had been.

Baz's gaze slid to Kai's left hand, where a U-shaped scar marred the surface of his Eclipse tattoo. The Unhallowed Seal that cut off his access to the magic in his veins. The *U* had many meanings: unhallowed, unfit, unbalanced, unworthy of magic–all the same, in the end. It was the only thing keeping Kai from becoming something other, a shadow self, as twisted and wrong as the Shadow was believed to have been.

Beneath it all, Baz imagined he could feel the ghost of Kai's power, a silver beast put to sleep in his veins.

"You look . . ."

"Like shit?" Kai supplied with a cold laugh.

Baz didn't know what to say. It was true that Kai didn't look well at all–dark bruises under his eyes, skin emaciated, once-luscious hair falling in limp, oily strands down to his shoulders. A haunted man in a haunting place.

Suddenly he couldn't stand seeing Kai like this, in this Tides-forsaken prison. He realized the pain of missing him these past few months had been a dull thing compared to what the sight of him now conjured. Never had he longed so ardently for their late nights in the commons, with Kai sprawled on the sofa and he on the chair beside him and the briny breeze billowing between them. He hadn't realized how much he missed the easy silence of mornings spent waiting for the coffee to brew, or the long conversations about the book they both loved. The solidarity that sprang from being the only two of their house. Tides, he even missed their training sessions where Kai turned Baz's fears and nightmares into bone-chilling reality.

Kai didn't belong here. His place was in Obscura Hall–with him.

Anger rose in Baz, sharp and quick. "Tell me you didn't do this on purpose. That you didn't deliberately push yourself to Collapse just to see what might happen."

Kai's eyes darkened. "I did what I had to."

Silence settled between them like ash.

"I thought you said you weren't stupid enough to try it," Baz said on a shaky breath. "How else did you think this experiment would pan out?" He shook his head furiously. Then, without thinking, "Do you know what it was like to get back from my sister's funeral and find out you were *gone*, just like that?"

He knew how pathetic he must sound, yet all this pent-up resentment in him didn't care as it came bursting out. He'd needed Kai's steady presence this summer, the only thing keeping him afloat in the ocean of grief he'd been drowning in after Romie. He needed the people around him to stop *leaving*. His father who Collapsed, his mother who checked out, his sister who drowned, Jae who never stayed put for long, and now Kai, who'd barreled headfirst into trouble without thinking of what it might do to *Baz* to lose him like that.

He'd never quite understood the acute pain of it until now, the gutting sense of abandonment he'd felt upon returning to the empty Eclipse commons. With his father, things had been different: Baz had *seen* his Collapse happen, had lived through it, and so his getting sent to the Institute made sense to him, a natural conclusion to the events he'd witnessed. With Kai, he felt he'd missed a beat, like climbing down stairs and thinking there was one last step, heart in his throat as he met solid ground instead.

"I've been carrying around this guilt because I *knew* you were obsessed with this idea and I didn't take you seriously," he said, too worked up to keep things bottled up now. "And then, what—you waited for me to go home so I'd be out of your way? Why'd you show up in my sleep the night before? To say goodbye? And *still* I didn't clock in that you were going to do this."

"I knew you'd try to talk me out of it if you were there," Kai said. "I thought it'd be easier this way."

Baz scoffed. "You did this for yourself and no one else. This was so selfish of—"

"Are you seriously calling *me* selfish? *You?* The guy who hasn't visited his own father in nearly a decade because the thought makes him too uncomfortable." A joyless laugh. "I knew you wouldn't understand. Look at me, Brysden. I'm a shade of what I used to be, and I've only been here for a few months. The ones who've been in this shithole for years? It's like they exist, but they're not really *here.*"

A shiver licked up Baz's spine. He thought of his father, locked away in a room just like this one somewhere in the correctional wing, withering away to nothing.

Empty and hollow.

"You really have no idea how hard it's been," Kai said. "So don't call me selfish when I'm the only one trying to figure out what it is they do to us, because there's something shady going on here, Brysden, and no one else but me and Jae seem to be taking it seriously. They believe me; why can't you?"

Baz stilled. "What do you mean, *what they do to us?*"

Kai settled back against the wall and ran a hand over his face, still simmering with anger. He toyed with the moon-and-sunflower pendant at his throat. "They do experiments on us or something. They haven't done it to me yet, as far as I can tell. But I hear others sometimes, screaming in the night. The power in here flickers in and out like it's the end of the fucking world. Whatever it is has everyone scared. No one will talk to me, but I see it in their eyes, that *fear.* And the Regulators, they don't care about us." Kai's gaze fell on the chess piece on the bedside table. "We're all pawns in whatever fucked-up game they're playing." He suddenly knocked the piece over, letting it roll onto the floor. He pierced Baz with a stare. "So why are you here, Brysden? *How* are you here?"

Baz shifted uncomfortably. "Someone helped me deactivate the wards and pick the lock on your door."

A pause–then Kai laughed in utter disbelief. "I leave you alone for

a few months and you turn rogue? Where was this rebelliousness hiding all this time?"

"I went to see the Veiled Atlas."

That seemed to wipe the smile off Kai's face.

"I asked them about the missing epilogue. They told me about Adriana, how she might have known where to find it, and how both you and Romie had been there before, asking the same questions."

Dreamer.

Stay out of my way, nightmare boy.

"You two were trying to find the epilogue, weren't you?"

Kai peered at him curiously. "I thought you didn't care about the epilogue."

"I care because Romie did." He pulled the note from his pocket and handed it to Kai. "Whatever competition I assume you two had going on, this senseless search for the epilogue . . . It's what led her to Dovermere. To her *death.*"

Kai remained quiet as he stared at the note. Finally, he said, "I didn't know she was going into those caves, Brysden."

There was enough anguish on his face to convince Baz he was telling the truth.

"Then what happened?"

"After I went to the Veiled Atlas, I found your sister in the sleep-scape. Asked if she'd had any luck finding Adriana or the epilogue." He snorted. "She told me to fuck off and mind my own business. And it did become a sort of competition between us then, to see who might get to it first. Until we realized we were both hearing that same song in our sleep and decided to help each other instead."

"What?"

"Romie was adamant it was Adriana calling us to the epilogue. Or at least a clue to finding it. Night after night, we tried to fol-low the song deeper into the sleepscape. We went further than I've ever been, until everything felt distorted and heavy and it was hard

to breathe. But we could feel it, how close we were. One night, the umbrae came. Too many of them. I tried to keep them back, but it's like they weren't responding to my magic. I was on the verge of Collapsing. Romie could have kept going, could have left me behind while she pushed further, but she didn't. She pulled me out of there, and that was the last time I saw her, both in the sleepscape and out. I don't know if her going to Dovermere had anything to do with it, but I know she was as eager as I was to get the epilogue, and willing to do just about anything to get it." A frown as he looked at her note again. "Where'd you find this, anyway?"

"She left it in Clover's manuscript."

Kai raised a brow. "*The* manuscript?"

Baz nodded solemnly; he knew Kai understood the weight of it, this fabled, mythical thing that was the manuscript, usually off-limits to the public eye. "I don't know how Romie managed to get access to the Vault," he said, "but it looks like she must have left this note there in a hurry."

He'd been puzzling it over since finding the note. Had she meant to take it with her but was caught and forced to leave it behind? Or had she been meaning to leave it in the manuscript all along, maybe for someone else to find—like Kai?

"Wasn't she friends with that girl who works there?"

Baz blinked at Kai. "Who?"

"The Sower girl. The clerk who works the permissions desk."

Nisha Zenara—whom he'd just seen with Keiran and Emory. *Of course.* If they'd been close, she was likely part of whatever Romie had been involved with too.

"How . . ."

Kai shrugged. "Your sister and I got to talking in the sleepscape." He frowned. "Does the book *Dark Tides* mean anything to you?"

"*Dark Tides*?"

"The last time we were in the sleepscape, Romie was mumbling

this . . . rhyme. *There are tides that drown and tides that bind.* I don't remember the rest, but it was strange enough that I looked into it after she drowned, thinking it might have something to do with the epilogue. It led me to this title: *Dark Tides*. I didn't get the chance to read it before I . . . Well." He shrugged as if to downplay his Collapsing. "Might be worth looking into."

Baz watched him carefully. "How did you Collapse, Kai?"

He gave a long, frustrated sigh, like he'd known this was coming. "Last time Romie and I were in the sleepscape and I almost Collapsed . . . I can't describe it, Brysden, this sense of peace I felt. I was on the brink of Collapse, that darkness pulling me forward, and all I could think was that it didn't feel so threatening at all. Not a curse, but a dam about to break to let something *good* through. I had this gut feeling that I'd be okay if I just . . . let myself succumb to that pull." He shook his head, staring into the middle distance. "After Romie drowned . . . I knew if I went back to the sleepscape without her, followed the song further than we'd gone together, I'd Collapse. And maybe with all that power coursing through me, I would finally reach the epilogue."

The look he threw Baz set his insides aflame.

"I knew I had to try. So I went to sleep in Obscura Hall, thinking if I did Collapse, at least the wards would contain the blast, and no one would get hurt. But then I started fucking *sleepwalking*, and suddenly I was on the beach down at Dovermere Cove. Almost like the song was calling my subconscious deeper into the sleepscape, while it called my body closer to Dovermere. I don't know. I only woke up after the umbrae found me in the sleepscape. I almost had it, I think. The epilogue. But then I Collapsed. The blast woke me, pulled me from the sleepscape, and someone must have seen it all happen, because next thing I knew, some Regulator was snapping damper cuffs around my wrists and bringing me here to get branded with the fucking seal."

"Kai . . ."

The stark light over their heads flickered.

Kai swore. "And now it's happening again."

"What is?"

"This is how it starts. Whatever it is they do to us."

A distant, muffled scream broke the quiet.

Baz nearly leapt out of his skin as Vera opened the door, a panicked look on her face. "We need to go. Something's happening down the hall."

He looked to Kai and thought, if he and Vera had come this far undetected, he might help Kai escape. The same thought seemed to occur to Kai. Baz saw it in the twinkle in his eyes, like the first glimmer of stars in a night sky. He saw it in the way Kai's body tensed, as if ready to pounce. He could follow Baz and Vera out of here and be free.

But the Unhallowed Seal would forever paint a target on his back, wherever he went. Kai flexed his hand, like he, too, had come to the same conclusion.

Another scream, and the stars in Kai's eyes glowed brighter, his features set with fierce determination now as he settled back on his bed. "Go. I'm not leaving until I figure this out."

Baz's heart broke. "Please. We can go back to Obscura Hall—"

The lights flickered on and off again, more quickly than before.

"You need to go, Brysden."

Baz thought he saw a silvery track of veins on Kai's neck, as if his slumbering magic was stirring despite the seal on it. Baz frowned, mouth open to ask if he felt his magic waking, but Vera tugged on his arm with renewed urgency as another bloodcurdling scream rose, and before Baz knew it, he was out the door, holding on to that last glimpse of Kai as it slammed shut between them.

"Come on," Vera urged him.

They hurried down the corridor. Power surged all around them

when another scream echoed. Baz faltered as someone pleaded, "Stop, please, don't take it," and for a second he thought it might have been his father, though it sounded nothing like him. Vera pulled at his sleeve, swearing as footsteps sounded ahead of them— and a Regulator rounded the bend.

One with an all-too-familiar face.

"Jae?"

Baz stared incomprehensibly at Jae Ahn. They were clad in a Regulator's charcoal uniform, a panicked look in their eye.

"Basil, what in the Tides' name—"

Nearby voices cut them off. Baz whipped around. The screaming had stopped, and the voices—they were coming from that same direction. Jae's face turned ashen with fear the likes of which Baz had not seen from them since . . . since his father Collapsed, he realized. Confused bits of memory from that day swirled in his mind, but before he could say a word, Jae motioned him and Vera down the hall.

"We need to get out of here," they whispered. "Quickly now."

The three of them ran as quietly as they could.

"On the left," Vera wheezed as they came to a crossing. Baz recognized it, knew the door they'd come through was just past this next bend—

"Hey!"

Two Regulators appeared behind them at the other end of the corridor. They tore toward them. Panicked, Baz considered what it would be like to freeze them in time. Pausing time for immaterial objects was one thing, but *people*, whole living organisms, was something he'd never dared attempt. Yet what choice did he have?

But then—a wall materialized out of thin air between them and the Regulators, severing the corridor as if it had always stood there.

"What the fuck?" Vera exclaimed.

Jae was smiling rather smugly. "That should give them pause."

Jae shook their sleeves—no longer wearing the stiff charcoal Regulator uniform, but their usual frilly shirt and vest combination. They caught Baz's eye and winked at him. "Let's go."

Vera stared after Jae with her mouth slightly agape. "What the fuck?" she repeated.

"They're an Illusionist," Baz explained breathlessly.

A little harmless illusion work to get me through the door, Jae had said about getting into the Institute. But what were they doing here in the middle of the night?

Angry shouts echoed behind the illusioned wall, making his pulse hike. He and Vera ran down the empty corridor after Jae. He could barely remember how to breathe as they reached the exit. The knot of tension in his chest didn't ease in the slightest even as they burst into the night.

Breathe in, hold, breathe out.

They made for the wooded area at the edge of the Institute, and only once they were there did Jae finally stop, rounding on Baz.

"When I suggested you come visit your dad," they said tensely, "I didn't mean break into the Institute in the middle of the Tides-damned night. What were you *thinking*?"

"I might ask the same of you," Baz retorted angrily. "And what were you doing dressed as a Regulator?"

Jae pointed to the Institute. "I was trying to figure out what *that* was. That's why I'm in Cadence, Basil. There's something odd going on at the Institute, something to do with Collapsed Eclipse-born."

"I know. Kai told me. That's who I came to see, not Dad." He glanced back at the building. "Did you find anything, at least?"

"No. I was heading toward the screaming when I bumped into you. You need to stay far away from here from now on, understood? I don't want you anywhere near what's happening."

Baz didn't need to be told twice—but the idea of Kai being left behind to fend for himself, and his father, too . . .

As if they read his mind, Jae put a reassuring hand on his shoulder. "I won't stop digging until I figure this out, Basil. I promise." They glanced at Vera. "How did you two get here?"

Vera nodded toward the road. "Motorbike. You?"

"Illusioned myself a cab," Jae said with a wink and a nonchalant shrug. As though such a feat was nothing to them.

But that kind of magic . . . It was incredible, even for such a powerful Illusionist as Jae. Baz knew it must have taken a toll on them. He watched them warily, imagining the worst, his mind full of silver veins and blasts of power and bone-chilling screams.

Jae caught his eye and said, "You go on ahead now before they come looking for us."

"What about you?"

"Don't worry about me. I'll find my own way back." At Baz's hesitation, they added, "The fall equinox is coming up. We'll meet then and go over all this together. Until then, *stay out of trouble*."

A branch snapped in the near distance, making them all startle. Jae mouthed *Go* before retreating deeper into the woods. Vera pulled on Baz's sleeve, and they hurried toward her motorcycle.

It was only as Cadence came into view that Baz broke down in silence, angry tears drying in the wind as if they never existed. He shut his eyes tight against the hurt, but it didn't help. All he saw was Kai's face burned into the backs of his eyelids, the fleeting hope Kai had lit up with at the prospect of escape, his grim determination as he decided against it.

A part of Baz regretted coming to see him at all. He should have stayed in the commons, kept to his books. Then he wouldn't have to feel this sickening pain in his heart.

15

EMORY

THE DECRESCENS LIBRARY FELT ENTIRELY DIFFERENT AT night—not the safe harbor Emory had come to know it as during her morning sessions with Baz, but this cavernous beast with mysterious things lurking in the shadows. Blood rushed to her ears as the current cohort of Selenics led her through the rare books collection on Dreamer magic, past the restricted Reaper aisles, and all the way to the far end of the empty, darkly lit library. They had all unmasked, yet somehow felt more mythical and unattainable to her than before.

None of them had said a word since the lighthouse.

Keiran stopped her before the narrow staircase Emory knew led into the Vault. The others were already descending, an eerily grim procession that had her stomach in knots.

She glared at him once they were alone. "You knew I was a Tidecaller."

"I had my suspicions, yes." He leaned against the archway, not a trace of remorse on his face. "When you saw me healing that bird

and thought the Selenic Mark was what gave me such power."

"You let me believe we were the same. Why? So I'd walk into whatever trap tonight was and reveal my magic? So you could claim me as this *thing* you wanted to add to your little Selenic collection of rarities?"

Keiran flinched slightly at that. "That was never my intention."

"You had to have known the kind of hostility I'd be facing if I showed my hand like that. Artem was *this close* to bringing me into the Institute—"

"I wouldn't have let him." His eyes sparked fiercely in the semi-darkness. "Trust me, you were never in any real danger."

She scoffed, crossing her arms. "As if I could ever trust you now."

Keiran pushed off the arch, taking a tentative step toward her. "I would never have put you in that position unless I was sure I could get the Council to side with you. They needed to see your magic to be convinced of what you might bring to the table. *I* needed to see it. And you performed brilliantly, Ainsleif."

"And if I hadn't, would you have let them take me to the Institute?"

"Of course not."

Emory eyed him warily. "Why did you put yourself on the line for me like that? Artem was right to fear me. I don't know anything about these powers except that they started after Dovermere. For all I know, I did something that night to make the others—" She bit back the words, shaking her head. "Yet you're still willing to take me in. To trust *me*. Why?"

Keiran took another step closer. "Because I think we were meant to find each other, you and I. There's a reason you went into those caves, a reason this magic chose to manifest in you that night, a reason our paths have kept crossing since. I've been trying for so long to unlock the secrets to wielding all lunar magics, and here you are, able to do just that."

The intensity in his gaze left her breathless.

"That kind of power . . . It's incredible."

Emory shook her head. "It's unnatural."

"No." Keiran closed the gap between them, his fingers brushing a strand of hair from her face. She was too stunned to move as he gently tilted her chin up. "It makes you *exceptional*, Ainsleif."

An involuntary shiver ran up her spine. It was such a different reaction to how Baz had acted when he found out. There was no fear in Keiran's voice, no accusations. Just this undiluted awe and the warmth of his hand as it cupped her cheek.

It was exhilarating.

"I knew there was something about you the moment I found you on the beach, but I never dreamed it might be this," he mused, letting his hand fall to his side. "I told you I know what it's like to search for answers after losing someone to Dovermere. Your magic is the very answer I've been seeking."

"How?" she asked, enraptured despite the warning bells in her mind.

The corner of his mouth lifted. He laced his fingers through hers and said, "You'll see."

Emory let him guide her down into the Vault. She'd never been before, and marveled at the towering shelves, the cascading water in the center. The Vault was empty, the others nowhere in sight. Keiran brought her to the *S* aisle, at the entrance of which a free-standing wrought-iron staircase sprouted from the stone floor and spiraled up to the high ceiling above. He ran a hand along the intricate motifs of frothy waves and lunar flowers woven in the metal. A spiral like the one they both bore was hidden among them. At his touch, the base of the stairs unfurled, stone grumbling to life in the Vault's half-light. Beneath their feet, the staircase wound on, and on, and on. An odd, bluish light shone at the bottom.

Their steps echoed ominously as they climbed down. Damp cold seeped through Emory's dress, making the fine hairs on her arms

stand to attention. She wished she'd taken a jacket, wished Keiran would tell her what exactly she was walking into. The sound of water was deafening as they neared the bottom, where the stairs spilled into a large circular chamber carved into stone.

A cavern.

For a second, everything in Emory seized. She was back in Dovermere, in those algae-slick caves that would become a death trap once the tide rose, and that was the sound of the sea rushing in, ready to take her under–

But no. The water came from above, a continuation of the Fountain of Fate's sacred waters that spilled into the heart of the Vault and into this chamber below. It pooled into a great basin in the middle, the sides of which were adorned with weathered carvings of the moon's phases. Soft light shone from the bottom of the basin, making the water refract turquoise light on the walls around them. Sixteen chairs lined those walls, carved into the stone itself. A throne for each tidal alignment, she realized. The rest of the Selenics sat upon them, an echo of the Tidal Council from earlier, though much less formal. Indeed, Virgil was sprawled carelessly on his chair, legs draped over a throne arm, cheek resting on his hand in an almost bored way. He winked at Emory.

"Welcome to the Treasury," Keiran said at her side. "The crown jewel of the Selenic Order."

The name slithered over her bones. The Selenic Order–which she had agreed to swear an oath to, become part of, for whatever that meant.

"This was the first seat of our Order," Keiran continued. "According to our records, they were the ones who built Aldryn College, selecting this precise location for its closeness to Dovermere. They say the Fountain of Fate flows with water from the heart of Dovermere, which the first Selenics believed was the very birthplace of the Tides themselves."

He ran a hand through the glowing pool. "It's with this water that they made the first synthetic magic, the diluted kind you saw earlier tonight. And it's with this water that we were able to experiment with something stronger. Our way of accessing other magics no matter our tidal alignment or the moon phase ruling the sky."

Emory looked at the pool, at the thrones and the Selenics sitting upon them like kings and queens. "Why not hold the soiree here instead of the lighthouse?"

"The Treasury always belongs to the current cohort," Virgil drawled from his seat. "Those old bags had their time in the limelight when they were at Aldryn. Now it's ours."

This earned smiles from Louis and Javier.

"The Tidal Council watches over the Order at large, but here at Aldryn, we're the ones steering the ship," Keiran added. "The introduction soiree only serves to present candidates to the Order's alumni, and we take care of the rest. We make the initiates swear their inaugural oaths, give them their preliminary trials, prepare them for the Dovermere initiation, and finally induct those who survive it into the Order."

He moved to stand in front of her. The subtle smell of his cologne was intoxicating, his eyes more teal than hazel in the glowing pool's ethereal reflection. "And tonight, we welcome the first Eclipse-born into our ranks. Our very own Tidecaller."

A sneer from Lizaveta. "Call her by her proper title, Keiran. She's a Tidethief." Her contempt was icier than the cavern's damp seeping into Emory's bones. "That's what it is, isn't it? You leech magic off those around you, magic that doesn't *belong* to you. Just like the Shadow stole the Tides' magic from them."

Virgil snickered at that, and Lizaveta snapped, "Something funny, Virgil?"

He waved his hand toward Emory in a nonchalant manner. "How is her magic any different from what we've been doing with the

synths? We took Nisha's blood to borrow her Sower magic." He craned his neck to look at Nisha. "I don't see her complaining about how we leeched off her."

Nisha threw Lizaveta an apologetic look. "I feel fine, honestly. It's like Louis said when we tried it with his Healer magic during the new moon. It doesn't feel at all like bloodletting outside of my lunar phase; my magic doesn't feel depleted in the slightest." She peered at Emory with open curiosity. "Maybe it's the same thing when she uses her Tidecaller magic. She's calling on other magics without depleting their bearers' reservoir."

Lizaveta crossed her arms. "Whatever. It doesn't change the fact that she's Eclipse-born." She gave Keiran an accusing look. "I can't believe you of all people are okay with this. After what happened to your parents? To my dad?" A quiver broke through her voice, but Lizaveta quickly gathered herself. "Artem was right. We should have let him take her to the Institute before she inevitably Collapses and kills someone."

Horror dawned on Emory. Was *that* what had happened to Keiran's parents, to Lizaveta and Artem's father?

"No one's bringing her to the Institute," Keiran commanded, and Emory had to wonder again why he was so intent on helping her join the Order, especially if he had suffered such a loss at the hands of Eclipse magic.

His eyes found hers, glowing with something more than just the pool's reflection. "She's going to help us call the Tides back to our shores, and once they return, we'll ask them to bless us with the former glory of their magic."

A laugh nearly escaped Emory's mouth, but the solemnity in his voice, on his face, was not feigned; he truly believed the Tides were more than myth, that they could somehow be brought back to life. The others looked just as serious.

"What are you saying?" Emory asked.

Keiran took a step closer. "This is what our cohort has been try-ing to achieve. The rest of the Selenics . . . They've forgotten the original purpose of our Order, content with these small magics they've fabricated over the years, but never pushing for more." He motioned to the others sitting on their thrones. "*We* have sought to make the synths stronger, hoping to use that magic to bring back the Tides."

"And how do you suppose you'll bring them back?"

"I'm not sure yet. But you're a Tidecaller. If the power of all four Tides runs in your veins . . . you might very well be the key to wak-ing them."

Your magic is the very answer I've been seeking.

This was the reason he'd fought for her back at the lighthouse. Why he'd been so willing to risk his position within the Order. He needed her. Her power. And if they succeeded in waking the Tides, returning magic to what it once was . . . then her own Tidecaller magic might not be viewed as such an aberration. She might even be praised for her role in bringing back the Tides–*if* such a thing was even possible, and that felt like a stretch.

Keiran seemed to read her hesitation. He drew closer again, making her heart race. "If we're the ones to wake them, to bring them back to these shores they once ruled over, think of what they could do for us, the favor they might grant. They hold the power to everything. Life, death. Rebirth." His eyes danced with a fervor that both scared and enthralled her. "They could bring back Romie. Farran. All those we've lost."

The words were slow to settle in her mind, like feet sinking in wet sand.

Emory had only wanted answers about her friend's death, but this was better than anything she had dared let herself hope for. If there was even the slightest chance this was doable, if she might be able to see Romie again . . .

"We're Selenics." Keiran turned to the others. "Our Order has pushed the boundaries of magic for centuries, and we owe it to ourselves now to try this one great feat." He looked at her again. "But only if our Tidecaller is willing."

A charged silence filled the cave. Only Lizaveta still looked at Emory with that icy guardedness, but the rest of them seemed genuinely curious—and most of all, hopeful. There was no trace of fear in them, only sheer wonder at what she might accomplish. They looked at her, she realized, the way everyone had always looked at Romie. It made her feel valued—*wanted*—like she'd never been before.

Purpose thrummed at her fingertips, as if the strings of an old instrument had finally been tuned somewhere deep in her soul, and the melody it produced rang clear and true.

She'd always felt lacking significance. A mediocre Healer, not better or worse than any other, but middling. Unimportant. Now her power promised greatness. Made her into someone noteworthy—someone who might hold the key to *everything*: waking the Tides, throwing the floodgates of magic open wide for all, and bringing Romie and the others who'd drowned back from the dead.

She lifted her chin, her blood singing.

"Where do we start?"

It started with an oath.

Keiran handed her a small silver flake like the one she'd seen Virgil imbibing earlier. *An Unraveler synth,* he explained. *It'll force you to tell the truth when swearing your oath.*

A distant, drowned-out part of her had a terrible sinking feeling as Keiran led her to the large pool. They waded through the shallows until they stood waist-deep in the center of the basin, just out of the cascade's reach. The rest of the Selenics gathered around her, forming a tight circle in the order of the moon's phases. All

Emory could think of was how surreal they must look to the outside eye, dressed in their sopping wet suits and gowns, their faces cast in dancing turquoise light.

"Here before us you must share three truths," Keiran intoned. "A painful memory that haunts you, a dream that calls to you, and a secret that burdens you. Let these truths serve as a reminder of the Order's secrets you carry, and those of yours we now hold."

It was a reminder, she realized, that if she should ever betray the Order, her deepest, darkest secrets might be used against her.

Keiran and Virgil helped her lie floating in the pool with her face turned to the dark ceiling above. The water was cold, the salt on her lips a bitter shock. The rest of the Selenics grabbed on to her limbs, holding her aloft.

"Speak your truths," Keiran commanded, his voice made distant by the water filling her ears.

Emory spoke slowly. "A painful memory . . . is the one I have from the initiation, of waking up on the beach next to those bodies." There was a faint, pleasant hum at her fingertips, as if the synthetic magic delighted in the truth of her words. She knew she couldn't lie even if she wanted to. "Sometimes I feel this phantom impression of a corpse brushing against my skin, and I wish the sea had taken me, too, so I wouldn't have to carry this guilt with me."

She swallowed past the lump in her throat, focusing on the cascading waterfall. She couldn't look any of them in the eye.

"A dream that calls to me . . ." She thought of Romie, of the note Baz had found, of her own odd dreams of Dovermere. It called to mind another Dreamer, and the truth slipped from her lips before she could think twice on it: ". . . is to find my mother, who abandoned me at birth. To finally know her and discover all the ways we're different and alike. I dream of her coming home so we can be a family together."

Her cheeks flushed at the thought of sharing such private

thoughts—something she had never fully been able to articulate in her own mind—with people she barely knew. Her heart picked up speed at what she needed to share next.

"A secret that burdens me . . ."

They already knew she was a Tidecaller, and no secret was more of a burden than that. Unless . . . The words came to her too fast, but she forced herself to speak them slowly, to weigh each one so she wouldn't say more than she should.

"The night Travers washed ashore was when I first used Tidecaller magic. At least, the first time I remember using it. While I was trying to heal him, everything came rushing up to the surface at Lizaveta's amplifying touch. I couldn't stop it." Her eyes found Virgil. "I felt the Reaper magic at my fingertips, and it was so overwhelming that I was afraid it would kill Travers. That *I* would be the one to kill him. I . . ." She bit the inside of her cheek, trying to find the words to work around the Unraveler magic—she didn't want to drag Baz into this by revealing he'd helped her. "The magic stopped before it could kill him." Her throat worked for air. "But Travers died anyway, and I'll always feel responsible for it."

Your fault.

Emory heaved a breath, somehow lighter for having admitted the truth of that night. She found genuine empathy in Virgil's eyes.

"Let us seal these truths in the water," Keiran said solemnly. He bent closer to murmur, "Don't fight it."

It was her only warning before her head was shoved underwater.

She thrashed against the seven pairs of hands that held her down, screaming her surprise. This had to be part of the oath-taking ritual, but primal instinct kicked in, a tidal wave of terror that threatened to fill her lungs, pull her under. Visions of dark, turbulent depths rose to greet her, and all around her were bodies, their eyes fixed and unblinking in death. The logical part of her knew it wasn't real, knew it was just her mind conjuring

her worst fear, but still her nails dug into someone's wrist as she fought against their hold, her screams near soundless in the water.

And then, just as suddenly, it was over. They pulled her up, and Emory broke through the surface, choking on a gulp of air. She clung desperately to Keiran as he pushed wet strands of hair from her face, something dark and lovely and powerful in his eyes.

"The Order welcomes you, daughter of the Eclipse. Arise as a Selenic."

She did, and nothing had ever felt so right.

Someone popped a bottle, and a flute of sparkling wine was handed to her. They drank in the ethereal light of the pool, and all the while Emory did not mind her sopping gown, her damp hair, because here with Keiran's jacket draped over her shoulders and the Selenics' curiosity about her magic—not the academic intrigue tinged with dread that Baz treated her with, but pure, sheer wonder—she was made to feel important, valued.

She slowly learned about the others—that Louis and Javier were an item, melting into each other whenever they were together, that Ife was kind and warm, that Nisha had a quiet magnetism that had her begrudgingly understanding Romie's infatuation with her. Only Lizaveta kept her distance, and as she and Keiran held a tense conversation at the other end of the grotto, Emory couldn't help feeling bad for her.

If Lizaveta had lost someone to the violence of a Collapsing, it was no wonder she was so cold to her.

Virgil walked up to her and refilled her glass. There was a disarming earnestness to him as he said, "You know, what you said about Travers . . . Don't beat yourself up over it. If you *had* used Reaper magic, it would have been a kindness, I think. No one should have to suffer the way he did."

Emory remembered the way he'd looked when Travers's body

was taken away, the profound grief written on his face. She considered him. "Have you ever . . ."

Virgil lifted a bemused brow. "What, *killed* someone?" A booming laugh. "Tides, no. You do know most Reapers have never and will never actually reap a life, yeah? We have too much respect for it. Death magic isn't all doom and gloom. It's rarely ever about death at all and more about *endings*. The peace of a cycle coming to its end so that it may start again or not at all. Drying up a rose to preserve its beauty forever, for example. Helping farmers remove crop residues or rid their fields of pests and diseases so that newer things can take root and grow."

He smiled peacefully, a dreamy, faraway look in his eye, so different from his usual flair. "There's a classroom in Decrescens Hall that's as full of life as any of the Sower greenhouses. Vines and flowers fill every inch of it, and in the center is this massive tree. We Reapers practice making the seasons turn, changing the leaves from green to yellow and red and crisp brown until everything is bare. Our own perpetual autumns and winters at our fingertips."

Virgil seemed to catch himself, and that sardonic smile of his came back. He nudged Emory with a shoulder. "We're a real catch with Sowers, I can tell you that."

"I didn't know that room existed," Emory said, mesmerized.

"Ah yes, well. We're a secretive bunch over at Decrescens Hall. But I'm sure I could sneak you in one day, teach you how to use Reaper magic the way it was meant to be used."

"I'd like that." She realized she meant it wholeheartedly, now oddly at peace with her Tidecaller magic and all the possibilities she might unlock with it.

A sudden commotion drew their attention. Lizaveta was storming out of the Treasury, leaving a tired-looking Keiran behind.

Unease was swift to swallow Emory up again. Virgil tracked her line of sight and said, "Don't worry about Lizaveta. There's

history there, and, well . . . Let's just say she's not so trusting of Eclipse-born."

I don't blame her, Emory wanted to say. She peered at Virgil. "And the rest of you? How do you feel about having an untrained Eclipse-born in your midst?"

"I can't speak for the others, but us Reapers? We understand more than most, I think, the kind of challenges the Eclipse-born face. The distrust that follows both our alignments." He looked to where Lizaveta had disappeared. "I'm sure she'll come around eventually. But in the meantime, just know you've got at least one person in your corner." A wink. "I'm rooting for you, Tidecaller."

Emory hid a smile. She caught Keiran's eye from across the room, and nothing else mattered as he made his way toward them. Virgil excused himself, saying he'd better go check on Lizaveta—*I'll put in a good word for you*—making Emory wonder if there might be something between the two of them.

She hoped he was right, and that this animosity Lizaveta had for her would dissipate.

"I hope we didn't overwhelm you," Keiran said as he sidled up to her.

She laughed, the wine and tension of the evening going to her head. "Oh, not at all. This is just a regular weekday night for me."

He smiled that dimpled smile at her, full of genuine mirth. It was disarming.

"Ask me again tomorrow," she amended, "when all this doesn't feel so much like a fever dream."

"Fair enough. Shall I walk you back to your dorm, then?"

There was so much she wanted to ask him still, but her mind went blank under his stare, and all she could do was duck her head to hide her blush. "Sure."

As they reached her room, it felt to Emory like she was dancing upon a precipice, heart racing to a wild tune in anticipation of

the drop. They lingered in front of her door. In the quiet corridor, Keiran's features were shadowed, edges limned in faint light. His eyes slowly traveled down to her lips, making her stomach go taut at the intensity in them.

"Now that you've sworn your oath," he said, voice lowered to a husky tone, "I can show you what the Selenic Mark *actually* does, if you want." A nod at her door. "Can we . . . ?"

Emory opened the door, heart beating so fast she thought it might burst. Keiran brushed past her into the room, and she leaned back against the door, unsure of what to say or how to act now that they were here. Her room felt too small; she couldn't quite make sense of his presence in it as he strode over to her desk, his hands reaching for the bloodletting instruments she kept there: a shallow bowl, a vial of salt water, a knife. Things every magical adept kept close, but that she didn't need anymore, she supposed, now that she was Eclipse-born.

Emory watched with growing anticipation as Keiran poured a bit of salt water into the bowl, every movement precise, loaded. His tattooed hand hovered over the bowl. His eyes didn't leave hers as he slowly dipped his hand in the water, all the way past his wrist. Something changed in the air between them, and when he lifted his dripping hand, Emory could plainly see the symbol on his wrist, glowing faintly silver. A prickling sensation drew her attention to her own wrist, an echo of the burning that had birthed the mark on her skin–which was now glowing just like Keiran's.

"This is what the mark does," he said in her ear, making the fine hairs on her neck stand to attention.

Emory drew a sharp inhale, expecting to see him beside her, so clear had been his voice, the murmur of breath against her skin. But he still stood across the room from her, casually leaning against her desk.

"How . . ."

"It's a calling card of sorts. With it, you can call on anyone else who bears the mark, no matter how far away you are."

She saw his lips move, but again his voice sounded right beside her, as if he stood there whispering in her ear. There was something oddly intimate to it, with his gaze so intent on her; it made her glad to be standing so far away, while at the same time yearning to be closer.

She glanced at her own marked wrist. "Show me how to do it."

Keiran motioned to the bowl. "Salt water activates it."

Emory pushed off the door and came to stand beside him. He looked at her in a way that made her pulse quicken as her hand tentatively grazed the surface of the water.

"It's all about intention," he said over her shoulder, both through the mark and not. She shivered at his nearness. "You have to really think about who you wish to call on, let their essence wash over you. Focus on the act of calling out to them itself."

Emory conjured his face in her mind. It wasn't hard to do, with his breath on her neck and his faint aftershave in her nose. *I want to speak to Keiran Dunhall Thornby,* she thought. She sensed something at the edge of her vision, felt a prickle on her wrist. When she lifted her hand from the water, the symbol was bright silver.

"Like this?" Her voice sounded normal to her ears, but she felt it, somehow—the way it traveled to him through whatever magic, sending a jolt through her spine.

His voice caressed the back of her neck. "Exactly like that."

Emory turned to find him standing inches from her, his face so beautiful it hurt to look at.

"You truly believe it, don't you?" she asked, marveling at the way his throat undulated as he stared at her lips. "That we can bring the Tides back."

His hand brushed hers, twin spirals glowing in question and answer to each other. "I believe there's power in intention. It's what

makes the magic in our Selenic Mark come alive, what lets us call on each other, a gift we have no explanation for because whatever its original purpose might have been is lost to us now. Intention is how people of old were able to touch all magics, because so long as they honored the Tides, power flowed freely through their veins. Magic from all moons and all tides. Like yours."

He looked at her from beneath thick lashes. "I think if we truly set our minds to it, if we set out with intention and use your magic for this one great purpose . . . why shouldn't we be able to call upon such a force as the Tides themselves?"

Emory supposed it was possible. Up until tonight, she didn't know such a thing as synthetic magic existed. Before that, she didn't think her own magic was possible, still couldn't believe how she could go her entire life thinking she was a Healer and suddenly be something as fabled as a Tidecaller, her blood running with the dark power of the Eclipse. And until moments ago, she never let herself hope—dream—that she might see Romie again.

Nothing was impossible.

"It's late," Keiran whispered. "I should go."

Emory swallowed down her disappointment as he pulled away. What had she hoped for? That he would stay and—*Tides*. She needed to keep her head straight.

Keiran lingered by the door. "Do you see now why I was so adamant to back you at the lighthouse? Why I asked you to trust me? If this works . . . it'll change everything, Ains."

"And if it doesn't?"

"It will."

"How can you be so sure?"

His mouth lifted in that boyish grin, though his eyes—his eyes darkened in a way that made her knees weak.

"You underestimate how tireless I can be when I chase after something I want."

Dovermere finds her again in sleep. Dream, memory, memory dream—the lines too blurred to know one from the other.

Around her, the cave walls drip with not water but tiny stars that plummet slowly to the ground, fading as they reach the growing darkness at her feet. Romie stands alone before the great hourglass with its shifting black sands and wilting flowers trapped inside. A silver spiral burns on the surface where her hand touches the glass.

"I read that there are symbols like this everywhere, strewn about in the deepest, darkest places in the world."

Romie's voice echoes strangely around them. Her hair is a wet mess, her skin bloated and wrong. "Some say they were put there by naiads and sirens as a way to contact each other. A bridge between the world's many bodies of water."

Her lightless eyes find Emory's. Behind her, the spiral unfurls into a golden sunflower that burns through the glass and the flowers and the sand. The remaining ash spills from inside, and it is not ash at all but claws of shadow that slither over Romie's arms and neck.

Her lips are blue with cold death. Water trickles from the sides of her mouth as she tries to speak, but no sound comes out. Her distorted voice echoes ghostlike in Emory's ears instead: "The water guides us all, even when it claims us."

"I don't understand," says Emory.

Tendrils of darkness crawl into Romie's eyes, her blackened throat. Her voice sounds all around and nowhere at all. "There are tides that drown and tides that bind, tides with voices not all kind . . ."

The breath is squeezed from Romie's throat. She points a single finger to something behind Emory. A great beast of shadow erupts.

It is darkness

fear

nightmare

bound in a soulless form that sets hungry, fathomless eyes on Emory. The beast lends wrongness to the dream, and when it swipes for her, she knows it will devour her and leave her bones to feed the ancient stone.

She runs toward Romie, but Romie is not Romie anymore. She is stardust that turns to ash that sinks below the stone to depths unknown.

A voice sounds in Emory's ear, velvet as the night:

"That way lies madness, dreamling."

Emory's eyes flew open, glancing wildly around her in the dark. The dream was already fading, but that voice . . .

Only a dream, she told herself before falling back asleep.

16

BAZ

The printing press haunts his nightmares once more.

Baz peers at the grandfather clock in the corner. He knows by now how the scene plays out, down to the very second. Knowing does not lessen the horror.

It starts with his father's arms wound tight around Baz's middle, silver veins rippling beneath his skin. Ten seconds from now, the roof will cave in. In twenty, one of the printers explodes and metal bits of machinery start flying. In thirty, the screaming stops, death come to claim its fill. The ink on his father's hands always turns to blood then, and that is how Baz knows it is only a nightmare.

"It's going to be all right," says his father—yet it is not his voice Baz hears but another's.

He looks up and glimpses Kai before him.

"This isn't real," the Nightmare Weaver utters with a frown, as if to convince himself more than Baz.

A second later the world is burned in silver.

Baz woke with a start, blinking up at the ceiling through tear-blurred eyes. Dazedly he realized he was not in his own room but in Kai's. He hadn't meant to fall asleep, had only come in here thinking it might appease this guilt he felt at leaving him behind. It hadn't, but now that he was here, he didn't want to leave.

Kai's painted constellations swirled over him in the dark. *Not real,* Baz thought, and wistfully drifted back to sleep.

SONG
OF THE
DROWNED
GODS

PART III:

THE WARRIOR
OF THE WASTES

There is a world somewhere between near and far where things grow from nothing.

Sturdy trees with suits of armor sprout from inhospitable soil, while mighty beasts hatch from delicate stones and molten rock yields swords of gold. Fierce warriors are carved from the most fragile of hearts, and things like courage and love ignite like flames in the dark.

This world is a forge. Brutal and scorching and full of finely crafted things.

A warrior sprang from this world as improbably as the flowers that bloom in its arid wilderness. She was not a warrior at first, but something else she does not care to remember. (A sword does not recall the lump of metal it came from; it knows only the hand that wields it and the sun that kisses its blade and the life that bleeds at its fateful end.)

Now the warrior takes lives and defends lives and binds them too, weaving a ballad of life and death, flame and steel. Metal sings in her hands as it does in a smith's; the battlefield is her forge. She crafts victories out of impossible odds and wins her people's love with every beast slayed. Around her, empires rise and burn just as the sun dies and reawakens, and through it all the warrior remains unchanged because she is the heart of her world, the bright burning core of it.

And here come the blood and the bones like moths to a flame, eager to rally her to their cause. To answer the call that she, too, has heard between the stars.

This is her story now as much as it is theirs, and here it begins.

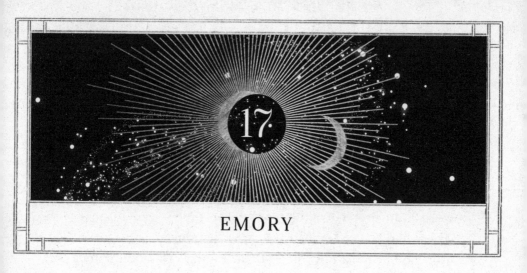

EMORY

THE MORNING AFTER EMORY'S OATH-TAKING FELT LIKE waking up to a new world, a new *her*. She was a whetted blade sharpened by intention, and all she wanted now was to be worthy of the Selenic Order's purpose, of Keiran's belief in her abilities—all of it to see Romie again.

Waking the Tides. It seemed an impossible feat, yet how many impossible things had she witnessed and done herself since the start of the term?

She needed to master her magic, and fast. The problem, she realized, was the frayed state of things between her and Baz, the only one who might help her hone her power and keep her from Collapsing in the process. He wasn't in the Decrescens library at their usual appointed hour, and after their little spat in the greenhouse, she feared he might no longer want to see her at all. She couldn't blame him, really, but it hurt all the same.

No time to dwell on it. Now that Emory knew her Tidecaller magic didn't come from her spiral mark, her thoughts were full

of Luce, wondering why and how her mother might have hidden the true nature of her magic. This, at least, she could tackle on her own. It was easy to find where the lunar almanacs were kept in the archives. She pulled up the one from the year she was born and found her birth date–the second day of a new moon in the dead of winter, at the lowest point of a rising tide. She flipped to the day before it, the first day of the new moon.

There had been a total solar eclipse that day.

Her mother must have lied about the date to hide the fact she was born on an eclipse. It didn't explain why she'd only ever had Healer magic until now, or why the selenograph confirmed her as such when she was younger. And though it only added to the mystery of Luce Meraude, here was a tiny morsel of truth, at least.

She truly was Eclipse-born.

This single, incomprehensible fact brought about a tangle of emotions she couldn't begin to understand. Her whole identity lay shattered at her feet. How was she supposed to build herself anew?

In her early years at Threnody Prep, she'd been endlessly fascinated by all things Eclipse. Especially Baz's magic. She remembered thinking how singular it made him, how desperately she wanted that for herself. She had wished she'd been born in House Eclipse then, with magic that would set her apart–until she realized such magic meant those of House Eclipse were doomed to remain on the sidelines because of it.

It seemed she'd gotten her wish.

"You look lovely with a frown, Ainsleif," a voice murmured in her ear.

A delighted shiver ran up her spine. Keiran leaned casually against her table, mouth upturned in that dimpled smile. He peered at the almanac. "Research so early?"

"Just trying to make sense of all this." She voiced the thought that

had been nagging her all night. "What if my magic isn't enough to bring back the Tides?"

"Nonsense. Power like yours was meant for greatness."

"But how exactly am I supposed to wake them?"

Voices drifted to them as a few other students came into the archives. Keiran pushed off the table. "Let me show you."

A suggestive lift of his brow was all it took for her to follow him deeper into the archives. Quiet footsteps offset the quickening of her pulse as she struggled to catch up with him. Keiran disappeared behind a shelf, and when she rounded the corner, she nearly collided into him, catching herself just in time. He was browsing old files and finally tugged one of them free.

Keiran skimmed the text. "The Selenics used to keep ledgers of their activities hidden in nondescript school files such as these, lost to us for years because of it. Until Farran and I started doing some digging. He always had a knack for unlocking old mysteries."

Emory watched him flip to the next page. "You said the two of you grew up together?"

"We did. Him, me, Lizaveta, and Artem, we were practically family. Our parents were all part of the Order and remained close after their heyday at Aldryn. The four of us wanted so badly to follow in their footsteps." A quick, sad smile. "Farran was the one to push this idea of waking the Tides, actually. Back when we were still at prep school. It was his way of getting us to focus on something other than our grief after what happened to our parents. A way for us to continue their legacy, ensure their deaths weren't in vain."

Even though she thought she knew the answer already, she asked, "How did you lose them?"

Keiran stared at the papers in his hand. "They were killed in a Collapsing accident."

He said it tightly, in a way that made Emory uneasy thinking that

she might Collapse one day. Yet he was putting all this faith in her anyway.

Before she could say anything, he handed her one of the papers, where an illustration of eight people forming a circle around a fountain had been drawn over the text of some nondescript administrative form.

"What am I looking at?"

"Look closer."

She realized the lines of the drawing were formed of words—tiny, nearly illegible script, hidden in plain sight.

"It details the archaic rituals that were observed back in the days of the Tides," Keiran said, "when people called upon them to use their magics. These rituals have been forgotten over time, no longer useful since magic was splintered. But the first Selenics still performed them, believing they might summon the Tides back from the Deep."

"Clearly, they never succeeded." She peered at the drawing. "What makes you think we'll be able to do it now?"

There was a fierce glimmer in his eyes. "I'm sure they never had a Tidecaller in their mix. With you joining our ranks, lending your own abilities to this kind of ritual . . . our summons will be stronger than theirs ever could be."

Emory frowned. "Did Romie know about all of this?"

Baz had been closer to the truth than she suspected he knew, with his talk of cults and songs and Dovermere. If Romie had known Keiran meant to summon the Tides back from the Deep, perhaps she'd likened it to the story in *Song of the Drowned Gods*. Maybe the note she left was her way of hinting at where she was going in case she didn't make it back. A way for her to say, *Romie Brysden is about to do something reckless (again) and here is where you'll find her.*

"No," Keiran said, shutting that theory down. "The initiates knew

about synthetic magics, but not this. We were going to let them in on it after Dovermere. Those who got the Selenic Mark, that is."

Emory ran a thumb over her wrist. Keiran tracked the motion. "Aside from the fact that it allows us to communicate with one another, we don't know much else about it. Clearly, the original Selenics knew enough of the power of Dovermere to craft their initiation ritual around the Hourglass. It's the only ritual we've kept since the Order's inception. Every year is the same: we round up the eight most promising new students, two of each of the four lunar houses, and have them undergo a series of preliminary tests to see who might have the countenance for synthetic magics. Only those who pass, if any, are invited to the final initiation: vanquishing Dovermere."

"And those who don't pass these preliminaries?"

"Memorists like Vivianne make them forget. They go about their lives unaware of the Selenic Order."

Emory made quick calculations in her head. "So last year, every candidate passed the preliminaries, since there were eight of them in Dovermere. What about the rest of you? Were you all the same year?"

"All of us except Virgil. He's a year younger than us." He looked away, voice laced with something bitter as he said, "There were only seven of us who went to Dovermere my freshman year. Louis, Ife, Nisha, Lizaveta, Javier, me, and Farran. The other Waning Moon candidate didn't make it past preliminaries, and Farran, as you know, drowned at Dovermere."

A shadow fell on his face. "The four of us, Farran, Liza, Artie, and I, we grew up seeing firsthand the prestige that came with being a Selenic. We knew that once we joined, anything we wanted would be ours for the taking: the best postgraduate programs, the most exclusive internship placements, the highest-ranking jobs, access to synthetic magics. Artem was older than us, so he got in first,

made sure to tap us for initiation when we got to Aldryn. We were riding a high then. Thought we were unstoppable. But when Farran died . . . I couldn't shake this anger, at first. All of that hurt, and for what? Morsels of fabricated magic, the kind of power that wasn't worth risking our lives for in Dovermere."

"So why stay?"

"Because Farran had shown us the potential for *more*. We wanted to honor his memory by steering the Order back to what it used to be. To go beyond the glamorous parties and networking and do the one thing no Selenic before us had done."

"Waking the Tides."

"What could be more worthy an endeavor than that? When Artem's cohort graduated and I took over the reins, we started going through what Farran had found, testing all these rituals and playing around with synths in the hopes of becoming powerful enough to summon the Tides. That first year I was in charge, I also wanted to ensure the preliminaries were harder to pass, hoping it would limit the deaths. Virgil was the only one who made it past his preliminaries; he survived Dovermere all on his own."

Another Reaper to replace Farran, Emory thought, wondering if it were mere coincidence.

"The year after that," Keiran continued, "all eight students we tapped for initiation made it to Dovermere. They were just that good." A bob of his throat. "You know how that worked out."

Eight names etched on a silver plaque at the Tides' feet: Quince Travers, Healer. Serena Velan, Darkbearer. The twins, Dania and Lia Azula, Wordsmiths. Daphné Dioré the Wardcrafter and Jordyn Briar Burke the Soultender. Harlow Kerr, Unraveler. And Romie— the fierce, secretive, bright Dreamer.

"It was such a promising group," Keiran lamented. "The most powerful young mages the Order had seen in years. And with the strides we'd been making developing stronger synths, I thought we

might finally have what it took to wake the Tides." He shook his head angrily. "Their deaths weigh on me still."

Emory felt a grim kinship with him, to know that he, too, blamed himself for their deaths. She wanted to tell him it wasn't his fault, that he couldn't have done anything to prevent this, that only Dovermere was to blame. It was the lie she told herself every night she woke in cold sweats, plagued by this nightmarish guilt.

"At least their loss wasn't entirely in vain," Keiran said quietly. "It brought us you."

Her cheeks burned furiously at the ardent look he gave her.

"I meant it when I said we'd try to get Romie back," he asserted. "She and Farran and all the others. And if the Tides won't grant us this one thing, then I promise we'll pull them back from the Deep ourselves if it's the last thing we ever do."

Emory blinked past the sudden sting in her eyes, looking at the ritual drawn on the page. "And this will bring them back?"

"Not quite. Think of waking the Tides as opening a door. But that door is locked; the Tides barred from our world. So first we need to unlock it." He rustled the page. "This is how we might do it. It's a fall equinox ritual, where the first Selenics made offerings of their magic to the Tides. They believed there was power on the fall equinox, since it marks the beginning of the end of the cycle, a bridge between summer and winter. They thought the Tides would hear them and be inclined to answer their call."

"The fall equinox is in less than a week," Emory said slowly.

Keiran nodded. "And with the festival happening at the same time, the whole campus will be otherwise occupied. No better time to hold our first ritual with our Tidecaller, I think."

The fall equinox festival was widely celebrated at Aldryn. Students gathered on the banks of the River Helene to cast boats out to sea, a way to entreat the Tides to guide them into autumn. A handful of students from each house were selected to stand upon

their respective houses' boats and perform feats of magic representing each of their lunar houses as they traveled down the river toward the sea. It was a grand spectacle, and an opportunity for the chosen students to showcase their talents to important dignitaries from grad schools and institutions that sought to recruit them.

House Eclipse was always omitted, likely for fear of its students Collapsing while performing their magic.

Emory watched Keiran as he pocketed the ritual drawing, thinking again of the stark difference between his and Baz's reactions to her magic. How Baz, Eclipse-born like her, seemed more wary of it than Keiran, when it should have been the other way around.

"Why aren't you scared of me?" she asked. For all he knew, she could Collapse at any given moment, yet there wasn't a trace of fear in him. "I'm Eclipse-born. Surely–"

"Surely I must hate all Eclipse-born because one of them killed my parents?" Keiran finished for her with a snicker.

The words were too raw, slicing between them like a blade.

"Maybe I did once." His brows scrunched together. "I was fifteen and looking for someone to blame, and it seemed so easy then to despise all Eclipse-born for destroying my family. But that was a long time ago, and I don't think that anymore. I'm not afraid of you, Ainsleif."

"Why not?"

A hint of his dimpled smile. "Would you prefer it if I were?"

"Of course not. But it would make a lot more sense than . . . this." Whatever *this* was, this thing between them.

Keiran seemed to grasp her meaning. She wished to drown in his molten gaze.

He tugged on her hand then, and she had no choice but to follow as he pulled her deeper into the archives. She hadn't even known the archives were this big to begin with, and the farther they went,

the older everything got, a musty smell clinging like cobwebs to the shelves. He helped her climb up a narrow wrought-iron ladder to a hidden attic that was plunged in darkness.

Keiran's hand left hers to flick on an everlight lantern. And suddenly dozens of the same light shone around the room, that single lantern reflected in a dizzying array of mirrors of every shape and size, all perfectly aligned to refract the light around them.

It felt more like an abandoned museum than an archive attic. Unhung frames lined the walls, great oak dressers and old bookcases and lecterns gathered dust, and in every corner were things that did not quite belong: swords and bows and arrows, scrolls of parchment so ancient they'd begun to disintegrate, broken clocks and chipped vases, golden string instruments, an easel with a half-painted canvas of wildflowers in a sunlit field.

"Farran dubbed this the Forgotten Place," Keiran said at her side. "We found it during our freshman year while scouring the archives for anything we could find on the Order. A lot of it is junk, but—"

"Are those the photographs you're restoring?"

She reached for a silver plaque like the one she'd seen him working on, displayed on top of a claw-footed dresser. The surface was no longer mottled but polished enough to reveal the outlines of three people posing for the camera.

"One of them, yes," Keiran said. "This one's not done yet. I think with more work I can restore it enough that we see their faces."

"It's amazing, the things you can do with your magic."

"I'm glad you think so. You know, I used to resent being a Lightkeeper," he admitted with a bashful smile. "I wanted to be a Memorist or a Seer or an Unraveler. I thought there was only so much I could do with Lightkeeper magic, and I wanted more. That's what drew me to the Order. We're taught that there's the magic we're born with and ways to excel at it, to push this

singular ability we have to its limits. But I wanted to *exceed* those limits. I wanted no limits at all."

He looked at her like she was the answer to that dream. A way to attain all magics. She ducked her head, studying the shadows on the silver plaque. They were very clearly the outlines of three men dressed in an older fashion, sitting in what might have been a lavish taproom. Only their faces remained tarnished, rendering them featureless.

"My father's a Lightkeeper," she said quietly. "He tends a lighthouse for a living. He doesn't have enough magic to wear the Full Moon sigil, but that's what he does. And he loves it. It's where I grew up, in this tiny lighthouse in Harebell Cove."

The thought of home made her wish she were there. "I always feared I might end up like him. That I wouldn't pass the tests, wouldn't get to wear my house sigil, wouldn't get to study here at Aldryn." Emory laughed sullenly at the admission. "I always felt unremarkable as a Healer, and now I have this impossible magic and I'm afraid I'll mess it all up."

Keiran reached for her hand, his thumb brushing her marked wrist. "You won't." He drew her attention to a large painting propped up against the wall. "This is what I wanted to show you."

It was strangely beautiful in the refracted light of the mirrors. Dark, muted colors in loose brushstrokes depicted a young man lying in a pool of water and blood and sea-foam, his hands folded neatly on his chest. He was smiling, even as blood ran from a wound in his middle.

"What is it?" It was an odd thing for him to show her, Emory thought.

There was something like reverence on Keiran's face as he beheld the painting. "It's a mystery. There's no signature, nothing known about the painting or its maker, nothing in the technique that might echo another artist's work. I don't know why I'm so drawn to it.

It's exquisite in a morbid sort of way. The darkness of it, the featurelessness of the man. The way he's smiling even at the end. I suppose it reminds me there's beauty even in death. That's what Farran always believed."

Emory thought of what Virgil had said about Reaper magic. She studied the painting again, trying to see it through another set of eyes.

"My parents were in Threnody for work when they died," Keiran said softly, still fixated on the painting, like it was easier to speak if he didn't look at her. "Collecting pieces for their gallery. It's part of why I like this place so much. It reminds me of them." He cleared his throat. "There was nothing left of them for us to bury. That's how strong the Collapsing blast was. I remember sitting at their funeral *hating* the person who'd done this. I didn't care that it was an accident. I needed someone to blame and make into a monster for taking my parents away, and I was glad to see him sent to the Institute to receive the Unhallowed Seal."

An impossible realization dawned on her. Blood pounding in her ears, Emory asked, "Who was it, the Eclipse-born who killed your parents?"

He met her gaze with a sad, knowing smile. The sorrow on his face broke her.

"Say it. Please."

His throat bobbed. "Theodore Brysden."

Baz and Romie's father.

Emory shook her head, refusing to believe it. But it made sense—the timeline of it all, the way Baz had locked up at the sight of Keiran with her in the quad. The way Lizaveta had seemed to despise her from the start, even before she knew she was Eclipse-born, likely because she was Romie's friend, and Romie was a Brysden as much as Baz.

"Tides, Keiran. I'm so sorry. Did Romie know?"

"She did. I never held it against her," he added quickly, "nor her brother. It was an accident, after all. And we are not our parents."

Emory couldn't fathom what it must be like, to lose one's parents like that. To be torn between blame and acceptance, rage and forgiveness, at the thought of the person who'd taken their lives. It made even less sense to her that he'd accepted her—*fought* for her—with such eagerness. An Eclipse-born he was putting all his trust in after living through such horror.

But maybe, she realized, he wished to bring his parents back from the dead too.

Your magic is the very answer I've been seeking.

Keiran frowned at the painting. "I couldn't stay in Trevel after their deaths. Too many painful memories. Dean Fulton was a good friend of my parents. She offered to take me in, so I continued my prep school education right here at Aldryn under her tutelage. When I first got here, I was so angry. I couldn't understand why Eclipse students were allowed within these sacred halls, why institutions like Aldryn would put everyone else at risk like that. Then my first year staying with Fulton, a Reaper undergrad killed another student. It was a gruesome accident. A slip of magic, the heat of the moment. A mistake. But it made me realize that a Reaper could just as likely cause death and destruction as any Eclipse student might. That any one of us could slip up at a moment's notice. Maybe not in the same way as those who Collapse, but that doesn't mean the rest of us are exempt. Magical accidents can happen to anyone."

He turned to her once more. "You asked me why I'm not afraid of you." His fingers brushed her brow, tucked a lock of hair behind her ear. "The truth is, I am. But only because I see your potential. Your power. Only in the way all of us both fear and are enthralled by death, this inevitable, unconquerable force we'll all bow to in the end."

Such a force might have scared Emory, once. But standing here

before him, as enthralled by him as he claimed to be by her magic—
by *her*—she found she did not fear it in the slightest.

It was on her way to the greenhouse that evening that Emory
finally caught sight of Baz. He looked even less put-together than
he usually did, hair disheveled and glasses skewed and shirt only
half tucked in his pants. He didn't notice her even as she sidled up
next to him, his eyes trained on the book in his hands.

"Hey."

His head snapped up. "Oh." He slipped his book under an arm.
"Hey."

"I didn't see you in the library this morning." She gave him a
demure smile, hoping whatever this thing was between them
wasn't yet broken.

Baz averted his gaze, his face shuttered. "Yeah. Sorry. Long
night."

His shortness made her falter. There was something different
about him. A heavier weariness to him than usual. She wanted so
badly to tell him everything would be fine. That she would bring
Romie back and they would both see her again, hear her laugh.
But she couldn't, not when she'd just sworn an oath to the Selenic
Order. It felt dangerous to involve Baz in something she herself did
not yet fully understand, *especially* given his and Keiran's history.

If she managed to do this—wake the Tides, have them bring Romie
back to life—Baz would understand and forgive her lies. He had to.

"I was heading to the greenhouse," she said, "but if your offer to
train in Obscura Hall still stands . . ."

Baz watched her over the rim of his glasses, a tightness in his
jaw, as if waiting for her to say something else. Finally, he let out a
long sigh. "I can't right now."

It felt like a punch to the gut. "Oh."

"Sorry. I'm late meeting Professor Selandyn."

"Of course."

If Baz heard the disappointment in her voice, he didn't let it show, only left with that distracted look in his eyes. Emory tried not to let his dismissal sting too deeply. She couldn't expect him to always be at her beck and call. She'd been the one using his feelings for her to get what she wanted, and maybe he'd finally come to realize it.

So why did it bother her so much?

And how in the Deep was she supposed to practice on her own?

Power like yours was meant for greatness, Keiran had told her.

Maybe she didn't need Baz at all. If she'd performed magic without incident last night in front of the entire Order, she could do so again in the privacy of the greenhouse.

But someone was already there. Nisha could have been Anima herself, standing in the middle of all these dead plants, head tilted up to the sky as if to implore the moon. She wore a burgundy pinafore dress over a cream turtleneck, her black hair unbound and lips unadorned.

Her eyes, Emory saw as they met hers, glistened with tears.

"Are you all right?"

Nisha wiped furiously at her cheeks. "Sorry. Yes. I was just on my way back to Crescens Hall when I finally mustered up the courage to come in here." She looked around the space with melancholy. "I miss Romie. It feels strange being back here without her, doesn't it?"

Bitter defensiveness rose in Emory's throat. What did she know about missing her? She hadn't known Romie like Emory had—her grief couldn't compare.

"You know she spoke of you all the time?" Nisha said with a tentative smile. "She always said she wished she were more like you."

"Me?" Emory sputtered, taken aback. *She* had always wanted to be more like Romie, so self-assured in her skin and in her dreams, so vibrant and easy to speak with.

"She said she wished she had your drive and focus." Affection warmed Nisha's voice. "You know how scattered she could be."

It was true; Romie wanted everything so much, but she always got distracted by the next big idea, the shinier dream. Nothing ever truly satisfied her. She'd leave things behind without a look backward if she no longer felt the desire to pursue them, her goals always shifting. It made for very little follow-through on her part.

Emory was the opposite. When she set her mind to something, she didn't waver.

"She once told me she felt like she didn't entirely know herself, because she was always changing, just like her interests and dreams," Nisha continued. "But she could always count on you to remain the same. She saw you as this force to be reckoned with, someone who stayed true to herself and her friends no matter what. She loved you for it."

Tears prickled at Emory's eyes. Could Romie not have told her any of this herself last year, instead of pulling away from her in favor of Nisha? Anger and jealousy sharpened to something ugly inside her.

"She didn't say much about you," Emory said, perhaps a bit too viciously. To temper her words, she added, "Then again, she didn't say much to me at all in the end."

"That makes two of us."

"I thought the two of you were close."

"She became distant with me too. It wasn't just about the Order. There was something else preoccupying her that she wouldn't share with me." Nisha swallowed with difficulty, tucking her hair behind her ears as she eyed Emory. "Did she ever tell you about us?"

"The Order? Of course not."

"Not the Order. Me and her."

Emory frowned incomprehensibly. And then it dawned on her.

"Oh."

Oh.

Nisha smiled sadly. "I'll take that as a no. But yeah. We were seeing each other."

All the pieces fell into place so quickly that Emory wanted to smack herself. Romie had always liked both boys and girls, that much Emory knew. But she'd never suspected Nisha might be more than a friend, so clouded by her own jealousy of their friendship that she couldn't see the truth behind it.

Nisha ran a finger along a dead leaf. "This is where we'd sneak off to. The Order sort of frowns on present cohort members dating initiates–favoritism and all. And then, of course, I knew a bit about Keiran's and Lizaveta's history with Romie's father. . . . But I didn't care. I couldn't keep away from her. She was so . . . magnetic. So full of life. It's a wonder she wasn't a Glamour."

Nisha's open vulnerability caught Emory off guard. "I know what you mean."

"Anyway. She kept talking about how she wished she could wield other magics, and here I was sitting on the secret of synthetics. So I gave her a push in the right direction, told her if she wanted in, she'd have to convince Keiran, since the Order already had their two Waning Moon candidates in mind. She barged into his dreams, and that was the end of it. We picked her over the other Dreamer candidate."

Nisha's smile twisted into a frown. "Do you hate me? For introducing her to the Order?"

Emory pondered the question. She *had* hated Nisha for taking her friend away from her–but she wasn't any better herself. They both dealt with guilt, she ·realized, wondering what they might have done differently to save Romie from her fate.

At last, she said, "I think Romie would have found a way to do what Romie wanted, as she always did."

"She did have a mind of her own, didn't she?"

A smile, like they were sharing a secret. Because that was a little bit how it felt to be close to Romie—like being let in on a secret, holding the key to the mystery she was to everyone else.

"Well. I'll leave you to it, then."

Nisha made to leave, but Emory stopped her with a whispered "Wait." She fiddled with a loose thread on her sleeve. "Do you think . . . Do you really believe we can bring her back?"

A fierceness shone in Nisha's eyes. "I have to believe it. I love her too much to accept a world without her in it."

They looked at each other from across the wilted space, understanding blooming between them.

"I'm scared I'll fail," Emory admitted quietly.

A twinkle of mischief lit Nisha's face. "You know what Romie always said of failure."

"Fear of failure's the bitch that holds you back from success?"

They both laughed, all hostility between them now dissipated. Nisha grew serious again, voice soft as she said, "You're not alone in this, Emory." She trailed a hand over a dead plant, cocking a brow at her. "Do you want help practicing?"

BAZ

THE MORNING OF THE FALL EQUINOX, BAZ FOUND HIMSELF in the Vault again.

Professor Selandyn had come through for him, pulling strings with Dean Fulton to get him permission for *Dark Tides: Rare Tidal Movements through the Ages*–though not without some convincing on Baz's part. The Eclipse professor had narrowed her eyes at him upon hearing the title, and when Baz mentioned Romie's interest in it, hoping that would sway her, she'd gone very quiet.

"Does this have anything to do with you meeting those crackpots that call themselves the Veiled Atlas?" At his befuddled expression, she added, "Jae filled me in. I hope you didn't take anything those fanatics said at face value."

"I thought you of all people might be open to their ideas."

Selandyn had huffed a laugh. "My dear boy, surely you've worked with me long enough to know there's a difference between provable theories and silly fantasies. The Veiled Atlas have taken this business with the epilogue entirely too far. People lose all sense

when it comes to tracking that thing down. It's become a danger-ous game, and anyone who plays it is a damn fool."

"What about Jae?"

"Jae's interest is purely academic. They don't concern them-selves with this absurd treasure hunt. Promise me you won't get involved, Basil."

The promise was a bitter lie in his mouth as he found himself picking *Dark Tides* up off the shelf.

It was an innocuous little book. Plain dark leather binding, silver title nearly worn away from use. Baz flipped it open to the epi-graph and recognized it as the rhyme Kai had alluded to:

> *There are tides that drown and tides that bind,*
> *tides with voices not all kind,*
> *moon-kissed tides with pitch-black eyes,*
> *and those that dance 'neath stranger skies.*

The words felt like nothing more than poetic ramblings, yet they made the hairs on the back of Baz's neck stand. Someone had carefully drawn the eight phases of the moon atop the four lines, as well as two other symbols beneath them, meant to represent the lunar and solar eclipses. A swirling constellation of childishly ren-dered stars wove around and over and between the words in blue ink. They looked exactly like the stars Romie would draw whenever they tried recreating illustrations of the Tides—of Quies especially, the Waning Crone always portrayed with her head tipped up to a heavy blanket of stars.

She's like in my dreams. So many stars.

Baz brought the book back to the permissions desk for Nisha Zenara to stamp its checkout card. Romie's name wasn't on it. He'd asked Nisha about it earlier, noticing her brief flicker of recogni-tion as he mentioned *Dark Tides*. She'd feigned innocence, looking over her ledger and stating that Romie was never listed as having

come into the Vault. Baz knew better. If they'd been as close as Kai suggested, Nisha had probably let Romie sneak in unofficially.

Too eager to wait until he was in the Eclipse commons to start reading, he did so as he climbed the narrow stone staircase that led into the Decrescens library above the Vault. He'd just walked through the slender archway at the top, where two marble busts stood as solemn sentinels, each one wearing a crown of gold-leafed laurels, when he deigned to finally look up.

The book dropped at his feet.

Keiran Dunhall Thornby stood before him.

"Brysden," he said in a voice that was eerily calm.

Time stopped as they stared each other down. It wound back in Baz's mind until he saw Keiran as a fifteen-year-old boy in a court-house, alone and angry at being robbed too soon of his family, hazel eyes full of hurt and hate as they swept over Baz.

By some unspoken agreement, the two of them had always given each other a wide berth at Aldryn, knowing full well they'd inevi-tably clash if they got too close. It was nothing short of a miracle they'd never once been in the same room together, at least not without others there to act as buffers.

But now, as Keiran's face shed the perfect mask of civility and nonchalance he always wore, Baz realized with no small horror that for the first time, they were indeed alone.

He took an involuntary step back as Keiran lunged—not at Baz, but at the book he'd dropped on the floor. Keiran smirked at his cowering and read the title. He stilled, and Baz thought he might have imagined the unease on his face, the tightness in his shoul-ders. Slowly, Keiran lifted his eyes back to him, and there was vio-lence brewing in their depths, a storm on the brink of unleash. As if he knew what this book was, what it meant that Baz had it.

Before either of them could say anything, Dean Fulton appeared.

"There you are, I've been looking all over for you."

This seemed to be directed at Keiran, though her voice was tinged with a casual note that threw Baz for a loop. The dean faltered when she spotted him. "Oh, Mr. Brysden. I didn't see you there." Her gaze bounced between the two of them in the ensuing silence, no doubt noticing the tension. "Is everything all right?"

"Everything is just fine," Keiran said with a sharp-edged smile. "Isn't that right, Brysden?"

"Of course," Baz gritted out.

Fulton looked at him for a second longer than necessary. "Well, it was nice seeing you, then, Mr. Brysden. I hope you'll enjoy the equinox festival tonight. Mr. Dunhall Thornby, my office, please." Her tone brokered no argument as she turned on her heel.

Keiran handed Baz his book back with a scornful curl of his lip. "Happy reading."

"*Doors to the Deep*," Vera read, peering at the book as they made their way to the equinox festival. She shoved it unceremoniously back into Baz's hand. "I've heard of them before. Water holes that drain the sea into their seemingly bottomless depths. They're said to be remnants of old, collapsed sea caves, no?"

"Yeah."

Baz thumbed the pages of *Dark Tides* as they kept walking. There was palpable excitement in the air as students made their way to the site of the festival on the banks of the River Helene. Everlight lanterns dangled from branches arcing overhead, lining the path down to the river, which slithered through the woods that hugged the hill upon which Aldryn College stood. The magicked lanterns were barely needed on such a night: the waxing gibbous hung high in the sky, its silvery light flooding the woods.

There was no sign of Jae. They'd sent word to Baz the morning after the Institute, letting him know they were safe and confirming they'd come to the equinox festival. It was the only reason Baz was

here at all. He never came to these things–too many people, an absolute nightmare. He was grateful to have Vera with him at least. She'd been eager to tag along, claiming she'd never been to such a festival before. *They don't have them in Trevel,* she'd said. Baz suspected she also just wanted to see Jae again, so fascinated had she been by their magic.

He couldn't wait to pester Jae for their thoughts on *Dark Tides.* It was a truly odd book. Obscure theories on rare tidal movements said to influence magic in strange ways, stranger still than any ecliptic event ever did. Rip currents that brought deadly plagues or incredible fortune to whatever shores they unfurled on. Tides that gifted people with astoundingly long life, and others said to spawn transformations that could only be the stuff of myth, tales of merfolk and men who howled at the moon like wolves. And these water holes that acted as portals believed to take you to distant ports and continents or other worlds entirely.

It was exactly the kind of reading material Professor Selandyn loved to pore over. Impossible magics and theories that weren't exactly plausible but that she'd entertain nonetheless, often proving them right or wrong. Baz had thought of going to her first about what he'd read in *Dark Tides,* but after what she'd made him promise, he'd decided a third party might be best.

"But do you think there's any plausibility to these things being *actual* doorways?" he asked Vera excitedly. "Here, look–"

He stopped under a lantern and flipped to a particular passage that had drawn his eye.

> *The tide sinks and swirls out of sight through*
> *these holes, carrying along whatever or whoever*
> *falls into them. It is said that the Tides sank down*
> *into such water holes to bring the Shadow into*
> *the Deep, thus spawning this long-standing belief*

that they are doors to the Deep itself; portals into
the dark hellscape that lies at the bottom of the
sea. Others believe these carrier tides unfurl onto
distant shores, though none have ever survived to
tell the tale.*

*   *The authors of this work urge their readers*
caution where these "doors" are concerned,
and remove themselves from all responsibility
following any disappearance, injury, or death that
should arise.

Vera frowned at the page. "You think Dovermere is a door to the Deep? That it's the way to other worlds?"

"I think, at the very least, that's what my sister believed."

"Except Dovermere is very much still a cave, not the old remains of one. It's not . . . whatever this door is supposed to look like."

Baz groaned and shoved the book back in his bag. She was right. It felt like he was grasping at straws. And yet . . .

A portal on a page, a door to the Deep, a song heard between the stars. Whatever it was, it all came back to Dovermere.

Jae would have answers—Baz was sure of it.

He buried his hands in his coat pockets, savoring the crunch of leaves under the soles of his shoes. The trees had only just begun turning, but some were already shedding their leaves, creating a carpet of rusts and golds to lead the students to the festival. They made their way down the path in clusters of twos and threes, laughing and talking excitedly about the night ahead and the various parties planned after the ritual itself.

"You know, my mother always said that if anyone were to find the epilogue, it would be Adriana," Vera said suddenly, kicking at a pinecone. "When she got an idea in her head, she wouldn't let it go. She was so young when she made it out here. Sailed across the

seas all on her own, hitting every port town and coastal point of interest where she thought the epilogue might be hidden. Aldryn was the one she had her sights on the most, of course, since Clover studied here."

The path before them branched off in two directions: downriver to the left, and upriver to the right. Those chosen to perform feats of magic on their house's boat would head right to the wooden quays where the boats were set to launch. Baz and Vera turned left to where students were gathered on the riverbank on wool blankets. Kiosks were scattered among the crowd, selling drinks and treats to be enjoyed during the performance. Vera pulled him to one selling fried dough and hot cocoa.

"And you really have no idea what happened to her?" Baz asked as she handed the kiosk worker a few coins.

Vera shut her eyes as she took a sip of cocoa, puckering her lips. "She disappeared. Whether that's because her ship capsized or someone beat her to the epilogue and killed her for it or because she found a door to the Deep and slipped into another world, she's gone. And that's the end of it."

She shoved the paper bag of fried dough under his nose, all but forcing Baz to take one.

"I thought being part of the Veiled Atlas meant you'd be the first one to go looking for the epilogue."

Vera laughed, licking sugar off her fingers. "I'm part of the Veiled Atlas because I was born into a family that believes in the magic of other worlds. And I do too. But take it from a magical reject like me: some powers are beyond our understanding, and it's best we leave them alone." She stuffed the last of the fried dough into her mouth. "Just something to think about before this obsession you seem to have with Dovermere gets you killed. Now, can we *please* hurry up and find a good spot? I don't want to miss the spectacle."

Vera caught him glancing around for Jae again and said, "I'm

sure they'll turn up. No point trying to find them in this large a crowd anyway. Come on."

Baz knew she was right. Still, unease made his stomach turn, and he suddenly regretted eating that fried dough–especially as he caught sight of Emory.

She sat not ten feet away next to a dark-haired girl Baz thought was called Penelope. Emory gave him a tight smile he didn't know how to respond to. They hadn't seen each other since the other day in the quad, and though Baz felt bad for postponing the training session he'd promised her, he told himself it was for the best. He didn't think he could handle much else at the moment, and yet . . . he hadn't realized until just now how he missed their quiet mornings in the library. How much he missed *her*.

Vera nudged him. "Friend of yours?" At Baz's noncommittal response, she cocked an eyebrow. "Let's go say hello."

"No, Vera–"

But she was already introducing herself to Emory and Penelope, who invited her to sit with them. Baz had no choice but to follow. Penelope was wedged between Vera on one side and Emory on the other, and this was Baz's worst nightmare. Panicked, he sat beside Vera, who gave him a withering look as if to say, *Not here, stupid.* Too late. He jerked his chin toward Emory in an awkward hello before glancing uneasily around for Jae again, trying not to think of all the ways Kai would make fun of his gaucheness if he were here.

As Vera chattered enthusiastically with Penelope–who apparently had family in Trevel and knew people who went to university with Vera–someone else knelt at Emory's side. Baz's stomach fell. Keiran was leaning in close to whisper something in her ear, and Baz didn't miss the way Emory ducked her head to hide a smile.

So that's how it was, then.

Something in Baz dimmed. He looked away, but not before

Keiran's gaze met his, an ember of that earlier storm he'd seen brewing in his eyes.

Happy reading.

Did Keiran know about these doors to the Deep? What they might have meant to Romie?

Baz thought it odd that Keiran was here at all—he would have imagined he'd be part of his house's delegation, given his grades. Then again, he'd likely already secured a prestigious position without needing to resort to such fanfare.

A few students farther upstream suddenly exclaimed loudly. The thrum of conversation died down as the boats appeared in the distance, sleek things of beauty with dark wood gleaming under the moonlight, each one adorned with artfully arranged bouquets of lunar flowers that filled the air with a sweet summery scent at odds with the autumn chill.

The spectacle was starting.

Vera's elbow wedged itself into his side. "I didn't know Regulators came to this thing."

She pointed to a nearby elm where a charcoal-uniformed Regulator stood with a pretty redheaded student. They seemed caught in a tense conversation. The Regulator tossed a look over his shoulder, and Baz noted the similarities in his features and the student's. Something silvery passed from his hands to hers.

"Yeah, like that's not suspicious at all," Vera muttered sarcastically.

The student pocketed whatever it was and turned her back on the Regulator. There was something familiar about her—about both of them—but they disappeared in the crowd before Baz could make sense of it. He thought he saw Keiran glancing their way. But just then, the New Moon delegation's boat glided on the river in front of them, drawing all their attention.

The four students chosen to perform their magic—one of each alignment—stood at the prow wearing robes of midnight velvet

with fur collars and sleeves crusted with what looked like glittering snow. Utter darkness fell, spilling from the Darkbearer student. The narcissus flowers that decorated the sides of the boat came to life, glowing like diamonds in the night. A faint breeze picked up, steering the boat steadily down the ribbon of water. Baz heard a rippling gasp drawn from the students gathered closest to the water, and as the breeze reached him, brushing against his cheek, he understood why.

There was healing in that gentle caress. The faint headache he'd had receded, and he found he could breathe easier, as if unburdened from whatever aches and torments had previously ailed him. Beside him, Vera looked at her hands in amazement at whatever cut or pain had likely been healed. A collective sigh of contentment blew from the crowd.

Then—a cry of surprise broke through the night. Baz felt the air shift ever so slightly as murmurs rose in the ensuing quiet. A chill ran up his spine. He knew those voices did not belong to the living. The Shadowguide was at work.

The Darkbearer lifted their arms up to the sky, manipulating the darkness so that it danced above them. Another delegate stepped up to their side, pressed their hand on their arm. The Darkbearer unleashed the gathering dark, making it plume toward the calm waters. The river erupted, a tidal wave of dark water that splashed the students on the banks. Curious droplets that were neither liquid nor solid nor gaseous reached Baz, and in them he saw—what did he see? It was his own face reflected on the multiple facets of a prism, old and young and not quite himself, but versions of him that could be. The work of the Seer, then.

This was big magic, Baz thought, an impressive feat for those who needed to rely on bloodletting tonight—every house except for those of House Waxing Moon who answered to the waxing gibbous

phase. He had no doubt that every student who performed would be showered with offers of internships and coveted positions.

His gaze cut to Emory, who watched the procession with a look of rapture, maybe even longing. It stirred something in him, reminding him there was beauty in this kind of magic. He found it hard to take his eyes off her–her slightly parted lips, the way her hair framed her face, fringe brushing her brows, curling slightly at her temples. The silvery glow the moon cast around her, like an ethereal aura.

Beautiful.

He only looked away once the Waxing Moon delegation appeared. The four students wore high-collared dresses made of diaphanous panes that shimmered palest blue to deepest indigo, cinched at the waist by a thread of silver. A sudden melody filled the air. One of the students plucked away at the strings of a guitar and began to sing in a language Baz wasn't familiar with, voice low and soft. Another student wound her voice in the song, lovely and bright, and it was as if Baz could see the reverberations of the music in the air around them, gliding over the river along with the boat.

Everything the notes touched grew and bloomed, heeding the music's call: fish curved out of the water like synchronized swim-mers; algae crept along the sides of the boat, interweaving with the great vines of hollyhock that adorned it, the vegetation dancing in time with the strings; nightbirds and crickets and frogs lent their own voices to the song, and the night became an orchestra, the river a stage, with the two singers as their conductors.

A third student joined their voice in the mix, compelling the crowd to dance. Baz felt a presence brush against his mind, the stroke of a finger along the walls of his innermost self. *And why not dance?* he thought as the rhythm pulsed. He tapped his foot to it, felt every-one around him stir. Beside him, Vera broke out in a laugh as she

stood and gave an elated twirl, heeding the call of the Glamour's compulsion.

It was only when the music subsided to deafening applause that a distant part of Baz thought this sort of magic was wrong, but it was so innocent a thing, and the music had lifted his heart in a way he hadn't known in a long time, that he simply let it go, eager to see more.

The Full Moon students did not disappoint. There was a single bare-chested boy and three girls wearing dresses made of gauzy silver panes that left little to the imagination. White orchids over-filled the inside of their boat like a blanket of nebulous clouds. The bare-chested student stepped to the prow, and the magicked lan-terns dangling from trees on the riverbank were extinguished in one great sweep, their light gathering to his outstretched hand. Hundreds upon thousands of little drops of light detached from the beam in his hand to hang in the air. The beads shot up in the sky and burst like great fireworks. A shower of light rained down on the river, glittering and mesmerizing, and when it touched Baz, he felt cleansed of all his worries and anxieties, the air he drew in his lungs crisp and cool and heartening. His soul lifted, light as a feather, at whatever purification magic this was.

A faint wind made orchid petals lift and scatter, dancing along the riverbank. Baz couldn't help the smile that tugged at his lips as one of them brushed against him. There was protection in that faint caress, a feeling of safety, making all the tension he carried in his body ease. More light burst above them like fireworks, and students laughed in wonderment, giddy with this fabricated hap-piness raining gently down on them. The Lightkeeper unleashed the remaining light in his hand, willing it to run through the depths of the river like a ribbon of color to guide the boats down to the sea, then sent it back to the lanterns, once more illuminating the riverbank.

Everyone applauded, and Baz couldn't tell if it was his own joy or the fabricated one still fluttering around inside him that made him smile.

The mood sharpened when the attention shifted to the Waning Moon boat. The joyful light vanished, replaced by a heaviness, a soundless sort of quiet, as if a thick blanket had been laid over the world. The breeze picked up, chilly and dark, and Baz's eyes became heavy with sleep, his mind wiped blank with the peace of it. Arches of deep purple poppies adorned the sleek boat, beautiful blooms that seemed to be the only color in the suddenly bleak night.

Frost crept over the river, reaching for the yellowing grass and decaying leaves on its banks, the willow manes that brushed the water, the poppies on the boat. Everything it touched froze and withered, a death touch that held infinite finesse. There was beauty to it, as if the frost were cleansing the world, purging it of its old hurts to remake it anew.

Baz's breath fogged around him, and in that breath he saw—a *memory*. Him and Romie as children, reading under the willow tree behind their home. The fog faded, and just as Baz wondered if he'd imagined the memory, his gaze caught on the river, where great castles of glittering ice and snow rose from the water, made of moonlight and starlight and waking dreams.

Then the shapes on the water wound backward—wisps of dreaming unraveling back to whatever realm they'd come from. The memories fogging the riverbank were undone, reversed by Unraveler magic, just as the languidness of sleep was lifted from the crowd. The Waning Moon students took a solemn bow.

Baz looked at Emory again, thinking of Romie and how much she would have loved to see this—of how she would have no doubt been on that Waning Moon boat, entrancing everyone with her own magic.

But Emory was no longer there, and neither was Keiran, and Baz couldn't make sense of the unpleasant emotion that surged inside him. Penelope looked just as disappointed as he felt.

He startled as a hand fell on his shoulder, turning to find Jae smiling down at him.

"Sorry I'm late." They dipped their head at Vera and cast an uncertain look at Penelope, who was gathering her things with a forlorn expression. "Should we . . ."

"I've got this." Vera looped her arm through Penelope's. "Let's go grab some of that cider I saw over there."

The girl blinked in surprise. "Oh, you don't have to—"

"My treat. I insist. I'm homesick, and you can tell me more about that Trevelyan family of yours." Vera looked at Baz pointedly over a shoulder, as if to say *You're welcome.*

"I won't keep you long," Jae said once they were alone. "I told Beatrix I'd meet her for a nightcap."

"Did you find anything?"

Jae shook their head. "Couldn't get back in. The Institute was closed to visitors after our little breach." A wink. "I'm guessing they got spooked."

Baz gulped. "Do you think they know—"

"No, no. We're fine."

"Good." Trying not to think of Kai, Baz pulled *Dark Tides* from his bag and handed it to Jae. "Then I'm hoping you can tell me what this is."

Jae read the title, then the epigraph. Their forehead creased. "I've never heard of *Dark Tides*, but this here"—they tapped the strange riddle—"*this* I've seen before."

"Where?"

"In Cornus Clover's personal journal. Well, *journal* might not be the right word. Alya let me have a look at it once—the Veiled Atlas has the only known copy. Clover wrote everything in it,

from class notes to random lists of names to important dates and rendezvous. Even some passages that appear to be early attempts at *Song of the Drowned Gods*. Like this." Jae tapped the epigraph again. "Clover wrote this. I remember because there was a first draft of it, with lines and words crossed out and rewritten all over the page, and on another page was a cleaner draft with all these ideas for *Song of the Drowned Gods* written around it. Plot threads and character names and descriptions of the other worlds and such. Even some quick illustrations he sketched."

Jae glanced at the book's spine, searching for an author name Baz knew wasn't there. Another peculiarity of *Dark Tides*, that it was written anonymously.

"Whoever wrote this had to have seen Clover's journal," Jae concluded.

"Could it have been Clover himself? Or someone from the Veiled Atlas, maybe?" Vera, at least, hadn't seemed to recognize the epigraph.

Jae hummed pensively, flipping through the rest of the book. "Could be. I'm guessing you got this in the Vault?"

Baz nodded. "Kai told me about it. Said Romie was mumbling those exact words in the sleepscape. Did he tell you they were looking for the epilogue together?"

Jae's brow arched in surprise. "No, he did not."

"They both went to the Veiled Atlas and became obsessed with finding it. It's how Kai Collapsed."

Jae swore under their breath. "This is why I dislike the Veiled Atlas. Putting all these crazy ideas about the epilogue in people's heads, *especially* impressionable students who can't differentiate between academic interest and—"

"But what if everything they believe in is true?" Baz interrupted. "Or at least some of it. Look." He showed Jae the passage about

doors to the Deep, watching their face closely as they read. "This is why Romie went to Dovermere."

"Basil." Jae sighed deeply. They pinched the bridge of their nose, pushing their tiny half-moon glasses up, and for the first time Baz truly noticed how much they had aged. It was more than just the silver strands in their hair or the subtle lines around their eyes and mouth. Exhaustion hung heavy on them. They looked world-weary; bone-tired. As if all their years of research and traveling had finally caught up to them.

It made Baz wonder how his father must look after wasting away at the Institute for so long.

"I swore to your parents I'd watch over you," Jae said quietly, "and in truth, I've never really had to, because you've always been bright and cautious and smarter than most people I know." Their dark eyes were imploring. "Please, for my sake, for the sake of your poor mother and father, don't go down this road. You've seen what it does to people." They shook their head. "Stay away from this, Basil."

The Institute, Dovermere, the epilogue—it felt to Baz like he was a child being warned away from all the things that were hazards to him, but completely innocuous for the trusted adults around him. It angered him to realize how coddled he'd been all his life. With Jae and Professor Selandyn. With Kai, who hid from him what he was planning to do in some odd attempt to spare him.

Tides, even Baz's father, as he was being carried away from the devastating scene of his Collapsing, had seemed more worried about Baz than his own gruesome fate.

Was he really so fragile?

Baz opened his mouth to tell Jae exactly what he thought—and shut it, the sorrow on their face giving him pause.

The printing press flashed in his mind, a startlingly clear image of that world-shattering day: the three clients who'd come in and

cornered Jae, the damper cuffs one of them had taken out, threatening to bring Jae into the Institute if they didn't cooperate.

Baz had no memory of what was said during the heated exchange that took place right before his father Collapsed, nor why those people were at the printing press at all. But he suddenly remembered how scared Jae had looked–much as he did now.

"The people who came to see you at the printing press," Baz said slowly. "Were they there about the epilogue?"

Jae looked at him strangely. Before they could answer, Vera and Penelope appeared at their side. They mentioned something about a party, but it was the furthest thing from Baz's mind.

"I think I'll just walk with Jae back to campus," he said. "Call it a night."

"Suit yourself, party-pooper," Vera teased. She linked her arm with Penelope's again and waved at him. "See you around."

Jae knew Baz well enough than to suggest he stay and enjoy the festivities. They smiled at him knowingly, and together they started up the path back to school. Neither of them mentioned the printing press again.

Baz found himself glancing around for Emory. He thought of how enraptured she'd been by tonight's display of magic. How beautiful she'd looked. He clung to that image, promising himself he'd find her tomorrow to make good on his offer to train her. He wanted to see that enchantment on her face again, the pride she lit up with whenever she used her magic.

The thought scared the shit out of him. *She* scared him–but maybe that was exactly what he needed. Someone who didn't treat him like a child in need of coddling, but as an equal.

Someone who believed in him when it was so hard to do on his own.

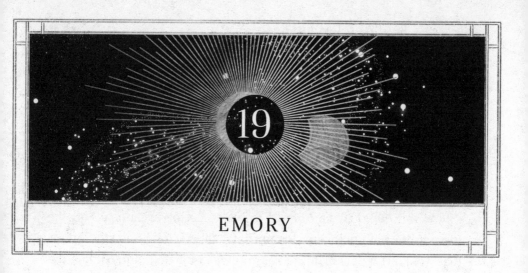

EMORY

"SO, YOU AND BRYSDEN," KEIRAN SAID AS THEY MADE THEIR way through the woods, a slight crease between his brows. "How close are you exactly?"

Guilt churned in Emory's stomach. She'd been waiting for this question ever since Keiran sat next to her on the riverbank, mortified at the thought of him and Baz confronting each other. The tension that simmered between them had been like a beast looming in the dark, waiting to pounce. And she felt responsible for it. The unwitting glue that brought the two of them there together.

She scoffed, the lie coming to her with ease. "Not at all."

Suddenly it was like she was back at Threnody Prep, shame and fear surging in her at the thought of being associated with Baz when everyone else steered clear of him. She tried to tell herself she was doing it for Baz's sake, keeping him as far away from the Order as she could, but really she was *embarrassed*; she didn't want anyone in the Order to know what she was up to with him—especially not Keiran, given their history.

Keiran gave her a sidelong glance, as if seeing right through her lie.

"Well, I mean, we *used* to be, back at prep school," Emory amended. "But that was a long time ago. We hardly ever speak nowadays."

"And tonight?"

Was that jealousy she heard in his voice, or just unease at the idea of her being close to his parents' killer's son? She studied his features in the dark. His expression was guarded, a mask like the porcelain faces of the Tides. She couldn't imagine what it must be like to constantly be reminded of his parents whenever he saw Baz. Whenever he'd seen Romie, too.

"He doesn't know you're a Tidecaller, does he?" Keiran asked at her silence.

"No. Of course not."

The thought briefly crossed her mind to tell him what really happened on the beach the night Travers appeared, how Baz had saved her from her own power by reversing time. But just as quickly, she pushed the impulse away. Sharing that would be like betraying Baz. He'd made it clear he wanted nothing to do with her and her magic anymore; the least she could do was respect him enough not to drag him into this mess.

"Good. It's best no one else knows what you are." Keiran drew closer, brushing the curls at her temple. "Easier to protect your secret this way."

Warmth flooded her. "I won't tell a soul."

She was all too aware of her own heartbeat, of her parting lips, as his eyes flickered to her mouth. Keiran leaned in—only to brush past her, saying, "We're almost there."

Tides damn her. She needed to get a grip on herself.

Emory caught up to him. Sure enough, the river appeared up ahead, gleaming silver under the gibbous moon. It was narrower

here than it was downriver where the festival was, and calmer, too. Rustling willow trees brushed the water's surface.

"Remind me again why we're doing this along the river and not the Aldersea, or even Dovermere?"

"No one's going back to Dovermere until we know for certain how to wake the Tides," Keiran declared. "I'm not risking any more lives. Besides, the Tides rule over more than just the sea. The river might not hold the same power as the sea or as Dovermere itself, but it's where the first Selenics held their fall equinox rituals. We've done it a few times before, but it always felt like there was something missing." A glance at her. "Of course, we didn't have a Tide-caller then."

Emory looked away, cheeks burning.

"Even if tonight's summons yields nothing," Keiran said gently, "it's the perfect way to test your power."

She hoped she'd live up to it, this expectation he placed on her.

The rest of the Selenics were already gathered on the riverbank. Nisha gave Emory a bright smile to which she responded in kind, grateful that things between them had mended.

Somewhere behind them, a branch snapped loudly. Emory whipped around to see Lizaveta brandishing a metal case. "Got the synths," she declared.

Lizaveta inked everyone's Selenic Mark with the synthetic magic, which was imbued with a mixture of both Waxing and Full Moon magics. *To honor Anima and Aestas, who used to rule over summer and autumn,* Keiran explained.

In the oldest versions of the myth, the cycle of the Tides started in spring, with Bruma taking seed, followed by Anima tending those seeds in summer, Aestas shining over the plentiful harvest of autumn, and Quies quieting the world with the cold winds of winter, so that the cycle could start anew in spring. Nowadays, those associations had been skewed to fit a more modern perspective:

Bruma was attributed to the dark barrenness of winter, Anima to the growth of spring, Aestas to the bright lushness of summer, and Quies to the dwindling of autumn.

Since tonight was the fall equinox, the transition from summer to autumn, they would honor the old ways and use magic belonging to both the waxing moon that shone upon them and the full moon it would very soon become. They were fitting magics for such a ritual: speaking their intentions to make them true like Wordsmiths; using Glamour compulsion to will the Tides to hear them; shining their light like a beacon, the way Lightkeepers guided ships to safe harbor.

Protection, purification, mindfulness, manifestation—it had all the makings of a powerful summons.

If waking the Tides was opening a door, as Keiran put it, this was them trying to first unlock it.

At Keiran's insistence, Emory was inked too, on the basis that it might help open her senses, make it easier for her to access these other magics at her disposal.

As all eight of them formed a circle in the order of the moon's phases—Ife and Louis of House New Moon, Lizaveta and Nisha of House Waxing Moon, Keiran and Javier of House Full Moon, Virgil of House Waning Moon, and Emory, standing between Virgil and Ife for House Eclipse, the link between the first and last phases of the moon—she thought she felt the synth working. A beat drummed in her ears, the melody of seven beating hearts synced to the rhythm of her own. Something tugged at the edge of her vision, smudges of color that clung to each Selenic, shifting and swirling in mysterious ways.

The air was cold, their breaths fogging around their mouths. She could feel the others' breathing like whispers against her flushed cheeks, her exposed neck, making gooseflesh rise on the skin hidden away beneath the heavy folds of her coat. There was a

sharpness to the air, an expectant sort of clearness, as if the night itself was eager for magic to fill it.

"The Tides watch over us this night." Keiran's voice commanded power as he looked at each of them in turn. "Much as summer spills into autumn, this river spills into the sea, carrying with it all its strength. The first Selenics would pour their magics into the River Helene so that she might carry them to the Aldersea, an offering to the Tides, a plea for them to hear their fervor. It was a way for them to say, *We remain. We remember.* Tonight, we send out this initial call to make our intention known. To show the Tides that we still remain, still remember the ways of old, and that we mean to bring them back."

His gaze settled on Emory last. He looked at her in a way that sent her stomach into knots and her skin tingling with anticipation. "If nothing else, let this be our way of testing our Tidecaller's magic."

Keiran gave a nod to Ife and Louis, who intoned as one: "To Bruma, who sprang from the darkness."

Then, Lizaveta and Nisha: "To Anima, whose voice breathed life into the world."

Keiran and Javier: "To Aestas, whose bountiful warmth and light protect us all."

And Virgil at last: "To Quies and the sleeping darkness she guides us through at the end of all things."

"From the Deep we seek to raise thee," Keiran continued. "With this ritual, our word becomes oath; let it bind us to thee. Let us pour our magics into the river and see them flow."

His eyes found Emory's again as he shucked off his coat, began unbuttoning his shirt. Emory glanced nervously at the others, all of them undressing quietly in the moonlight.

Virgil was the first to strip down to his briefs. He ran to the river, followed closely by a shrieking Nisha in dainty lace under-garments. When they hit the water, Emory gasped. Impossibly,

she felt the shock of that cold water against her own skin. Virgil dragged Nisha beneath the surface, and Emory staggered back slightly at the feeling that settled over her: a sudden hush, pressure on her eardrums–the muffled weight of the river above and below and all around her, as if she'd been submerged herself.

Sound returned once Virgil and Nisha emerged, laughing and sputtering, and Emory realized she could *feel* what they felt, every sensation, every breath. It was as if all of them were linked by an invisible string, their souls and bodies bound under the bright eye of the gibbous moon by whatever magic had been imbued in the synths.

As the others headed into the water, Emory's attention darted back to Keiran. He hung back, watching her intently. Slowly, he peeled off his shirt, the moonlight limning his bare torso. He worked on undoing his pants next, lifted a brow at her as he did.

An invitation, a challenge.

One she felt entirely up for, curiously devoid of fear.

She slipped out of her clothes down to her undergarments, heart pounding wildly, breaths coming in quick, short bursts. She shivered at the cold wind that bit her skin. Keiran's gaze traveled down the length of her, dark and deliberate, and she realized the nebulous cloud around him was his *aura*, the kind Soultenders dealt in. The impression it gave her was one of desire, and she knew hers responded in kind. They gravitated toward each other like starved celestial bodies. They didn't touch, letting the breeze run like silk in the inch of space between them.

If this was how this strange magic felt when they weren't even touching, Emory could only imagine what it might be like if they did. She couldn't muster the energy to chastise herself for the thoughts that crossed her mind, to *focus*. Keiran smiled knowingly. He laced his fingers through hers, and all her nerve endings stirred, tingled, awakened. She craved more, wanted to erase the

distance between them, but Keiran pulled her toward the river, and together they dove into a world of muted silence and murky darkness.

Emory held her breath—and when she exhaled, realized she could breathe underwater.

Protective magic. Wards like the kind that Wardcrafters could wield.

It felt different than when she used her Tidecaller magic. That was like opening a door to let the different powers of the lunar cycle rush through her, familiar and somehow part of her. This felt . . . strange. Intimate. Like she was drawing power from some-one specific. Like she could *feel* the person the synthetic magic belonged to, their very being coursing through her blood. It was almost intrusive, yet somehow all the more thrilling for it.

Keiran reached a hand up toward the surface, calling forth the light of the moon that filtered through the water. He began to glow like a faintly burning star, illuminating the depths so that all of them could see the tiny fish darting between their legs, the rippling algae below, their own limbs kicking about to stay suspended here beneath the surface.

Keiran swam over to the person nearest him. He wound a hand behind Louis's head to draw him near, laid the other on the Healer's bare torso. Emory watched with curious intent as Keiran rested his forehead against Louis's in a gesture that was somehow both tender and sensual, like Aestas herself. Light pulsed from Keiran's hands, and when he pulled away from Louis, the Healer was aglow with his own light. Tendrils of it swirled around his chest, his arms, snaking around his fingers as he brought them up to his face in wonderment.

And Emory could *feel* Louis's awe through whatever bond was linking them. The light was power, transformation, abundance, healing; it was everything the moon's entire spectrum embodied,

and it lifted Louis's soul as well as her own. His aura turned to gold and silver, beautiful and serene.

Keiran kicked his way over to the next person and paused, glancing back at Emory expectantly. He wanted her to mimic him. To wield the Lightkeeper magic he was using as her own.

And why not? She held the key to it, did she not? All she needed was to set it into the proper lock and open the door.

Emory called forth her own burst of light, letting the moon's might wrap around her. Her breath hitched at the comforting warmth of it. The sheer *power* of it, sensual and vast and true.

Her eyes flickered to Keiran again, studying the way he drew closer to Ife. They wound their hands together, and Ife broke into a smile as Keiran transferred the light to her.

The inner workings of the magic came to Emory almost instinctively as she watched them. She turned to Nisha, who swam closest to her, her long, dark hair flowing gently around her. Emory brought a shining hand to the base of Nisha's neck, holding herself afloat by snaking her other arm behind the girl's back. She willed a plume of light to transfer to her, and Nisha's lips parted in a soundless laugh, bubbles of air rising from her mouth as the colors around her shifted to an elated white gold.

Emory felt as gleeful as Nisha did, and all the more powerful for it. She swam away from her and caught sight of Keiran a few feet away, wrapped in what looked like a sensuous embrace with Lizaveta. The girl's red hair moved like a dancing flame. She brought Keiran's head down into the crook of her neck as his light hit her body, a beatific smile on her parted lips.

Emory felt a tinge of jealousy as she wondered how close they actually were, but it paled against the faint reverberation of Lizaveta's delighted shiver, which Emory felt through their bond.

A hand glided over Emory's arm. Virgil pulled her in closer, longing etched on his face, desire for this power they all shared. Emory

laid a hand on his chest, and as she made the light flow toward him, she couldn't help but want *more*. More of this magic that made her feel formidable, indomitable.

A glimmer of mischief appeared in Virgil's eyes, as if he could hear Emory's every thought. His chin dipped to where Lizaveta glowed. His intent was clear: If Emory wanted more, she could have it. Could amplify her own power.

Yes, Emory thought, reaching blindly for Lizaveta's power.

The amplifying magic surged into her, but it didn't feel like *taking* anything from Lizaveta, she realized, just as using Lightkeeper magic didn't feel like taking power away from Keiran, either. She wondered if she needed to draw the magic from someone else first at all—if she needed to be in contact with a user of that specific magic for it to flow through her—or if she could call on whatever magic she desired, as her title suggested.

The light around her and Virgil flared brighter with the surge of amplification, like a supernova in the making. Emory directed it toward the others, amplifying their own light. Great threads of gold and silver and faintest blue and purple wove between the eight of them, making tangible things of the curious bonds that linked them. The colorful auras around them shimmered brilliantly, drawing soundless gasps from each of them as they observed their glowing limbs in the water. The threads of light rearranged themselves, shooting up toward the surface of the river in a great burst of power.

If someone were to look down from the sky, Emory knew they would see a mark etched in moonlight on the river's surface: a spiral just like the one burning silver on all their palms. The Selenic Mark, sacred and dear to the Tides.

Please hear us, Emory thought, willing the deities to heed their call, to absorb this magic and rise so they might bring Romie back.

Distantly, she thought of Baz and all his warnings, but she was fearless in this moment. There was no concern or dread at the power that flowed through her, nor the fate that could snap its jaws over her at a slip of her toe across that precarious line Baz described.

What was the point of having such power if she couldn't use it? If she had to keep a permanent leash on it?

She was a Selenic, the first Eclipse-born to hold such an honor. That had to mean something.

Emory met Keiran's gaze, full of admiration and awe and something she couldn't quite place. And here in the water, she finally believed it: that perhaps this sort of magic could indeed bring back the Tides.

She'd find a way to make it work, if only to keep him looking at her the way he did now.

They emerged shivering against the cold and raced to pull their clothes on. Distant music and laughter drifted to them, students no doubt keeping the fall equinox festivities going. The Selenics didn't join them. They stayed here by the river, with a spread of blankets and a roaring fire and the bottles of wine and flasks of liquor Virgil had brought for everyone to share.

As the others danced to the music that Lizaveta amplified to ring louder around them, Emory watched Keiran stoke the flames. He caught her looking at him over the fire. Heat pooled in her stomach at the half smile he gave her, a crooked upturn of his lips. He jerked his head in wordless invitation. She followed him without thinking.

They sat in a patch of flattened tall grass a ways down the river. Keiran handed her the bottle he'd snuck and leaned back, propping himself up on his elbows, legs sprawled in front of him. She felt his eyes on her as she took a sip, acutely aware of the hunger in them. She glanced at him over her shoulder.

"You're staring," she breathed.

A hint of that dimpled smile again. "I can't help it. You were stunning tonight, Ains."

His voice was thick with—was it lust? Affection? He frowned like he was trying to figure it out himself, like whatever it was had taken him by surprise. Emory ducked her head shyly, tucked her still-damp, messy hair behind an ear. Words eluded her. When she handed the bottle back to him, Keiran sat up and reached for her instead.

His hand cupped her cheek, trailed behind her head. Her heart was beating so fast she thought it might burst as his lips brushed hers, ever so soft. It was everything her treacherous heart had dreamed of.

Desire pooled in her stomach. Emory kissed him back, desperate for more. And he obliged her. She couldn't catch her breath, couldn't believe this was really happening. The synth's effect was gone, but his kiss was every bit as electrifying as she imagined it would be, and she never wished it to end.

But Keiran eventually pulled away, fingers caught on her chin, darkened eyes on her mouth.

A delectable shiver ran through her.

"We can head back if you're cold," Keiran suggested, eyes still on her lips.

She wasn't, but it didn't matter. Not when he looked at her like that, and she understood that he did not mean to return to the fire at all, but to school. Where they'd be alone. Together. "Let's go."

They barely made it to the quad before he drew her near again, stopping her beneath the cloisters. His hand trailed lightly up her arm, tilting her chin up with delicate fingers.

"You keep surprising me," he whispered, brushing aside a strand of her hair with heartbreaking tenderness, brows scrunching slightly as he scanned her face. "It's more than just your magic. It's

the heart you put into it. It reminds me why we're doing this in the first place."

Her knees weakened as he leaned in close. He lifted her hand, pressed it against his neck, and curled her fingers around it in a loose chokehold. "That's the kind of hold you have on me, Emory Ainslief." His breath caressed her face. Beneath her thumb, his pulse was as quick as her own. "And I don't mind it for a second."

Emory didn't know what to make of the way he looked at her. It was like he saw her for all that she was and could become—like he *desired* her, every single part of her, something she'd had little experience with in her nineteen years, least of all from someone like him.

He looked at her, she realized, the way everyone always looked at Romie. Like she was the most magnetic, important person in his eyes.

She let her hand slide down so that it rested over his heart, this thing he was slowly letting her in on like a secret. She wanted to know more of it.

"You too," she breathed.

He waited, eyes searching hers. As if asking for permission. Emory nodded. She wasn't sure what she was agreeing to exactly, but it didn't matter, not as Keiran's mouth found hers again, and everything in her soared.

Her hands wove behind his neck, savoring the supple feel of his hair between her fingers. It moved something in him, and when he kissed her again, it was full of intent, an eagerness she responded to in kind. Lips parted and tongues collided. Keiran pressed against her, trapping her between him and the column at her back. He tasted of champagne, heady and sweet and utterly intoxicating.

And just as his lips grazed her neck, drawing a small sound from her throat, the loud creak of a door made them both pull away. At the other end of the cloisters, a student sleepily padded on by,

bleary-eyed and oblivious to them—a sleepwalking Dreamer, no doubt.

A breathless laugh slipped past Emory's lips. Keiran looked as if he wanted to capture the sound, eyes sparking as he drew closer again. She tilted her head up. His hand cupped her cheek, thumb skimming her bottom lip. She couldn't help but arch toward him, eyes fluttering hungrily to his mouth. It hovered just above hers, made her burn with anticipation as he slid his hand down her neck.

He winced suddenly, frowning down at his hand. The spiral on his wrist glowed faintly silver. His eyes grew distant as he listened to whoever was calling him, then focused on her again. "Artem wants to know how our summons went," he said with mild annoyance. "He's waiting for me at the gate. I should go."

Emory swallowed back her disappointment, though he made no move to pull away, his thumb still pressed against the heartbeat at the base of her throat. "Or you could stay," she breathed.

She thought he might oblige her, breach the small distance between them and kiss her once more. Instead, he tucked her curling hair behind her ear, eyes dark and heavy with want as he said, "Don't worry, Ainsleif. Plenty of time ahead of us." He pressed his mouth to her temple, sending shivers up her spine. "I'm not nearly done with you yet."

He kissed her brow, which felt more intimate than anything they'd done, and left her there with a dimpled smile that lingered like a promise.

She dreams of Dovermere again.

Flowers and plants bloom at her command as she walks in a cave slick with moss and algae. Sunflowers adorn little pools of standing water. Great vines of philodendrons trail in her footsteps. Everything is aglow in soft whites and blues,

pinks and greens, linked to her by shimmering threads of silver that pulse in time with her heartbeat. Every step she takes is full of life, and everything around her has a voice, a seed of consciousness, down to the barnacles on the rock, the minerals in the water.

She commands them. She is them. They are her and everything is connected, everything belongs.

She reaches the great beast's belly, though it feels more like a womb. In its middle is the towering silver hourglass full of slowly dripping black sand. She lays a hand atop the cool glass, feels a prickle against her palm. A single poppy sits atop the sand, calling to her.

Emory, Emory.

She feels the bloom suffocating in its prison of glass. Its need for air strains her own lungs. Silver blood drips from her hand as she breaks the hourglass and it shatters into a thousand pieces, melding with the fine black sand in its midst. She reaches for the poppy. It crumbles at her touch, withering away to dust.

Emory, Emory.

The voice is music, and it comes from a door. The door is set at the bottom of the hourglass, an opening through which the sand starts to vanish, sinking, swirling. She takes a step past the sharp shards of glass and into the receding sand.

She falls

into

darkness,

and finds it is a strangely loving embrace. It is the sea's beating heart, its doting hands pulling her home. Her feet wade through the shallows of this great nothingness, water cold as ice. More voices call her name now, an orchestra of sound, a tune half remembered guiding her through the dark,

and she wants so desperately to follow it. She knows the song and knows the voices, for they are a part of her in some inexplicable way.

She takes a step to meet them.

Hands hold her back, and Romie is there in the dark, stars forming a corona in the depthless expanse above her head.

"Emory." Her voice is the melody of crystal, clear and pure. "You're alive."

Of course I'm alive, but this is a dream, she thinks confusedly, even as a part of her wonders at how real Romie's hands feel, how bright her eyes shine, how even the sea seems to pause at the intrusion, as if her presence here is not right, not quite the dream's doing.

"Where are you?" she asks of her friend, because suddenly she knows she is somewhere other than here.

Romie opens her mouth, but only water spills from it as the sea wraps clawed, shadowed hands around her, eager to pull her back into its depths. The music around them is sharp now, angry. Romie reaches a desperate hand toward Emory, and on it there is a spiral burning silver.

All around them, nightmares erupt: blank eyes and stretched limbs over empty souls.

A screech makes Emory's ears burst and bleed.

A bloody tidal wave pulls her friend under. Her voice shouts Emory's name.

The shadows reach for Emory now, eager for her blood, her power–

Another pair of hands grips her arms. A different voice, this one close to her ear, velvet and darkness and the cold death of a burning star:

"Wake up."

✳

Emory woke with a gasp. She could swear constellations were swirling above her on the ceiling, an imagined sky that had followed her into the waking world. Her window was thrown open, clamoring against a sudden gust of wind. Outside, the sky flickered wildly with light, an electrical storm blowing past.

Brine and sea salt. The smell of the sea.

Already her dream was fading from memory—everything but Romie, the crystalline quality of her voice. And the other voice that pulled her from those deadly shadows, away from the dream itself . . .

Emory glanced at her wrist. The spiral scar shone faintest silver. A trick of the moonlight, perhaps. But she knew how it felt to have a Dreamer show up in her sleep. Romie had done it before, and Emory always remembered those dreams upon waking, how real Romie appeared to her in them. Just like she had now.

She grabbed a sweater, heart pounding with conviction. The dream was a message, a revelation, and Emory knew where she had to go.

But she couldn't go alone.

BAZ

BAZ COULDN'T SLEEP. HE TRIED TO READ BY THE FIRE-place, tried to distract himself by playing with Dusk, but nothing could ease the sharp ache that seeing Kai at the Institute had left him with. Kai's absence was everywhere, and it was unbearable.

He felt like the night sky outside, restless with a brewing storm.

With a frustrated sigh and his copy of *Song of the Drowned Gods* tucked under his arm, he headed out of the commons, hoping the Decrescens library might bring him the kind of solace he used to find here. When the elevator gate creaked open at the top, Baz swore, nearly dropping his book.

Emory was pacing in the corridor, looking half-crazed in a too-big sweater and striped pajama pants, her hair hanging in messy curls.

"Thank the Tides," she breathed with visible relief.

"What are you doing here?"

"I wasn't sure the wards would let me through." The tears lining her eyes gave him pause, and there was a desperate, pleading note

in her voice as she said, "I saw her. I saw Romie in a dream just now, and it was *real*, Baz."

His brow furrowed. "What are you talking about?"

"I dreamed of her in Dovermere. But it didn't feel like a normal dream. It was Dreamer magic, I'm sure of it." A sob that might have been a laugh slipped from her lips. "Romie's alive."

Baz blinked. Frowned. Shook his head. "That's impossible."

"I thought the same about Travers," Emory pressed, "yet we both know he wasn't quite dead when he washed up onshore."

"No. I had a Shadowguide look for her beyond the veil for precisely that reason. Romie's gone."

"What if she isn't?"

"She is. The Shadowguide told me—"

Baz stopped himself. Alya had told him there was nothing of Romie for her to find beyond the veil—that, like Adriana, her spirit had most likely moved on.

Spirits who aren't tethered to this plane sometimes seek horizons even us Shadowguides can't reach.

Emory grabbed the sleeve of his cardigan. "It was Romie. I could *feel* that she was alive, Baz. I don't know how, if it's because of my magic, or Dovermere, or . . ." She let go of him, clutching her tattooed hand to her chest. "I just know I have to go back there. I have to go to Dovermere, because what if she's there? What if she comes back like Travers did?"

Baz palmed the back of his neck, a thousand emotions fighting for control as he looked around the corridor, desperate for something to make sense of. Behind him, the elevator door still stood open. His mind went to the secret passage in the commons that led down to Dovermere. If there was a chance Emory was right . . .

To hell with everyone's warnings.

Baz met her gaze squarely. "Let's go find out."

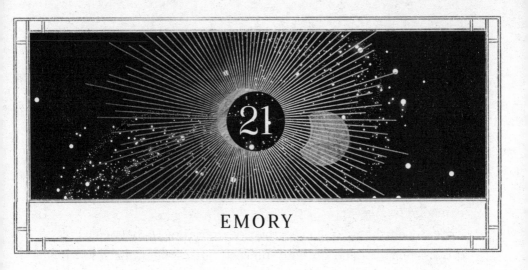

EMORY

EMORY WASTED NO TIME ONCE THEY GOT TO THE BEACH. She shucked off her shoes, waded into the sea, and plunged her hand into the cold, dark water lapping at her shins. She could feel Baz staring at the back of her neck, wariness and confusion coming off him in waves. She didn't care if he saw the silver light of her Selenic Mark. She didn't care what he thought as she closed her eyes and called on Romie with every fiber of her soul.

It's all about intention, Keiran had said.

She summoned every ounce of it as she thought of Romie, picturing her coming back to their room after long hours spent in her greenhouse: ruddy-brown curls wild around her round face, smudges of dirt streaked like paint over her freckled skin, earthy smell clinging to her clothes. Her brow would crease in concentration as she tried to find the perfect spot to put her newly potted plant in their dorm—much like Baz looked when he was reading.

I want to speak to Romie Brysden, Emory thought.

She opened her mind to Romie. Her fingers were going numb in the cold water, but there was no prickle on her wrist, no indication that the mark had even awakened. She called for Lia Azula and Jordyn Briar Burke, the other two students whose bodies hadn't been recovered, desperate for one of them to heed her call. For someone to answer.

Please, she begged the sea, the sky, everything in between.

Dovermere looked on with interest, but nothing answered the call.

Emory's eyes flew open. Furiously, she stepped deeper into the water, not giving a single thought to the pieces of broken shells that sliced her feet. Dream twisted into reality, reality into dream, and in every shadow she saw things of nightmare, thought she heard an echo of that song calling her forward.

I want to speak to Romie Brysden.

Ominous clouds swallowed up the stars. Behind her, Baz shouted her name, but she didn't listen.

Romie, please, answer me . . .

There was salt on her cheeks, her lips–from the sea or her tears, she couldn't tell. A wave threatened to knock her off-balance. Fingers dug painfully into her arm to keep her steady. Baz's face was inches from her own, eyes wide and distraught behind his glasses. She realized they were standing waist-deep in the water as another wave broke against them, making her lurch toward him. The Aldersea was stirring, as if angered at their presence. Wordlessly, they pulled each other back to shore, Baz's hand still tight around her arm. They stumbled onto the beach, falling to their knees on the wet sand. The cuts on her feet burned, but it was a distant sort of hurt. She didn't bother healing them.

"Are you *crazy*?" Baz bit out on a shaky breath.

Emory drew her knees close to her chest, trembling against the cold. Baz lingered at her side, shoulders tense, as if he thought she might flee into the water again. She pulled the coat he'd lent her more tightly around her. It was warm and dry and smelled like him.

"I know what I saw was real," she said forcefully. "I was dreaming of Dovermere. There was a melody . . . someone calling my name . . . I followed it into the sea and there she was. Her voice was crystal clear, Baz. Then the nightmare creatures came and pulled her into the waves, and someone told me to wake up, and I just *knew* I had to come here."

Emory's eyes drifted to the water, those cliffs. When she looked at Baz again, she noted the concerned line of his mouth, his utter stillness as he watched her.

Her shoulders slumped. "You don't believe me."

Baz held her gaze, and it felt like the whole world hinged on what he would say next. Something flickered in his eyes. Not quite reproach, not quite anger, but perhaps as close to it as it would ever get with him. It banked, disappearing as quickly as it had appeared, and when he spoke, his voice was soft, nearly drowned out by the waves.

"You told me you don't remember everything that happened that night. That there are pieces missing. And with Travers and everything that's happened . . . It can't be easy, to live with that kind of trauma. That guilt." His throat bobbed. "But Romie's dead, Emory. It took me this long to come to terms with it myself. But she's dead, and the sooner we accept it, the sooner we can move on with our lives."

Emory shook her head, wiping furiously at her tears, desperate to deny it. But his words broke something in her. He was right: Guilt chipped away at her soul. Guilt at not remembering exactly what occurred in Dovermere. Guilt over what happened to Travers

and Romie and all the others, which she could never know for certain wasn't her doing.

Everything might have been her fault. The result of her Eclipse magic unlocking at whatever strange pull Dovermere had on her. And even if the Selenic Order *did* find a way to bring back the Tides, and the deities managed to return those they'd lost to them, Emory would forever carry that guilt.

She tried to find an answer in Baz's eyes, searched for that glimmer of accusation she'd feared to see so many times, the resentment he surely harbored toward her. But the way he looked at her . . . There was none of that. Only a heartbreaking sort of understanding.

"You should hate me." Suddenly she couldn't stand his silence, his softness. An angry sob tore past her lips as she shoved at him. "Why don't you hate me, Baz?"

He reached for her as she moved to shove him again, freezing fingers wrapping around her wrists. Emory fought weakly against his hold, tears falling in earnest down her cheeks now.

"Emory . . ."

She came undone, sagging against the curve of his arms, and then he was holding her close, a solid weight to keep her from shattering. And here in the dark, with the angry sea and Dovermere's looming presence, with the crushing sadness and guilt and dream madness pressing down on her, *this* was the only thing that felt real. The sound of her name on his lips, the solidity of his embrace, the faint smell of coffee and bergamot that enveloped her, soothing, grounding, familiar.

Emory tilted her head up to his. She caught the shadow that fell on his face, the way his lips parted slightly, his throat bobbed.

She caught sight of something else, too, just out of the corner of her eye.

A figure rising from the water.

Emory gripped Baz's arm. He leaned in, mistaking the gesture for something else before he noticed the widening of her eyes, the leeching of color from her face. He turned around and startled, falling back with a swear.

"What is *that*?"

Emory was already on her feet, recognition spurring her to action as the figure drew nearer. She knew that small frame, those dark tresses. They were a mirror of another girl, another body that had found its way onto these shores. But where the other Azula twin had been strewn on the sand with her limbs bent at odd angles, this one was alive.

Unchanged.

Lia Azula stepped out of the sea, looking for all the world like she was emerging from a leisurely midnight swim. Her eyes found Emory's.

The night paused between them.

And then Lia collapsed on the sand.

Emory rushed to her side, barely hearing Baz calling out to her. She grabbed hold of Lia, who looked up at her with pleading eyes. Her mouth fell open, but no words came out, only a trickle of water.

Just like Travers. Just like Romie in her dream.

Emory braced for Lia's body to start disintegrating as Travers's had, readying her healing magic, but by then Lia was screaming, a wail that pierced the night. She staggered out of Emory's grasp and back toward the water. Her hands flew to her neck as her screams turned desperate, then faded to a gargled whimper, then to nothing at all. Emory flung her healing magic at her, desperate to stop whatever afflicted her.

Lia fell limply to the wet sand. She went utterly still, eyes fixed on the night sky. The spiral on her upturned wrist was black. Her

mouth hung agape, clouds of steam wafting from it, and Emory stumbled back at what she saw.

Baz fell to his knees on the other side of Lia's body, the whites of his eyes gleaming in the moonlight, as horror-struck as Emory's own.

The inside of Lia's mouth was charred down to her very throat. Burnt to a crisp.

And her tongue was missing.

BAZ

THERE WERE DIFFERENT KINDS OF SILENCE:

There were those Baz could comfortably sink into, like the peaceful lull of the Decrescens library with its featherweight fluttering of pages and steady heartbeats of clocks, or the early hours of the morning in the Eclipse commons when the world had yet to rise.

There were those he found unbearable, the awkward pauses and long silences he always felt the need to fill but never quite knew how.

And then there was the knife-edged kind, too full of unsaid words yet too fragile to break, the sort of silence that meant everything was about to change.

Such a silence lingered in the Eclipse commons, punctuated only by the steady drip of brewing coffee, Emory's soft breathing where she slept on the sofa, the screeching of gulls outside as the morning sun ascended. But even those sounds were quiet, hesitant. As if scared to cut themselves on the sharp truth of it all.

Baz feared if he listened close enough, he might hear Lia's bloodcurdling scream trapped somewhere in that silence.

He kept seeing it, the way she'd clawed at her throat. The way the sound had suddenly been wrenched from her lungs as the inside of her mouth and throat and tongue were burnt to a crisp. The mark on her wrist a muted black. Her eyes staring unblinkingly at the sky, at the waxing moon that birthed her.

We are born of the moon and tides, and to them we return.

The saying had come to him on the beach and would not leave him. Nothing felt real.

Emory's eyes met his from across the room. The soft morning light drew out the gold in her hair, which had dried in messy curls draped over the arm of the sofa. It was strange seeing her there, in Kai's favorite spot. She wore a too-big flannel shirt and slacks she'd borrowed from him last night, her own clothes left near the window to dry.

Baz tried not to blush.

"Hi," she said, and he was glad not to be the one to break the quiet.

Just like that, reality came crashing down around them. The weight of what they'd seen, what they'd done, so much starker now in the daylight.

Emory sat up, glancing warily at the window that overlooked Dovermere.

"Is she . . ."

A shake of his head. "Someone must have found her."

A fisherman, a student, anyone but them. It was what they'd intended when they left Lia's body on the beach: that someone might find it at dawn, and they'd assume it was simply brought in by the tide.

He and Emory had decided on it by some unspoken agreement as they knelt in the sand, reeling from everything that happened.

Afterward, Baz had led her back up the secret stairs to the Eclipse commons, where they'd gotten out of their wet clothes and fallen asleep on the sofas, too spent to even talk about it.

The coffee was ready. Baz poured two cups and handed one to Emory as he sat in the chair across from her.

She drew her feet under her, wrapped her hands around the warm cup. She looked around the shabby space, as if seeing it for the first time, with the cloud of urgency and veil of darkness from last night finally lifted.

"Doesn't it ever get lonely down here, all by yourself?"

"Sometimes."

Not presently, he thought, and when her gaze met his, he was sure she understood. It felt . . . nice, to have her here. Like this was something they'd been heading toward all their lives, and now she was here, in her rightful house. With him.

Emory took a sip. A sunken feeling gripped Baz at the widening of her eyes.

"What is it?"

"Nothing, just . . . Tides, I get it now, why you never drink the coffee I bring you." She took another gulp. "This is *divine*."

Baz couldn't help it—he laughed, the sound unfamiliar to his own ears. It eased something in his chest to see the laughter reflected in her eyes. The weight of last night wasn't so heavy, he thought, carried as it was between the two of them. Still, as Emory's attention drifted to the window again, brows scrunching together as if she could see the scene replaying on the beach below, Baz decided they desperately needed a distraction.

"Come on." He set his coffee down on the table. "Let me give you the official tour of Obscura Hall."

He could have shown her the precariously stacked books, the initials carved in the tapestry, the bedrooms upstairs. But the true

glory of their house was just outside the Eclipse commons themselves. Emory faltered as he opened the door and parted the lush mane of leaves draped over the other side. Tentatively, she followed him out. She turned on her heel to puzzle over the great willow tree they'd emerged from, the door carved in its trunk left slightly ajar.

Baz tried to see it all through her eyes. The field of wild grass swaying in the breeze. The beaten path that cut through patches of boneset and gorse, hyssop and snakeroot, bordered by a rope fence that ran down the gently sloping hill toward a strip of white-sand beach and the sea beyond. The ceiling-less expanse above their heads, open skies and puffy white clouds.

Emory ran her fingers through the yellowing feather-reed grass, and Baz knew she must be grappling with how real the illusion felt, how impossible it was that this should be in the lower levels of Aldryn. He saw it in the wonder on her face as she took in the sky, the sea, as she breathed in the smell of brine and grass on the air and strained her ear to the sound of gulls and the buzzing of bees and the melody of songbirds.

"I didn't quite believe it last night," she murmured. "It all felt like a dream, but now . . . How is this possible?"

"Illusion magic. This path through the field is really just a corridor, and the sea isn't really there—well, it is, but there's technically a wall between us and it. Same with the willow tree. The common room inside it is real. The rest of it is just a trick of the mind."

It was a remnant of the magic that Illusionists had wielded over the years, though the shape of the illusion itself was entirely dependent upon the students presently occupying Obscura Hall. It changed to suit the preference of the oldest student there, taking on a scenery that held some meaning to them. And since Baz was the only Eclipse student remaining . . .

"It reminds me of the fields behind Threnody Prep," Emory said. "The ones we used to run in with Romie, remember?"

Baz felt his face heat. Of course he remembered. It was the image he cherished the most, the ideal he had of happiness. A simpler time he often wished he could return to.

One particular day always came to mind. It had been gloomy all week, storms battering the seaside town of Threnody, and when the sun at last pierced the sky, Romie had coaxed Baz and Emory to slip out from the boarding school while the rest of the students were at some assembly.

The images were imprinted on his soul, how the light hit Emory's face and made her hair shine like gold. He remembered the sound of her laugh and the way she'd smiled, the blue of her eyes, how everything had felt right in the world before it all got ripped apart days later by his father's Collapsing. He remembered the weightlessness of running downhill through singing tall grass, the sharp briny smell in the air, and the coarse sand beneath him as the three of them fell in a heap on the beach, heads turned to the clear blue sky.

Look how free they are, Romie had said of the gulls soaring above them. She'd pushed herself up and run into the water after them, arms extended on either side of her as if she, too, were about to fly away.

He remembered stealing a glance at Emory's rosy-cheeked face then and thinking he would like to stop time, freeze the here and now and live in it forever. She had smiled at him, and his heart had never been so full.

Baz cleared his throat, wondering if that day meant the same to her as it did him. Likely not. It had gotten him through the darkest days of his youth. A memory he'd clung to in the aftermath of his father's Collapsing, the place he went to in his mind when he sought reprieve. It had planted a seed in his heart, and hope that

she might feel the same about him made it bloom–only to wilt away to nothing when she'd pulled away from him like everyone else.

But that was long ago. And now . . . Now he didn't know. Didn't want to let himself hope again only to see it crushed.

Still, he replayed the moment right before Lia had appeared. How close they'd been. The glimmer in Emory's eyes, as if she were finally seeing him.

Baz kicked at the dirt path. "Speaking of Romie . . ." He palmed the back of his neck. "I stayed up all night going over everything in my head. Trying to make sense of the pattern between the two bodies that washed ashore."

They had reappeared on a night that corresponded to their respective lunar houses, each succumbing to strange magics that seemed to twist their own: Travers, a Healer, withering away to a husk of a person; Lia, a Wordsmith, robbed of her ability to speak.

And Emory–always Emory at the heart of it. As if her mere presence at Dovermere had called to them somehow, drawing them back to these shores from the depths that had claimed them.

She seemed to read his thoughts, her gaze drifting to the imagined sea. "Maybe it is all my fault."

The quiet despair in her voice compelled him to reach for her, just like he had last night.

Why don't you hate me, Baz?

Instead, he shoved his hands in his pockets, too scared of screwing up whatever tentative, fledgling thing might be between them. "It doesn't matter now," he offered weakly.

"How can you say that after what happened?"

"Passing around blame won't bring Romie back. What we need now is to figure out what the hell's going on so we can save her."

He had just started to accept her death and move on, as

everyone around him said he should. But that was before Lia showed up without a tongue. Certainty now thrummed at his fingertips, because of this he was sure:

Romie was alive.

Alive.

It felt almost too big, too impossible to even think it, but it had to be true.

He eyed Emory's wrist, where he'd seen the spiral on her skin glow silver. "You put your hand in the water last night, and that mark glowed." Her silence spoke volumes. Baz pressed on: "Tell me what it is. What you were trying to do with it."

She chewed the inside of her cheek, and he thought for a moment she would lie again, tell him it was nothing. "It appeared that night in Dovermere." The words came haltingly, as if she were weighing each one. "I'm not sure how, exactly, but when I woke up on the beach, there it was. The others . . . the ones who didn't make it . . . They all had it too, though theirs was black. I thought maybe Dovermere marking us this way might connect us. That if Romie was alive, maybe I could . . ."

"You thought you might reach her somehow?"

Emory nodded. She studied him, a crease forming between her brows. "That note you showed me of Romie's. Why do you think she went to Dovermere because of *Song of the Drowned Gods*?"

Baz hesitated for only a second. A part of him still wasn't sure he could trust her—she was clearly still hiding something from him, yet she'd trusted *him* enough to come straight to him after seeing Romie in her dreams, despite how her involvement in all of this made her look. She was just as eager for answers as he was—that much he believed. And now they held the secret of Lia between them and needed to figure out what was going on before it happened again.

So he told her everything: Romie's interest in the relation

between Dovermere and *Song of the Drowned Gods*, her search for the missing epilogue and belief in the existence of other worlds. His own research into the parallels between the Tides and the drowned gods, the Deep and the sea of ash. The song heard between the stars and the doors to the Deep and the spiral Emory bore, a symbol somehow tied to all of it, just as she seemed to be.

She stroked the scar on her wrist, a pensive look in her eye. "You think the four students who vanished–Travers, Lia, Jordyn, Romie . . . They all went through a door inside Dovermere. To answer the call of fictional gods that may or may not be the Tides themselves."

"Possibly." The look on her face wasn't as skeptical as he'd have thought, which was a relief. "What else might explain how two of them have come back now, still alive and seemingly fine? Not a scratch on them, no bloated skin, not a single sign of starvation or *anything* when they first appeared. No one can survive that long inside those caves. Unless they're not *inside* the caves at all." His thoughts raced. "Do you remember seeing anything that might resemble such a door?"

He almost felt bad for asking as he glimpsed the haunted look in her eye.

"No," she breathed, "nothing like that."

Baz knew it couldn't be that easy, yet he refused to let it go. "You said you heard a melody in your dream. What if it's the same one Romie was hearing?"

A beat as they shared a look.

"You think it's the song in *Song of the Drowned Gods*," Emory said.

"*Something* is calling you to Dovermere. Just as it called Romie." And Kai.

Baz pressed on, too worked up now to stop: "There are

four heroes in *Song of the Drowned Gods.* Four people who cross through worlds to find the sea of ash. And there were four students that night whose bodies never made it out of Dovermere."

Four students born of four moon phases, each with a different magic: Healer, Wordsmith, Soultender, Dreamer.

Blood and bones and heart and soul.

"What about the four students who washed up onshore with me that night?" Emory asked.

In her eyes he thought he could glimpse those bodies, could imagine the horror she must have felt when she came to on the beach, surrounded by death.

There are tides that drown and tides that bind . . .

"Maybe they just . . . died. Drowned by the tide. Maybe the door only admits four. You didn't go through it either."

"That still doesn't explain how Travers and Lia came back," Emory argued.

"That's the real question, isn't it? Because if the four of them did somehow go through a door they'd been searching for, be it to the Deep or the sea of ash or some other distant shore, what would make them turn back? And most importantly, what might make them suffer such horrible deaths once they returned?"

The image of Lia's burnt insides and Travers's withered corpse flashed between them.

Emory looked at Baz expectantly, brows slightly arched. "Clearly, you have a theory."

A rush of excitement and growing certainty vibrated through him. "If the missing epilogue is the key to traveling between worlds, they must have never found it. They tried to do it without this key element, and now they're stuck."

"Stuck where?"

. . . and those that dance 'neath stranger skies.

Baz pushed his glasses up the bridge of his nose. "In another world."

He knew how it sounded, knew it made little sense—and yet, maybe there was truth to Clover's story after all. Maybe the Veiled Atlas had it right.

"Whatever it is," he said, "Romie and Jordyn are still alive *somewhere*. We just have to figure out how to get to them before the same thing that happened to Travers and Lia happens to them, too."

EMORY

A LETTER WAS WAITING FOR HER UNDER HER DOOR.
Emory had been about ready to cry as she rushed back to
her room, intent on changing out of Baz's clothes and getting her
thoughts in order. The sight of her father's handwriting on the
envelope finally brought her to tears.

A pang of homesickness washed over her as she opened it. Her
mind conjured her father in stark detail: reddish-blond hair a tangled mess that fell to his shoulders, a big smile in the middle of his
beard. Emory imagined burying her face in the rough-spun wool of
his sweater, the scent of brown bread and chowder in the kitchen,
playing cards together in the evenings while a fire crackled in the
hearth. She could almost hear his gruff voice in her ears as she
read his words:

> *My dearest Emory,*
> *I hope the issue with your magic's been resolved—*
> *maybe it was only nerves?*

I'm not sure how Luce could have lied. I've been
trying to think of anything strange she might have said
or done, but she was a mystery wrapped in charm,
wit, and quick smiles–everything about her was
peculiar, in the best of ways, of course, but nothing
out of sorts comes to mind.

I did find something of hers she must have left
when she brought you to me, or maybe before that,
I'm not sure. It seemed useless at the time–I probably
stashed it in a drawer and forgot all about it. I think
it's broken, but it's yours to do with what you please.

I hope you're happier than when I saw you last.
You know I'm just a train ride away.
Dad

Her heart lurched at the last line. After Dovermere, the summer months she'd spent at home had been a mess for both of them. She'd been inconsolable with grief, a ship unmoored, and he'd been so patient with her, a steady presence to count on. And as much as she knew it worried him to see her leave in the midst of all that, she knew he was relieved, too. He hadn't known what to do with her, and it had pained her terribly to see him fret so much.

She reached for the heavy object at the bottom of the envelope and frowned at it. It was a pocket watch, or a compass. Both, somehow. An intricate design full of needles and cogs and wheels she could see no apparent use for, frozen there behind the scratched glass. She turned it over, and on the brassy gold were initials so weathered she could barely make them out: *VA.*

The name of a ship, perhaps. Or a plundered treasure.

Emory threw it into a drawer. The only thing of her mother's she owned, and it was utterly useless.

She was a mystery wrapped in charm, wit, and quick smiles, her father had written. More like a mystery veiled in lies, deceit, and abandonment.

Her gaze caught on the vials of salt water and the bloodletting bowl on her desk. She rubbed at her spiral mark, wondering if she should contact Keiran and tell him everything that had happened, because if anyone could make sense of it, she thought, it was him.

But then she'd have to admit to Baz's involvement, tell Keiran the truth about what Baz knew, how he'd been helping her all this time. She'd lied to Keiran when all he'd done up until now was trust her implicitly. He'd put all his faith in her, and now Lia was dead, probably because of her.

She couldn't tell him the truth now, after everything that had happened.

Her selenography textbook sat beneath the bloodletting bowl. With a start, she realized today was her makeup exam—which she was going to be late for if she didn't hurry.

Emory headed to class, trying to recall everything she'd been studying. Her mind went blank as she reached the classroom and saw everyone waiting outside whispering behind their morning newspapers. There was a thrum of tension in the air, subdued excitement. She caught a glimpse of the headline visible on the front page, and it was like déjà vu:

BODY OF ANOTHER DROWNING VICTIM FOUND AT DOVERMERE.

Lia.

She grabbed a discarded paper and flipped to the article in question, eyes roving over the text in search of anything incriminating. But it was as she and Baz expected: some fisherman had found the body at dawn, and since no one saw the gruesome way Lia died, it was simply assumed her body had washed in with the tide. It said an inquiry was to be made, autopsy and all,

but there was no mention here of her charred mouth or missing tongue.

No doubt keeping those gruesome details quiet.

She spotted Penelope with a newspaper in hand, blinking back tears.

Penelope looked at her as if in a daze. "I wonder if her parents know. I should give them a call, right?"

"Nel, I'm so sorry . . ." Emory hadn't thought of it until now, how Lia's body being found would affect her friend. The devastation on Penelope's face was heart-wrenching. She wished she had some comfort to offer her. At least, she told herself, Penelope hadn't seen it. At least now, Lia's body could be lain to rest next to her twin sister, Dania.

"What can I do to help?"

"Nothing." Penelope tried for a smile. "I'm fine, really. I just . . . I need to go. Will you tell Professor Cezerna?"

"Of course. I'm here if you need me."

Guilt knifed through Emory's heart. This was all her fault, in the end.

It was no small miracle that she passed her selenography exam, and that she managed to focus long enough to finish at all. She left the class wondering if Professor Cezerna might have been more lenient at grading her than he normally would, given the situation.

One less thing to worry about, at least.

She was waiting in line at the coffee cart when Virgil sidled up to her. "Thanks for saving me a spot," he greeted her lightly. "I'm in desperate need of caffeine this morning." He winked at her, ignoring the nasty looks he got for cutting in line, and asked, "Did you see the newspaper?"

"I did," Emory said, reminding herself that Virgil didn't know what really happened.

"Bit odd she washed ashore on the same night we did the ritual," Virgil mused.

She hadn't considered that. "Do you think it might have had something to do with it?"

"Maybe it was the Tides' way of letting us know they heard us." He gave a nonchalant shrug. "At least whatever fucked-up thing happened to Travers didn't happen to her, right?"

Emory met his gaze, and she wondered if he saw beneath her mask–if he could somehow sense Lia's death on her.

This disquieting thought followed her all day. With the news of Lia's body, there were bound to be questions from the rest of the Selenics. From Keiran, too. She couldn't keep hiding the truth.

She called on Keiran through the mark that very evening. There was a brief silence, and then his voice sounded in her ear, here and not but wholly his.

"Ainsleif?"

"We need to talk. It's about Lia."

A pause. "Where are you?"

Minutes later, Keiran was on her doorstep, and for a second she was just a normal girl standing in front of the boy she kissed last night and wanted so very much to kiss again. If things weren't so Tides-damned screwed up, she might have done just that. As it was, Emory couldn't even look at him, didn't want him to see her pathetic tears, the wobble of her lip. She turned to the window. Behind her, the door closed with a soft thud. Keiran rested a warm hand on her arm and gently turned her to face him. His hazel eyes searched hers.

"Whatever it is, you can tell me."

Emory drew a breath. "I was there. It's my fault she's dead."

She told him everything–how Baz had been helping her try to hone her magic, how he'd gone down to the beach with her last night after she'd seen Romie in her dreams. She shared Baz's

theories on doors and Dovermere and that Tides-damned book of his, and doing so felt like betrayal on her part. But she owed Keiran the truth. He'd fought for her, kept her secret, trusted her despite his history with the Eclipse-born, and this changed *everything* they were working toward.

By the end, she sat on her bed, feeling utterly depleted. Keiran watched her quietly by the window.

"I think my presence at Dovermere is what called Travers and Lia back. Both times, I was at the beach, in the water." Emory traced her Selenic Mark. "I tried reaching Romie through the mark last night. What if I somehow called Lia back instead? If our ritual made it possible for her to hear me?"

"That wouldn't explain Travers, though," Keiran argued. "There was no ritual that time."

Emory groaned, grabbing her head between her hands. "Then maybe it's like Baz thinks, and there's this impossible dream song calling us to other worlds like in *Song of the Drowned Gods*." She laughed a little hysterically. "I don't know what to think anymore."

Keiran sat beside her, his warm hand caressing the back of her neck. She melted against his touch.

"If we're to assume Romie and Jordyn are still alive," he surmised, "maybe Brysden is right about them being stuck. Not in another world, but some kind of in-between. A purgatory between here and the Deep. Not quite living, not quite dead."

At the perplexed look Emory shot him, he added, "I've done my own fair share of research on Dovermere and these supposed doors to the Deep, read everything I can in preparation for waking the Tides. We know for a fact that Dovermere holds power beyond our understanding. I'm sure you felt it when you were there, the dark pull of the Hourglass. Like a beast you know you shouldn't approach but want to touch regardless."

In her mind she heard an echo of her whispered name as the caves filled with water.

"If Dovermere's both the place the Tides were birthed in and vanished to," Keiran continued, "it would make sense for it to be a gateway to the Deep itself. And maybe it opened last spring because, for the first time in the Order's history, the circle around the Hourglass was complete. With magic not just of the four lunar houses, but of House Eclipse, too."

Cold licked up Emory's spine. If her mere presence had opened this door to the Deep, then *she* had sent the four of them to purgatory.

She might as well have sentenced them to death.

As if reading her mind, Keiran ventured another guess. "What if by escaping death that night, you formed a link to those Dovermere *did* claim? Maybe that's how Romie could contact you in your dream, why Travers and Lia both came back when you were near Dovermere. Death left its mark on you all."

Emory shook her head. "But if I called them back to the world of the living, why did they *die*?"

This seemed to throw him for a loop. He stared into the middle distance. "The Deep demands payment," he said quietly. His gaze sharpened, focused on her. "Think about it. No one has crossed through those doors and lived to tell the tale because such a crossing demands payment. Because no one can step into the Deep and return to the living without first paying the price. If Travers and Lia had one foot in the underworld before crossing back into the world of the living . . . it might explain their strange deaths."

Emory's heart raced. "They both lost their magic in some strange reversal of their power." A Healer withering away to bones. A Wordsmith losing the ability to speak things into being. "You think that was the payment demanded by the Deep?"

Keiran nodded grimly. "Their magic—their very lifeblood—in

exchange for the act of crossing into the underworld. Maybe Brysden's theory about the lost epilogue isn't too far off. This idea of holding a key to cross through worlds . . . it makes sense. Take Reapers and Shadowguides, for example. The veil to the Deep is thinner for them than it is for anyone else. They have the countenance for it, have been blessed by the Tides with gifts that have them closely intertwined with death. But even they can't *physically* find themselves in the Deep. They'd need some kind of protection to survive it."

"You mean the epilogue?"

"Maybe. Or something the epilogue might have hinted at. If Romie was researching such a possibility, she might know how we can go through that door and come back from the Deep unscathed. It's the missing piece to what we've been trying to achieve."

"Romie's the key to all of it," Emory breathed.

"And she found a way to contact you in a dream." Keiran's eyes glistened. "With your power . . . you could wield Dreamer magic too. Reach her in the sleepscape, find out what we need to wake the Tides. To save her too."

Emory shied away from the intensity in his expression. The kind of magic he was asking her to do was far beyond her reach. After last night's ritual, she wasn't even sure how this Tidecaller thing worked anymore. Would she need to come into contact with a Dreamer first to mirror their magic, or could she call on it through her own power? It was too much to think of.

"Hey." Keiran pressed his forehead to hers, fingers weaving through her hair. "We're so close, Ains. I know you can do this."

His words—this utter faith in her he seemed to have—thrilled and scared her in equal measure. "If this fails, I'm blaming you," she said lightly, forcing the corners of her mouth up.

"There it is," Keiran whispered. "That smile."

A featherlight brush of his lips against hers had her eyes fluttering

shut. Warmth rushed to her face as he trailed delicate kisses down her jaw. She was burning and nothing mattered–until Lia's incinerated mouth flashed in her mind.

Emory pulled away with a start, fresh horror on her face.

"What's wrong?"

"I'm sorry," she said. "I just ... with everything that's happened ..."

"No, of course." Keiran kissed her forehead. "I'll go."

She pressed a hand to his arm as he started to get up. "Wait."

It wasn't that she didn't want to go further with him–because Tides, she did. And it wasn't that she'd never gone further than kissing before, either. Her first time had been a fumbling experience with a boy at Threnody Prep; her second, a drunken romp with another New Moon student during her first week at Aldryn. Both instances had been disappointing and fleeting, fueled by mindless attraction and this nagging sense that she needed to *catch up*. It was silly, really, but all she could do then was compare herself to bold, experienced Romie, whose generous curves and aura of confidence turned heads wherever she went. Meanwhile, Emory was always overlooked, for who would spare a glance at her, the timid, reserved, bland girl, when they were blinded by the blazing sun that was Romie?

But this thing with Keiran, whatever it was . . . It felt different. Suddenly *she* was the sun, and he looked at her like she was everything he'd ever wanted. She'd never known this kind of rush–this kind of budding intimacy. And she wanted so desperately to see it flourish.

"Stay with me?"

She flushed as the words left her mouth. A part of her didn't think it was her place to ask such a thing of him, but the thought of being alone–of falling asleep and possibly dreaming of Romie again, or not dreaming of her at all–was unbearable.

Understanding lit Keiran's eyes. He settled back against the

headboard and drew her into the crook of his arm. They stayed like that for a while in comfortable silence.

Thinking of Lia, Emory asked, "Did Farran . . . Was he lost to Dovermere, or did his body . . ."

"We got to bury him," Keiran murmured.

"What was he like?"

"He was the kindest person I knew. He saw only the good in everyone, in the world itself. He was a hopeless romantic that way." His hand drew slow circles on her arm. "It ate away at his heart to see anyone in pain. Back in prep school, he was dating someone in secret. An Eclipse-born. He thought none of us knew, but we did. It was so painfully obvious how smitten he was. We never brought it up, though, thinking he'd tell us on his own terms. But after what happened with our parents . . . I think he thought he had to choose. That staying with an Eclipse-born would be an affront to us and the memory of our parents. He was different after that, wanted so desperately to ease our hurt that he threw himself into this endeavor to wake the Tides, and nothing else mattered."

Then, so soft she might not have heard him: "He shouldn't have felt like he had to choose. I always regretted not telling him that."

Emory supposed she understood better now why he was so quick to accept her being Eclipse-born. He thought he'd failed his friend by making him feel like he couldn't be with who he wanted to be, simply because they were from House Eclipse.

But the mistake of a single Eclipse-born wasn't all of theirs to shoulder.

When she finally drifted to sleep, she wished with all her being to be carried back to Romie. But her dreams were void, her friend nowhere in them.

BAZ

EMORY FOUND BAZ IN THE DECRESCENS LIBRARY FIRST thing the next morning.

"What do you know of the sleepscape?" she asked without preamble.

He shot her a skeptical look. "Why?"

She spread her hands on the table. "I want to try reaching Romie in dreams. And before you say anything, I know this is complex magic that's far bigger than anything else I've wielded, and I *know* you think I'm reckless and not ready to start training yet, but unless you thought of something better, this really is the only option we have."

For Tides' sake. His coffee hadn't even properly kicked in yet.

Before Baz could object, Emory angled her body toward him, leaning in close. "Let me at least try. For Romie's sake."

There was a hitch in his breath at her sudden proximity, the softness of her plea. His eyes caught on her lips. Images from the other night tugged at his memory: the way she'd held on to him as waves

crashed around them, how close they'd been before spotting Lia in the water.

His throat bobbed. He tried to come up with an argument against her plan but couldn't. She was right: it was their only recourse. "All right."

She pulled back in shock. "Really?"

"Yes, really."

"All right, then." Emory sank in the chair across from him. "The problem is I don't know the first thing about accessing the sleepscape."

"Neither do I." A field of purple-black poppies glared at him from the stained-glass window above. Baz sighed, pinching the bridge of his nose. "But I know someone who does."

Emory lifted a brow. "No one else knows about me being a Tide-caller, Baz. We can't exactly waltz up to any Dreamer and have them show me how it works."

"Not a Dreamer," he said darkly. "A Nightmare Weaver."

SONG
OF THE
DROWNED
GODS

PART IV:

THE GUARDIAN
AT THE GATE

There is a faraway world where things grow like a song builds to its crescendo.

There is always music there. Melodies that make and unmake beneath strangely dancing skies. Symphonies of lightning and thunder and whispering winds. Dissonant chords plucked in the space between stars like faint echoes of worlds beyond.

It is atop the highest peak hidden in the clouds that a boy gives audience to this divine orchestra. He sits by the icy gates he is tasked with guarding, lonely but never alone. The music keeps him company, the winged horses, too, and he has his lyre to play when he aches for something more attuned to his moods.

But mostly he listens.

Not many people listen, and so the moon and sun and stars share their secrets with the boy. They sing visions that swim in his eyes and chant prophecies that prickle at his skin. They whisper of bloodstreams that are also lungs and rib cages that wrap around hearts and the hollow at the center of it all where a once-sprawling sea turned to ash and its once-mighty gods were left unmoored.

Listen, they whisper. *Hear the blood and hear the bones and hear the fiercely beating heart.*

They fill his soul with hope, longing, purpose, and soon the boy is too unstrung to merely sit and listen.

It is his turn to make music now, to voice all the secrets he cannot keep alone.

Thus he picks up his lyre and begins to play.

Can you hear him? The boy who sings of silver and

marble and gold? The gods speak through him, and he lets them, thinking himself the cleverer adversary. *Come,* he beckons the scholar and the witch and the warrior whose souls are an echo of his own. *Seek me as I see you.*

He wills the chords of his lyre to draw them a map among the stars, and the skies weep to hear the sound.

Patience, they whisper. *Take heart.*

They will find him among the stars—he is certain of it.

And so the boy waits by his gate, still lonely, but not for long.

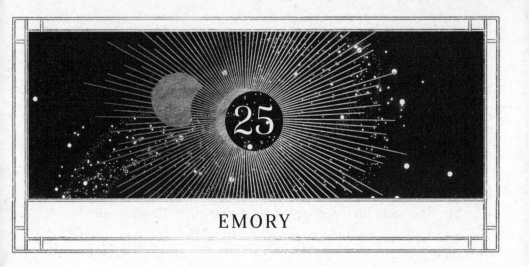

EMORY

THE SIGHT OF THE INSTITUTE MADE EMORY'S SKIN CRAWL.
She was caught off guard again by the New Moon sigil on
Baz's right hand as they climbed out of the cab. He met her gaze,
face bloodless.

"This will work, right?"

Emory ground her teeth. "Let's hope."

It had been Baz's idea to mask his Eclipse sigil to get inside the
Institute—*a little illusion work to get us through the door*, he'd
said—but the inspiration behind it had sprung from her. They'd
been in Obscura Hall under the twilit hues of its imagined sky, trying to figure out how to get into the Institute—notorious for turning
away Eclipse-born for no reason, according to Baz—when she had
reached for Baz's magic, wondering what it might feel like to bend
time to her will.

It had felt like plunging into shockingly cold waters, her lungs filling with it as she gasped for breath. She didn't know which way was
up or down, how to pull away from this magic that felt terrifyingly

foreign, vast and complicated and crushing in a way she would never understand. She'd finally sputtered out of its grasp, eyes wide and clutching at her chest, to find Baz reaching for her as if he'd meant to shake her out of her stupor.

His voice trembled. "What in the Tides' name was that?"

Emory hadn't known how to describe it, how scary it had felt. She'd thought Eclipse magics might somehow be easier for her to wield, that being Eclipse-born herself would create an affinity for them.

"Tidecallers drew on the lunar magics of the *Tides*, not the Shadow's own magic," Baz had argued like it was the most obvious thing in the world.

But Emory was undeterred. Now that she'd tried it, she wanted to see how far she could go, test the limits of her power. "What if I tried with another Eclipse magic?"

Somehow, she managed to sway him, and it was how she found herself reaching for the Illusion magic around them. It wasn't as overwhelming as Baz's magic, though it still felt dangerous. Like treading murky water without knowing when she might drop into an abyss. She got the sense that one wrong step would bring her to Collapse faster than it would take Baz to reach for his magic to stop her.

In the end, she'd painstakingly succeeded in making a single sunflower appear in the fields of rippling tall grass. It felt like using Sower magic, in a sense, but so much harder, given that she was conjuring something from nothing.

After practicing enough times to get the hang of it, it was with this same Illusion magic that she'd made the dark moon and sunflower of Baz's Eclipse tattoo disappear, leaving his left hand perfectly unmarred, while on his right was a near-flawless rendition of the dark moon and narcissus of House New Moon's sigil. Same as hers.

Baz caught her smiling at her handiwork and flexed his hand. "If it gets too hard to hold the illusion . . ."

"I know." She could already feel the strain of it on her magic, how difficult it was to keep the illusion up. The sunflower had felt easier: once sprung into being, it had stopped draining her power, though the illusion had then slowly withered away to nothing. For this, she needed to keep a hold on the magic long enough at least to get them into the Institute–*without* Collapsing.

A stern-faced Regulator greeted them at the door. "Purpose of your visit?"

"We're visiting a Collapsed patient," Baz answered with surprising calm. "Kai Salonga."

The Regulator noted the New Moon tattoos on their hands. "Identity cards."

Emory felt Baz stiffen ever so slightly as the Regulator looked at their cards, searched their faces. For a moment, she thought it wouldn't work. But the Regulator handed them back their cards and motioned them through the next door with a bored jerk of the head.

Baz blew out a sigh. Emory forced a smile; the magic was already taking its toll. *Just a while longer,* she told herself as an attendant led them through the maze of corridors. The edges of her vision began to blur.

"Let go of it," Baz muttered at her side. "*Now.*"

She didn't need to be told twice. Emory sighed in relief as she let go of the illusion. Baz tugged on his sleeves, hiding the back of his hands. She hoped it would be enough.

They were brought to a small inner courtyard where another attendant watched over four patients: an aging man and a middle-aged woman playing chess, a girl not much older than Emory huddled in the corner drawing in a notebook, and Kai, sitting cross-legged on a bench with a book open in his lap. Without

taking his eyes off his reading, he swept his shoulder-length dark hair back, tying it in a low bun. The sunlight caught the delicate chains he wore around his neck, complementing the warm undertones of his skin, and Emory thought she saw the edges of a tattoo peeking out from his shirt.

Kai finally caught sight of them as he lifted his head. His eyes narrowed in on Baz, and the air between them grew taut in a way Emory didn't quite understand.

"Back so soon, Brysden?"

Emory seized. That voice . . .

There was a curious glint in Kai's gaze as it fell on her. She stood completely hypnotized.

"This is Emory Ainslief," Baz said with an awkward clearing of his throat. "She's a friend. Of Romie's."

"You were in my dream the other night," Emory blurted.

Kai's brow shot up. "Was I now?"

There was no mistaking his voice, like a midnight breeze.

That way lies madness, dreamling.

Wake up.

"You were there when I saw Romie. You woke me from my dream."

"In case you hadn't noticed where I'm currently being kept," Kai sneered as he motioned to his branded hand, to the heavy damper cuffs around his wrists, "I can assure you I'm in no position to be walking into anyone's slumber."

Something in his tone, in the faint recognition he tried to hide from his eyes, told her he knew *exactly* what she was referring to.

"How else would I have dreamed of you when I've never even met you?" She'd seen him around campus a few times, had heard of him sure enough, but this went beyond that.

"You know what they say," Kai said in a wry way that reminded her a bit of Virgil. "Dreams are manifestations of our unconscious

desires." He gave her a disinterested once-over. "I'm flattered, though you're not exactly my type."

Did she imagine the way his eyes cut to Baz? Baz was frowning between them, looking completely oblivious to the insinuation. "I think I saw you too," he said to Kai. "After I came to visit you. I had the nightmare again . . ."

He trailed off. A loaded look passed between him and Kai, and Emory felt like she was intruding on something deeply personal.

"I thought I was seeing things," Baz breathed, "but you were really there, weren't you?"

Kai watched Baz for a beat, and something changed in him, as if having Baz admit that he'd also seen him in his sleep had settled something. Whatever pretense he'd been assuming vanished. He spoke in a sinister undertone: "Told you they were doing weird shit to us."

"Wait—what weird shit?" Emory asked, feeling completely out of the loop.

"The night I visited Kai," Baz explained grimly, "the Regulators did something to one of the Eclipse-born here. There were screams and weird power surges. That's the night I saw Kai in my sleep." He frowned at the U on Kai's hand. "But it doesn't make sense. How can you access the sleepscape if your magic is sealed?"

"Fuck if I know," Kai groaned. "The first time it happened, I thought I was going crazy. I tried doing it again, but it never worked unless the Regulators were making someone scream. Then I'd find myself pulled into the sleepscape, like whatever they did messed with the seal on my magic, and it managed to slip through the cracks some-how. Last time it happened was on the fall equinox."

"That's the night I saw you," Emory said. It felt a tad violating to have had him in her head, even if he *had* snapped her out of that twisted dream. "Why me, though?"

"No idea. I have no control over it. Usually it's the nightmares of

those closest to me that call. Or those of other Dreamers." He tilted his head to peer at her New Moon sigil. "But you're no Dreamer."

Baz shot Emory a sidelong glance. "That's the thing," he said slowly. "She kind of . . . is?"

At Kai's dubious expression, Emory explained, "I'm a Dreamer, and a Healer, a Lightkeeper, a Sower, an Illusionist . . . I'm all of that and more, or can be if I choose to, because I'm a Tidecaller."

It felt strangely empowering to say it aloud—until Kai snickered at her, full of disbelief.

"Sure you are. And I'm the Shadow himself." He looked at Baz. "Don't tell me you believe this nonsense."

"I've seen her use Tidecaller magic myself."

"And I've seen nightmares that would make you both gouge your eyes out—doesn't make them real."

"You just admitted to using magic even though you have the seal," Emory shot back. "You might want to reevaluate what can be real or not."

"Trust me, I think I have a fairly decent ability to tell reality from fantasy."

Kai's gaze pierced her soul, and for a delirious moment, she wondered if that cold sense of foreboding she felt was his magic, still alive somehow despite the brand that sealed it off. Baz took a step forward. He spoke Kai's name in warning, as if he, too, wondered if his power might not be as slumbering as it should be.

The feeling subsided as Kai settled back against the bench. He gave her a thin smile. "All right, say you're a Tidecaller. What is it you're here for? I'd throw you a welcome party, but seeing as I've been basically kicked out of House Eclipse myself . . . what does this have to do with me?"

"I need your help understanding how the sleepscape works. How to reach someone in their dreams."

Kai huffed a laugh. "Walking through the sleepscape isn't exactly

a quaint little stroll down the beach. Navigating it takes years of practice, and even the best Dreamers can get lost, trapped, or worse." He cut a disbelieving look at Baz. "What's so important that you'd risk all that?"

"Romie's alive," Baz said quietly.

Something shifted in Kai's eyes, a softness that was there and gone again before Emory could make sense of it. "I thought we went over this already. She's gone, Brysden."

"She might not be."

"Romie used Dreamer magic to speak to me," Emory asserted. "You were *there* in the dream. Didn't you see her?"

Kai said nothing, his expression undecipherable.

"Please, Kai," Baz pleaded. "We need your help."

Again, something passed between them, a silent conversation Emory wasn't privy to. Kai heaved a sigh and threw an arm on the back of the bench. "Fine. I'll walk you through it."

Emory wondered if Baz saw it, this devotion the Nightmare Weaver seemed to have for him.

The corner of Kai's mouth lifted. "But Brysden's got to do something for me in return."

Baz looked like he was about ready to disappear. "What?"

"I know which room the Regulators bring us to when they do whatever the fuck it is they're doing to us. I can't get to it without eyes on me. But you can."

"How do you know which room it is?"

Kai hesitated just a moment, and then: "Your dad told me."

Baz blanched. "You saw him?"

"They usually keep him in a different wing, but they transferred him just the other day. He told me the Regulators took him to this room and did something to him, though he can't remember what." At the devastation on Baz's face, Kai added, "He seemed fine, Brysden. But I need to know what's in that room. Jae hasn't

been back, as far as I know, so it's on us now to look into it."

Baz shuffled uneasily on his feet, blinking away what looked like tears. "I'll go look around."

"Good." Kai's attention turned to Emory. "Then listen carefully, Tidecaller. Sleepscape 101 starts now."

"So what's the deal with you and Brysden?" Kai asked as she sat next to him on the bench.

She met his penetrating stare with a raise of her brow. "What's the deal with *you* and him?"

Neither of them answered the other.

Theirs was an odd friendship, Emory thought. She'd always considered Baz a recluse, more at ease with fictional characters than with real people, so his evident closeness with Kai took her by surprise. She couldn't imagine what they might possibly have in common. Kai with his sharpness, Baz with his softness. The master of nightmares and the boy plagued by too many fears. From what little she'd gleaned of their dynamic, Kai seemed to like tormenting Baz, pushing his buttons in a way she would have thought would scare him off, make him shut down around himself. But it seemed to have the opposite effect—like Kai coaxed him out of his shell a bit.

Maybe she didn't know Baz as well as she'd thought.

She drew her legs up under her and eyed the Unhallowed Seal on Kai's hand. "Do you miss it, your magic?"

"Every damn day." He motioned to her New Moon sigil. "Scared they'll take yours away next? Maybe they'll throw you in a cell next to mine and you can tell me all about how this curious magic of yours came about."

"No one's going to find out."

"You're putting an awful lot of trust in someone who has literally nothing to lose in here."

The thought should have unnerved her, yet she felt certain her secret was safe with Kai. "You won't say anything."

"And now she pretends to know me enough to predict my actions."

"I know you wouldn't betray Baz. He's involved in this. Surely they wouldn't be too kind to him for harboring such a secret if word got out."

It was, apparently, the wrong thing to say. Kai pinned her with a glare, and it felt like falling through ice into a cold, dark lake.

"If anything happens to him," he said, a dangerous bite to his voice, "I'll make your life a walking nightmare."

"I wasn't saying–"

"I'm sure you know how principled he is when it comes to magic. Him helping you with this? It goes against all his precious rules. Which means he trusts you. And that's the thing about Brysden: under all that worry, all that anxiety, his loyalty, once you earn it, is unswerving." He leaned in threateningly close. "Don't fuck that up."

There was a sudden thickness in her throat at the shame his words conjured. She'd been treating Baz as a necessary means to an end, and for Kai to see the truth of her so easily . . . Was she really leading Baz on so strong that it was *that* obvious?

She thought of that fleeting moment on the beach, the way Baz had leaned in. Recalled the quiet emotion on his face the next morning, his evident pride as he showed her around Obscura Hall. And this subtle shift she'd noticed in him since, like he felt more confident around her, more at ease . . .

Maybe she'd beguiled Baz into helping her long enough, and she should stop. Especially given how close she and Keiran were becoming.

Baz trusted her more than she deserved, of that she was painfully aware. But she *needed* him. They needed each other.

And yet . . . she really didn't want to hurt him.

"I won't," Emory told Kai in earnest. It was a promise to him as much as to herself.

"I'll hold you to that."

The skepticism in his voice made it obvious he didn't trust her to keep her word. It should have irked her, but all she could think was how lucky Baz was to have Kai on his side. Maybe their friendship wasn't so strange after all. Kai was like a keeper of fear where Baz was concerned, protective of him in his own way. A fierce friend— or maybe something more. Something she suspected Baz couldn't even see.

An odd feeling swept over her at the thought. Before she could dwell on it, Kai leaned back against the bench, the threat of his words evaporating around them.

"All right, then. The sleepscape. What is it you want to know?"

BAZ

BAZ SLIPPED FROM THE COURTYARD, LEAVING KAI AND Emory to their lesson. His thoughts raced with the idea of Kai and his father–of his father being subjected to whatever it was the Regulators were experimenting with. The screams he'd heard the night he visited Kai . . .

They needed to get to the bottom of this.

He found the room that Kai had described, thankfully not bumping into anyone on the way. It had no windows and was locked, but Baz had learned the hairpin trick from Vera, figuring it might come in handy one day and prevent him from using magic to do so. He proceeded to unlock it and found–

Nothing.

At least, nothing out of the ordinary. It was a medical room, clinical and spotless, with surgical instruments locked away behind glass cases. Cold crept up the back of Baz's spine. Before he could investigate further, he heard the jangle of keys outside.

Baz backed out of the room, leaving the door unlocked before

he disappeared down another corridor. An older attendant looked his way, brows furrowing slightly as if in recognition, but someone called their name, drawing their attention away as Baz rounded another corner.

His eyes zeroed in on the label next to one of the doors.

Theodore Brysden.

Heart pounding in his chest, Baz peered through the slender window, noting the small comforts that made the room almost homey. A pile of books. A knit blanket thrown at the foot of the bed–his mother's handiwork, no doubt. A picture frame on the desk held a sepia-toned memory of another life, a better time. Four smiling figures that were unrecognizable now.

Breathe in, hold, breathe out.

Baz had been repeating the mantra to himself ever since getting out of the cab, trying to stay grounded. But he suddenly forgot how it went as he spotted his father on the bed, his profile nearly unrecognizable, thanks to the passage of time and something crueler still.

Baz's throat worked for air that would not come, everything in him locking up as memories of that day erupted behind his eyes.

School had been on holiday, and fifteen-year-old Baz couldn't wait to spend an entire week holed up in the printing press, reading quietly in an empty office or listening to Jae tell stories against the backdrop of melodical machinery. He distinctly remembered the three clients who'd come into the printing press at noon, the chime over the door announcing their presence. He'd looked up from his book with disinterest, and only suspected something might be wrong when he heard raised voices and saw his father standing between Jae and the clients–two men and a woman–his arms extended as if to stop a fight.

Baz remembered how scared he'd been as one of the men lunged for Jae, damper cuffs in hand, and Jae responded by flinging

illusion magic his way and Theodore screamed at everyone to stop, to please just *stop*.

Then: a blast like that of a star in collapse. Screams and silver veins and the wet glimmer in Theodore's eyes as the Regulators who eventually showed up subdued him. As they took him away to be branded with the Unhallowed Seal and become *this*. A frail, pale imitation of the man he'd once been.

You'll be all right, his father had said to him before Baz was wrenched from his arms. *Everything will be all right, Basil.*

He watched his father now as he flipped the page of the book he was reading. It felt surreal that only a glass window separated them after so many years. Theodore's back suddenly went rigid, his face lifting toward the door, as if he could feel his son's presence on the other side of it.

Baz stepped out of sight before his father could see him. And then he was sprinting down the corridor, lungs burning, everything in him holding on by a flimsy thread. He made it back to the courtyard just in time to see the patients being herded away by an attendant. Something about it being lunchtime, he was distantly aware of Emory saying as she sidled up to him.

Kai spotted him from across the courtyard. His shoulders fell at whatever he saw on Baz's face. There was nothing to say. No time to say it.

Only when Kai disappeared did Baz's knees give way. He crumbled against a wall, and it took everything in him to get a grip on his breathing. In and hold and out and in again until the world stilled, quiet and safe once more.

His name spoken softly brought him back to himself. Emory knelt in front of him.

"You okay?" she asked.

"I saw my dad." His eyes squeezed shut. "After all these years, I still couldn't bring myself to face him. He killed those people. And I

know it was an accident, but I always wondered how it could have happened in the first place."

Theodore was a *Nullifier*—it had felt to Baz like that should be the safest kind of Eclipse magic to wield, yet he still Collapsed.

"If I could have stopped it . . ."

"Hey."

Emory's hand gripped his, soft and real and warm. He looked into her stormy eyes and found them to be grounding.

"You were a kid," she breathed, "and there's nothing you could have done. But if you need to see him now, if you want to go back . . ."

"I can't."

"Then come on. Let's go home."

Home was a funny word, Baz thought. Once, he had never felt more at home than when he was at the printing press with his father and Jae. And when he'd had that ripped from him, home became books, the stories they contained. When he thought of home now, he thought of Aldryn, of the warded sanctuary of Obscura Hall, the warmth of the Eclipse commons. But that home wasn't one at all, he realized, without Kai there to share it with.

He needed to bring this—whatever was happening at the Institute—into the light. He'd had enough of Eclipse-born hiding in the shadows.

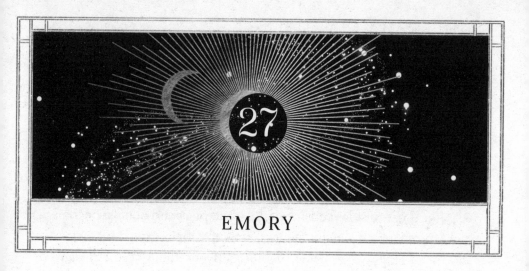

EMORY

"O W." EMORY WINCED AT THE STING OF THE NEEDLE. "DO you have to jab that in quite so hard?"

A withering look from Baz as he pulled the syringe, releasing the sleeping drug into her muscle. "You say that every time, and every time I try to do it more gently."

If there was one thing she hated in life, it was needles.

"My arm's still sore from yesterday and the day before that," she gritted out. A pinprick of blood formed between blooming bruises on her arm.

"Why don't you just heal the pain away?"

Emory leaned back on the sofa, her muscles already going heavy. "I keep hoping it'll motivate me to get it right for once."

The drug was sleep magic imbued in salt water, a tonic that some Dreamer students used during their training to make themselves fall asleep, thus facilitating their access to the sleepscape. Baz had somehow managed to borrow a small stock of it from a teacher in Decrescens Hall.

They'd been experimenting with it for a week now, and still Emory wasn't able to access the sleepscape.

The first couple of tries, she'd merely fallen into a deep, entirely normal slumber. According to Baz, she even snored a few times, out like a light until the effects of the drug began to wear off and she woke to Baz's nervous pacing.

After those first few unsuccessful attempts, she'd at least become aware of herself as she slept. It was like being on the brink of sleep yet still awake, when the line between thought and dreaming blurred. It was in this state that she was supposed to find the sleepscape, a thing much easier said than done.

"Just follow the darkness," Kai had instructed her at the Institute. "All sleep is dark, in a way, but sleepscape darkness is different. You'll know when you see it."

Emory thought she glimpsed it once. Blackness so impenetrable it felt tangible. But she'd been under too long already by then; before she could reach it, the sleeping drug wore off, and she was pulled back into waking.

She hoped this time would be different. Outside, the sun was setting, casting the Eclipse commons in warm golden light. The last sliver of a waning moon was already visible in the darkening sky, though if the last few days were any indication, it had no influence at all on Emory's power and would likely not make using the Dreamer magic any easier now.

As sleep sunk its claws into her, slow and deliberate, Emory's gaze found Baz sitting across from her on his usual rust-colored chair. She could tell he hated this, watching her go where he couldn't follow, wield magic he could not see. There was a permanent weariness to him since the Institute. They hadn't spoken of it, but she knew it bothered him, not knowing what was going on. He must be imagining the worst happening to his father and Kai, and with good reason. The Institute was a vile place.

Emory tried giving him a reassuring smile before she went under, but it only hardened the look in his eyes.

And then she was sleeping.

Her mind fought for clarity in this strange, floating state. She opened her senses, grappled for the Dreamer magic that was still so elusive to her. She couldn't see anything, all of it dark, a blank void of nothingness.

But there, at the edge of it all, a darker smudge on the horizon.

She flung her consciousness in its direction. In her mind's eye, she saw a semblance of a door, gleaming black obsidian.

She reached for it.

It unlocked.

And Emory stepped into impossible, velvety darkness, onto a path laden with ethereal stars that appeared both near and far, motionless and swirling, above and below and dizzyingly all around.

The sleepscape, at long last.

Her mind was her own again, and she was awake—at least here, in this strange in-between world. There was a living, breathing sort of quiet, at once peaceful and crushing, like the weight of being underwater. Her movements were slow and heavy, as if she were trying to move against a current. She inched toward the edge of the path, which curved in either direction, dipping away into darkness. Beyond the light of the stars lining it was a great vast *nothing*. She had the peculiar sensation of looking over the edge of a steep cliff. Yet that nothingness called to her, and she found herself wanting to go toward it.

What could hurt her here? This was the domain of dreams, lovely and enchanting. A realm of endless possibility.

The cold hand of Kai's half-remembered words pulled her back from the edge. "First lesson of the sleepscape," he'd said, his voice a midnight caress, "is never veer from the path."

"Where does it lead?"

"No one knows. If you venture too far down in either direction, you start feeling overextended. It's like diving too deep under-water, reaching that point where everything becomes a crushing weight. Depths you were never meant to exist in. You risk losing yourself, your connection to your waking body. But you won't need to go that far."

Emory glanced at the glowing orbs around her, reaching tenta-tive fingers toward a winking star above her head.

"Every star is a dream," Kai had explained. "Dreamers can just reach out to one, cup it in their hands, and step into that dream. But first, you need to find the star you're looking for. That's the tricky part. Thankfully for you, though, Dreamers recognize each other in the sleepscape. They're like beacons to each other, so find-ing Romie should be easy enough. *If* she's there."

"And what of the darkness beyond the stars?"

"That," Kai had said with a dangerous tilt of his mouth, "is the realm of nightmares. It's where the monsters we call umbrae dwell. You know that feeling when a dream shifts and becomes a hor-ror you can't escape? That's the umbrae. They devour dreams like black holes gobbling up any star that moves too close. Dreamers are trained to recognize the signs. As soon as they sense an umbra's pull, they need to escape. They need to wake. If they don't . . . the umbrae claim them."

The umbrae. She'd heard Romie speaking of them only briefly, these things made of something worse than nightmares.

"The body those Dreamers leave behind in the waking world keeps functioning, at least for a while," Kai had continued. "But in the sleepscape? Their consciousness is devoured. The umbrae feast on it until there's nothing left and they become just another black hole of nothingness." He'd pointed his chin at a passing attendant pushing a middle-aged man in a wheelchair. The man appeared to be sleeping. "That's a Dreamer who never woke, his soul taken by

the umbrae. There's a whole wing dedicated to them, what we call eternal sleepers."

"Is there no chance of them waking?"

"Not that I know of."

Emory had watched the Dreamer with blank horror. "Please tell me the umbrae haven't somehow found a way into the waking world. They can't escape the nightmares they haunt, can they?"

"I thought I might have pulled one into the waking world with me once when I brought something out of a nightmare. But I didn't. It stayed in the sleepscape. Couldn't follow me out into the waking world, I guess. As far as I know, they're contained to the sleepscape."

"And what do they make of Nightmare Weavers?"

"They tend to let me be."

Emory had wondered if it was because they sensed Kai had the power to destroy them, or if they recognized in him—in his magic—some of the same darkness they were made of.

"But you're something new," he'd told her. "Something the umbrae have never seen before. They'll be drawn to you like moths to a flame. If you get so much as a prickling of their presence, you need to wake yourself up. Immediately."

Cold ran up Emory's spine now as she looked out at the impossible dark. The thought had crossed her mind to draw on Kai's power instead of Dreamer magic—that maybe by using Nightmare Weaver magic, she, too, would be left alone. But given how hard it had been to draw on Baz's magic, how bottomless and inaccessible it felt . . . something told her Kai's magic would be the same, too vast for her to grasp.

She took a deep breath, searching for any sign of Romie. Distantly, she was aware of the sleep drug starting to wane, but she was so close, had finally made it into the sleepscape . . .

And she had no idea how to find Romie.

She glanced down at her wrist and wished she had a vial of salt water to activate the Selenic Mark. Instead, she looked helplessly at all the stars around her, hoping for something to spark that recognition that Kai spoke of. She shouted Romie's name, her voice echoing strangely around her, like a sound muffled underwater.

No answer came. There was nothing but darkness and crushing silence.

And then—a horrendous scream, or a distant echo of one. Screeching like nails along a blackboard.

The umbrae.

Emory bit back a sob. "Fuck." She barely knew how she'd made it *into* the sleepscape—she didn't have the faintest clue how to wake herself up before the sleeping drug did it for her. Kai had merely said to find the link back to her body, whatever that meant. And she'd been mindless enough to not press him for more.

Another inhuman scream. The darkness seemed to close in on her.

She cast a desperate look around her, hugging her arms. She could do nothing but wait. Tentatively, she sent her power flying down both sides of the path. It reached and reached until it could do so no more, stretched too thin and too far for her to control.

She sensed nothing, still nothing.

Clawed hands rose at the edge of her vision. She might have screamed, but then the darkness around her receded, and her eyes opened wide to the twilit Eclipse commons.

Baz was on his knees in front of her, hands gripping her shoulders to shake her awake. He slumped back onto the floor, looking deflated. "What happened?"

Emory curled her hands into fists. "I made it, but I couldn't sense Romie anywhere. Then the umbrae showed up."

Baz swore. He took his glasses off, ran a hand over his haggard

face. "I heard you calling out to her. Then you started trembling and I–"

"I want to try it again."

"Emory . . ."

"Again."

"No. We'll pick this up tomorrow. You look like you're about to pass out."

She fell back against the sofa, sighing deeply. He was right, of course—she felt like she'd just cycled up the hill from Cadence to Aldryn about a dozen times. "It's like she's too far away for me to reach," she mused. "Like something's blocking her from me."

Baz sat beside her, his arm brushing hers. "We'll try again tomorrow," he repeated softly.

Emory drew her knees up beneath her and turned to face him. He still hadn't put his glasses back on, and his eyes were closed as if in sleep. She studied his face openly. These past few days spent here with him in Obscura Hall had shifted something between them. Or maybe it was Kai's looming threat, the fierce protectiveness he'd shown Baz, that made her see him in a new light. Whatever it was, it felt easy with him. Comfortable in a way she hadn't counted on.

"You look different without your glasses."

His eyes fluttered open. This close, she could make out the faint freckles on his nose, the various shades of brown in his irises.

"Different how?"

"Less scholarly, maybe. Not so tragically serious."

A shy smile from him. "What if I like being the serious scholar?"

"Is that why you want to become a professor? To study books in peace with your endless supply of tea and coffee?"

She'd meant it teasingly, but Baz seemed to consider the question in earnest, eyes unfocused as he looked out the window to the Aldersea.

"I don't know. I think I mostly want to help other Eclipse-born

find their balance. Teach them what I know of control to limit their chances of Collapsing as much as I possibly can. I know there's not much I can do to prevent it, in the end. But if I can make this place into some kind of . . . sanctuary, a place where they can feel safe, then that'll be enough."

He ran a self-conscious hand on the back of his neck. "It probably sounds silly."

"No. You're good at this, Baz."

It was the truth. Despite all his trepidations, he was truly in his element here, helping her practice her magic. And seeing this side of him, hearing him voice his motivations aloud, made her understand him in a way she hadn't before. She'd viewed him as this frightened boy who downplayed his power and let life pass him by, content to keep his nose down and buried in books. But maybe this was his own way of trying to fight for something. He had all this incredible power coursing through his veins, something she was keenly aware of after having tried to use it herself and feeling just how vast and depthless it was, yet he chose not to utilize it. He chose instead to help other Eclipse-born in whatever small way he could so that they wouldn't know the same fate as his father, as Kai.

Perhaps she'd been too quick to judge him all those years ago, writing him off as someone too withdrawn, too quiet, too dull. There was something noble in his goal. A steady optimism to him that she found particularly endearing.

"I wouldn't have made it this far without you," Emory murmured.

She didn't know what compelled her to brush his hair back from his brow, curling it around his ear. He stilled at her touch; something heated in the browns of his eyes, so rich and inviting and soft without his glasses to hide behind. She couldn't deny a part of her was rather enjoying it, the attention, this attraction she'd been noticing more and more from him. For a second, she imagined what

it might be like to kiss him, if only just to see if there was something there. If she might return the feelings he'd once harbored for her, and maybe still did now.

He looked at her with hopeful anticipation, like he knew exactly what she was thinking.

Emory pulled away.

Tides. What was she *doing*? "I should go." She pretended not to see the disheartened sag of his shoulders, reaching instead for her satchel. "See you tomorrow?"

She was spending entirely too much time with him lately, and taking advantage of this soft spot he had for her was blurring the lines between what was real and what was not. There was nothing here but friendship, wouldn't ever be a chance for something more because that wasn't what she wanted. It was Keiran who filled every part of her mind, Keiran who excited her and made her feel important. It was him she burned for–*not* Baz.

So why then did she feel so wretched leaving him?

Attending a party at Decrescens Hall was just what she needed to purge Baz from her mind.

It was, admittedly, a very exclusive upperclassman party that Emory hadn't technically been invited to, though Keiran *did* mention she should pop by if she had the chance after her training. They'd both been so busy this past week, she with her sleepscape sessions with Baz, he with his photograph restoration, a sample of which he meant to present to interested museums and art curators. She needed to see him. If only so his lips could erase all lingering thoughts of Baz–the soft feel of his hair on her fingers, the little flip her stomach had made as she realized how close they were.

She was in dire need of a drink.

Outside the Decrescens upperclassman dorms, Virgil was laughing boisterously on the porch with a group of students Emory didn't

know. Wine spilled from the bottle he held as he noticed her.

"Emory!" He slid down the porch railing and threw an arm over her shoulder. "So glad you could make it. Let me show you around our humble Waning Moon abode."

There was nothing humble about the dark, opulent common room they stepped into, full of velvet settees and lounge chairs, diaphanous curtains billowing in the breeze coming in through an arched window. Candles were lit haphazardly on shelves full of old grimoires and silver instruments, and music played from a scratchy gramophone. Emory spotted the other Selenics in the fray of students: Javier and Louis laughing together on a settee, Nisha chatting up a girl by the overflowing drink cart, Ife dancing, and Lizaveta slyly passing a velvet pouch to two handsome boys in exchange for what looked like a wad of bills.

"Is that . . ."

"Synths," Virgil confirmed. "The mild version. We bring them to these kinds of parties sometimes. It's a bit of an unspoken rule among the buyers not to say a word about them. One of Aldryn's most well-kept secrets. After the Order itself—and your secret alignment, of course." He winked at her, then nodded at someone in the distance. "Ah. Here comes our fearless leader."

Keiran had never looked more handsome, she thought. His hair was perfectly styled, and he wore a fine-knit black turtleneck that hugged his chest. His mouth quirked up when he saw her.

"Don't think we all haven't noticed *that*," Virgil whispered in her ear. With a flourish, he picked up two coupes of sparkling wine off a passing tray and handed her one, clinking his coupe against hers before downing it in one go. "Enjoy."

He wagged his brows at her and left, just as Keiran appeared at her side.

"Come here." Keiran gently tugged on the hem of her sweater to pull her close, trapping her mouth in a kiss.

Her blood sang. Purging successful. She wanted to kiss him forever and think of nothing else.

Still, she found herself pulling away slightly to say, "I made it into the sleepscape."

His eyes lit up. "And?"

"I couldn't find Romie. But I have an idea. I'm not sure it'll work, exactly–" The disappointment blanketing his face made her go quiet. "What is it?"

Keiran heaved a sigh, running a hand through his hair. "We can't go forward until we know what to expect beyond that door. Until we find the epilogue. It all hinges on you contacting Romie."

"I'm trying, Keiran."

"Not hard enough."

He must have seen her flinch at the hardness of his tone. His voice softened. "I'm sorry. I know you're trying. It's just that everyone's growing restless, and with everything else . . . It's taking a toll on me."

"I'll find a way," Emory promised. She couldn't stand to see him so disheartened.

He squeezed her hand with a smile. "Let's hear this idea of yours, then."

"I was thinking I could try calling her through the mark while I'm in the sleepscape. See if that might get through whatever's blocking her from me."

Keiran came to the same conclusion as her: For it to work, she would either have to activate the mark before she slipped into dreaming or bring salt water with her in the sleepscape so she could activate the mark there. But neither of them had ever heard of taking things *into* the sleepscape, only out of it.

Keiran was suddenly pulling her toward where Lizaveta sat with the two boys she'd sold the synths to.

"Hey, William. Question for you." One of the boys, fair-skinned

and brown-haired, lifted slightly glossy eyes to Keiran, who asked with smooth assurance, "Can you Dreamers bring stuff *into* the sleepscape?"

"Why?"

A shrug. "Call it academic interest."

"I suppose it's possible, though I don't see why we'd need to bring something *in*. It's taking stuff *out* of dreams that interests most people. Only one Dreamer I know of could do that as easily as breathing. Rosemarie Tides-damned Brysden."

He spoke her name like she was a legend, and Emory couldn't help but perk up with pride. She realized with a start that, before, such a comment might have prickled her jealousy. But now . . . she was starting to realize that she, too, had worth. She might have had a hard time recognizing it before, what with her living in Romie's shadow, but not anymore.

She was a Tidecaller, something new and powerful. She wasn't lesser than, wasn't mediocre at all–she was just as worthy as Romie.

As the Dreamer turned to his friend in search of more party-appropriate conversation, Keiran gave Emory a knowing smile. They had their answer: if there was even the slightest possibility it might work, she'd make it happen.

But this was a party, and now she would have some fun.

"The game is called Kiss the Moon," Lizaveta explained with a devilish smile. "You pick a card from the deck, and you kiss someone with that alignment. Then that person goes next."

She pulled a card out of the navy-painted deck she held and flipped it for everyone to see. Silver waning crescents were drawn in the corners, and in the middle of the card was a cloaked silhouette with skeletal hands holding a scythe. The Reaper.

Virgil sputtered on his drink and pulled himself up so swiftly he spilled wine all over the carpet.

"Here, darling!" he hollered as he made his way to Lizaveta.

She rolled her eyes at him, though her red painted lips curled up in a smile. She pulled him closer by the lapels of his unbuttoned shirt and kissed him to lewd cheers and whistles.

Emory took a long sip of wine. The thought of being chosen—and worse, having to choose someone in turn and kiss them in front of all these people—was mortifying. Yet weirdly exciting, too.

Virgil picked a card of his own. The illustration was of a bright lighthouse, with the full moon drawn in the corners. Lightkeeper. He pointed at Keiran. "Come here, you beautiful bastard!"

Everyone laughed and hollered as Virgil grabbed Keiran's face in both hands and kissed him firmly on the mouth. Emory couldn't help her own smile as they finally pulled apart and took a deep bow to loud applause.

Keiran took a sip of whiskey before he reached for the deck. "My turn, then?"

Emory's heart seized as he held up the Eclipse card, illustrated with a wilting sunflower, with the sun and moon in eclipse in the corners.

For a second, she imagined the scene playing out in her head—him coming over to kiss her, outing her to all these people who weren't supposed to know. But the moment dissolved into nothing as someone shouted, "Pick another!"

"Unless you want us to go find the Timespinner?" someone else asked.

Laughter rang in Emory's ears. A sick feeling crawled under her skin. She couldn't make out the expression on Keiran's shadowed face as he tossed the Eclipse card and reached for another.

He pulled out the Amplifier card.

Surely Lizaveta couldn't be the only Amplifier here, but Keiran's eyes immediately went to her. He cocked a brow. She answered with a feline smile.

"Well?" Lizaveta said, leaning back in her chair. "It's nothing we haven't done before."

Emory's stomach plummeted. She'd suspected a history between the two, what with their shared childhood and Lizaveta's hostility toward her, but to have it confirmed . . .

It's just a game, she tried to tell herself as she watched Keiran brace his hands on either side of Lizaveta. He lowered his face to hers, and Lizaveta bowed toward him like a starved plant under the sun. One dainty strap of her silky dress slid down her shoulder, her lips parting in anticipation.

Keiran moved past her mouth to brush a delicate kiss on her temple instead. His words were low, but everyone heard them well enough. "Best we leave the past alone, don't you think?"

He drew himself up and discarded his hand. Lizaveta's icy composure and sardonic smile never wavered, though her breathless chuckle sounded a little too forced as she said, "Your loss."

Emory didn't know what to think as Keiran walked away. He looked back at her before disappearing through a door. She followed, leaving the others to their game, suddenly disenchanted by it all. And then eager hands were drawing her into the shadows and Keiran was trapping the sound of her surprised laugh in his mouth and everything was right again.

"There's the Eclipse kiss I was owed," he breathed against her lips.

"Lizaveta wouldn't be pleased."

"That," Keiran said, pulling her close as he leaned back against the shelves behind him, "is not what I want to be discussing right now."

Neither did she, but still she asked, "Was it serious between the two of you?"

"We were young. Had our fun." He caressed her face. "You're who I want, Ains."

He kissed her again, and all thoughts disappeared from her mind except this ache in her soul, this need to be closer to him. *This* was what she wanted too–someone bold and charismatic and passionate, someone who made her feel important, who excited every part of her.

Someone who wasn't Baz, she thought.

It seemed to her they were the only two people in the world until a sound made them pull apart. A girl who was clearly very drunk stumbled into the room. With a start, Emory recognized her.

"Nel? What are you doing here?"

Penelope's eyes were slow to focus on her, her movements sluggish as she lifted a bottle in the air. "Trying to have some fun, of course," she hiccupped. She took a swig from the bottle and stumbled again.

Keiran reached her before she could fall, throwing Emory a concerned look. Something dark crawled along her senses. This wasn't like Penelope–she *never* partied, her idea of a late night out consisting of books in a library.

"Nel, are you okay?"

A huff. "Oh, so *now* you care?"

"Of course I care. You're my friend."

"Where have you been, then? I tried to be there for you, and then Lia's body washes up and you can't be bothered to check in with me."

Emory realized with a pang of guilt it was true. She'd been so obsessed with trying to get to the sleepscape, she'd completely ignored Penelope outside of class.

"Nel–"

"No." Penelope pushed out of Keiran's grip. "Just let me have some fun."

Emory followed her into the common room, where the Kiss the

Moon game was still going strong. William, the Dreamer from earlier, looped an arm over Penelope's shoulders and said, "Over here, darling, we're missing a Darkbearer."

Keiran stopped William with a hand to his chest. "She's clearly drunk."

He scoffed. "Whatever."

"I said she's done."

It was as if Keiran held the kind of power that Glamours did without being one; William let Penelope go with a bored look. She doubled over, retching on the floor, and Emory was at her side in a flash.

"I just want to forget," Penelope sniffled. "This hole in my chest."

Emory's heart broke. "I know."

"Her tongue was missing. It makes no sense."

It became difficult to breathe. The truth of Lia's death still wasn't public knowledge; her family and close friends must have been let in on it after the autopsy. Emory cast a weary look around her. Everyone had turned away with disinterest, and Keiran was exchanging tense words with the Dreamer by the foyer. The only person close enough to hear—the only one who wouldn't write this off as the senseless ramblings of a drunken girl—was Lizaveta. There was none of her usual hostility as she said, "Let's get her back to her room."

"No." Penelope tried to shove both of them off. "I don't want my roommate to see me like this."

"Then we'll go to my room," Emory suggested. "Come on, Nel."

Penelope let herself be carried back to the underclassman dorms, where she quickly fell asleep in Romie's old bed. Emory begrudgingly thanked Lizaveta for her help.

"Guys like that always take things too far," Lizaveta said with her arms crossed. "The fucking prick deserves to get punched in the face."

Emory huffed in agreement, surprised to see Lizaveta's vehemence directed at someone worthy of it, for once.

Lizaveta hovered by the door. "Are you going back to the party?"

"I'll stay with her, make sure she's all right. Could you let Keiran know?"

She couldn't tell if it was jealousy that flashed in those icy eyes, or something else. There was a long pause before Lizaveta said, "He told us what you're doing, trying to reach Romie in the sleepscape. That you went to the Nightmare Weaver for help. Did Keiran ever tell you about Farran? That he used to date Kai?"

The floor tilted, then righted itself beneath her. The Eclipse-born that Farran had dated—was *Kai*?

"Farran and I were always closer than the others," Lizaveta continued without waiting for a reply. "I was the only one he trusted with this secret relationship of his. Do you know why he initially wanted to wake the Tides? He wanted to prove to us—to everyone—that the Shadow was never the Tides' enemy. He wanted to bring them back so they'd tell us we'd gotten it all wrong, that the Eclipse-born were never stained by the Shadow's sin, because he believed, like Kai had led him to believe, that the Tides and the Shadow were, in fact, allies. Friends. Lovers. That they left these shores together for the love they bore for each other."

Lizaveta scowled at the idea. "Farran chased that dream all the way to Dovermere and died for it. And as much as I think this idealism of his is ridiculous, I just want him *back*." She gave Emory a look dripping with contempt. "But I'm not willing to risk another Eclipse-born hurting me and my friends for the slim hope of seeing him again. So if you don't think you're strong enough to reach Romie in the sleepscape or wake the Tides, I think we'd all rather you give up now than pretend you can do this." Lizaveta looked down her nose at her. "I wouldn't want to be in the caves with you when you push yourself too far and Collapse. You Eclipse-born

have robbed me and mine of enough happiness already."

"I'm not backing down," Emory said through gritted teeth. "I can do it. Wake the Tides. Keiran believes it, and so do the others. Why can't you?"

Lizaveta searched her face for something. "I know how easy it is to fall under his spell, you know. We're all a bit infatuated by him and his grand plans. He's always been like that, has this way of making you feel like you alone hold the key to all the answers he seeks." She pulled the door open. "But don't confuse his interest in you with his obsession with power."

Lizaveta left, but her words stayed with Emory, mixing with Keiran's earlier comment that she wasn't trying hard enough. All Emory wanted then was to prove to them both that she would find a way. That she could do this. Once she was sure Penelope was sound asleep, she gripped a vial of salt water and begged sleep to find her, too, thoughts of *Not good enough* following her into the sleepscape. She nearly cried with relief at the vial that remained in her hand, carried with her into dreaming. But it was a small victory, cut short too quickly as she activated the mark and called out for Romie with every particle of her being, and still no answer came.

In that impossible darkness, she thought she glimpsed a glittering hourglass down the starlit path. Lizaveta's words rang all around her. *I wouldn't want to be in the caves with you when you push yourself too far and Collapse.*

She knew then what she had to do.

BAZ

THE DAWN WAS UP BEFORE BAZ WAS, AND SO, APPARENTLY, was Emory.

He nearly fumbled down the last few steps to the commons when he saw her pacing near the window. Emory stilled as she spotted him, gripping the strap of her satchel tight.

"Morning," Baz mumbled awkwardly. He slid toward the coffee counter and busied himself with filling the filter. His heart thudded an uneven rhythm in his chest. He wished he could stop time, rewind it so that moment on the sofa last night never happened. Or maybe relive it so that *more* could happen.

Tides. He was losing his mind.

The words she'd said to him were a battle drum in his ears.

You're good at this, Baz.

I wouldn't have made it this far without you.

The sheer belief and confidence in those words . . . It made him feel like he could tackle anything. He'd never been so vulnerable in sharing his quiet goals before, but doing so hadn't been as

terrifying as he'd imagined. Something about her made him want to shed his fears, throw all caution to the wind, and though the thought scared him to death, it also excited him.

He felt awake. Alive.

He felt, for the first time in a long while, like the island he'd made himself into didn't stand so far apart from the rest of the world. From *her*. She made him feel like that invincible boy who saw the world so innocently and brightly before his father's Collapsing, the boy who thought magic was beautiful, not a thing to constantly fear and keep bottled up. He wanted to let himself sink into this feeling, keep chasing it like an elusive sunset until he might bask in it forever.

And yet.

She had pulled away, and all his fears came rushing back to the surface, the sunset fading behind the horizon with her leaving. Who was he kidding? He must be imagining things, making up stories in his head. Besides, there was the Keiran Dunhall Thornby of it all. He hadn't seen them together since the equinox festival, but he knew she was still hanging around him and his friends. And who was he compared to Aldryn's golden boy?

No. Whatever it was he felt between them was the result of working so closely together and nothing more.

But then: her fingers curling around his ear, that look in her eyes, the breath they'd both held.

He'd never been so confused in his life.

"You're here early," he said, wishing the coffee were ready so it could banish these thoughts from his mind.

"I'm going back to Dovermere."

Baz's hands stilled. Slowly, he turned to Emory.

Her face was smooth, expressionless. Her voice steady as she said, "I think the reason I can't feel Romie in the sleepscape has something to do with Dovermere, with the wards set up around it. If I can get past them, if I'm near enough to the Hourglass, I think I

can reach her." She stood a little straighter. "Today's a new moon. Which means if our theory is right, my presence at Dovermere won't be a risk to Jordyn or Romie. It's the only thing I can think of to make this work. The one thing we haven't tried."

Everything always came back around to her and Dovermere, Baz thought grimly. The caves were like a darkness at the edge of his vision that kept growing and growing until there was nothing left. Much like the deadly tide that would fill them.

It was madness, and she knew it.

Those damn storm-cloud eyes had him transfixed. They were a rain-battered sea that conjured the moment they'd shared last night, the smell of something fresh and faintly citrusy that had made him want to draw her closer, twine his fingers around her hair.

He saw the flicker in her gaze, like she, too, was remembering that moment. It had been so small a thing, yet it felt to Baz like it had changed everything. Like a door had been eased open between them, and now they stood on either side of it, waiting to see who might cross it first.

Or maybe he was being delusional.

But then . . .

But then she drew nearer, the sunrise catching in her eyes like on the water's surface. She ducked her head before he could make sense of the conflicted shadow in those blue depths. Her hand rested on the counter a hair's breadth from his own, and nothing else mattered except this, how close they stood, the way his heart stopped and then started again.

He wanted to freeze time, make it stretch so he could live here forever.

"I know what you'll say," Emory said softly. "It's dangerous, and I know that. But it won't stop me from going. This is what I have to do."

Baz realized she was waiting for him to say something, tensing as if for a fight. She knew this was a suicide mission. To reach Romie, she would need to go into the sleepscape, and for that, she needed to *sleep*. What if the tide came rushing in while she was still under?

She needed time on her side.

Understanding rippled between them.

"You need me to come with you. To pause time."

Emory's chin dipped, and it was answer enough.

"You don't have to," she said weakly. "I'll manage on my own if I need to." She squared her shoulders then, but even he could tell her bravado was false, fabricated. "I have to try. If the roles were reversed, Romie would do the same for either of us in a heartbeat."

For Tides' sake.

Baz gripped the edges of the counter to keep himself together, because this was *madness* and he was unraveling and Emory was holding all the strings and he was absolutely, foolishly, maddeningly fine with it.

She was going to get him *killed*, and he was too far gone for her by now to even care.

"All right," he bit out. "I'll go with you."

Outside, Dovermere seemed to sigh, contented by this dark bargain struck, the cogs of fate clanging into place with an unsettling note of finality.

"There's something powerful about the two of us going in there together, don't you think?"

Emory's words made the hair on Baz's skin rise. The bright midday sun painted her gold as they came upon the jagged cave mouth at the base of the cliff, unveiled by the receding tide. He'd gone back and forth on his decision to come with her a dozen times since she came to see him this morning, and though his pulse was beating erratically and his hands were moist and a voice at the

back of his mind kept nagging at him that this was wrong, this was so, so wrong and they should turn back now before it was too late, there was something oddly comforting about Emory's presence at his side. A feeling that they were indeed meant to face Dovermere together.

"Let's get this over with." He threw a wary glance over his shoulder; he couldn't shake the feeling that someone was watching them.

They forged into the cave, defiantly holding up their lanterns to light the darkness within. Neither of them spoke. The only sound was the dripping of water, the scuffle of their feet against rock, the splash of their steps through shallow pools lining the way.

Baz kept glancing at his watch, careful not to slip on the algae-slick rock. He walked behind Emory, the walls around them too narrow to allow them to be side by side. She looked over her shoulder, arching a brow at the half-folded map in his hand.

"Where'd you find that, anyway?"

"An old cartographer's journal. Thought it wouldn't hurt to bring a map of this place."

He knew a map wouldn't be the thing to save them here; only time and magic and a bit of Tides-damned luck might do the trick. But still, having the map comforted him.

"Any luck with the missing epilogue?"

Baz grumbled in answer. He'd been searching every avenue he could think of, had asked Jae and Alya and Vera to get him in contact with anyone who might have more information, but he'd still come up empty. Adriana Kazan was a ghost, and the epilogue was indeed lost.

He looked at his map again and stumbled. Emory reached a hand to steady him. His fingers wrapped around her wrist, and in the pause that followed, the space became charged with memories of the last time they'd been this close, the last time their skin touched. Baz swallowed audibly as he released her arm.

Emory glanced at her watch. "We need to keep moving."

She trudged on ahead. Her grim determination should have been reassuring, but it only widened the pit in his stomach. Time dripped, slipped, stood still, as they walked on in silence. Baz had an awareness of it he didn't usually have, and it felt both deeply unsettling and oddly familiar to him.

This place was strange.

At last, they reached the Belly of the Beast. The cavern opened like a womb around them, dark even with their lanterns to illuminate it. Its jagged teeth cast shadows in every direction, and at the very center of the grotto, perched on a natural platform, stood what Emory had called the Hourglass: a towering formation made up of a conjoined stalactite and stalagmite that clung to each other by a mere thread, veins of silver running along its sides. It looked nothing like what he'd expect of a door to the Deep, if it even was one at all. The doors he'd read about were described as water holes close to shore, the remains of collapsed sea caves. But this cave still stood, and the Hourglass with it.

While Emory faltered at the sight, Baz went right up to it, marveling at the spiral etched on the stalagmite, which glowed a faint silver. The same Tides-damned spiral that was on her hand.

"This is where you all got those marks, isn't it?" he asked.

Emory nodded. Slowly, she stepped onto the promontory beside him. Her hand hovered over the strangely striated rock, a frown knitting her brows together. She reached for the symbol, and a dread like he'd never felt before gripped Baz. He pulled her hand away before she could touch it.

"Don't."

She blinked at him incomprehensibly.

"Look what happened last time you touched it." Four students dead, and four more disappeared. "Let's just get this over with without touching anything, okay?"

Emory seemed to snap out of whatever pull the rock had on her and nodded. Baz took the syringe and sleeping drug out of his bag. Glanced at his watch. There were four hours left until high tide. He locked eyes with Emory, who'd pushed up her sleeve, waiting.

Baz hesitated. "Maybe we should just–"

"Baz, I swear, if you don't jab that needle in *right now*–"

He stuck the needle into her arm, eliciting a hiss of surprise from her.

"There," he said darkly as he pulled the needle out.

She wiped a thumb over the pinprick of blood on her arm. "Was that so hard?"

Baz bit back a retort. Emory pulled her sleeve down and stepped off the platform. She sat leaning against the rocky ledge, hands braced on the wet floor, readying for sleep to pull her under.

"You'll keep an eye on the time?"

"Of course," Baz promised as her eyes fluttered shut. If it got too late, he would pause time, wait for her to wake up. And hope it was enough.

Emory mumbled what sounded like a thank-you before slumber took her, and into the waiting arms of the sleepscape she fell.

Baz was going to be sick.

He paced in front of the Hourglass, eyes flitting back and forth between his watch and Emory's sleeping figure. The silver hands on his watch moved to and fro, slow and fast. Here in this strange place, a minute could last an hour, and an hour could slip away to nothing in the space of a blink. Time made little sense, and the fear coating Baz's mouth only grew thicker as he wondered if it would bend to him at all, or if it only answered to one master here. To whatever old magic ruled these depths.

It called to him, that magic. A susurration that grated against his

senses, that set every part of him aflame with how strangely familiar it felt. How *inviting*.

Breathe in.

Hold.

Out.

He tried to resent Emory for convincing him to come. All his life,
he'd lived in his perfect little safety bubble. Never reaching, never
daring to dream outside the confines of his make-believe worlds
and narrow existence contained to the library and Obscura Hall.

His skin still crawled at the thought of the magic he'd used last
time there was a new moon, when he'd kept Emory's magic from
running rampant on the beach. And though a part of him remembered how good it had felt to use it, and every fiber in him knew
he'd barely scratched the surface of the power he kept such a tight
lid over, he didn't want any of it. Had never *dared* to want it.

But he would have to now. And for Emory–for Romie, too–he
could try. Maybe there was power in finally stepping over that
carefully drawn line if it was for them.

Still, it did nothing to ease his nerves.

Baz looked at his watch. Ten more minutes, he told himself, and
then he'd try to wake Emory, whether she'd found Romie or not.
They were cutting it too close, and all this pacing around wasn't
helping him. His breathing exercises did nothing to appease him.
He needed to do *something*.

The dark pull of the magic around him seemed to agree, trying
to coax his power out.

Come play, it whispered.

Tentatively, Baz answered the call.

He extended the barest sliver of his power out to the Hourglass,
gently probing as he tried to find the threads of time that might
have seen it open once.

But this was not such a simple lock to pick.

So many threads wove through it. A great entanglement of them that he couldn't begin to make sense of, much less know which one to tug on. Too many moving parts surrounded its inner workings, complicated clockwork that was out of Baz's depth. It wasn't as simple as turning the dial of a small object back in time, or even like what he'd done with Emory's magic the night of the bonfires. It felt more complicated still than what he imagined pausing the threads of time for people might be.

But if he concentrated enough, if he reached for this one part, bigger than the others . . .

Emory mumbled in her sleep, and Baz's concentration slipped, his magic going back to slumbering in his veins. He took a step toward her as she uttered what sounded like Romie's name.

Then her mouth opened on a scream.

Baz's heart was in his throat as he reached for her–and Emory's eyes shot open.

She drew an unnatural breath, arms grappling for purchase as if fighting some invisible demon. Baz took her face in his hands. Her wide eyes settled on his.

She was awake, alive, out of the sleepscape–

And darkness had followed her into waking, he realized, as the stuff of nightmares erupted around them.

EMORY

EMORY OPENED THE DOOR TO THE SLEEPSCAPE AND stepped onto that curved path lined with impossible stars. She immediately reached into her pocket, breathing a sigh of relief as her hand closed around the vial of salt water she'd brought. She poured it into her cupped hand and rested her marked wrist in the little makeshift pool.

The Selenic Mark glowed silver as it activated, and with it, Emory called out to Romie.

I want to speak to Romie Brysden.

She threw every ounce of magic into this place of dreams and nightmares, trying not to think of Baz in the Belly of the Beast, of the minutes trickling down like sand in an hourglass, each grain bringing them closer to the rising tide.

Something, at last, answered.

Emory, Emory.

A prickling on the back of her neck. She turned, scanning the darkness.

And there Romie stood, a little farther down the path.

Romie turned slowly toward her, looking just as she had the night of the initiation: soft brown curls framing her freckled face, clad in a simple collared shirt and corduroy pants that hugged her generous curves, so different from the plaid skirts and frilly tops she usually wore. More practical. Everything about her was the same as it had been last spring, down to the shadows under her eyes, which widened as they fell on Emory.

"Em? Is that really you?"

A broken sob escaped Emory's lips. She ran to Romie, and Romie to her, and here in the space between waking and sleeping, they hugged each other close.

"I found you," Emory cried.

Romie was *here*, in the sleepscape. She was *real*—and yet still not real enough, she realized. It was as if a watery film were separating them. They could touch each other, sure enough, but it felt almost like an illusion about to shatter.

They pulled apart, and when Romie spoke, it sounded like Emory was hearing her from underwater, the sound distorted and far yet near enough to touch.

"How are you here?" Romie asked. Horror struck her, and her fingers tightened painfully around Emory's wrists. "How are you *here*, Em? Did you go through the door?"

"No, Ro, we're in the sleepscape. This is just a dream."

Her grip eased. "You didn't go through the Hourglass?"

"I'm calling you through the sleepscape, just like you did."

With a frown, Romie searched the darkness around them. "Did a Dreamer bring you?"

"Sort of? I'm . . . Well, I can use Dreamer magic."

"How–"

"It's a long story. I'm not sure how much time we have."

Her eyes narrowed. "But you're alive?"

"Yes, Ro, I'm alive. You're the one who had me thinking you were dead."

Romie swore, wiping furiously at her tear-stained face. "Well, I'm not."

She drew Emory in for another hug, biting down a sob, and Emory didn't care that the weight and feel of her felt off, only that she was *here*.

And then Romie pulled back, shoving at her.

"Ow," Emory bit out.

"You stupid asshole. Why did you have to follow me that night? What the fuck were you thinking, going to Dovermere like that?"

"*Me?* What about *you*? Risking your life to join the Selenic Order just so you could get a taste for other magics?"

Romie flinched. "You know about that?"

"Yes, I know about *that*." Emory showed her the glowing mark on her wrist. "I'm one of them now."

Romie lifted her arm in mirror to Emory's. Her own mark glowed silver—not black, thankfully.

"I can't believe you didn't tell me." Emory pushed her sleeve down. She couldn't quite keep the anger from her voice. "We're supposed to tell each other *everything*, Ro."

Color rose in Romie's cheeks. She crossed her arms defensively. "I couldn't say anything, could I? It's called a *secret* society for a reason."

"Yeah, well, it sucked. All this time, you had me thinking you didn't want to be friends anymore. That you'd finally had enough of me."

"Don't be ridiculous."

"How am I being ridiculous? This is what you do, Romie. You get bored of things and people and leave them behind to chase after more exciting prospects."

"I would never do that to you."

"You *did*, though." Her voice broke. "You did. And look where it got you."

She expected Romie to counter with more defiance, but was taken aback when she deflated, looking contrite. "You're right. I'm sorry, Em. I didn't mean for anyone to get hurt. I just . . ." Romie cast a look around the sleepscape. Unshed tears glistened like stars in her eyes. "Did the others make it?" she asked quietly. "Serena, Dania, Harlow, Daphné?"

Four broken bodies on the sand.

"I'm sorry," Emory said. "They're dead."

Romie only nodded, swallowed. As if she had expected this.

"What happened to you, Ro?"

Romie blew out a breath. "When the tide rushed in . . . I had my eyes open through the whole thing. The waves were spinning us around the Hourglass, and it *opened*, Em. It really opened, and before I knew it, I was through."

"The door to the Deep."

Romie pursed her lips. "I'd been dreaming of it, you know. There was this song in my sleep, always calling me to Dovermere. Just like in *Song of the Drowned Gods*." She laughed harshly. "I became obsessed with finding the epilogue because I was *so sure* it was the key to lead me to the next world. I thought having access to the kind of magic the Order has might help me find it. Instead that fucking ritual brought me to the Tides-damned sleepscape."

Emory frowned. "The sleepscape? You mean all this time, you've been asleep?"

"No, that's why it doesn't make any sense, because I'm *awake*." Romie glanced around them with a frown. "It's as if I'm in the sleepscape but not. Like it's some sort of . . . in-between, and I'm stuck here whether I'm sleeping or waking. I've tried reaching for dreams, but it feels off. I only managed it with you, and even

then, it was hard to do. Like trying to call out to you from too far a distance."

Emory repressed a shiver. "We think . . . We think you might be in some kind of liminal space between our world and the Deep."

Romie gave a harsh laugh. "Purgatory, huh? Figures."

"Is Jordyn with you?"

"He is." A hesitancy in her eyes, her voice. "An umbra got to him early on. I've been tending to him, making sure he doesn't succumb to the umbrae's pull, but he hasn't been the same since."

Romie hugged her arms. "I wanted to keep looking for the epilogue because I can *feel it*, Em. It's here somewhere, and it's the key to everything. It still calls out to me, that fucking song I can't shake. We tried going after it together, the four of us, but the others . . . They didn't acclimate well, not like I did. The farther down the path we went, the worse it got. They'd start bleeding from their noses and ears and would find it hard to breathe. So we had to turn back and stay here. I watched over them, fighting the urge to follow the song, because without me, I don't know . . . I don't think this place is meant for those who aren't Dreamers." She frowned at Emory. "However it is you got here, you need to be careful."

"I'll be fine. But what happened to Travers and Lia?" Emory asked, hoping Romie could provide an explanation for their washing up onshore. Wondering if she even knew of the horrible fate they had suffered.

"First it was Travers," Romie said grimly. "He kept hearing a voice. But not like my voice, not like the music in my dream. He said this voice was calling him home. I thought it was the sleepscape taking its toll on him, but . . . One day, he was there one minute and gone the next. Vanished in what I can only describe as a wave of darkness. Like a riptide.

"We couldn't make sense of it. And then the same thing happened to Lia. I *saw* her running and crying to the voice she said

was calling her home, and she vanished, taken by this strange tide just like Travers. I tried to follow her through that darkness, but it only took her. Only her."

Romie's voice came out thick with emotion. "A part of me hoped they did go home. That whatever purgatory this must be, it'd finally come to pass for them."

"They did come back," Emory said painfully. "But not . . . Romie, you can't let Jordyn follow that voice. *You* can't follow that voice."

"Why? What happened?"

"We found them. Travers and Lia."

"Alive?"

Emory shook her head. Devastation darkened Romie's brown eyes, and Emory couldn't bring herself to tell her the gruesome truth of their deaths. Didn't want to give her a false sense of hope by telling her they'd been alive when they'd first washed up, even if it was just for a moment. They had to make sense of this before Romie or Jordyn tried to follow those voices and suffered the same fate.

But they also couldn't stay here—that was clear enough. They needed a way out that wouldn't get them killed.

Romie's eyes narrowed onto a point over Emory's shoulder. She stiffened. "Jordyn, what are you doing?"

"Jordyn?" Emory echoed, whipping around.

He was a dark shape down the path, his movements slow and uncoordinated, almost as if he were drunk. There was a gaunt, haunted look about him, and down the side of his face were three long, black gashes. He didn't seem to hear Romie or see Emory as he leaned dangerously close to the edge of the path. Stars shied away from him and the gathering shadows beneath him.

A clawed hand materialized from the dark then, made of shadows itself. Slowly, it reached for Jordyn, whose own hand lifted in a mirroring gesture.

Romie tore toward him. "Jordyn, *no!*"

Those monstrous claws sank into Jordyn's flesh. Cords of black sinews raced up his arm and neck and into his open mouth, and just as Romie reached him, darkness burst all around them. Emory thought she might have screamed, thought she heard Romie crying out to her, saying something that didn't register, but all she knew then was chaos and cold and fear—

Emory stumbled back into waking.

She opened her eyes to another tenebrous space, to another Brysden shouting her name.

She was awake—but so was the stuff of nightmares.

The darkness had followed her. It expanded and twisted and stretched, looking to fill the cavern. A chilling breath blew through the Belly of the Beast, knocking over the lantern she'd left on the cave floor, leaving only the one in Baz's hand, a weak beacon in the void.

There was silence. Neither of them dared to breathe or move, all too aware of the presence that loomed.

Baz saw it first, the shape that lengthened behind Emory out of the darkness. A slender thing of bone and shadow, humanoid in theory but stretched too long and too thin, with fathomless eyes and clawed hands tipped in black.

An umbra. Nightmare personified.

I thought I might have pulled one into the waking world with me once, Kai had said.

But it was impossible. He'd claimed they were contained to the sleepscape, and yet—

A low rumble rattled her bones, the only warning sign before the umbra swiped for her.

Baz wrenched Emory out of the way just in time. *"Run!"*

They bolted for the exit, feet slipping on the wet cave floor as the creature behind them shrieked and screeched, darkness and fear

given form. Emory felt its cold breath on the back of her neck as she stumbled forward. She fell to her hands and knees, the breath knocked out of her.

"Baz!"

Pain lanced through her ankle as claws pierced her skin. She kicked at the creature, desperate to extricate herself from its grasp. Baz's feet sloshed into a shallow pool as he came to an abrupt stop, turning toward her. The umbra let out a piercing wail and recoiled, as if blinded by the light Baz was holding up to it.

Emory scrambled to her feet. As Baz reached for her, the lantern slipped from his grasp, shattering on the ground.

"No!"

Emory shot her hand out—not to grab the lantern, but to pluck the last flickering ember of light from it before it died. The Lightkeeper magic came instinctively, and she was glad she'd had practice wielding it on the harvest moon. The feeble light twisted around her outstretched hand, kept safe in her grasp.

"Look out!" Baz yelled.

Emory glanced over her shoulder and stared into the face of nightmares—into eyes so black they seemed to drown out every bit of light in her soul.

They devour dreams like black holes gobbling up any star that moves too close.

She thought she might have glimpsed something human in those depthless orbs, but then the umbra's power seeped into her, and Emory screamed.

Fear was a blade and it ripped through her, bright and burning.

30

BAZ

COLD SPEARED THROUGH BAZ'S SOUL. FEAR WAS A SEED in his chest that bloomed into a thing he might choke on as the umbra turned its empty eyes on him, making images come to life in his mind:

A blast of power. Blood and rubble and veins shot through with silver. His father telling him everything would be all right. His mother's singing that he hadn't heard for years and Romie's baking that he would likely never taste again. His sister's name on a silver plaque and caves that beckoned and the stormy-eyed girl who pulled away from him over and over. The ache in his heart every time he watched her drift into a world where he could not follow. The empty commons and the dismal absence of Kai.

Everything he'd ever hoped and dreamed and feared, pulled to the surface by the umbra's magic as it sought to make him hollow.

This was so much worse than the kind of magic that Kai would use on him, because he could trust Kai to make it all stop, to end the nightmares with a look, a touch, a single note of his midnight

voice. But this . . . If nightmares were but a single droplet of fear, *this* was an entire ocean of it. Baz felt himself slipping, tumbling through fear after fear–until the umbra scrambled back with a shriek of pain.

Beams of light shot from Emory's hands as she stood defiantly in front of the umbra, the gash on her ankle already healing. She cast the creature back into the depths of the cavern, creating a barrier of light between them. A light to keep the nightmares at bay. A reprieve–if only temporary.

"What happened back there?" Baz gasped. "How did an *umbra* follow you out of the sleepscape?"

Emory ignored him, taking a careful step toward the creature that writhed in the darkness beyond the light. Baz tried to stop her from getting any closer. She shrugged him off.

"Jordyn . . ." The umbra stilled at the name. "Jordyn, if you're still in there . . ."

Bleak, horrible understanding dawned on Baz. If this was Jordyn, then Emory must have found Romie in the sleepscape too. But there was nothing of the student behind the umbra's eyes. It was a predator assessing its next move, and as Emory took a step closer, it pounced.

The umbra clawed at the barrier of light, and Emory buckled beneath the impact, biting back a sob. Baz's hand shot out to steady her.

"He's gone, Emory. That's not Jordyn anymore."

The umbra's wails turned piercing as it sought to disperse the slowly waning light. Emory couldn't keep it back forever. They had to stop it, but could a nightmare be killed? Could fear be conquered?

The walls rumbled around them, giving even the umbra pause. There was a sound like a great thunderclap, so loud it rattled his bones.

The tide rushing in.

Baz glanced at his watch. The hands had slipped, and now they were out of time, with nightmares closing in on both sides. The umbra pushed back against Emory's light, using their distraction to its advantage. She faltered, leaning heavily against Baz's side as she held trembling hands out to keep the light from dying.

Out of time out of time out of time–

They needed more of it, or for it to stand still.

Baz reached for the threads of time, this power he was familiar with if only in a distant, scholarly sort of way. It was knowledge that existed without experience, and as his eyes focused on the hands of his watch again, he tried not to think of it, this nagging inadequacy he feared had become him.

For so long, he'd kept his power in check, shying away from his ability and that damn line he'd drawn between small magic and big magic.

What if in pretending to be mediocre, he had become so?

What if he couldn't wield his magic now, the one time it counted?

A trickle of water appeared at the mouth of the cavern. Baz thought of Romie, of how any hope for her would drown here with them if he couldn't bring himself to save them now.

Stop, he thought as the water streamed in, so much quicker now.

Please, he begged.

It was a language he had not spoken often, but it came rushing back to him all the same. Familiar and lovely and strange and entirely his. The whole world seemed to pause for him. Time held its breath. He knew it by the way the pools of water at his feet stopped rippling, by the droplets of water that hung untethered in the air. He and Emory were still in motion, as was the umbra still testing itself against the light, but time, Baz knew, had stopped around them. *For* them.

The hands of his watch were frozen where they stood, but he

could see their subtle vibration, as if they longed for that forward motion ingrained in the very fabric of their design, trying to break free of Baz's hold.

Quickly now, his magic murmured in his ear. It wouldn't hold forever.

But Baz didn't need forever; only long enough.

He tugged at Emory, pulling her wordlessly toward the tunnels as she focused on keeping the umbra at bay. Shallow water nipped at their ankles, then all the way up to their knees. In the narrow corridor outside the Belly of the Beast, they came upon a large wave frozen in time, like a great, watery hand stopped mid-motion as it reached for them.

Baz ran tentative fingers along the wave, watching in amazement as the motion rippled slowly through the particles of water. A little farther down, the frozen wave rose into a veritable wall between them and the next bend in the carved corridor.

The only way out was through.

"You think there's any chance the umbrae are deathly afraid of water?" Emory asked. She sagged against him, weakened light pouring from her hands. The umbra lay in wait in the dark.

"It's fear itself. I don't think getting a little wet will be much of an issue for it."

"So what do you suggest?"

Baz considered her. "Can you swim while holding the light?"

A nervous, near-hysterical laugh bubbled past Emory's lips. "I don't have much of a choice, do I?" Something dawned on her face then, an idea taking shape. She grabbed his hand in hers.

"What are you doing?"

"As soon as I release the light, we make a run for it."

"Wait, no, you can't let go of the—"

Baz gasped as sudden warmth enveloped him. It started in his hand, where his fingers were laced through hers. His skin glowed,

as if his entire body was suffused with light, like a protective second skin. He blinked at Emory, who was shining just like him. The beam at the end of her other hand intensified, a bright sunburst that swelled and pulsed.

"Now!"

She released the light. It blasted the umbra back, and Emory shoved at Baz, shouting at him to *run* as the umbra let out a deafening shriek.

They hurried toward the frozen wave. Baz barely had time to take a deep breath before plunging into its ice-cold depths. Emory was instantly at his side, and together they moved through the odd, gravity-less water like brightly burning stars making their way across the dark recesses of the sky, at once eternally slow and impossibly quick.

His pulse beat too rapidly, like the needle of a watch out of sorts, jumping from one line to the next in erratic motions. Before long, his lungs screamed at him, his body rebelling against him, desperate for air.

This is it, Baz thought. He would die in this time-still wave before he could emerge, and then time would speed up again and the tide would rush in with all the sea's power at its back, and he and Emory would drown, and everything would be lost.

He broke the surface.

Baz breathed in a painful gasp of air, clawing at the wet floor of the half-submerged tunnel. Emory helped pull him up, and together they fell to their hands and knees, both of them still glowing in that protective light. They were in an odd bubble of waterless space created by the curve of the immobile wave. The distant sound of crashing waves reached them, strangely muffled in the quiet, and for a horrible moment, Baz thought he'd lost his grip on time. But the hands of his watch were still frozen, the water around them still motionless.

"The sea," Emory gasped out. "We have to be close to the exit."

That was what they heard: the rising tide battering against the cliffside, the outside world unaffected by Baz's magic. If they made it out of here unscathed, those deadly waves would no doubt make quick work of them.

You could stop time for them, too, his magic whispered in his ear. *A single wave, an entire ocean, the world itself. Nothing is out of your reach.*

There was little comfort in the thought.

"We can make it," Emory said. "We just have to–"

The umbra emerged from the time-still wave at their backs. Darkness filled the space around them, and Emory screamed as it sank its claws into her side despite the light still wrapped around her.

The umbra dragged her toward the watery depths.

"No!" Baz lunged for her, wet fingers slipping against hers.

Emory's eyes widened with unspeakable fear, mouth open on a soundless scream.

The light around her flickered out.

And then she was gone.

EMORY

THE STRANGE, STILL WATER MUFFLED EMORY'S SCREAM. Bubbles rose and remained suspended around her in the dark as she fought against the umbra's hold—against *Jordyn's* hold.

Cold seeped into her even as a great fire raged in her lungs, and memories of another tide of nightmares rushed in: a voice in the deep, four bodies on a beach, Travers's emaciated face, and the scream that tore through Lia's throat and burned it to a crisp.

Fears and nightmares, crushed dreams and dwindling hopes—the umbra feasted on all of it, *delighted* in her pain. The sorrow she'd felt as a child every time ships sailed past, taking the idea of her mother further away from her. The sting of Penelope's words as she accused her of not caring. The spark in Baz's eyes when he looked at her, full of soft yearning she feared she might never quite reciprocate—or worse, that perhaps she did, or was beginning to, and it might break everything between them, this rekindled friendship that was becoming so dear to her.

The umbra wasn't afraid of her here in the dark. The light was

gone, and soon her life would follow. Water was already filling her lungs.

She'd been so close, Romie and Jordyn just within reach for one blissful moment before the umbrae erupted from the darkness beyond stars and claimed Jordyn as their own.

The relief on his face . . . It was almost as if he'd *wanted* to become one of them.

It all came back to her now, as if pulled up to the surface of her mind by the umbra's power. When Jordyn had emerged in his new form, unrecognizable save for that glimmer of humanness still in his black eyes, Romie had pushed Emory back, yelling at her to wake up, to get out. But Emory had only stared, frozen, at the monster that rose from the dark.

A person who'd become a shade. A Soultender robbed of a soul.

He wasn't supposed to follow her back into the waking world.

She wasn't sure how it happened. His wraithlike hands had wrapped around her throat, and then: the feeling of tumbling through stars, the cold of the cave and the hard rock beneath her and the sharp, acidic taste of fear in her mouth as the umbra emerged behind her. It shouldn't have been possible—wasn't a full moon—and a distant part of her wondered if she had unwittingly called on Romie's Dreamer magic to take him out of the sleepscape.

But no . . . This was no mere illusion, and it did not dissolve to dust.

What once was Jordyn pulled on her now with the intent to destroy her. Her vision blurred. The sea would claim her at last, and this would have all been for nothing.

Emory, Emory.

There it was, the Beast calling her back to its depths and into death's waiting arms.

She had cheated death, once, but for the life of her, she couldn't remember how.

Yes—*life*. She had walked hand in hand with it before. Its power had flowed through her veins, answered her call.

And didn't all magics unlock at her touch?

Emory reached for the one that had always come to her the easiest, the magic that had shaped and saved her time and time again. It jolted through her like an electric current, lending strength enough to fight back against the umbra's hold.

Heal, she thought, and it was so very eager to comply.

But she couldn't heal away the water in her lungs, couldn't create air she desperately needed, and there was no light to call upon here, no saving grace, no hope. Only this dread that filled every part of her. How had they managed to breathe underwater at the river? A distant part of her knew the answer, something about wards, magic she wasn't skilled enough to call on, didn't know how, because she was so damn mediocre.

Emory stopped fighting.

Let this nightmare drag me down where I belong, she thought.

But something else reached for her then, pulling her in the opposite direction. The tide, it seemed, wanted a piece of her too.

Except the tide had hands. A face. It yanked her out of the water, gifting her a second life. Or perhaps, more accurately, a third.

Emory fell back against the rock, fighting for every breath. Baz's soaked figure bent over her. She clung to him desperately, not quite believing it was him, unable to grasp that she was still here, alive, with him at her side.

"I've got you," he breathed. His shaking hands smoothed back wet hair from her face, eyes wild behind his skewed glasses. "I've got you."

She wanted to break down in his arms, but the nightmare wasn't over. The umbra emerged from the water again, towering over them. Tendrils of dark water wrapped around its elongated limbs as an angry shriek wrenched free of its throat. Cold frosted the

frozen wave, and before either of them could move, the umbra lunged.

It wrapped its claws around Baz's throat, as if in retribution for taking Emory away. Baz's legs kicked wildly as the umbra lifted him from the ground, his hands searching for purchase, trying to escape the umbra's hold.

Emory couldn't see the invisible shadows that plagued him, but she *felt* it, the way the umbra feasted on Baz's fears. She saw it in the tears that lined his eyes, and when his limbs stilled, the fight waning from him, Emory uttered a desperate cry.

She drew herself up, soaked and dripping and fearless as she opened her senses wide. She reached for whatever remnants of light she could grasp, reached for darkness and death and life and protection, for the illusion of hope and dreams and fears, anything to fend off the very real nightmare before her. The thing that was trying to *devour* Baz, snuff out his light and make him into a shade of what he was.

Emory wouldn't let it. She couldn't let the umbra destroy the boy in the field, the boy she'd looked up at the stars with, the boy who'd helped her time and again despite the crushing weight of a thousand fears.

He had saved her; she owed him the same kind of courage in return.

She screamed as magic rushed through her, blinding, searing. It tore at her, silver in her veins, blood that sang, a great crashing in her ears as it sought to burst forth.

Her power was a tidal wave unleashed. And though Emory knew it might be the end of her, she let it consume her.

BAZ

BAZ SUSPECTED EMORY'S POWER WAS CLOSE TO SLIPPING past that invisible line. Her skin rippled with strange light, like moonlight over water, her veins shining silver just beneath the surface, pulsing brighter and brighter. A star on the verge of implosion.

The Collapsing readying its fateful blow.

And even with the umbra's claws around his throat and fear like he'd never known seeping through him, all Baz could think of was her. The pain of knowing she would become like his father, like Kai, her magic eclipsing everything she had once been. The girl who made dead things grow back, who made sunflowers bloom in an illusioned field, who made facing his fears a little more bearable than it had been before.

Baz tried to reach for his magic, this thing singing to him just past the cold, dreadful terror wresting for control. A beam of blinding light burst from Emory's chest. It shot toward the monster holding Baz in its grasp, made it shriek, shrink back in pain. Fear dug its

claws out from him, and Baz slumped onto the rock below, head spinning as silver flooded his vision.

Emory cried out in pain as another beam of light shot from her. There was a crack, a sound that ripped through the world as a piece of the cave ceiling came loose.

And suddenly, Baz was back in the printing press, with his father's arms wrapped around him and machinery raining down on them as the blast of his Collapsing razed everything it touched.

His worst fear reenacted. His darkest memory replicated.

He couldn't let this happen again. Not to her.

Baz pulled on all the threads around him.

The rock froze midair. The umbra stilled, stumbled back, disappeared into the motionless water. The silver light around Emory receded as Baz wound back the figurative clock that sent her Collapsing back to a time it had not yet happened. And this was so much bigger than the death magic she'd wielded on another new moon night, when he had stopped that, too. And he was so very far past that line between small magic and big magic, but still he trudged on deeper and deeper, watching as the silver in her veins dulled, then darkened to blues and reds and purples.

She was a dying star in reverse, until at last, there was just Emory. No longer shining with ethereal light, but shaking with the impossible weight of what was and then was not.

"You're okay," Baz rasped. "Everything's all right."

He had done that. He had *stopped* her Collapsing.

Emory sagged against him. "Thank you."

Baz wrapped his arm around her, his cheek pressed against her wet hair, and realized he would do it all again in a heartbeat.

The sea heaved the two of them onto the beach, boneless and utterly spent.

They'd gone into the caves at the lowest point of the noonday tide

and emerged just before it reached its peak. An entire afternoon had somehow passed in the blink of an eye, though it felt, peculiarly, like it had spanned a lifetime.

Baz's ears still rang with the echo of monstrous shrieks and falling rock, and all he could see were Emory's silver veins and that blast of power that almost tore the cliff down on them. He watched the rapid rise and fall of her chest now as she lay sprawled on her back with her head turned to the horizon. Her veins were a normal color under her skin.

They'd wordlessly dragged each other out of the caves before the umbra could return. The incoming tide hadn't been so bad after all, half-hearted waves battering against the cliffside. The shoreline had been close enough to swim. The whole cliffside had seemed to shake when Baz released his hold on his magic. Rocks had fallen as time resumed, and as they swam for the shore, Baz felt the strange caress of Dovermere against his magic, pleading, *Wait, don't go.*

He reached now for one of the wool blankets they'd left on the beach and wrapped it around Emory. Sunken eyes met his, and in them he saw everything that felt too big and impossible to say.

He'd saved her from Collapsing—had *reversed* it, this thing that was supposed to be inevitable, unconquerable. It should have eclipsed her entirely and left nothing but raw, destructive power in its wake, but here she still was, still *her.* Still safe.

Emory grabbed his hand, searching for signs of silver in his own veins. "Are you . . ."

"I'm fine."

Unease filled the space between his lungs where the words had been lodged. He was absolutely, completely fine. There had been no bottom to his magic, no end in sight, nothing to warn him that he might have gone too far past that line, and so he was *fine.*

Too easy. It shouldn't have been so easy to wield such magic. *He* should have Collapsed trying to prevent her from doing so herself.

Adrenaline coursed through him, made him dizzy with wonder. If he had enough control over his magic to stop other people's Collapsings . . . it could change *everything*. Eclipse-born students might truly find sanctuary at Aldryn with him there to protect them.

It was such an impossible, ludicrous thought, something Baz would never have even let himself *dream* of before. It felt like the whole world was unfurling before him, rife with possibility.

Emory looked at him like she was thinking the same thing, like she was seeing him for all he could be if he finally shed his fears, and it was a rush all its own, to have her look at him in such a way. Their labored breaths fogged the air between them as they held each other's gaze, the waves clamoring against the cliffside serving as a stark reminder of what they'd so narrowly escaped.

And suddenly they were wheezing with delirious laughter, the tension and horror and impossibility of it all coming to a crest. Emory leaned into him, and he wasn't sure if her shaking was from laughter alone or cold and shock as well. His cheek pressed against her sopping hair, fingers numb as he gripped the blanket around her. She tilted her face up to his, so close they breathed each other in. There was no laughter now, only stark reality, the warmth between them that proved they were still alive.

Nothing is out of your reach.

For once, Baz didn't think.

Before he knew what he was doing, he grabbed her face between his hands and kissed her.

His mind went blank at the sea-salt taste of her lips. Emory hesitated for the briefest, most terrifying second before her mouth moved against his, soft and warm and inviting in a way he hadn't known he'd craved until just now. A small sound rumbled at the back of his throat as she deepened the kiss. But then she was pulling away, holding him at arm's length.

Baz blinked incomprehensibly. Emory was frowning down at her

hand, where the sacred spiral glowed silver on her wrist. For a terrible moment, he thought she might have Collapsed after all. He reached for her arm, fear coating his mouth.

"Emory . . ."

She had a faraway look in her eye, as if she saw something he could not.

"What happened?" she breathed.

A sick, sinking feeling tugged on Baz. "I'm sorry, I thought–"

"Keiran, what are you talking about?"

Keiran?

Baz scanned the beach. There was no one here but them. Emory still had that distant look, all color leeched from her skin. He shook her lightly, his mind racing. She blinked. Swore. Finally, she came back to herself, her eyes clearing to focus on him.

"Are you all right?"

"It's over," she said as if still in a daze.

"Emory, what–"

"The dean found out I'm a Tidecaller." She wrenched herself away from Baz, wiping furiously at her face. "She knows you've been helping me train. She's on her way here to deal with us right now." Her lip trembled. "I'm so sorry, Baz."

"Emory, slow down." What the fuck had just happened? "Fulton can't possibly have found out. I'm the only one who knows . . ."

He eyed the mark on her wrist again, no longer faintly glowing. His shoulders fell as he put the pieces together. "You were talking to Keiran through the mark."

Just like she'd tried with Romie the night Lia reappeared.

"Does he know you're Eclipse-born?"

"Baz . . ."

The remorse in her eyes was all the answer he needed. And it was a knife twisting in his gut, this realization that he wasn't the only one to bear her secret, to have earned her trust. That she would

share such a thing with Keiran Dunhall Thornby, of all people . . .

Horror and anger and hurt rose in his throat. "He's part of this, isn't he?"

Dovermere, the drownings, those marks on everyone's Tides-damned wrists . . .

Baz had known from the start that Emory was keeping things from him, and all along he'd been too blinded by his feelings for her, too scared of losing the fragile, rekindled bond between them to dig deeper.

But this–*this*, he couldn't overlook.

"Is Keiran the reason Romie's gone?"

"Of course not. He's trying to help me *save* her."

Baz huffed a cold laugh. "You can't trust him, Emory. Whatever he's told you, whatever it is you're involved in . . . There's no way he would ever work alongside an Eclipse-born unless he had some ulterior motive. He doesn't care about saving Romie. He clearly doesn't care about you if he betrayed you to the dean."

"It wasn't him," Emory asserted. "And you've got him all wrong."

"His parents were killed in a Collapsing incident."

"I know. He told me everything."

Baz flinched. "And did he also tell you who their killer was?"

She looked away, and it was confirmation enough.

"My father took his family away from him. Ever since, he's had it out for me, for Romie, for the entire Brysden family and every single Eclipse-born there is. Tides, he even broke up Kai and his former lover because he couldn't stand the idea of his friend being with some lowly Eclipse-born."

This seemed to startle her, but she quickly composed herself. "It's not like that. *He's* not like that." She drew herself up angrily, a defensive gleam in her eyes. "He sees the value in my power and has never once been afraid of it. Unlike you."

"Then he must be a damn good liar, and you must be more of a

fool than I thought. Tides, it makes *me* the even bigger fool, because despite everything in me screaming that I couldn't trust you, I did. I took a chance on you, and I–"

He bit back his words, shaking his head, trying to make sense of this emotional whiplash. A moment ago, he was kissing her, thinking nothing had ever felt so right in his life. For the first time, he'd put himself out there, laid bare his heart, and dared to hope she might feel something of the same toward him.

How very wrong he'd been.

"Were you just using me?"

The words came out as broken as he felt.

Emory opened her mouth but caught herself as her eyes landed on something behind him. Baz whipped around. Dean Fulton was making her way toward them on the path that led down to the beach. She wore a grave expression and a long trench coat that fluttered in the wind.

The dean of Aldryn jerked her chin at them. "Come with me, both of you."

She turned on her heel, and Baz started after her. Emory reached for him with a desperate plea. "Baz–"

He brushed past her, dutifully following the dean back up to the school to face whatever fate awaited him.

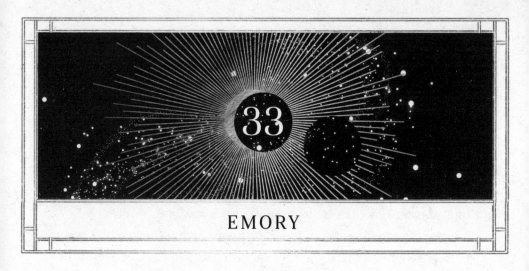

EMORY

THE DULL RINGING IN EMORY'S EARS WAS THE ONLY sound in the reception room outside Dean Fulton's office. It kept her company as she sat alone on an upholstered bench, staring at the tapestried wall in front of her without really seeing it. At some point, someone had taken a sample of her blood, the sting of the needle now a dull throbbing in the crook of her arm. Her clothes were still damp, but she'd been offered a rough blanket to keep warm, at least.

Baz had been in and out of the dean's office without so much as a passing glance at Emory. The rupture between them was deafening, tearing wider with every step he took away from her.

That kiss still lingered in her mind, on her mouth.

It had taken her aback, though it really shouldn't have. She'd done this—had known how Baz felt about her and used it to her advantage, pushing at it like a bruise, leading him on without a care for the pain it might bring him.

She'd never meant for it to go this far—for him to actually kiss her.

And yet.

She recalled the fluttering of her heart, her body's treacherous response. She had *liked* kissing him, and she had to wonder if a part of her had wanted it to go that far, if the feelings she felt for him—this fearless, heroic version of him—were real.

Emory flinched as the office door opened, and there stood Dean Fulton, looking as put together as ever. The tightness around her eyes and mouth was the only thing that betrayed the direness of the situation as she wordlessly beckoned Emory inside.

Emory had been here once before, on another new moon. She was more alert now than she was last spring, noting the dark, gleaming wood, the silver and brass trinkets that adorned every corner, the impressive collection of carefully labeled water vials, the leather-bound tomes that looked as old as the school itself.

Dean Fulton sat behind her large desk. "Have a seat, Ms. Ainsleif."

The ringing in Emory's ears grew louder under the dean's scrutiny. Fulton drew a hand over her closely shaven salt-and-pepper head, leaning back in her chair. A heavy silence cloaked the room, punctuated only by the ticking of a clock, the faint metallic whirr of an instrument on the dean's desk, the sizzling of embers in the chimney. The window was closed, yet Emory thought she heard that voice again, calling to her, mocking her.

Emory, Emory.

"I've tested your blood." Fulton motioned to the selenograph on her desk, a much newer model than the one Emory had used in the library with Baz. "It clearly marks you as Eclipse-born." She fixed her with a piercing gaze. "This is the part where you explain yourself."

Emory stared at the hands folded in her lap, at the New Moon sigil she had once been so proud to wear, the dark moon and silver narcissus she couldn't stand to look at now.

She told the dean as much of the truth as she could. That she'd uncovered her new Tidecaller powers after Dovermere. That she'd since been training with Baz, too scared to come forward for fear of being administered the Unhallowed Seal. It was no use lying about it now; if what Keiran had told her through the mark was true, Tides-damned *Penelope* had already told the dean everything, including Baz's involvement.

Emory couldn't fathom how Penelope might have found out, nor why she would have done such a thing. She'd been racking her brain to see if she'd slipped up at any point, if Penelope might have seen her with Baz, overheard their conversations about her magic. Penelope had still been fast asleep when Emory left her room earlier this morning–she couldn't possibly have known she was at Dovermere.

The dean leaned back in her chair, a calculated look in her eye. "Obviously, you'll need to be stripped of your New Moon identity and receive the mark of House Eclipse. Though whether or not you should be branded for hiding the true nature of your powers remains to be seen by the Regulators." She shook her head, looking suddenly haggard. "You should have gone to them as soon as these powers started manifesting."

Just then, a knock came at the door, and whoever it was didn't wait before barging in.

"Dean Fulton," Keiran said smoothly.

He looked dapper, dressed in a tweed suit that made him look older than he was. He held himself with such commanding power, Emory felt the knot of nerves in her stomach start to untangle, the last words he'd spoken through the mark washing over her with a sense of relief. *Hang tight, Ains. I won't let anything happen to you.*

Faint annoyance lit the dean's eyes. "Keiran. You can't simply waltz in here however you please."

"I only need a moment, if you'd allow it." Keiran strode over to where Emory was sitting. "I'm here to plead Emory's case."

"I'm sure you don't know what you're talking about."

The hand he rested on the back of her chair was a small comfort, as if he were saying, *I've got you, Ains.* "I know she's Eclipse-born, Sybille. I've known for a while."

Though the dean didn't bat an eye at his casual use of her first name—Emory was reminded that she'd taken Keiran on as her ward after his parents died—she seemed utterly taken aback by the revelation.

"And you never thought to share this knowledge with me?"

"She's under the Order's protection."

The dean huffed. "Is she now."

Emory's pulse raced. Keiran was lying—the Order had told them they'd rescind any protection of her should she ever be found out. That *he* would be held responsible for her. She had to wonder how much the dean knew of the Order; Emory didn't think she was part of it, didn't remember seeing her at the lighthouse. But the dean seemed to know enough as she considered the thinly veiled threat beneath Keiran's words.

A carefully contained storm brewed beneath the dean's pinched face. "I've often turned a blind eye to what your Order does on this campus, Keiran, but you and Ms. Ainsleif have put this entire college at risk by keeping her magic a secret. If anything had happened—"

"Except nothing did happen. I've seen her use her magic. I can vouch that she's taken every measure to ensure control over her power."

The dean gaped at him in disbelief. "Your parents must be turning in their graves to see you defending such reckless behavior from one of *them*."

Emory tried not to flinch at the unrestrained loathing that seeped into Fulton's words. As dean, she was supposed to be impartial, but here was the truth of her at last, her tone giving away just how much she disliked and mistrusted the Eclipse-born.

Emory half expected Keiran to agree with her. The dean was right, after all. If Keiran had seen just how close she'd been to Collapsing in the caves . . . Would he still defend her so ardently, knowing she'd had no control?

But Keiran didn't know, and so he only looked at Fulton with a complacent smile. "All the more reason to take my word for it." A pause. Then: "The Order is willing to recompense the school greatly if this is kept under wraps."

"Absolutely not. This needs to go to the Regulators. Ms. Ainsleif will be stripped of her New Moon tattoo and marked with the Eclipse sigil. There will be an inquiry—"

"And what do you think those conducting such an inquiry will say of the fact a Tidecaller was under your nose this entire time?" Keiran interjected. "They'll say Aldryn College didn't do its due diligence in testing its students for admission. They'll interrogate every single professor who never saw the truth of her power. They'll look into the drownings Emory is associated with and draw conclusions that would taint Aldryn's reputation for years to come, and yours by association. They'll gut this school alive, Sybille, unless you keep this secret contained to this very room and let the Order handle the mess for you. Your involvement will forever remain confidential. You have my word."

A silent battle of wills took place between the two of them. Finally, the dean conceded: "This will require the utmost discretion. Ms. Ainsleif will continue to pose as a student of Noviluna Hall, keep attending all her regular classes as if nothing

has changed. No one must suspect. Of course, we'll have to get Professor Selandyn on board to start training her properly and in secret."

"A fair arrangement," Keiran agreed.

"And then there's the matter of the girl, Penelope West. She's being brought here as we speak. Is she part of your Order, or is this something else we'll have to contain?"

"We have a Memorist who can take care of it," Keiran said coolly. "I'll have her come here straightaway."

Horror struck Emory at the thought of someone taking away Penelope's memory of this—but what other choice was there?

The dean's eyes found hers. "One step out of line, and I don't care what they do to me or this school—I'll send you straight to the Regulators to receive the Unhallowed Seal. Understood?"

"What's going to happen to Baz?"

"I've already advised Mr. Brysden that he's on academic probation until further notice. But as for the rest . . ."

Fulton looked at Keiran expectantly, and for a second, Emory feared he would suggest getting the Memorist to wipe Baz's memories too.

Please, anything but that.

But Keiran only said, "He's kept Emory's secret so far. Besides, isn't he Professor Selandyn's assistant? That could be useful. And if suspicions were ever to arise, his friendship with Emory provides the ideal cover."

"Then the secret will be contained to the people in this room, the Order, and those of House Eclipse only. Is that clear, Ms. Ainsleif?"

"Yes."

Fulton looked at Keiran again. "I'm doing this for the love I bore your parents. But for your sake, I hope you know what you're doing."

Keiran dipped his head in thanks and led Emory out of the office.

Penelope stood on the other side of the door, eyes wide and red-rimmed. Her lip wobbled. "Em, I'm so sorry . . . I don't know what came over me . . ."

"Save it, Nel. It's done." With the sudden realization that this might be her last shot at the truth before Penelope's memories were taken away, Emory asked, "How in the Deep did you even find out about me?"

"I don't know. Em, I swear, I would never do that to you."

A mirthless huff. "And yet here we are."

"That's the thing. I don't know how we got here. I just remember the party last night, and then I was in your room, seeing you and Lizaveta Orlov . . . Then it's just this weird distortion in my head and–"

The dean's voice cut her off. "Ms. West, please come in."

Penelope gave Emory one last pleading look before she stepped into the office. Emory banished her tearful face from her mind, trying not to think of what would happen when the Memorist arrived.

She felt numb as Keiran led her through the corridors.

"You didn't have to do any of that for me."

"Of course I did." Keiran stopped her beneath the cloisters, drawing her into a shadowed alcove. "Tides, Ains. The Order is *furious*. They were ready to shun you completely if this got out. I managed to convince them I could get Fulton to keep quiet. That it was better for everyone this way. Less risky to keep it contained to a single person the Order has influence over than the world at large."

The lengths to which he was willing to go to fight for her . . . She didn't think she deserved it. "How'd you find out, anyway?"

"I was on my way to see Fulton when Penelope came out of her office in near-hysterical tears. It took a little gentle coaxing, but she told me everything: that she'd seen you and Brysden going down

to Dovermere, that she knew you were a Tidecaller and had told Fulton." His throat bobbed with emotion. "You scared me, Ainsleif. I thought the caves might take you this time."

There was such anguish in his eyes it took Emory aback. "I'm fine. I made it out." *Barely.* She rubbed absently at her arms, thinking of Penelope. "I don't understand how she could have known. I never said *anything* to her, I swear."

"Do you think she might have spied on you?"

Emory blew out a laugh. The idea was absurd. Except . . .

The grief in Penelope's eyes after Lia's body was found. The party she'd gone to that was so unlike her usual self. The vehemence in her words as she berated Emory for being such an uncaring friend.

And the book Penelope had been obsessed with, about a Darkbearer who would cloak herself in shadows to spy on people . . .

Maybe it wasn't so far-fetched a thing. And it would serve Emory right—she *had* been a terrible friend to Penelope. Had set her eyes on the Selenic Order and nearly forgotten everything and everyone else in the process.

"I don't know," she said at last. "Possibly."

The worry on Keiran's face made Baz's words ring in her ears. And though she didn't want to give him the satisfaction of heeding his warning, she had to ask.

"Why did you get close to me? If it was to get some kind of revenge on Baz and Romie for what happened to your parents . . ." Keiran stilled, but she kept going: "Is that why you tapped Romie for initiation? You hoped Dovermere would take care of her so the Brysdens would hurt like you did?"

A loss for a loss.

"I can't believe you'd think that."

The hurt in his eyes made her want to take it all back.

"I got close to you because I *saw* you, Ains. I saw you at your

most vulnerable when you washed up on that beach. I saw the pain and grief you came back with, the resilience it took to face everyone when your whole world had been ripped away. I see how incredible you are, and *that* is why I got close to you."

Something in her broke then. The words came out in a sob. "I'm sorry. Everything is too much, and I just . . ."

"It's all right."

Keiran pulled her in, a light in the dark as he'd always been. She clung to him as whatever dam she'd built around her crumbled and everything came pouring out–everything that happened in Dover-mere, the sleepscape, Jordyn. The only part she left out was her close call with her Collapsing, too scared and ashamed to admit to it.

And that kiss.

When she was done, Keiran tipped her chin up, hazel eyes searching hers. He wiped her tears, trapped her hands between his, and pressed them against his chest. "You're safe. That's all that matters."

Safe. But at what cost? Penelope would have her memories taken. Baz was on academic probation and still liable for her secret–still at risk should something happen down the line. And she would have to keep the farce going, pretend to be a Healer for the rest of her life.

A small price to pay, Emory supposed, for keeping her magic and her place within the Order.

For so long she'd dreaded being found out and sent to the Reg-ulators. She'd been scared to see her former self eclipsed by who she'd become, horrified at the idea of ever wearing the golden sun-flower and dark moon of House Eclipse. But now, as she stared down at the untruth of her New Moon tattoo, the prospect of hav-ing to keep lying forever felt more daunting than anything else.

She'd discovered what it meant to have Eclipse magic, had

started to imagine what it would be like to study in Obscura Hall, to belong to its house.

At least she had the Order, she thought, and perhaps that was where she truly belonged.

Baz wasn't in the dining hall or the library or even the greenhouse when Emory went looking for him that night. To apologize. See what could be salvaged between them, if anything at all. She was on her way back to her room, defeated, when she finally glimpsed his lanky form slipping into Obscura Hall.

"Baz, wait!"

She followed him inside, catching him in front of the elevator.

"Professor Selandyn filled me in on everything," Baz said in a clipped tone. "You shouldn't be here."

"Baz, I'm so sorry."

His jaw was a hard line, and his eyes . . . There was no softness there. Nothing of the boy who'd kissed her on the beach, of the friend who'd kept her from shattering time and again this past month.

"You're angry with me."

Baz pressed the button to call the elevator. "I'm angry at myself."

His voice was barely above a whisper, and that made it so much worse.

"I should never have agreed to any of it. Helping you, keeping your secret. It was reckless. Foolish." His throat worked. "Ever since you came into my life, it's been nothing but near-misses and inexplicable deaths, and it's too much, Emory. I can't do it anymore."

Guilt threatened to choke her. "What about Romie?"

"We're no closer to finding out how to bring her back."

"So you're just giving up?"

"I'm asking *you* to give up. Us going to Dovermere . . . It was a mistake." The rickety elevator dinged as it reached the top, and Baz

stepped inside. He couldn't look at her as he said, "Everything you touch crumbles to dust."

An ocean of words rose in her throat, but none of them came out. All she could think was that she'd done exactly what Kai thought she would: betrayed Baz's trust, his loyalty. She'd fucked it all up.

"Did you tell Keiran you almost Collapsed?"

She couldn't respond.

Baz nodded tightly as the door began to shut. "I hope you know what you're doing, because I won't be there to save you next time."

Baz disappeared, and Emory left, trying to keep from breaking down into angry tears. His words crawled over her, seeping into every corner of her mind. He was right. Everything was her fault. Travers and Lia, called to their deaths by her proximity to Dovermere. Jordyn's soul devoured by the umbrae. Romie stranded in a place that would not let her go. Penelope driven to such grief and resentment that she had outed her to the dean. And Baz, who couldn't even look at her anymore.

It all came back to her, the source of everyone's suffering.

She was a suffocator. A stormy sea leaving only ruin in her wake.

Emory should never have come back to Aldryn. Should have stayed home after the summer, safely tucked away in her father's lighthouse, with no other soul for miles around. No one for her to damage.

Had she not followed Romie into the caves, she would still be a Healer, nothing more than mediocre, but none of this would have happened, and she'd still have her friend at her side.

Emory had dared to reach for it all, everything that wasn't hers to take. Everything she'd felt entitled to, all in the name of finding herself, of becoming someone noteworthy.

And what was left, in the end?

Her feet led her right to Keiran's doorstep. His face and hair

were mussed from sleep when he opened the door. Torso bare. The smell of his aftershave wrapped around her, warm and inviting.

"Can I stay with you tonight?" she asked, not bothering to wipe the tears on her cheeks.

He wordlessly pulled her to him, and in the circle of his arms, tucked under the warm covers of his bed, she found safety. Comfort. She pressed a kiss to the side of his mouth, cupped his face in her hand. His cheek dug into the heat of her palm. She ran her other hand through his supple hair, let it fall to the back of his neck, trailed it down his shoulder.

Keiran's eyes fluttered shut. "What do you want, Ains?"

"I want . . ."

I want. It was what had gotten her into this mess to begin with, but here in the dark, she couldn't deny this ache for him. This need to feel wanted, desired. The need to know that someone, at least, didn't hate her.

Faint light fell on Keiran's face, so close to her own. Those dark-lashed eyes looked at her with the same intensity that always set her aflame.

I saw you, Ains.

It was all she'd ever wanted, to be seen. To have someone see her for everything that she was and wasn't and deem it enough.

"I want you," she whispered. "I want this."

Emory lifted his hand between them, pressed it against her neck, curled his fingers around it like he'd done to her before. "You have a hold on me too. You have all of me, and I don't mind it for a second."

With that simple admission, Keiran took what she offered, gave as much in return. Pleasure came in waves, breaking and remaking until they were utterly spent, and lust gave way to something else then, raw and intimate. A kind of fragile state that might shatter as

soon as they pulled apart. And in that delicate embrace, with the melody of their quiet panting wrapped around them, words rose to Emory's mind. Big words, impossible ones. Words she could not speak, for they lodged themselves in her throat, stuck there by their own too-muchness. She only clung tighter to Keiran, her mouth pressed against the crook of his neck as her tears pooled onto his skin, and hoped this was enough to convey what she dared not say.

They fell asleep in each other's arms, and maybe that, too, was enough.

She dreams of the sea.

Great waves wrap around all the people in her life, pulling them under one by one until Emory is the only one left, alone and adrift at sea. And she is the sea, she realizes, or at the very least the one who commands it, dragging those around her to their watery ends.

Suddenly Romie is there in a sea of a different making. Stars swirl around her, reflected in her eyes. They form a corona atop her head, a crown of stars for the one who rules this realm of dreams.

"I'm going now, Em," says Romie, her voice crystal clear. "There's no one here but me anymore, so I'm following the song to wherever it leads."

"You can't. What if it leads to the Deep?"

The stars cast Romie in a queenly glow. "Only one way to find out."

"It'll kill you. The epilogue–you need a key."

"The epilogue's not what we thought. Not a key, exactly, but . . . It's like in the book: The travelers never needed a key. They were the key, each one of them a piece of the whole. I

hear their song calling me forward. The pull of Dovermere, of other worlds. It's what I was meant for, I think. To find the others beyond the door."

"Please don't leave me again. Let me find a way to bring you home."

"I love you, Em. But I have to go."

"No," Emory says. "Wait," she begs.

But already another wave comes crashing in. It coils around Romie and draws her toward a deeper sort of darkness. "Tell Kai I left it for him to find."

Romie disappears, and then Emory is truly alone.

Emory's eyes fluttered open, and for a panicked moment she didn't know where she was. The sight of Keiran's face dappled in the morning light anchored her. She felt split in half, with her body here in his bed, limbs tangled with his, while her mind was still in that dream, the sound of waves growing fainter in her ears.

Keiran cracked an eye open and smiled sleepily at her. "Morning, Ains."

Emory sat up, hair spilling over her bare shoulders. Grim determination sang in her blood as she reached for her clothes.

Keiran's hand snaked around her torso. "Come back to bed."

He pressed a kiss to her spine, and she wanted so badly to stay here and relive what they'd done last night time and again, but all she could see was Romie being dragged farther off to sea. The same way she'd described Travers and Lia disappearing.

I love you, Em. But I have to go.

It didn't matter that Emory's dreaming self had begged Romie not to go; Romie wouldn't listen. She would do as Romie always did, following whatever held her fancy without thinking of the consequences or who she might hurt in the process.

Emory had to tell Baz.

She pulled on her sweater and felt her resolve slip. Could she truly put him through this again? Half-formed hopes and theories and reckless plans that ended up hurting those around her, him most of all.

Everything you touch crumbles to dust.

No. This was her burden to bear now. Her wrong to right.

She turned to Keiran. "We have to go to Dovermere. Right now."

He froze, his hand still on her waist. "We're not ready."

"Romie's trying to leave that in-between space, and I can't let her." She told him of the dream. "If all we need to open the door is a ritual with the five houses like we did last spring, then we can open it again. Today. I don't care that we don't have the epilogue or know what's needed to survive crossing into the Deep. If I don't stop Romie, she's going to die just like Travers and Lia."

Keiran frowned in thought. "What did Romie say about the key, exactly?"

"Something about the book characters never needing a key to travel through worlds because they are the key."

"That's it," he muttered, more to himself than to her. "We don't need the epilogue at all. We have you."

"Me?"

"Think about it. The door demands payment both to go in and out. The ritual around the Hourglass—an offering of blood, of one's mortal life, to enter the world of the dead. And to reenter the world of the living, an offering of magic. A piece of one's soul."

A Healer withering to bones, a Wordsmith robbed of a voice.

"For all we know, the door can only open from one side," Keiran continued. "*This* side. It didn't open until you touched the Hourglass last spring. And Travers and Lia couldn't escape their purgatory until *you* were near Dovermere. What if the door is keyed to your blood? Maybe it doesn't need blood from the five houses to

open, only yours. A Tidecaller who holds all the moon's phases in her veins."

"No. I–"

"You bled on the Hourglass during the initiation ritual. You cut yourself walking along the beach the night of the bonfires, right before Travers appeared, remember? And didn't you tell me you were in the water when you found Lia, too?"

The blood leeched from Emory's face. A new moon for Travers, a waxing gibbous for Lia. She'd stood near Dovermere on both those nights, blood pearling on her feet as she waded through the shallows toward it. Toward a door that called to her, and her to it.

Emory, Emory.

I hear their song calling me forward. The pull of Dovermere, of other worlds.

The same pull Emory felt.

Her thoughts scrambled to make sense of it. Romie had said she wasn't able to follow Travers or Lia when they heard that voice calling them home. *Her* voice. Her *Tidecaller* blood. If their moon phase had anything to do with their being able to return to the world of the living, it stood to reason that Romie couldn't follow them, because it wasn't her time. Wasn't her *tide.*

And Jordyn . . . Jordyn had become something else when he'd crossed back over. Something *other*, not quite living or dead. Maybe as an umbra, the moon had no consequence on him anymore.

Emory's blood had called them all home, and in doing so, she had doomed each one of them, sealed their fates.

"With that rare eclipse in your blood," Keiran said, "I think you'll be able to travel to the Deep and back unscathed. It'll protect you. It's just as Romie said: the key was never the missing epilogue, nor any physical object at all. It's you, Ains. *You're* the key."

Emory's heart thudded painfully. If Romie had indeed found a way out of the purgatory she'd described–if she believed *she* was

the key, able to travel through worlds unscathed even though she wasn't a Tidecaller–Emory feared she would be lost for good.

"We need to do the ritual, Keiran. I can't let Romie meet the same fate the rest of them did." Guiltily, she thought of the last time she'd gotten too hasty–the near Collapsing she had yet to tell Keiran about. But this might be her last chance to save her friend. She wouldn't wait around and gamble with Romie's life. "Please, I have to at least try."

She braced for him to react the same way Baz had. To tell her how senseless and dangerous this was.

But Keiran drew himself up and put on his clothes. "Round up the others," he said. "Tell them to meet us in the Treasury."

"Where are you going?"

"To get us some synths. If we're going through this door, we need all the help we can get." He stopped and looked at her with something she couldn't quite place. "You're sure you want to do this?"

Emory righted her spine, strengthened her voice. "Yes, I'm sure."

"Then we're going back to Dovermere–at noon, once the tide is low." An ardent glimmer lit Keiran's eyes. "I don't suppose it'll have any consequence on us opening the door, but it is rather fitting, I think, that there should be a partial solar eclipse today."

The words struck a deep resonance in her soul. It felt like an auspicious omen, and suddenly she believed with all her being that this would work.

She'd first opened the door as a Healer, under the new moon sky she thought had governed her. And now . . . now she'd do so again as a Tidecaller, under the proper sign.

Emory might never wear the sigil of House Eclipse, but she belonged to it all the same.

34

BAZ

B AZ FOUND HIMSELF AT THE INSTITUTE AGAIN.
He had faced all his fears in the confines of those damned
caves. Nightmares given form, wrapped in memories that hurt so
much he didn't remember ever holding them inside. And here he
was, alive and whole. Still breathing despite it all.

He didn't want to be afraid anymore. Not of this.

Vera was an all-too-willing accomplice. She accompanied him
to the Institute once more, deactivating the wards again for him to
slip in unnoticed while she waited outside this time, ready for their
getaway. Baz made it to Theodore's room and opened the door.

Bare and white and clinical. The small comforts of books, a knit
blanket, the Brysdens caught in a framed sepia photograph, a
memory trapped in amber.

Breathe in. Hold. Breathe out.

His father turned to him slowly, blank smile at the ready, no doubt
expecting to see anyone else but him standing at his door. His smile
faltered as he took Baz in, made sense of the person before him.

In. Hold. Out.

"Hi, Dad."

A flicker of recognition, an ember of hope sparking behind his eyes.

"Basil?" his father croaked. "Baz. It's really you?"

"Yeah, it's me."

Baz stood awkwardly by the door. The last time he'd been alone with his father was just before that fateful day at the printing press. He'd visited him once at the Institute after that with his mother and sister, and that was it.

He looked at his father's left hand. The Eclipse sigil was broken by the Unhallowed Seal, stark and slightly ridged against his skin. A singular *U*. Unhallowed. Unfit. Unbalanced. Unworthy. The sight of it still jarring after all these years.

Theodore was the first to speak. "I thought I saw you the other day. Must be my mind's playing tricks on me."

Baz shifted uncomfortably. "I'm sorry I didn't visit you sooner. I couldn't . . ."

"It's all right, son. It's all right."

You'll be all right. Everything will be all right.

Baz adjusted his glasses. Now that he was here, he didn't know what to say. His father eyed Baz's Eclipse tattoo. He nodded, as if picking up the thread of a conversation they'd been having.

"It suits you. Aldryn, is it?"

Baz palmed the back of his neck, self-conscious about his unmarred sunflower in eclipse. "Yeah. I'm at Aldryn College."

His father's lips pressed into a firm line. "They brought another Aldryn student here. I warned him about it, told him how it starts. How they take it from us, then use it for themselves."

The words made little sense. Theodore threw a glance at the door behind Baz, and when he spoke again, it was barely above a whisper. "You've been able to control it?"

Baz frowned. "What?"

"Your magic."

"Of course."

A nod. "That's good. Very good. They can never know."

Baz's confusion deepened. "Know what?"

A sly smile from his father. "Precisely. The truth was buried in the rubble that day. No one will find out. Just you, me, and Jae."

A tingling sensation started at Baz's fingertips. His pulse beat quicker.

"Dad. What truth?"

His father blinked incomprehensibly at him before glancing at the door again. He lowered his voice. "Your Collapsing, of course."

Baz's heart broke. So this was what all these years in the Institute had done to Theodore Brysden: delusions and madness. "I'm not the one who Collapsed, Dad." *I'm not the one who killed those people.* "That's why you're here. In this place."

The corners of Theodore's mouth pulled down. He shook his head, eyes full of sorrow. "No, son. That's not why. I'm here to protect you. Our little secret, remember?"

Silver veins and rubble and blood—that's what Baz remembered, what had been plaguing his nightmares since the day it had happened. It was all too vivid, especially now, after reliving the memory through the umbra's cold, nightmarish pull.

Baz found that *U* on his father's hand again, the scarred lines marring the once-delicate sunflower. He remembered clinging to that hand that day as his father's arms wrapped around him, protecting him from the crumbling building and the blast of uncontrollable power that sought to take it down.

"I didn't Collapse, Dad," Baz said gently, hoping his father would see sense. "My blood doesn't run silver, for one thing, and—"

"Well, of course it didn't *stay* silver," Theodore interrupted with a note of exasperation. "The blood only stays silver for a day or so

after Collapsing before it settles back to red. It's why we thought we could hide the truth, make it seem like I was the one who Collapsed instead of you. So that you'd escape the seal and stand a fighting chance at a normal life. If Jae could do it, so could you."

The floor pitched beneath Baz's feet as he slowly made sense of what his father was insinuating. "If Jae could do what, exactly?"

"Well, hide their Collapsing, of course." Theodore's brows scrunched up in confusion. "Did Jae not tell you any of this? They've been Collapsed for years."

It couldn't be true—surely Theodore wasn't remembering it right, surely this place had addled his brain—yet he seemed so completely lucid and sure of himself in this moment, it made doubt bloom in Baz's stomach. Was that why those people had been at the printing press that day, threatening to bring Jae into the Institute? Because they'd found out Jae had Collapsed and had somehow escaped the Unhallowed Seal?

"Jae assured me they would keep an eye on you," Theodore continued. "That you'd be able to control it, just like they always did."

Baz shook his head against the impossibility of it all. "Why hasn't the curse gotten to Jae, then?"

"*Think*, Basil. The Shadow's curse isn't real, at least not the way they want us to believe. The Collapsing doesn't plunge us into eternal darkness. It's a threshold, and on the other side of it is this raw, undiluted power."

A single wave, an entire ocean, the world itself. Nothing is out of your reach.

Baz's hands went slack.

"Power like that," his father continued, "it has the capacity to corrupt, sure enough, to turn us evil, but not always. Jae is proof one can use that power for good. So are you."

"*I haven't Collapsed*," Baz gritted out, anger rising in him now. "I can't have. *You* were the one trying to stop those people from

hurting Jae. *You* were the one whose magic blasted the printing press apart."

"I was trying to push *your* power down, Basil. To nullify it, keep it contained."

Something about those words made Baz think of what he'd done for Emory in the caves. How he'd stopped her from Collapsing. He looked at his father's branded hand. His father the Nullifier. The same kind of magic used to dampen Eclipse powers in the silver cuffs and the Unhallowed Seal itself.

"You stopped time trying to save Jae, and it was too much for you." Again, Theodore frowned in bemusement, a note of desperation now in his voice as he asked, "Don't you remember?"

All Baz remembered was Theodore screaming at everyone to stop, and then . . .

With sudden aching clarity, he recalled the sense of deep, unsettling urgency he'd felt at seeing those people threaten Jae. The strange presentiment he'd gotten that he'd never see Jae again if they were taken away.

Please stop, Baz had begged everyone around him, and when no one listened, time answered his plea.

The ensuing blast of silver light . . .

It hadn't come from his father, he realized with a start. It had come from *himself.*

Silver veins on his own small hands, his father's large ones unmarred as his arms wound viselike around Baz—not to protect him, but to *contain* him.

To try to stop Baz from Collapsing.

It all came back to him now. The blast of light that tore from him. Power thrumming through his fingers. A pit in his stomach, a plunge deep within, pulling everything up and up and up. His father tried desperately to stop him, to save Baz from himself as that power slowly drained everything from him. Darkness gathered around

Baz's vision, pulling him under, and when he came to again, he felt that power receding somewhere deep, somewhere he could lock it up forever.

And then—his father at his side, silver veins rippling on his skin, while Baz's own skin was clear.

But it was an illusion. A pale imitation of the real thing.

He remembered Jae standing behind Theodore, devastation and determination warring with each other on their face. They were the one who'd wrought the illusion, a secret in silver blood.

It's all right. Everything will be all right.

The Regulators took Theodore away without ever suspecting. They tried him thinking he'd Collapsed, and Theodore confessed to it. The blast of power was his. He was the one who'd lost control, killed those people caught in the rubble.

He took the fall for everything, and Baz believed him. Believed the illusion that Jae and his father had constructed. Everyone did. He believed his father was the one to Collapse, and Baz never gave another thought to the power he felt in his own veins. Never prodded into this vast well within him for fear of drawing on too much power and suffering his Collapsing like his father had.

An unfounded fear, in the end, for he'd already *had* his Collapsing.

He was the one who Collapsed that day, not his father.

Those deaths were on *his* hands, not Theodore's.

Baz looked at him now through angry, disbelieving tears. "Why? Why did you take the fall?"

The Regulators had stripped Theodore of his magic, and for what? For nothing other than trying to protect his son.

A sad smile from his father. "To give you a chance." He reached for Baz's tattooed hand, held it in his own. "I don't regret it for one second, Baz. Your magic? It's a gift, and I would have laid my very life down time and time again to prevent you ending up here."

His grip tightened, urgency lining his voice. "But you have to be

careful. They want our raw power, and for that they need more of us to Collapse. They need us in here. And if they knew of the power you and Jae have . . . I don't want to imagine what they'd do to you. We're all pawns in their game, son."

"I don't understand . . ."

There was a sudden commotion outside the door, raised voices and sounds of a scuttle.

"You can't do this to me!" someone screamed, a voice made of velvet and cold night air. "Get your hands off me–"

We're all pawns in whatever fucked-up game they're playing.

Fresh horror sluiced down Baz's back as the pieces started falling into place.

"Dad–what is it they do to us, exactly?"

Theodore's face was bone white. "They take away our magic. Every last drop of it."

Baz knew he wasn't talking about the Unhallowed Seal. This was something much worse, the reason those who'd Collapsed had such hollow nightmares, the reason they were brought to that surgical room, the reason the power surged in such odd ways at whatever happened in that room.

The very room they were bringing Kai to now.

He needed to get to him–quickly.

Theodore saw the grim determination on his face, the way he reached for the door and hesitated. His father nodded. "Go. There's nothing they can do to me I haven't already weathered."

Baz pushed the door open. "I'll come back for you, Dad."

Outside, he caught a glimpse of dark hair as two Regulators dragged Kai around the corner. The exit was in the opposite direction, but Baz followed the sound of Kai's screaming and swearing, his heart beating so erratically he thought he might faint.

A door clicking shut. Kai's voice waning to nothing but muffled whimpers behind it as power surged all through the building.

Baz barged in to find the Nightmare Weaver strapped to a chair. A Regulator was drawing blood from him – silver blood, power and magic. Kai's pleading gaze found Baz's. He could see the light dimming behind his eyes, his very power, his life . . .

Baz reached for the threads of time.

"You weren't supposed to see that," someone said behind him.

A whack on the back of his head. Faint stars swam in his eyes, and then everything went dark.

SONG OF THE DROWNED GODS

PART V:

THE DAMNED
IN THE DEEP

There is a world at the center of all things where nothing ever grows.

Ash rains down from colorless skies and blankets the world in colorless grays. No wind blows, and so the ash amasses–a mere semblance of growth, for only that which is living can grow, and ash is the domain of death. It forms into piles and mounds, mountains that claw for the heavens (if such a thing exists), precarious peaks that might topple at the barest flutter of breath like waves cresting and breaking into naught but foam.

It is a burial ground. A netherworld. A delicate prison for indelicate souls damned to a timeless existence, gods and monsters and all manner of vicious beasts trapped in this sea of ash and dust and nothingness.

We have seen this place before through the eyes of our scholar. He has not yet found his way back, though he has traversed many worlds in search of it and the gods in its midst, which he seeks to set free. The skies still hold their breath to see him succeed, expectant, hopeful. Sorrowful, too, for they know what awaits the scholar once he breathes the right words, opens the right portal.

He will find himself here again, though this time not alone. Four of them will stand in the ash, each one a part of a whole.

Blood and bones and heart and soul.

This is where their story ends.

EMORY

THE TIDE WAS LOW WHEN THE SELENIC ORDER STEPPED onto the shores of the Aldersea, dark blue steel beneath sullen skies. The wind of a coming storm breathed down their backs. The sea would be ruthless today, and if what they attempted didn't work, it would be swift to swallow them whole.

The sun hid behind clouds. Its eclipsing could not be seen, but Emory imagined she could feel it lending her strength.

As they approached the cave mouth, Emory couldn't believe how quickly she and Keiran had managed to convince the rest of the Order of this irrational plan, if it could even be called that at all. They were attempting to open the door and call the Tides sooner than expected, all so she might save Romie.

Lizaveta was the only one who'd been opposed to it.

"This is madness," she'd nearly yelled at Keiran, at Emory. "We're not ready—we don't even know if what we're doing is going to work—and most of all, *we can't trust her*. Haven't we jeopardized our standing with the rest of the Order enough as it is?" She'd

turned to Keiran. "After what happened yesterday, the lengths you went to, to keep her secret safe . . . Are you seriously willing to risk it all on her?"

"Everyone else is on board, Liza. Don't you want to see Farran back?"

Her desire to see her friend again had won over in the end. Though it hadn't stopped her from accosting Emory as they'd made their way to the beach.

"You should have run when you had the chance, Tidethief. Whatever happens is on you now."

Emory tried not to let those words get to her.

Everyone had armed themselves with synthetic magic hastily inked on their Selenic Marks. Except her. She thought it best not to alter her magic in any way, so as not to mess with the door-opening ritual. The synth was imbued with a few different magics—one for every lunar house, she was told—so that the others' power would be amplified. It also carried a drop of her own blood, to serve as protection. A talisman of sorts to get them into the Deep and out unscathed.

Keiran had come through for her—again. He was a pillar of unshakable belief, a steadfast presence at her side, and that was all that mattered. He offered her a hand with a fierce, determined look in his eye. Emory took it, and it felt like anything was possible.

For a third time, she stepped into Dovermere.

The darkness greeted the Selenics as kings and queens, masters of death, as if the ancient rock around them recognized their magic, the power each of them had once wielded to survive these strange depths. It might have been what kept the umbra from their path, though Emory knew the creature must be waiting for them somewhere deeper, eager to feast on their souls.

Or maybe it was dead, though she doubted it could be so easily killed.

Together they advanced, the path before them illuminated by the lanterns each of them carried. Emory couldn't find it in herself to be scared. The others' presence was reassuring, and every step she took away from the beach and into this strange, dripping place only made her feel surer. Whatever weight had pressed down on her before lifted, and all she knew was this pull and the steady beat of her heart as she forged deeper into the cave, toward its own heart of stone and silver.

"We're here," Nisha said up ahead.

The Belly of the Beast opened around them. The umbra, Emory noted uneasily, wasn't here. She glanced furtively at her watch. Five hours left until high tide—until this place became the death trap they would once again have to survive.

Virgil whistled a low note as he approached the Hourglass. "Never thought I'd have to see this ugly thing again." He arched a brow at Emory. "You're certain this is it? It doesn't look the slightest bit like a door."

"Romie said the Hourglass opened for them the night of the initiation," Emory said.

"We have to believe it will again," Keiran added, "under the right circumstances."

With all five of the lunar houses and her to serve as key. The same as last spring. It struck Emory how nearly identical this was to then, though where there had been nine of them last time, there were only eight now. Still, all that mattered was that each house was represented: Ife and Louis of New Moon, Lizaveta and Nisha of Waxing Moon, Keiran and Javier of Full Moon, Virgil of Waning Moon, and Emory for the Eclipse.

"Let's get on with it, then," Lizaveta said stiffly, setting down her lantern at her feet. "The quicker we see if this works, the sooner we can leave."

Virgil smirked at her. "Is that fear I detect, Liza?"

"Bite me, Virgil."

"If that's an invitation . . ."

"Four hours and thirty-five minutes until high tide," Ife said pointedly. "Let's get into formation and do this, yeah?"

Emory did a double take at her watch. She had just looked at it–there was no way nearly a half hour had gone by in the span of what felt like mere minutes. But such was the nature of time down here, to slip away too quickly and without notice.

Keiran produced a switchblade and handed it to Emory. "The honor's all yours."

She sliced the blade across her palm. The blade was then passed from person to person, and once blood trickled from each of their hands, they stepped onto the platform the Hourglass was built on, forming a circle around it in the order of their lunar phases. Emory stood between Virgil and Ife, between the waning moon and the new one.

Across from her, Keiran gave her a reassuring nod, and Emory blew out a sigh.

"Here goes nothing."

In unison, all eight of them brought their bloodied hands against the column, intoning the sacred chant.

"To Bruma, who sprang from the darkness. To Anima, whose voice breathed life into the world. To Aestas, whose bountiful warmth and light protect us all. To Quies and the sleeping darkness she guides us through at the end of all things."

For a second, or perhaps a minute, or an hour–time, they knew, tended to slip in these depths–nothing happened.

And then everything was as Emory remembered: a change in the air, a prickle on her wrist. Silver droplets detached from the striated rock, hovering around them.

A whisper, a draft, like wind through a door left ajar.

A breath in, a breath out. The rhythm of the sea.

Bright, silvery light flooded the Belly of the Beast, and the droplets rearranged themselves in front of them, flocking to the middle of the Hourglass. They concentrated on that narrow finger of rock where stalagmite and stalactite fused together, creating a bright silver demarcation between up and down, and Emory thought it looked curiously like a lock. One that might open at her touch.

This was it. The way in.

And then—darkness. Great vines of it slithered around the Hourglass, snuffing out the silver light drop by shining drop. The shadows reached for the eight hands still tethered to the rock. Virgil swore as he tried to pry free, and Emory watched in horror as a rope of darkness wound around his wrist, snaked up his arm.

"What is this?" Nisha cried out, trying to wrest her hand from the rock.

Everyone's wrists were bound by darkness. Emory's first instinct was to look for the umbra, but the creature of nightmare wasn't here. She glanced down at her own hand, but it was unmarred by the shadows, and for a second, she thought *she* was the one doing this, that her magic had acted against her will. But it was still waiting for her beck and call in her veins.

Virgil swore again, and when Emory looked at him, the darkness had seeped into his mouth, his eyes, just as the umbrae had done to Jordyn—

His hand finally wrenched free of the rock. Those black tendrils wrapped around him in a viselike grip, and he fell like a deadweight at her feet, just as the others around him did.

All of them except for Emory—and two others.

Lizaveta took her hand away from the Hourglass. Her other hand gripped Keiran's wrist—amplifying his magic as darkness spilled from him.

Darkness, not light.

Keiran stepped back from the Hourglass and away from Lizaveta's

amplifying touch. The darkness flowing from his hand fell away to wisps of nothing.

"What just happened?" Emory swept wide eyes over the five bodies–Virgil, Ife, Nisha, Javier, and Louis–sprawled on the cave floor, gagged by these strange ropes of darkness. She frowned incomprehensibly at Keiran, then Lizaveta. "What did you do to them?"

Lizaveta looked away as if in shame.

"They're fine, Ains," Keiran said softly. "Just put to sleep."

Emory glanced at the Hourglass. The lock she'd seen appear in its middle was gone. "We were so close. The door was about to open–I could feel it."

"And it will. When the tide comes in, it'll open just like it did last time."

"I don't get it." She pointed at the bodies at her feet. "Why do this?"

Lizaveta held herself rigidly, still avoiding eye contact–and unusually quiet.

"Keiran." Emory searched his face for an answer, trying to reason away the creeping dread crawling along her skin. "Tell me what's going on."

"If we're to call the Tides back from the Deep," he said with a pained expression, "others need to take their place. To keep the Shadow contained."

"What are you saying?"

"It's like in *Song of the Drowned Gods*, Ains. The drowned gods needed the heroes to take their place."

Horror struck her. The unconscious bodies around her . . . he meant to offer them up as sacrifices to the Deep–to doom them to an eternity watching over the Shadow.

She thought those might be tears glistening in Keiran's eyes, but his jaw was set with resignation, his mind made up.

Emory stumbled back, denial making her limbs go numb. She looked between Keiran and Lizaveta. They couldn't possibly be willing to sacrifice the others' lives for this—their *friends*. Virgil with his mischievous smiles and booming laughter. Nisha's constant kindness and Ife's steadfast presence. Louis and Javier's quiet way of gravitating toward each other, their stolen kisses whenever they thought no one was looking.

"No," she said. "There has to be another way."

"There isn't. The Tides need replacements—just as they need a vessel."

"What do you mean, a *vessel*?"

"The Tides need to be reunited in a single vessel to come back from the Deep. A mortal body to leave that immortal place—one that is strong enough to contain their ancient power, hold all the moon's might inside."

Emory was slow to process his words. "And you think that's *me*?"

"Your magic is keyed to each of the Tides. You're the Shadow of Ruin reborn—the Tidecaller given flesh. The very symbol that stole the Tides' power from them, the reason they needed to disappear into the Deep."

Emory's ears rang as blood rushed to her head and she understood what he meant to do. "Keiran . . ."

"I'm sorry, Ainsleif." There was a softness in his voice she hadn't counted on. "The only way to set our lunar magics free, to reclaim the full might of the power that was once ours, is for the Tides to eradicate the stain of the Shadow and all of those who carry a piece of his power."

It was never about her, she realized. Keiran getting close to her, *seducing* her—it was about the magic in her blood and the way he might wield it. *You asked me why I'm not afraid of you,* he'd said. *The truth is, I am. But only because I see your potential. Your power.*

Her eyes found Lizaveta's. They gleamed in a way that said, *I tried*

to warn you. And she had–had told her not to confuse Keiran's interest in her with his obsession with power–but Emory had thought it mere jealousy on her part.

"Baz was right about you." Emory hated the way her voice trembled. How small it was. Tears burned her eyes, but she refused to let them fall. "This is about what happened to your parents, isn't it? You said you didn't blame Eclipse-born for their deaths, but you do, don't you? All this time, this was about revenge."

"It's about *justice,*" Lizaveta said, though her voice lacked its usual vehemence.

"Justice and revenge are the same when you're willing to sacrifice all these lives for it."

Lizaveta's throat bobbed. "It's the price we have to pay to see Farran again. To see our parents, too."

Emory hoped Keiran would deny it all. He couldn't meet her eye as he said, "You're right, it did start out as revenge. After our parents' deaths, Farran's idea to wake the Tides . . . It fueled our thirst for justice. Our parents thought the world would be a better place with the Tides returned, with the stain of the Shadow removed, and we believed it too. The Eclipse-born are a perversion, Ains. You were never meant to have this magic. You wrested it from the Tides, and that's why none of you can control it. Why you end up Collapsing and killing *us* in the process."

Tidethief.

The word echoed in the silence around them.

The look in Keiran's eyes turned fierce and smoldering. "But you're different than the others, Ains. You hold the key to ridding the world of the Shadow's stain. And by becoming the Tides' vessel, you'll be freed of that curse. The magic running through your veins won't be the Shadow's anymore but the Tides'. You'll be spared their wrath and made into something new and sacred and *formidable.*"

Keiran took a tentative step toward her. "So yes. It did start out as revenge, but it became so much more than that. I saw your power, the heart you put in everything you do, and I knew you were meant for something greater. I knew you were worth saving."

Emory thought she might die from the ache in her chest. She balled her hands into fists at her side to keep her heart from shattering any further. "So everything else—bringing Romie and Farran and the others back from the Deep . . . It was all a lie so you could use me against my own House? And what—save my soul from damnation in the process?"

"It wasn't a lie," Lizaveta said. "It's the whole reason I agreed to this in the first place. *I* couldn't care less about saving your fucking soul. But whoever frees the Tides might obtain their blessing, and with it, we'll bring them back. It's what the four of us promised each other back in Trevel."

"The four of you?" Emory repeated.

"Farran, Keiran, Artem, and I."

Something shuddered on Keiran's face. "This has become so much bigger than what the four of us set out to do, Liza. To reset the balance in the world, rid it of the Shadow's stain—that's the favor we have to ask of the Tides now. The one thing we need to focus on. We can't risk losing our one shot just to see our loved ones again." His throat bobbed. "Dovermere chooses those who are worthy of the Selenics' secrets—those who might go far enough to wake the Tides. Farran didn't survive. We did. Maybe what's dead is better left to the Deep."

Silence dripped between the three of them as the full weight of Keiran's words settled. Hurt and betrayal flashed across Lizaveta's face.

"We said we'd bring Farran back. The whole reason I agreed to this—*to sacrificing all our friends*—was to bring him back."

"So why did you try to sabotage our plan?"

Lizaveta's cheeks burned furiously, that icy composure of hers slipping.

"Don't try to deny it," Keiran warned, voice lowered in a chilling tone. "You got cold feet about what needed to be done, and you used a Glamour synth to get Penelope West to out Emory to the dean, hoping she'd get sent to the Institute and receive the Unhallowed Seal. You hoped we'd lose our vessel so you wouldn't have to stomach what needed to be done."

Emory's head snapped to Lizaveta. What Penelope had said about not acting of her own will . . . Tides, she'd been *forced* to do it. To betray Emory with information she hadn't even known— information Lizaveta had planted in her head.

And she'd had her memory *wiped* for it—all for something that wasn't her fault.

"How could you do that to her?" Emory gasped.

Lizaveta met her gaze, full of cold fury. "I did it for your own good, but you couldn't take a hint, could you?"

You should have run when you had the chance, Tidethief.

Lizaveta rounded on Keiran. "All I wanted was to get Farran back. But to do it like *this*? To sacrifice our friends? It makes us just as bad as the Eclipse-born who killed our parents, Keiran. Worse, because this is *intentional.*" She held herself a little straighter, blinking rapidly. "But I was willing to do it all the same if it meant seeing Farran again. This was *his* dream, the reason we started going down this road in the first place. What do you think he'd say if he saw all we were willing to sacrifice to do this one thing?"

"He wouldn't understand, because he was weak-willed, just like you. It's why you won't be coming with us, Liza."

"Like hell I am."

Keiran jerked his chin to the prone Selenics. "If you care so much about them that you were willing to risk our plan with that shit you pulled with Penelope, then save one of them. We have one offering

too many. Both Ife and Louis are of House New Moon, but we only need one to take Bruma's place in the Deep."

The sacrifices–there were five bodies on the ground, but he only needed four. One of each lunar house. One for each Tide. Virgil for Quies. Javier for Aestas. Nisha for Anima. And either Ife or Louis for Bruma.

"I'm sorry, Liza," Keiran lamented. "This is the way it has to be. So have your pick; save the one you want. Then leave before the tide comes."

"You selfish bastard."

Water sloshed at Lizaveta's feet as she took a furious step toward him.

All of them paused, glancing at the cave floor. Water trickled into the Belly of the Beast from the passage they'd come through, a marker of the rising tide. The water reached all the way to the dais at the center. Where it touched the striated rock, it lifted from the ground in a thin tendril that wrapped around the Hourglass, mingling with the silver that ran along the rock. Around and around the stalagmite the ribbon of silvery water climbed, gathering in the middle of the column, where it formed a spiral to match the symbol on the rock.

That lock formed in the middle of the Hourglass again. Gooseflesh rose on Emory's arms as she heard it: a melody calling her forward.

The door, readying itself to open in time with the tide.

There was urgency in Lizaveta's voice now. Fear. "I'm not letting you go through that door without me." Her fist closed around something at her side.

"Then I'm afraid this is where we part, Liza."

Lizaveta lunged with a desperate scream, the gleam of a knife flashing as she swiped for Emory's neck. Keiran stepped between them. He caught Lizaveta's wrist, tried to wrench the knife free from her grasp.

"You can't wake the Tides without your precious Tidecaller," Lizaveta seethed, no match for Keiran's strength as he pried her fingers open. "If I can't have Farran back, you can–"

Lizaveta's brows knit together in confusion, her red-painted mouth open on silenced words, as a trickle of blood fell from where Keiran had lodged the knife at the base of her neck.

BAZ

BAZ WOKE TO A WORLD OF FOG AND STARS.

Muffled voices sounded in his ears, at once very close and too far away. There was a dizzying pain on the back of his head. He tried to lift his arm to touch it and felt the cold bite of something against his skin, restricting the motion.

His hands were cuffed together.

Panic burst through the blur of unconsciousness. His surroundings came into sharp focus. He was in a small wood-paneled room, slumped against a bookshelf or an armoire that dug into his back. Weak light filtered in through a singular window on the opposite wall, where two people stood behind an antique mahogany desk. One of them was a man in a charcoal Regulator uniform; the other, a woman. Baz recognized neither of them. They didn't notice he'd woken up, bickering in voices that still sounded odd to his ears.

He tried to focus on what they were saying–something about blood samples and order–and went rigid.

At his feet was a body.

Baz bit his tongue to keep from screaming. Kai's face was pale, eyes closed in sleep or death; he couldn't tell. He wanted to reach for him, shake him awake, will him to not be dead–but there. Kai's chest rose and fell with faint breath. Not dead. Not yet.

It all came rushing back to him at once: the Institute, his father's secret. The Regulators drawing silver blood from Kai–taking his slumbering power, his very *life force*, from him.

You weren't supposed to see that.

Baz knew that honeyed voice, the way it dripped with thinly veiled condescension. With power. He'd only gotten a glimpse of chestnut hair before he was knocked out, but it was plenty for him to recognize Keiran Dunhall Thornby.

His gaze flickered to the Regulator and the woman across the room. He wondered how Keiran was involved in whatever screwed-up experiment this was–and where he had gone to now.

"Spare me the lecture, Vivianne," the Regulator was saying. "Are you going to help me clean this mess or not?"

"Wiping their memory would be a lot easier if it were a waning moon," the woman, Vivianne, bemoaned. "Calling on that much power through bloodletting is going to deplete me entirely."

"Trust me, that won't be a problem for much longer."

Vivianne snorted. "Because Keiran is going to wake the Tides and return our magic to its former glory? Come now, Artem. You can't be that foolish. Your dad went down this very road, and look where it led."

Artem. Why did that name sound so familiar . . . ?

"But we've got *her*, Viv. She's the key that my dad and Keiran's parents never found, the answer they never even knew they were looking for."

Artem's gaze cut across the room, and Baz quickly shut his eyes, pretending to be unconscious.

"The Tides will emerge from the depths of Dovermere and finally

rid our shores of the stain of the Eclipse. They'll give us back the power those Tidethieves stole from us." Baz heard shuffling feet behind the desk, the clear clinking of glass. "After today, we won't need to taint ourselves with their blood to know the full might of the Tides' power anymore. Our magic will be free-flowing and true, as it once was."

Baz's pulse quickened as he recalled the silver blood they'd extracted from Kai.

They want our raw power, Theodore had said, *and for that they need more of us to Collapse. They need us in here.*

"The rest of the Council won't be pleased you kept this from them," Vivianne said.

"You're wrong. The Council will *praise* us. The whole world will—"

The sudden blare of an alarm cut off his words. Shouts and footsteps echoed out the door.

Artem swore. "I need to go check on that."

"I'm not staying here alone with two Eclipse-born," Vivianne scoffed as if they were the scum of the earth.

"Then come with me and stay out of the way."

"What about them?"

"They're not going anywhere."

Footsteps treading past him. A door opening. The click and switch of it locking from the outside.

Baz tensed, daring to crack open an eye. They were gone.

He took a proper look at the cuffs around his hands and realized with a sense of relief they weren't the damper kind—just regular cuffs, locked too tight around his wrists. He fought against the haze still in his mind, tried to call on his magic, but it felt faint and far away. They'd likely given him some kind of sedative.

He crawled over to Kai, shaking him with his restrained hands.

"Kai."

His eyes fluttered beneath their lids, but he remained lost to unconsciousness. Silver blood had dried in the crook of his arm, streaking from where a needle had been. And it was as if in that silver blood Baz could feel the sleeping magic inside Kai waning, like an ember about to flicker out and become nothing but ash. He looked around wildly for something to help, overwhelmed by this horrible feeling that if he let that ember of power die out, it would take Kai with it. His gaze landed on the desk, where a vial of something silver shimmered in the faint light.

Silver blood. Magic in its rawest form.

Baz could feel it coming off the vial: pure, undiluted power. The kind he'd sensed slumbering in Kai's veins when he'd first visited him at the Institute, this vast power just beneath his skin that the Unhallowed Seal kept in check. The very seal that was supposed to keep the Shadow's curse at bay, keep them from slipping into something dark and uncontrollable.

Raw power—was that truly what happened when one Collapsed? If any Eclipse-born could survive it like Baz and Jae apparently had—if they managed to escape the suppression of the seal . . .

They could be limitless. Power unrivaled.

And if the Regulators were taking their blood—if they knew the kind of power a Collapsing wielded—Baz could only imagine what they might be doing with it.

He bit back a sob, racking his brain for what to do. Outside, alarms and shouts still sounded. Even so, he needed to act quickly before Artem and Vivianne came back. He tested his magic against the cuffs again, pulling on the thread that would unlock them . . .

A click, and at last they slipped off his wrists.

His magic was waking, stirring. Too slow.

He had to reverse the damage done to Kai, pull on the threads of time the way he'd done for Emory with her Collapsing. But that kind of magic . . .

That kind of magic might have once brought about his own Collapsing. But he'd *already* Collapsed.

All this time, he'd had this raw power coursing through his veins without even knowing. His fingers thrummed with the power of that revelation, his heart beating steadily, like the ticking of a clock.

You have to be careful now . . .

But Baz had been careful all his life, and what good had that done him?

He owed it to Kai—to the Tides-damned Nightmare Weaver himself—to shed his fears for good.

Baz blew out a breath. The threads of time appeared all around him. He seized the one tied to Kai, the one that would return the blood back to where it belonged, in his veins and not in any Regulator's vials. Fear was a distant thing, still there but shoved deeper down into Baz's vast well of power. And he marveled at it, this ease with which time unraveled at his command.

Life bloomed under Kai's skin, and that ember grew to a flame as magic thrummed once more in his veins. It was still contained by the brand, trapped like a flame in an oil lamp, but there all the same.

Kai opened his eyes, drawing a sharp inhale.

Baz fell back with a shaky breath of relief. "Nice of you to finally wake up, asshole."

Kai's mouth slanted upward at the echo of his own words mirrored back to him. For once, though, he seemed to have no witty retort of his own. He awkwardly pushed himself up, hands still cuffed together, and sat resting his head against the wall. His eyes closed as if this small action had taken everything from him.

"I thought I was gone there for a second." He peered at Baz. "I thought *you* were done for. Tides, Brysden. When you barged into the room like that . . ."

His throat bobbed with emotion as he swallowed whatever words he might have said.

Baz was almost too afraid to ask: "Do you remember what they did to you?"

"They took my blood. The power flickering in and out . . . It started the *second* they drew my blood. It felt like they were ripping my very soul from my body. Like they were bleeding me dry of everything that made me *me*." Kai's expression darkened. "You saw who did this, right? I swear if I ever get my hands on Dungshit Fuckby, he'll wish he'd never been born. Him and all the Regulators in this Tides-forsaken place."

A shiver ran up Baz's spine; he didn't think for a second that Kai was bluffing.

And it hit him then—truly hit him that *he* was the one to blame for what had happened to Keiran's parents, not his father. He was the one who'd Collapsed all those years ago and brought down the Brysden & Ahn printing press, not Theodore.

His father wasn't a killer. *He* was.

Keiran must not have known. If he had, Baz doubted he'd still be breathing.

"We need to get out of here," he said.

With a flick of his magic, Kai's cuffs unlocked. Kai looked around, rubbing at his wrists. "Where is *here*, anyway?"

"I don't know. A Regulator's office? There was one in here just now before the alarms went off. He and some woman were talking about—about taking Eclipse blood and using it for something."

"A ritual. That's what Keiran and the Regulator who came to get me said. They needed more power for whatever it was they were planning."

The Tides will emerge from the depths of Dovermere and finally rid our shores of the stain of the Eclipse.

Cold slithered up Baz's spine. "The others at the Institute . . . the ones who've been here the longest . . ." Kai had said their nightmares

were empty and hollow–that they felt like ghosts. "What if they're like that because the Regulators have been harnessing their sealed magic for years and it's depleting their reservoirs? Taking every last drop of magic from their veins?"

Kai swore, the look in his eyes turning violent. "My blood–"

"I fixed it," Baz said. "It's in your veins where it belongs."

A glance at the empty vial on the desk confirmed it. Kai watched him curiously. "How did you–"

The door unlocked, swung open. Baz scrambled to put himself in front of Kai, readying his magic to stop time, to keep Artem and Vivianne from coming in–

But stared dumbfounded at Jae Ahn instead.

"Jae–what are you doing here?"

"Saving you, clearly," Jae said with ragged breath. They snuck a look behind them before shutting the door, then strode across the room to the desk. The sight of their charcoal uniform was jarring, despite it only being an illusion. "Gather anything you can find, whatever we might use as evidence for what they did. Quickly now–that alarm should buy us some time but not much."

"How did you even know we were here?"

"I was coming to see Kai when I ran into Vera outside. She was worried sick that something happened to you." Their eyes cut to Baz. "I told you to stay away from here, Basil."

"We figured out what they're doing." Baz walked over to the desk. He held up the empty vial, watching Jae's face blanch at the remaining silver sheen. "They took Kai's blood. His *magic*."

Jae looked between Baz and Kai. "Are you . . ."

"I'm fine," Kai bit out.

"I used my magic to reverse the damage," Baz explained. "My *Collapsed* magic."

Jae's face fell. "Basil . . ."

They took a tentative step toward him, but Baz shook his head, angry now. "How could you let Dad wither away in here while I remained free?"

"Your father begged me. He knew I'd been living a normal life since I'd Collapsed, and he knew I would keep an eye on you, help you through it as best I could. Those first few months, I was so scared you might slip into that wicked power we're always warned of. But . . . you never did. At such a young age, you already had more control over your raw magic than I ever did. So I thought it best to keep you in the dark. Let you lead a normal life."

Baz felt Kai watching them with narrowed eyes as he pieced it all together. "How in the Deep aren't you both glowing like fucking silver stars? How'd you manage to escape *this*?" he seethed, shoving his branded hand in their faces.

Baz had been wondering the same thing. The answer was somewhere deep in his bones; he could feel it. The Collapsing was supposed to eclipse them until there was nothing left but this endless darkness, evil incarnate. The Regulators branded them because that sheer power was supposed to be a threat to everyone around them. But if Baz and Jae could live their entire lives with the raw power of their Collapsing coursing through their veins—if Baz could *control* it, this thing he'd suppressed all his life without even knowing what it was—then certainly, others could too.

Kai could.

The only thing stopping him was the U-shaped burn scar on his Eclipse tattoo. The Unhallowed Seal, this thing that sought to quiet the magic in their veins.

An idea started to take shape in Baz's mind as Jae pocketed the empty vial Kai's blood had been in.

"There's no time to explain," Jae muttered defeatedly. "I swear I will once we get out of here, but right now, we need *evidence.*

They're never going to stop coming after Eclipse-born if we have nothing to use against them."

Jae tried to open one of the drawers, which was locked. A quick, inquiring look at Baz. And though he still had a million questions he wanted to ask, he shoved all of them down to do this one task, pulling on the thread of time that saw the drawer unlocked.

Jae rummaged through it, slamming documents and ledgers and loose papers on the desk. Kai grabbed a small, black leather-bound ledger from the pile.

Fury swept over his features. He swore, handing the ledger to Baz. "Look."

It was opened on a page containing Kai's name, the date his blood sample was taken, how much of it had been harnessed. An earlier entry caught Baz's attention—*Theodore Brysden*. But his father's name was crossed out with a note written in the margin that read: *BAD SAMPLE–SYNTH DIDN'T WORK.*

Baz frowned at the term. *Synth.* He flipped to the start of the ledger, where a title was written neatly at the top: *S.O. Synthetic Magics.* Above the title was a spiral just like the one Emory had on her wrist—like the one on the Hourglass—and below it, a list of instructions:

To make synthetic:
Take 1 vial of blood from a Collapsed Eclipse-born–
needs to be in its silver state; the Unhallowed Seal
prevents the silver from leaving their veins.
Combine with 1 vial of blood from a magic user with the
desired tidal alignment. Note: To imbue synthetic with
more than one tidal alignment, use double the amount of
silver Eclipse blood.
Ink blood mixture into skin; to activate, wash in salt

water. The synthetic lasts approx. 6 hours & works
regardless of the moon phase.

Horror was slow to dawn on Baz, and then it hit all at once. "The magic they put to sleep after we Collapse . . . They take it from us to make some kind of synthetic magic out of it."

His father's sample must not have worked because he *hadn't* Collapsed. His magic hadn't yet become this raw, silvery thing in his veins, and so somehow, it had no consequence on these experiments.

Baz frowned at Jae. "Wouldn't they have seen that Dad's blood was red?"

"Doubtful. The illusion I placed on him makes it look like he bleeds silver, even now. I made sure my illusion was a sustainable one. An upside of Collapsing, to maintain that kind of magic with little effort."

"Wouldn't *your* blood be silver?" Kai frowned between Jae and Baz.

"No. The silver only stays for a short period after the Collapsing, fading back to red over time—unless, of course, it's stoppered by the Unhallowed Seal. It's why those of us who Collapse but manage to escape the seal can avoid detection. Our blood runs red."

Baz quickly went through the other journals on the desk, full of notes and theories and lists he couldn't decipher. His eyes caught on Emory's name, the newest entry at the bottom of one such list. Her date of birth had been crossed out, with another inked over it. A single day before it. Baz's eyes swept the list all the way to the top, where the title *Suspected Tidecaller Eclipses* had been penned. His spine tingled with understanding: these were people born across centuries on the same ecliptic event as Emory. A rare variant of a total solar eclipse.

He blinked at one of the earlier names that was underlined, had to reread it again to make sense of it.

Cornus Clover.

It couldn't be. Clover was a known Healer. Born on a new moon . . . unless he was like Emory. Born a Healer, only to become a Tidecaller.

His heart pounded. Cornus Clover, the author of his beloved book, the man who was believed to have written himself into his story. The scholar who could walk through worlds.

. . . magic runs in his veins as he runs through worlds like rivers to the sea and blood through arteries.

That very same passage was written in the journal, right in the margin next to Clover's name. Below it, someone had scribbled in bold letters: *AINSLEIF'S MAGIC = KEY. USE AS VESSEL.*

Vessel.

It sounded like what the drowned gods had needed to escape their prison in *Song of the Drowned Gods.* A key to unlock the door to the sea of ash, four parts of a whole to take their place inside it. Blood and bones and heart and soul.

Four parts like the four types of magic that Emory could call upon. The four Tides, the four lunar houses, the four tidal alignments within each house–all of them a part of her, all hers to command.

She's the key my dad and Keiran's parents never found, Artem had said. *The answer they never even knew they were looking for.*

Baz swore. "He's going to get her killed."

"Who?"

"Emory. Keiran and the Regulator who did this to us . . . They think she's the key to waking the Tides. A vessel of some kind."

All that talk of restoring magic to its former glory . . . Artem really did believe it, that the Tides could be woken. That the fabled deities were *real.* It was crazy, surely not possible, but after seeing what Keiran was capable of . . . Whether it was plausible or not didn't matter–if they were willing to go to such lengths to do something

so unfathomable, the only thing that mattered was that Emory was in danger.

"I have to stop her from going back to Dovermere. We need to grab Dad and get out of here."

There wasn't a chance in the world that he was leaving his father here for one more second with everything going on, especially when he hadn't even done what he'd been accused of.

Jae shoved all the ledgers and documents into their bag. The three of them pushed out the door into the corridor. They rounded a corner—and came face-to-face with Artem.

Kai swung at him with lethal speed.

"*Stop*," Artem said simply. "*Don't move a muscle.*"

Kai stopped.

All of them stopped, rooted in place by some compulsion— Glamour magic, Baz realized, spotting the Waxing Moon sigil on the Regulator's hand, the blood dripping down his fingers. He'd called on his magic through bloodletting.

Artem walked toward them with slow, arrogant ease, a look of pure hatred in his eyes. There was no one else in the corridor, the place completely evacuated as the alarms still blared loudly. A knife hung from Artem's hand. Vivianne was not with him, a fact that set off its own alarm in Baz's mind.

Artem had wanted Vivianne to wipe their memories. And if he'd come back without her in tow, maybe he'd decided to finish the job another way. There was no one here to stop him.

The cruel curve of Artem's smile lent credence to that sickening thought, and as he lifted the knife, it became clear he didn't intend any of them to walk out of here.

There was a sudden movement behind Artem—and with a growl, someone knocked him over the head.

The Regulator fell limply to the ground.

Theodore Brysden stood over him with a metal tray. "Someone deactivated the wards," he said with a satisfied smile. "Can we go now? I'm quite tired of this place."

They left Artem on the corridor floor and hurried out of the building. Vera was waiting for them in the wooded area where she'd hidden her motorbike. She didn't bat an eye at Theodore and Kai in their Institute garments.

"Where to?" she asked.

"Aldryn?" Baz suggested. "Dad and Kai can hide in Obscura Hall while we figure this out."

Kai gave him a death glare. "I'm not fucking hiding. I'm coming with you to Dovermere." He raised a brow at Baz's stricken expression. "That's where you're going, no? To stop Keiran, save Emory."

"Yes, but–"

"Then I'm going with you."

"You're still branded. Without access to your magic . . . it's too dangerous."

Kai balled his hands into fists. "I have these, and I'm itching to punch Dunhall Thornby in the face for what he did to me. It'll have to be enough."

Baz looked at the brand on the back of Kai's white-knuckled hand. That idea again took shape at the edge of his mind, bloomed into something that felt impossible yet right.

"We can bring your dad to the Veiled Atlas," Vera suggested. "No one will think to look for him there. And I know Alya won't mind." She winked at Jae. "No matter how much she pretends otherwise, she'd do just about anything for you."

"Then let's go," Baz relented.

Vera relinquished her motorbike to an all-too-eager Kai–she would go with Theodore in the car Jae illusioned into being. "Be

gentle with her," she screamed at Kai as he revved the engine. Baz held on tightly to him, throwing his dad and Jae one last look before they tore toward Dovermere.

The wind howled around them when they got to the beach. On the far side of the cove, the cave mouth was still visible, the tide having just slowly begun to rise.

A storm brewed on the horizon.

"I should have known you'd Collapsed," Kai huffed.

"How could you? Even I was in the dark."

"It was that fucking nightmare of yours. I always thought there was something odd about it, a truth hidden beneath it that you couldn't see and I couldn't quite puzzle out." Kai shook his head in disbelief. "And to think how scared you were of Collapsing."

Baz could see the resentment beneath Kai's grim smile. His thoughts raced faster than his pulse. "I think . . . I think there might be a way for you to get your magic back."

The wind tore Kai's hair loose from the ponytail he'd tied it into. "What are you saying, Brysden?"

"If Jae and I both survived Collapsing . . . If we could live with it our whole lives and still stay in control, then maybe everyone else can do the same. You could, too."

Kai shoved his branded hand in front of him. "Little late for that."

"What if I reversed the seal?"

Time time time time time time time time

Possibility crackled between them. Kai stood very still, his face impassive as Baz explained: "I could turn back time to when the seal hadn't yet touched your skin or put your magic to sleep. I could probably turn it back further still so that you'd never even have Collapsed in the first place."

Kai shook his head. "No."

Baz deflated. The world truly had to be upside down for *him* to

suggest something so reckless that Kai refused. "You're right. This is crazy."

"No, I mean I don't want you to reverse my Collapsing," Kai clarified. "But the seal? Fuck yes. Get that thing off me."

A million calculations ran through Baz's mind. He glanced around them, looked up at the stairs that led to the Eclipse commons. It would be best to do it there, as the walls of Obscura Hall were heavily warded in the eventuality that an Eclipse student Collapsed, so that the blast wouldn't bring down the entire college. But here on the deserted beach, with nothing but wild grasses and sand and rock for miles around . . .

Once the brand was lifted from Kai's skin, his magic would wake. He would once again be able to use it. But the seal served as protection against the full force of his Collapsing, and if Baz got rid of it, then that raw energy would be unleashed, uninterrupted and unrestrained. The blast might not damage the school, or the beach they stood on, but as for Baz . . .

"Just do it," Kai urged.

"Are you sure?"

There was a challenge in his eyes. "It's like you said: if you can survive it, then I sure as hell can."

And Baz had time on his side. He could shield himself from the blast of Kai's Collapsing with it, make it so it never reached him. A barrier to hide behind.

"I trust you, Brysden."

Those words settled between them, an agreement struck. Baz took a few steps back out of precaution. Kai straightened, steeling himself for what was to come.

The sight was an eerie one: the Nightmare Weaver in the pale clinical clothes of the Institute, standing in the middle of a field of tall grass that swayed in the wind. The dark sea at his back. Thunderclouds above his head.

Baz let out a grounding sigh. The threads of time called to him, and instinctively, he reached for them. He turned back the dial on the brand on Kai's hand, and it was easy to do because it was the same thing he'd done with Emory's Collapsing, the same he'd done again just now when he'd stopped Kai's magic from turning to ash. The seal disappeared to a time when it did not yet exist, and just like that, the Nightmare Weaver was free of his restraints.

Silver veins rippled beneath his skin.

Kai smiled, a dangerous thing.

And then he erupted—his Collapsing barreling forward like an overfull dam bursting in heart-stopping fashion.

Silver light leeched all the color from the world. Kai was a star in collapse, a great shaft of lightning burning through the field, and in that brilliant blaze, he came undone and was remade anew. A scream tore from his throat as the force of his Collapsing rippled through him. None of it touched Baz, the space between him and Kai held just outside of time, rippling with Baz's own magic.

Everything will be all right, Baz thought, his father's words ringing in his ears. He might have shouted them to Kai—he wasn't sure, couldn't hear himself breathe over the force of the blast.

Kai's screaming honed to a sharp laugh as he fell to his knees, an indistinct shape in the middle of a supernova. And just when Baz thought his Collapsing might have gotten the better of him, all the light extinguished, whooshing back into Kai. Silver veins still danced faintly under his skin, in the whites of his eyes, but when he looked at Baz, he was still alive, still Kai.

He smiled that sharp smile before falling limply to the scorched earth beneath him.

"Kai!"

Baz was at his side in seconds. His hands reached wildly for Kai's convulsing body, thinking something horribly wrong must have happened as he heard the sound wheezing from Kai's lips.

But then he realized Kai was smiling—that it was *laughter* he shook with. And not his usual snide or snark, but such pure, joyous laughter that Baz couldn't help the hysterical laugh that rippled through him, too.

There were tears in Kai's eyes when he finally stopped wheezing. He looked up in wonder at the storm clouds over their heads. "I told you, Brysden," he mused. "There's no Shadow's curse. Only this." His head tilted to face Baz. "I feel . . . whole. Like this is what being Eclipse-born is supposed to be."

And here beneath the storm-ridden skies, those words rang true in Baz's soul.

All their lives, the Eclipse-born lived in constant fear of losing control of their magic, this thing that had no limits but the Collapsing itself. The nature of such power made it undeniable, like the pull of the moon on the tides or the song that called his sister to the Deep. Hard to resist, harder still to control.

Magic sustains us like air, his father had taught him long ago. *Go without it and you suffocate. Keep too much in your lungs and you'll burst. The key is taking carefully measured breaths.*

But the truth was they could fill their lungs with it, this power. They could breathe it in and let it consume them, and once they breathed it out again, they'd be whole.

There was no Shadow's curse. The Collapsing didn't eclipse them, didn't eradicate who they were. It wasn't a limit at all but a threshold—a way to tear down the boundaries they'd created around themselves.

Their blood ran with all the power of the eclipse. Light and dark, fleeting and rare and beautiful.

Baz drew in a shuddering breath, his nose full of the smell of the sea. He pulled himself up and Kai along with him.

"Let's go to Dovermere."

They would show Keiran the full might of the Eclipse.

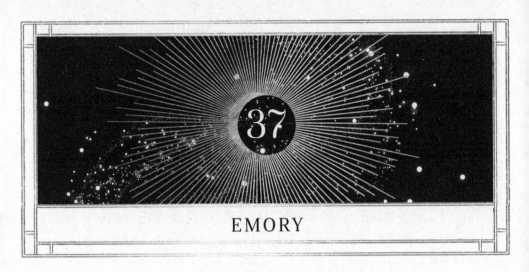

EMORY

LIZAVETA FELL LIMPLY TO THE GROUND, COUGHING UP
blood. Her hands fluttered to her throat, where the knife was
still lodged. Emory moved toward her, drawing on her healing
magic, intending to wrench the blade from her throat–

"*Don't,*" Keiran said.

A single word laced with Glamour magic, and all the fight
winked out of her.

Emory stared at Keiran, hoping to see something on his face
that would make this all okay, that would refute everything he'd
said, unmake the last few minutes, hours, until they were back in
his room, just two embracing bodies dappled in morning sunlight.

Yet even that thought made her sick.

"How could you do this?" She hated her voice for its brokenness.

"I did this for you, Ains, can't you see? To be the Tides'
vessel . . . Think of all that power you'll have coursing through
you. The full might of the Tides in *your* veins. There's nothing more
sacred."

Emory flinched away from his reaching hand. Hurt flashed in Keiran's eyes. He was gilded in the glow of lanterns, ever the embodiment of his tidal alignment, even now. A light in the dark.

Except he *was* the darkness.

Emory's fists uncurled at her sides. "Was any of it real?"

"Of course it was."

And there was such fervor in those words, how could she not believe him?

Yet Lizaveta's death-still body was at their feet and the others in their unnatural slumber around the Hourglass and there was no overlooking this, no way to spin this in his favor.

"I told you that you have a hold on me, and I meant it, Ains. This pull between us, this attraction . . . It's undeniable."

Emory drew back with a shake of her head. A wretched, rotten feeling twisted in her stomach, festered in her mouth. How easily she'd fallen under his spell. He'd known exactly what she wanted and had used it to his advantage—the same way *she'd* used Baz's feelings for her to her own, she realized with a pang of guilt. She'd craved to be seen and desired by someone like Keiran, someone magnetic and gorgeous who made her feel so very important, so much so she'd ignored all the red flags, ignored the suspicions she'd had when she first started this.

"I knew you were special," Keiran said. "And now you can be so much more."

A vessel for the Tides.

"But my power won't be my own," Emory refuted. Nor would her will, her mind. "It'll be the Tides pulling the strings."

She'd be a weapon used to destroy every Eclipse-born for what a single one of them had done to his parents.

The remnants of the Shadow's stain—that's what he thought was in her blood. The reason she could access all the moon's magics in some twisted, corrupt way. He thought her the Shadow reborn,

the great eye that shadowed the world, the unhallowed force the Tides had sent to the Deep.

Tidethief.

Once, Emory might have thought the same of her magic: that it was corrupt, wrong. Hadn't she hated it when she'd first discovered it? This burden she couldn't understand, this thing that had taken Romie from her and might as well have killed Travers and Lia and Jordyn and the four others who'd succumbed to Dovermere.

But she had seen the beauty in her magic too. Dead plants becoming lush again under her touch. Sunflowers blooming in an illusioned field. A path laden with stars.

And Baz at the center of it all, the quiet wonder that had started to replace the fear he'd once regarded her with, because he saw it too, the splendor beneath. He could deny his own power all he wanted, fear the Eclipse and the Collapsing and the destruction it could so easily wreak, but deep down, he had to know their magic had a place in the world. That it wasn't twisted or wrong or unhallowed, but magnificent and worthy of belonging.

Through her hand, the Tides would eradicate all that beauty, all those born under an eclipse, and Emory would be powerless to stop them.

She squared her chin. "I won't do it."

A shadow fell over Keiran's face. There was nothing of the Lightkeeper now in his features, nothing of his dimpled smile and easy manner.

"You will," Keiran said, voice low. "You'll unlock this door to the Deep, and you and I will walk through it together."

All this time, he'd made her feel important, significant, something Emory had always thought she was lacking. She'd wanted so badly to be someone worthy, someone who was more than just mediocre. Someone powerful.

But not like this. Not at the cost of losing herself in the process, of having her identity stripped away in the name of some greater, terrible power.

The words she'd thought to say to him last night were still lodged in her throat where she'd kept them safe. They threatened to choke her now, and she was glad she hadn't spoken them. They were the only piece of her Keiran hadn't gotten, and she would rather suffocate than share them now.

"I'm not opening anything for you."

Emory reached for her magic, calling to her the darkness that lived at the edge of the lanterns' light. Fury swept over Keiran. He stepped toward her, and she could feel the Glamour magic readying on his tongue as he opened his mouth to command her once more, bend her to his will.

Cold swept through the Belly of the Beast before he could utter a word, a dark breeze that made the hairs on the back of Emory's neck rise.

It was the coldness of stars, of the deepest ocean.

The chill of despair.

The hostility of fear.

Keiran whirled just as the umbra erupted from the darkness behind him, nightmare given form. It swept for him with its claws of elongated shadows, but Keiran was faster than it, shielding himself with a cocoon of shimmering light pulled from the lanterns. The umbra that once was Jordyn let out a bone-chilling sound that reverberated in the cavern.

Emory didn't think twice about what she did next: she wrested the protective light from Keiran's grasp, wrapped it around herself instead, and when the umbra lunged for him again, it found its mark.

Keiran screamed, falling to the floor. The umbra bent over his cowering form, and perhaps there was a piece of Jordyn left

in those fathomless eyes after all, seeking revenge on the person who'd no doubt filled his ears with promises of greatness and power.

Jordyn, Lia, Travers, Romie, all the Selenics lying around the Hourglass . . . Lizaveta . . . They'd been as much pawns in Keiran's scheme as Emory had been. There to open a door for him to take what was not his, their lives significant only in the way they'd been used on this sacrificial altar of power.

She watched numbly as the umbra feasted on Keiran's fears. She couldn't bring herself to feel guilty over the whiteness of his face, the horror in his eyes. He'd meant to *use* her. Erase her. Destroy everyone like her—all in some sick, twisted attempt to save her from this corruption he saw her magic as.

Keiran went limp as the umbra at last turned away from him. Its depthless eyes swept over Lizaveta. Her red hair was matted with blood as it pooled around her, her eyes turned unseeing to the Hourglass. She was dead, not a fear or nightmare left to plague her, but next to her . . .

With a piercing shriek, the umbra moved toward the sleeping forms around the Hourglass, as if in anticipation of the new nightmares it might feast upon.

Emory couldn't stand still, not for this.

She sent her light flying to the prone Selenics, but the thin cocoon that wrapped around them was too flimsy a barrier for the umbra. It clawed at Virgil first, hovering over him as it gorged itself on the Reaper's fears. Emory remembered all too vividly how it had felt to have the umbra draw upon her own fears, how she'd tried to defeat it with every ounce of magic she had, only to have it nearly ruin her. Silver veins aglow under her skin, the Collapsing eager to consume her.

Baz wasn't here to stop her from Collapsing this time. But if light and hope and dreams couldn't kill the nightmare, perhaps

the answer lay in the beast itself. In something that was just as frightening.

What could kill fear if not fear itself?

What could end a nightmare if not something more frightening still?

A distant part of her hesitated; this had been a person, after all, someone she'd known. But there was nothing of Jordyn left. Virgil had once told her it would have been a kindness for her to kill Travers. That death, if given, could be a mercy.

She had no choice.

Her own fears were so close to the surface, they were easy to call on. Romie going through a door she could not survive. Travers and Lia and Jordyn dead at her command, whether she willed it or not. The thought of Keiran using her against her own kind and the Tides erasing everything she was and who she wanted to be.

Never seeing her father again.

Emory felt it before she even knew what she meant to do. A sense of cold and foreboding that swept over the cave, just like when the umbra appeared, just like when it dragged her deep into that time-still water. But while the umbra had only leeched her memories, drinking them in like they were the richest wine as her worst fears plagued her mind, Emory made them *real*. Her fears wafted from her like wisps of black smoke, material and not, full of twisting shapes and faces, scenes from the bleakest depths of her psyche, images she wished never to see again.

The shadows slithered from her like a distorted aura, blending and reshaping to match the umbra bent over Virgil. A mirror image created from her own fears and nightmares.

A weapon for her to wield.

Her fabricated umbra drew itself up, gaining the attention of the beast that had once been Jordyn.

And it pounced.

There was a clash of shadows and teeth and water and claws. The walls of the cavern shook with the impact of the two monsters twining in a nightmarish dance. Her beast grew and stretched, filling the space within the cave until it became too big, a sentient thing with a will of its own.

There was a distant, thundering sound.

The water at her feet began to rise as more of it poured into the cave, quick and sudden with the force of the rising tide.

And Emory thought she might die here after all. At the hands of the umbrae or the tide or Keiran, it didn't matter; she was trapped here. Out of the corner of her eye, she saw Keiran push up on his elbows, the look he gave her promising death.

Emory took a step back, hit the rock behind her.

The Hourglass.

A way out. A door to somewhere beyond.

Emory whirled around to face it. She brought her still-bloody hand against the rock, where silver and water and blood swirled together into a great spiral at the middle.

Her blood was a key pressing into a lock.

The Hourglass became distorted. A bruise of darkness bloomed in its middle. It grew into a door, a fissure at the center of the Hourglass, a tear in the fabric of the world through which she glimpsed a sea of stars.

And she knew this darkness, recognized these strange tilting lights. Behind her, the shrieks of the umbrae and the roar of the tide were deafening, but they were distant things compared to the pull of what lay on the other side. It beckoned to her, called her forward like a million ghostly hands tugging at her, a thousand echoing sighs that seemed to whisper, *There you are. We've been waiting for you.*

Yes, her own heart answered.

But fear and doubt gripped her. She threw a glance over her shoulder, stomach turning at the sight of Keiran coming up on unsteady feet and the others still prone on the cave floor, lying in gradually rising water. She couldn't leave them vulnerable to the umbrae and the tide that would come crashing in.

But the door to the Deep called to her. And somewhere beyond it was Romie, fearless Romie, about to go where she could not. Or maybe she'd gone already and everything was lost. But Emory had to know.

She flung a hand behind her, and the flimsy light wrapped around the Selenics amplified, protection against the umbrae. She called on whatever magic she could think of–Dreamer and Unraveler and Healer alike–and thought a single word.

Rise.

She glimpsed the flutter behind Virgil's eyes, saw Nisha pushing herself slowly up on her elbows and Ife bringing a hand to her head, a dazed look on her face.

They had all made it out of the Beast once, had conquered the tide to claim their place in the Selenic Order; they could do so again. Emory only hoped they'd be fast enough to make it out before the tide trapped them inside.

She saw Keiran move toward her then.

"Don't," he commanded.

But his compulsion had no bearing on her now, not against the pull of this great darkness before her. She inched a toe across the threshold. The dark reached for her, drawing her forward like a tender lover. There was only this now. Everything else fell away: the Belly of the Beast, the hunger of the sea, the cold chill of nightmares still circling each other at her back.

The shape of her name yelled in the depths, a voice that told her to *wait.*

All of it faded until there was only that murmur brushing against her magic.

Emory, Emory.

The starlit void beckoned her forward.

Come, it whispered. *Seek us as we have sought you.*

And her blood was eager to answer its call.

BAZ

A SHRIEK ROSE IN THE DEPTHS OF DOVERMERE. IT PIERCED the quiet gloom and echoed oddly through the cave tunnels, giving Baz pause.

Kai turned dark eyes on him. The silver in his pupils and in his veins had dulled, but Baz could still feel it, the power that thrummed inside him in the wake of his Collapsing. Not an eclipsing of one's self, but an awakening. This he thought again for the hundredth time, not quite able to wrap his mind around it.

"Do you feel that?" the Nightmare Weaver asked.

Cold seeped through Baz as if in answer. The dread he felt was all too familiar.

The umbra he and Emory had fought against. Jordyn.

Baz broke into a run.

He recognized the great cavern mouth that loomed up ahead. Hope and fear twisted in his gut as he spotted Emory in the middle of the Belly of the Beast. Nightmares stretched in every corner of the wide space, with not one umbra but two of them, squaring off

in what looked like a brutal dance of shadowed claws and teeth. All around the raised platform were students slowly rising as if in a trance, and Emory stood in front of the distorted Hourglass, inching toward the impossible darkness that bloomed in the center of the column.

The door to the Deep.

Her name tore from Baz's lips, a desperate plea for her to stop, a last lifeline thrown out at sea. He thought she might have heard him over the chaos that reigned; she seemed to pause, her head tilting ever so slightly toward him, as if she'd recognized his voice through the madness.

Baz flung his magic outward, willing–*begging*–time to stop. To give him one more second, one last chance to make this right between them.

Please wait, he thought. A prayer spoken to the dark, to the cave itself.

The cave knew him and this strange magic that flowed through his veins. It was an echo of the same power that made up the fabric of Dovermere.

Time, in all its strangeness.

And so the cave stopped for him. Power surged outward from him, and everything that it touched stilled, like dominoes falling over in one fell swoop. The waking students went motionless first, as did the tide at Baz's back that had begun to rush in, nipping at his heels. The magic reached further still for Emory, for Keiran at her side, for the umbrae tearing each other apart–but it stopped before it could touch them, slipping from his grasp as a sudden force knocked Baz over, skewing his concentration. He thought it was the tide slipping past his magic's grasp, but *this* tide was made of light and dark, great tendrils that wrapped around him, binding, limiting.

The kind of magic Emory had once used.

His name spilled from her mouth as she turned at last from the Hourglass, her eyes wide with horror. And then Keiran was between them, fury twisting his features. Light and darkness spilled from his hands, twisting into something else, a magic not entirely his own. The binds around Baz grew tighter, and he realized it was Keiran who commanded them.

Kai snarled as he tore toward Keiran. The sound drew the umbrae's attention, as if these beasts of fear and darkness were called to the weaver of nightmares, answered to him now that he was Collapsed. They paused their thrashing as Kai pummeled into Keiran and the two of them splashed into the shallow water at the base of the Hourglass. Kai's fists met with Keiran's face, again and again and again. The two umbrae were at his back, leaning over his shoulder, and it almost looked like they were melding with him, lending him their cold, fathomless strength.

The Nightmare Weaver was dark fury, unleashing himself upon Keiran.

"Kai," cried Emory, tears rolling down her cheeks. She stepped off the dais toward them, stopped just out of their reach. *"Kai, stop."*

Kai's fist stilled midair, as if her words had frozen him–and at the fury on his face, Baz wondered if she had done just that, compelling him with Glamour magic. Beneath him, Keiran was unconscious, his face a bruised and bloodied mess.

"Please," Emory breathed.

Slowly, Kai drew himself up. He rounded on Emory, the umbrae at his back mirroring the gesture, shadows that seemed to bend to his command now. Baz tensed as he caught the gleam of silver in the Nightmare Weaver's eyes, like the glint of a blade under the sun.

Kai fixated on the open doorway at Emory's back. He took a step toward it, as if called by the velvety darkness beyond, but the

umbrae's claws gripped his shoulders, and Kai stilled, blinking away the silver fog in his eyes.

The Nightmare Weaver turned on the umbrae. *"Sleep,"* he said, and his voice was that of the lord of nightmares, quiet and commanding. The umbrae fell away to nothing but shadows, dissolving into the shallow water at his feet.

And then there were just the three of them in the stillness, staring at each other in the middle of the Beast. Three Eclipse-born standing before a door.

Even now, with the door to the Deep open and the vastness beyond within his reach, Baz heard no song, felt no pull, only the crushing disappointment of not being the chosen one like all the heroes in his stories.

He caught Emory's eye then, and relief pulled a breath from his lungs.

She was still here.

For a terrible, gut-wrenching moment, he thought he'd never see her again.

There was so much he wanted to say to her, but the sea at their backs pushed on his magic, raging at time's hold on it. And though the knowledge of his Collapsing made Baz less fearful than before, he knew there were still limits to his power, and the tide wouldn't hold forever.

He pointed to Keiran's unconscious form. "He meant to use you as a vessel," he told Emory. "Your magic, your blood . . ."

"I know." Her face was an obscure mask as she stared at Keiran. "You were right about him. He wanted to wake the Tides and have them eradicate all Eclipse-born."

Like the Tides had intended when they sent the Shadow to the Deep.

Baz's fingers went numb. There was not a sliver of doubt in his mind that Keiran's motivations lay with his parents' deaths. With

what happened to them—what Baz *did* to them. He felt Kai's gaze on him, as if the Nightmare Weaver sensed the tangled mess of feelings warring inside him.

"He really believes it, then?" Baz asked. "That the Tides are real and can bring lunar magic back to what it was?"

A grim nod from Emory.

"And you?"

Emory looked at the door. "I have to go through it, Baz. If Romie's there, I have to bring her back."

Understanding settled between them. She needed to answer the door's call—find Romie, save her, bring her home.

And Baz couldn't go with her. No one could, not if her Tidecaller blood alone was what might protect her in the Deep, the sea of ash, wherever this Tides-damned door led. Besides, he needed to stay here, hold back the tide, help these time-stilled students back to shore.

The idea of saying goodbye was unbearable. Emory had walked back into his life, carved herself a place in it despite all his trepidations, and though Baz doubted he would ever be fearless like Kai or Romie, he knew Emory had made him want to fear *less*. This girl who'd laughed in fields of gold, who'd made sunflowers bloom, who'd looked up at the stars with him and thought they were lost souls trying to find their way home.

Come back home, he wanted to say to her now. But the words felt painfully inadequate.

Emory's gaze swept over the frozen students around the dais. "Make sure they get back to shore," she pleaded. "They weren't part of this. It was all Keiran. He used them—was willing to sacrifice them. And he . . . he killed Lizaveta."

It was then that Baz noticed the redhead Emory was staring at. The knife lodged in her neck.

Emory rubbed at her bloodstained wrist, where Baz knew the

silver spiral was inked on her skin. Her throat undulated as she swallowed some emotion back. "I'm sorry for dragging you into this, Baz. If I could take it back . . ."

"I wouldn't. Not any of it."

Despite everything they'd gone through, he wouldn't change a thing, because it all brought her to him and him to her, brought both of them here, in this moment, standing in a cave dripping with time, before a door made of myth and story. And that felt a little like fate, Baz thought, even if it was a cruel one to pull them apart like this at the very end.

Emory's mouth quirked up in a sad smile, and those might have been tears lining her storm-cloud eyes, but he couldn't tell, not as she turned to Kai. "Romie said something to me in my dream. She said, 'Tell Kai I left it for him to find.'"

Kai and Emory looked at each other in silence, and that felt momentous too, in a way Baz couldn't quite explain. Here were the heroes of this story, he thought. The girl whose blood was a key and the boy of nightmares and the other girl somewhere beyond the door who'd dreamed too much and reached too far.

Finally, Kai dipped his chin toward the door, the swirling darkness beyond it. With a slanted smile, he told Emory, "Remember not to veer from the path, dreamling."

When Emory's eyes met Baz's again, they were full of fragile, expectant hope. Like she was waiting for him to come up with an alternative to this mad plan, or perhaps just for him to say goodbye.

The words wouldn't come.

She nodded as if she understood, started to turn toward the door.

"Wait," Baz said. *Stay*, he thought.

He knew that wasn't a possibility, so Baz kept the word trapped between his lungs. His resolve stood, a fragile thing, but Emory's

seemed to crumble entirely. In a blur of motion, she reached for him, arms draping around his shoulders, tear-stained cheek a perfect fit in the crook of his neck.

"Thank you," she murmured against his flushed skin.

Baz's arms encircled her. He breathed her in, engraved the feel of her against him. He wanted to tell her that he'd been wrong, that everything she touched didn't crumble to dust. Rather, she made the dust fall away, leaving things polished and new again in her wake. He thought she should know that but didn't know how to say it. It was what she'd done for him, in a way. For so long he'd held on to this image he had of their youth, not realizing they could never go back to that. Not realizing he didn't *want* to go back to that either. He'd learned too much, seen too much of the world, to return to such naivety. He'd finally shaken off some of his fears, and that was largely her doing. She'd pushed him to step outside the comforts of his limits, had shown him he could *try* at something and damn the risk.

Like that kiss.

He wouldn't take it back, wouldn't change any of it. He'd followed his gut, put himself out there, and for that brief, terrifying, exhilarating moment when she'd kissed him back, it had all been worth it. The world had felt right, his feelings vindicated. Proof that he wasn't crazy thinking there might have been something between them. What happened after the kiss didn't matter, not really, because at least he'd *done* something. For once, he hadn't kept everything bottled up inside.

She'd made him feel free, like all the gulls they used to chase down to the sea. She'd made him realize he couldn't fly with clipped wings, and only once he stopped letting his fears control him would he finally soar.

He had no regrets. They were about to be separated by an entire world, their paths diverging, and maybe that was okay, because at

least he wouldn't have to wonder what might have been. He could turn the page and be grateful for what they'd shared together. And if they happened to find each other again–*when* they found each other again, because she had to come back–well. It was like an epilogue yet to be written, and whatever awaited them, Baz would be content to have had this story with her at least.

Emory pulled away slightly to look at him. The tears staining her face reminded Baz of the taste of salt on her lips, and he wanted so badly to pull her mouth to his one last time to ingrain it in his mind forever. But he couldn't. If he did, he'd never let her go. Instead he let the space between them fill with words left unsaid that would forever remain in this place lost to time. And maybe that was okay too.

Emory kissed his cheek. A fleeting thing, the barest brush of lips. Like she, too, couldn't stand much else without breaking her resolve.

It felt like goodbye.

As she pulled away one last time, her gaze went to Kai, who quickly looked away, blinking back some emotion Baz couldn't figure out.

Then she turned her back on them both.

She took a step toward that darkness at the center of the Hourglass. Her name nearly tore from him again, fear like he'd never known threatening to choke him. But he bit back the sound, swallowed the fear. Emory's head tilted ever so slightly toward him, as if she'd heard him anyway and she, too, was gripped with a sudden dread, the same painful thought Baz had, that this was the last time they would ever see each other.

Her feet crossed the threshold before their eyes could meet. The darkness reached for her, drawing her in.

She disappeared like a star winking out of existence.

And out of the corner of his eye, something else darted past.

Keiran, no longer lying unconscious on the floor, but scrambling after Emory through the door. Kai shouted something. Baz sent his magic flying, willing time to stop him, but he was a second too late and the darkness was quicker, a stranger magic than his own, and it pulled Keiran through the door.

EMORY

EMORY TUMBLED THROUGH DARKNESS, AND IT WAS LIKE
free-falling into death's open arms, depthless, abysmal, until all
at once it stopped, and here she stood on a starlit path that was all
too familiar, in a silence she could choke on.

It was the sleepscape but not. The same darkness, the same
swirling stars and curving path. But it felt . . . clearer, somehow;
realer than it had when she'd found Romie in it just yesterday. As if
that had only been an illusion, like the sky in Obscura Hall, and this
was the real thing at last. Gone was the feeling of being underwater. She felt grounded.

Stay on the path, dreamling, Kai had cautioned, the words at
once unsettling and oddly comforting.

Emory took a careful step toward the edge of that star-lined path
and frowned as water sloshed beneath her feet. It flowed along
the path, trickling down the sides of it into the abyss. She peered
into the black velvet tapestry beyond the stars. There was a rift in
the blackness, she noticed: the still-open doorway that bled into

the caves she'd just left. The water was coming from the other side of it, from the Belly of the Beast visible through the rift. She could just make out the indistinct shapes within, but it was like looking through the surface of rippling water, trying to discern the shifting bottom. She wanted to reach for it, but the words Kai had parted with stopped her, made her pull back.

She needed to stay on the path and find Romie—if she was still here at all.

Emory glanced at her wrist, at the curved spiral glowing silver on her skin. *Romie,* she called through her silver mark, through the dark, through every bit of magic she had inside her.

Alone, she waited for the answer to come and the suffocating quiet to break. It didn't—and with a pang of fresh grief, Emory realized Romie might truly be gone.

Might truly be dead.

The only sound came from behind. Emory whirled in time to see Keiran appear on the path, beaten and bloodied and bruised, but still standing, if a little askew. His widening eyes took in the impossible darkness around them. A wheezing laugh blew past his split lips.

"So this is it," he mused. "The purgatory that leads to the Deep."

"It's the sleepscape," Emory said breathlessly.

Keiran pressed a hand to his side, wincing. "You said Romie couldn't pull herself out of this place like she usually could. That this couldn't be the sleepscape."

But everything was starting to make sense in Emory's mind. Why she'd been able to commune with Romie. Why Romie had survived this place longer than Travers and Lia and Jordyn had. Because as a Dreamer, she was used to inhabiting such liminal spaces.

And what was the sleepscape but a place between worlds? The space between waking and dreaming, living and dead. This world and the next.

Whatever purgatory this must be . . .

Romie and Travers and Lia and Jordyn had all been stuck in this nether region, lost in transit among the stars as they waited for the next train to arrive—for Emory to unlock the door again and pull them out.

This *was* the sleepscape. Not something *like* it, not the recreation of it that Dreamers visited in their sleep, but the real thing. A world of its own. Romie hadn't been able to escape it because she hadn't stepped into it like she normally did—hadn't accessed it through sleep at all. It was her body that had gone through the door that led her here. A physical door into a physical world made of dreams. And if both Romie's body and her subconscious were stuck here, in between the worlds of the living and the dead, then of course she couldn't wake, couldn't escape. There was nowhere to escape *to*, no body for her subconscious to flutter back to. She couldn't leave this world at all, not without paying in magic and blood as the others had.

Not without a key.

Romie, Emory called again, a desperate plea.

Keiran eyed her Selenic Mark. "Do you sense her presence?" he asked. "Is she here to answer your call?"

His mouth pulled down when she didn't answer. "I'm sorry, Ains. I really am." He limped toward her, his marked hand reaching for her. "Come with me. There's nothing left for us now but to find the Tides."

Emory glanced at the rift in the darkness between stars. She could have sworn it was shrinking, the door closing behind them.

"How did you figure out what my blood could do?" she asked Keiran. "All this time, getting close to me . . . Was it really all to get me here? To use me for your own gain?"

Keiran looked around him warily.

"There's nothing here but you and me and the dark," Emory said.

"The least you can do is to tell me the truth—for once."

His eyes found hers, bruises already blooming on his face from Kai's pounding. "I suspected there was something more to you last spring. When I saw what happened in the Belly of the Beast." He nodded at her frown. "I was there, Ains. I wasn't waiting for the others on the beach. I was in the caves with them."

It was impossible; there had only been the nine of them in the caves—Emory and the eight initiates. Keiran couldn't have been there too. She would have seen him.

He held his tattooed hand up to his face, dried blood marring the Full Moon sigil. "I told you once how I was never satisfied with being a Lightkeeper. How I always thought it was a terribly worthless tidal alignment . . . until I realized what bending light could be."

His hand disappeared—became *invisible*.

"With so many initiates last year, I was certain something would happen. That if there was ever a time for a door to the Deep to be opened, it would be when the circle was so complete. I followed the initiates into the caves, stayed invisible as they stood around the Hourglass. Nothing seemed to be happening at all . . . until you appeared.

"At first, I thought your presence at Dovermere had messed up the ritual. Then the night Travers returned, I made myself invisible and followed you to the water's edge, where you and Brysden spoke of your being a Tidecaller. I had to get you to trust me then. I knew if you thought I had the same twisted magic you did, you'd let me in, accept my offer to join the Order, and then our work could begin. So I made sure you saw me using synthetic magic."

The bird, the roses. She'd thought herself so clever to have caught him in the act, yet it had all been a trick to lure her in.

Emory swallowed past the tightness in her throat. "And my blood? When did you know it was the key?"

"It was Romie who gave me the idea, actually. She was obsessed

with this woman called Adriana Kazan, a member of the Veiled Atlas who was believed to have found the missing epilogue. I decided to look into her myself to see if there was any merit to that claim. You might know her by the pseudonym she adopted as she sailed the seas: Luce Meraude."

A dull ringing started in Emory's ears. She'd never told Keiran about her mother.

"It's a nice gift she left you," Keiran said as he pulled her mother's useless old compass watch out of his pocket. "I admit, when I retrieved it from your room, I thought it might be the key we were looking for. It's nothing, really, but it did lead me to the Veiled Atlas and the Kazans. Their family claims to have a shared lineage with Cornus Clover. That's how I discovered Clover was a Tidecaller himself. Born on the same auspicious eclipse as you. I then looked into others who manifested the same strange gift, and do you know what it led me to find? That by some fault in the design, a curiosity in your tides, those of you born under that rare solar eclipse always manifest Healer magic first. Most of you live your whole lives thinking that's what you are, children of House New Moon, because only those of you who encounter near deaths reawaken as Tidecallers. As if straddling the line between here and the Deep somehow unlocks your true nature."

Near deaths . . .

Emory had almost died last spring, had washed ashore half-drowned and with no memory of ever swimming out of the caves. All her life, her Healing magic had been her only power, until that fateful night at Dovermere.

But why would her mother lie about her birth? Had Luce or Adriana or whoever she was known what her latent abilities truly meant: that she might be able to open the door to the Deep, that she might one day be used as a vessel for the Tides? Emory wondered if her mother had cared about her after all, and in lying about her

birth, pretending she was born on a new moon instead of that rare eclipse, she had hoped Emory might never have such a near-death experience and would stay a Healer forever.

Maybe she'd simply wanted to protect her daughter.

Her mother was a sailor and her father a lighthouse keeper, and somewhere in between them, Emory was the sea. Both parents had tended to her in the way that suited them best, and maybe the only thing left to do now was to protect herself and others like her. Maybe the only way to ensure no one else ever sought to wake the Tides was to destroy the door that led to them. To destroy this place for good.

"I meant what I said, Ains. This whole thing might have started out as revenge, but my feelings for you are true. You took this hateful part of me and gave it new purpose. Something to look forward to—a better world, without so many limitations, without this underlying curse that plagues not only Eclipse-born but all of us it touches."

He offered her his hand again. "Please. Let me prove to you that I meant every word."

Emory looked at that rift in the dark. It was almost closed now, the world beyond it a distant echo. "I kept a secret from you too," she said.

Keiran lifted a brow.

"I didn't tell you everything that happened yesterday when I came to Dovermere with Baz. He warned me how easy it is to slip past that line, but I didn't believe him until then. One moment, I had control of my magic, and the next, *it* had control of *me*. I almost tore the whole cave down with me. Probably would have if Baz hadn't been there to stop me from Collapsing."

Slow realization dawned on Keiran's face. His hand fell at his side.

"You wouldn't," he said. "What about Romie?"

"I told you: I can't feel her. Which means she's already dead and I've got nothing left to lose."

In truth she refused to believe it—even though her call remained unanswered, even if Romie had followed the song somewhere she couldn't go without paying a terrible price . . . She refused to believe Romie was lost for good, but she was no longer *here*—that much Emory knew. Let Keiran believe she would do it. Call upon all the magics in her arsenal, let the blast of her Collapsing destroy everything. The door, the sleepscape, and them in it.

"If you destroy this place," Keiran warned, "we'll never reach the Tides. Whatever hope might be left for Romie, whether she's dead or gone or still here somewhere, she'll be lost for good."

"If we wake the Tides, *I* will be lost for good. And so will a lot of other people—people I care about."

Keiran approached her carefully, as if she were a scared animal about to scurry away. "I promise to leave you this one thing," he said, his hands coming up in a show of good faith. "If you come with me now, I'll beg the Tides to bring Romie back. I swear it, Ainsleif."

The same way he'd promised Lizaveta they'd bring Farran back.

Emory shook her head. "I made the mistake of believing you all this time. It stops now."

Romie, she called again, one last shot through the dark. *Please,* she begged, letting her magic sweep down the star-lined path. *Answer me.*

Something did answer her plea then.

But it wasn't Romie.

It sprang from the darkness beyond the stars. One umbra, then two, with three more on their heels. More of them materialized on the path, and this time Keiran wasn't as quick reaching for the light. But Emory was. She leapt out of the closest umbra's reach, wrapping herself in a film of starlight, just as a scream ripped from

Keiran's throat. Claws sank into his flesh with a wet sound. He tried to wrest free, but there were too many of them swarming him, hungry beasts looking to devour his soul.

This was their domain, and somehow Emory knew they were more powerful here, more *real*.

She watched numbly as Keiran went slack in their grasp, his face bloodless at whatever horrors he saw. Blood pooled from his middle, his shirt in crimson shambles. His eyes found hers from within the shadows that engulfed him, and she heard her name on his lips, a plea to save him.

She hesitated. Keiran hadn't hesitated when he drove that knife into Lizaveta's throat. He deserved every bit of this fate. So why couldn't she stand to watch it? Tears ran down her cheeks, the sight of him being *devoured* like this stirring up emotions she didn't want to feel.

So Emory looked away.

She did not move, not as Keiran spoke her name again, nor as his voice grew fainter until it was nothing at all. When she did look up, it was to glimpse the umbrae pulling him over the edge of the path. The last thing she saw of him were his bloodied hands seeking purchase among stars.

And then she was screaming.

A black-tipped hand wrapped around her neck, claws digging into skin. Fear like she'd never known before surged in her as she stared into the fathomless eyes of an umbra, and it was so much worse than last time, every vicious emotion and memory that rose to the surface of her subconscious chipping away at her soul.

Emory was being hollowed out, doomed to become nothing but a husk. Empty and lifeless.

Maybe she deserved it. Maybe she was no better than Keiran. Without her, none of this would have happened. No one would have died.

She could see nothing past the harrowing images behind her tightly shut eyes, could feel nothing but numbing pain and piercing cold and this never-ending despair and—

The slightest prickle on her wrist, not painful at all but comforting. Familiar.

Emory, Emory.

Her eyes flew open to see a star shooting toward her, carving a blinding path through the dark mass of umbrae. The star was calling her name. It had a voice she'd recognize anywhere, clear and bright and true, and eyes full of starlight, and freckles that were their own constellation.

Romie was here.

Romie was alive and she was *here*, barreling toward her like the unstoppable force that she was.

Relief, joy, love—they washed over Emory like a tidal wave, filling all the parts of her the umbra sought to extinguish. Light briefly surged around her once more as she fought to gain control of herself and her magic. It blinded the umbra. She fell limply to her knees as it let go, brought a hand to the bloody wounds around her neck and willed them to close.

But the umbra wasn't done. It found a new target in Romie, its black-hole eyes sizing her up with gleeful hunger. Gorged as it was on Emory's fears, it looked bigger, and all the more terrifying.

It pounced, faster than lightning, and Romie mirrored its gesture.

"Ro!"

Romie gave a ferocious grunt, but the umbra didn't touch her. It stumbled back, shying away from the brilliant light that shot from the glowing orb in her hand.

A star plucked from the darkness, a dream to hold the nightmare at bay.

Suddenly, Romie dropped the star as if burned, clutching her hand to her chest. Emory pushed to her feet, stumbled toward Romie as

more umbrae flocked around her, but her friend didn't need her, not as she grabbed two more stars, one in each hand, crying out in pain even as she held them up to fend off the onslaught of umbrae.

Romie looked at Emory, then beyond her, yelling something about closing a door.

The door.

The rift in the darkness was still open, and the umbrae were heading straight for it—for the caves beyond.

Emory froze, remembering how the shade that Jordyn had become had followed her into the waking world. She couldn't let that happen now, couldn't let the umbrae reach Baz and Kai, but they were moving undaunted toward the door, and how in the Tides' name was she supposed to stop them?

But Emory had unlocked it, that door. Her magic—her blood—had done so without her even thinking it.

And keys worked both ways. Something unlocked could be locked again.

She flung a hand out toward the rift, her magic singing in her veins. *Lock, lock, lock.* It started to close just as a trickle of umbrae reached it, a horde of nightmares eager to escape this tenebrous world that had birthed them.

"Come on, *lock*," Emory sobbed through gritted teeth.

The rift was stitching itself together too slowly, allowing screeching shades to slither through to the other side. Those that remained turned to her like they knew she was the one denying them access to the waking world. They rushed toward her, and Emory cowered, stumbling until she hit something solid. Romie, screaming in pain at the burning stars still in her hands. She dropped one of them with a broken whimper, and as its light vanished, they stood with their backs together, umbrae all around them now, a wall of impenetrable darkness closing in on them.

Emory knew this was how they would die, smothered by this tide

of nightmares. Romie's empty, bloodied hand clutched hers, the same thought no doubt crossing her mind. The star she still held in her other hand was dim now, nearly spent.

If this was death, Emory thought, maybe it was a small kindness that they were here together at the end of all things.

But this couldn't be the end–after everything they'd gone through, she refused to lose her friend here, now, when they'd just found each other again.

Emory gently pried the star from Romie's hand. It seared her skin, pain like she'd never known. She bit down on her lip, wondering how Romie had withstood it.

"What are you doing?" Romie asked in a small, panicked voice as Emory took a step forward, brandishing the star like a shield.

Emory didn't have an answer, only this odd certainty in her bones. She looked into the eyes of the umbrae and suddenly didn't fear them. They were like Jordyn–had been people once too, poor souls trapped here by whatever horrible means.

She thought of Serena, Dania, Daphné, and Harlow, who hadn't stood a chance against the tide; of Travers and Lia and Jordyn, taken somewhere they couldn't survive.

She thought of Kai, Baz, Romie–all of them trapped in the confines of their own fears or in prisons of others' making. *Her* making.

They deserved to be set free.

The fading star glowed brighter in her hand. Emory faced the nightmares with a single thought.

Heal.

The umbrae erupted in brilliant light. The blast was like that of a Collapsing, silver and bright and so powerful it brought Emory to her knees, tore a scream from her throat. She didn't understand the magic she was wielding. It was a symphony of all the things that might help the umbrae shuck off their pain and wounds and fears. Dreamer and Nightmare Weaver and Healer alike, Purifier

and Lightkeeper and Unraveler. Reaper–the magic of endings. Like what Virgil had told her about clearing diseased fields so that newer things could grow.

She gave the umbrae such an end. And in their unmaking, the sleepscape gained a new constellation of stars. Dreamers and Nightmare Weavers who'd lost themselves in the dark, in this space between worlds, to become shades of themselves.

No more.

The door shut at last, locked tight, sealed with that brilliant light.

Emory let go of her magic, and fell with Romie among newborn stars.

BAZ

IN THE QUIET, BAZ WAS AFRAID TO BREATHE.

Blood pounded in his ears as he stared at the place where Keiran had disappeared. He ached to step through the door, pay whatever price was needed just to see that Emory was okay.

She was gone. She was gone she was gone she was gone she was *gone*.

He thought of turning back the cogs of time, just a few minutes so he could stop Keiran from slipping through, but somehow he knew that even his magic couldn't reach beyond the Hourglass. Yet if he could just crane his neck through the dark, find Emory within it, make sure she was all right . . .

His hand hovered over the striated rock, just below that blooming darkness at its center.

"Baz."

He wrenched his hand back. Kai stood behind him, body tense. As if he'd meant to pull him away from the door if he tried to step through it.

"She'll be fine," Kai said. There was an almost pained note to his voice, a flash of something Baz couldn't understand in his expression before it yielded to steely resolve. "But we're running out of time."

He was right. Emory was gone and Baz couldn't follow, and they needed to get out of here.

Through unshed tears, Baz glanced at his wristwatch. The hands tremored slightly, yearning to inch forward. He felt the strain against his magic, the consciousness of the students frozen around him, the weight of the tide trying to break free at his back, an entire ocean battering against the time-still wave at the mouth of the cave.

With a breath, he released the students around the Hourglass from time's hold, careful to keep the halted tide under his magic's influence. Five upperclassmen Baz recognized staggered into motion, looking around in confusion. A sixth one—hair as red as the blood pooling around her—did not rise.

Someone uttered a scream that turned into a wrenching sob. Virgil Dade sloshed through the shallow water and bent over the lifeless body of Lizaveta Orlov.

"What the fuck happened?" he asked, blinking between Baz and Kai. Tears ran down his face. "What did you Shadow-cursed Eclipse-born do?"

Kai glowered at him. "That wasn't us. We're the ones who saved your asses."

"Then who killed her?"

"It was Keiran," Baz said miserably. Then, "Emory said he was going to sacrifice all of you to the Tides."

Disbelief met his statement.

"They went through the door, didn't they?"

This from Nisha Zenara, whose sorrowful eyes swept over the door to meet his. Baz nodded in answer. A muscle feathered in

Nisha's jaw. *She was quite the Dreamer,* she had said of his sister that day in the Vault. He wondered if she, too, felt this urge to go through the door, if she hoped Romie might be waiting on the other side.

"We don't have time for this," Kai urged. "We need to–"

Baz heard it before the widening of Kai's eyes gave it away: a low rumbling sound he mistook for the tide. But it wasn't coming from the right direction; not from the sea but from the gaping darkness beyond the Hourglass.

"Look out!"

Kai knocked Baz to the floor just as a searing pain singed his back. Darkness and light erupted from the door, and a horde of umbrae burst past the threshold.

Baz's hold on his magic slipped, and time resumed its fateful ticking, unleashing the tide. It was all too eager to rush in past the barrier he had erected, the full might of the sea pushing into the cave. Baz flung his magic out again despite the pain, desperately trying to stop the tidal wave surging in as he buckled under the force of it.

At his side, Kai sought to do the same with the nightmares spilling into the cave from the open door. Screams echoed around them as the umbrae found fear-ridden victims to leech from. The Belly of the Beast shook at the impact of these two opposing forces seeking to fill it. Rock and dust fell from the ceiling, and a piece of jagged stone fell right onto the Hourglass. A crack ran down its middle, and in the rupturing sound that thundered around them, the door disappeared, darkness and silver-laced tendrils of water receding, leaving only the precarious column of rock in its wake, split down the very middle.

"No!" Baz yelled.

He felt the magic of the door slipping, knew if the Hourglass fell, it would be destroyed–and Emory and Romie would be lost forever

behind it. But the sea pushed against his magic and the umbrae feasted on the souls around them, and Kai tried to command them to stop as he had earlier, but there had only been two umbrae then, not an army of them. It was chaos, and all Baz could do was hold on to the threads of time that made the tide batter against an invisible wall, chipping slowly away at his resolve.

Kai swore and stood tall. He was the Nightmare Weaver again, more fearsome than fear itself. The umbrae turned their depthless eyes on him. They flocked to him like he was a prince of darkness who commanded them. They enveloped him until Baz could no longer see him beneath, only this cloak of black velvet and claws, and he knew then that this was it. This was what would put an end to his friend. Not the Collapsing, not the magic the Regulators had tried to wrest from him, but *this*. The demons he had walked beside all his life.

The nightmares pulled in closer, a viselike grip around their weaver. But those were Kai's eyes Baz could make out in their midst, and that was a laugh like a midnight promise he heard vibrating against the walls.

The shadows seeped into Kai. He absorbed the nightmares until there was just him standing there, shadows dancing on his skin. Kai opened his eyes, blew out a breath. The shadows dissipated, his skin returning to its normal hue, his eyes to their normal blackness, and in the stillness, the Nightmare Weaver grinned at Baz as if to say, *This is what we can do now. What they tried to take from us.*

Power that felt limitless.

The crack on the Hourglass nearly cleaved the rock in two, but for now, it held.

Someone choked and sputtered. Baz looked down to see Keiran's battered form at the foot of the dais, half-submerged in a pool of blood and water and foam. His hands were clasped over his chest, where the umbrae had torn a hole in his middle.

Baz knelt at his side. He gripped Keiran's wet, bloodied shirt. "Where's Emory? Is she alive?"

Keiran laughed, white teeth a bloody flash in the dark. "With that door gone, she might as well be dead." He coughed up blood, eyes staring around him wildly until they focused on Baz. His throat worked as he fought to get the words out. "I see you got out of the Institute with your magic intact."

"Why did you do this?"

"You know why." Keiran laughed again, the sound drawing another bloody cough from him. His hands sought purchase on Baz's arm, his breath coming in an ugly rasp. "I only ever wanted justice for them. All of it was for them."

Baz knew he meant his parents. He didn't think he owed anything to Keiran, not after what he had done to Kai and Emory, but this was his one chance to come clean. He swallowed past the tightness in his chest. "The accident at the printing press . . . It was me. I'm the one who Collapsed and–and killed your parents."

Keiran's grip on Baz's arm loosened. He looked at him beneath wet lashes, the light behind his eyes already dimming. "How fitting I should die here with you, then."

Guilt sought to pull Baz under.

Those deaths were on *his* hands, not his father's. The truth buried in the rubble, in the deepest recesses of Baz's mind because of how horrible it was, how inconceivable.

What had Kai once said to him, about people suppressing their fears and memories and nightmares and childhood wounds until they were no longer aware of them?

It's always the quietest minds that hide the worst sort of violence.

But that was the thing, wasn't it? Maybe the real violence wasn't the one Baz had committed that day. That had been an accident, a slip of his magic as he tried to defend Jae, to keep them from being hurt by the very people who ended up getting killed in the

blast. There was no excusing what he'd done, but he'd acted out of fear, trying to save someone who was dear to him with magic he'd barely started to understand, let alone control.

No, the real violence was how his father had to sacrifice his own magic and mind and life to keep the truth of that accident a secret. To save Baz from the consequences of it.

The real violence was the fact that they lived in a world where people like Keiran and the Regulators *wanted* to see Eclipse-born Collapse, all so they could use their raw magic for their own gain.

The real violence, Baz thought, was how he'd been so conditioned to fear this supposedly corrupt magic in his veins, he'd never learned how to live without the crushing weight of it, that all-consuming fear. All his life, he believed he wasn't allowed to dream as his sister did. He never dared to want more than he had, to step past the careful lines he'd drawn around himself.

But it was an accident. It was a weight he'd carried until now and one he would shoulder for the rest of his life. Yet if he learned to breathe around this fear, to make peace with what he'd done . . . it might not feel quite as heavy a burden.

Blood and foam gathered around Keiran in the water. He looked oddly young. Innocent, even as he lay dying. For a moment, Baz thought he might be able to turn back time, make it so that none of this had ever happened. He would have never Collapsed, and Keiran's parents would still be alive, and both Romie and Emory might still be here because Keiran would have never sought revenge, would never have had to live with this ache in his chest where Baz had unwittingly torn out a piece of his heart.

But then Jae would be rotting away at the Institute. The truth about Collapsings would be silenced with them. Eclipse-born would keep living in fear of their own power as people like Keiran and his parents inevitably found ways to use their magic for themselves.

No. There was still a line Baz wouldn't cross. He might have

Collapsed and expanded his limits, but surely he was not limit-less. He couldn't disrupt the fabric of life like that, couldn't use his magic to fix everything that had ever gone wrong for everyone in the world, no matter how badly he wished to.

This was his doing. Now he needed to live with the consequences.

"I'm so sorry," Baz whispered.

Keiran rasped one last breath and died.

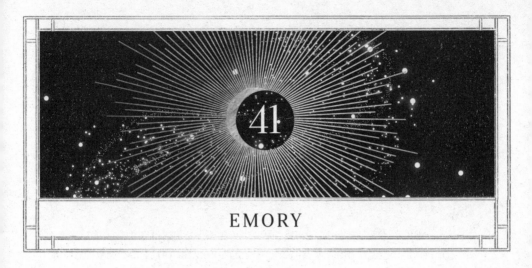

EMORY

EMORY'S EYES SHOT OPEN. SHE BROUGHT HER HANDS up–unmarred despite the white-hot star she'd held–and found no silver veins running along her skin, nothing to indicate she'd suffered her Collapsing. She *should* have Collapsed wielding that kind of magic. But other than being dazed and disoriented and completely depleted, she felt no different than before.

She pushed up onto her elbows. There was not an umbra in sight, and where the rift had been, there now was a silver door closed tightly shut.

"Ro?"

Romie lay beside her, face pale and clammy, lips cast in a bluish tint, and though her eyes were open, they stared ahead without any sort of awareness.

Terror seized Emory. *"Romie."*

At last, Romie blinked. "I can't feel my hands," she said faintly.

Her hands curled upward in a charred mess, burned right down

to the bone. It made no sense–Dreamers were used to touching stars all the time to enter dreams, and as far as Emory knew, they never got *burnt*. But maybe this physical version of the sleepscape didn't follow the same rules as its slumbering equivalent. Maybe stars weren't dreams at all here, but something else.

"I can't feel anything," Romie breathed weakly. Her eyes fluttered shut.

"Ro." Emory bit back a sob as she reached for her, trying to assess the burns through her own bone-deep exhaustion. "Stay with me, all right?"

Her eyes found the silver door again. She had to get Romie through it, bring her to a Healer. Her own magic was all but spent; she knew if she pushed further into her depleted reservoir, she would Collapse. Besides, this type of injury was far beyond her skill. Romie needed a proper Healer, someone who excelled at this magic.

As Emory drew herself painfully to her feet, Romie whispered a pleading *Don't leave me.*

It broke something in Emory. "I'm not–I won't. I'll be right over here." She took a step toward the door. "Just keep talking, all right? Tell me why you came back, why you didn't go through the door you found."

"I almost did," Romie mumbled. "I wanted to. I was certain it was my destiny. Then I thought about everything I did to get here, and I wasn't so sure anymore."

The secrets, the deaths. Emory had been thinking the same about her own poor decisions, but hearing Romie talk this way was startling; Romie never second-guessed herself on *anything*.

"I'm sorry, Em. Everything's gone to shit because of me, and now we're going to die in here, aren't we?"

"No," Emory said fiercely. "I'm going to get us out of here, Ro."

Rivulets of water trickled down the door's surface. A crack ran

down the middle, starting from one corner and ending in the place where a knob should have been.

Emory pushed at it and pulled and clawed, but the door did not budge.

The way back out was shut.

The starlit path felt unsteady under her feet. The door back to Baz was broken, maybe forever shut, and the space around her had never seemed so vast and fathomless.

The space between worlds, and she and Romie alone in it.

A distant, foreboding shriek made the hairs on her neck rise. She remembered what Kai had said, about the umbrae being attracted to new magic—like the kind she'd used just now to heal the umbrae. To *unmake* them.

They couldn't stay here.

Emory hurried back to Romie's side, trying not to break down in panic.

"Romie–"

She was convulsing, eyes going to the back of her head, ravaged hands clutched rigidly against her chest.

"Romie!"

She was going into shock, her body contending with the burns in the worst possible way, organs at risk of damage. She needed a Healer–*now*.

Emory reached blindly for her Healing magic, whatever dregs of it remained, this power she'd resented all her life for how mediocre it made her feel. She gritted her teeth at the strain it caused her. Trying to pull any ounce of it up to the surface was like grasping at ash blowing away on a breeze: elusive and hopeless.

Healing had failed her with Travers and again with Lia, but this was *Romie*, her best friend, the one person who'd always seen her worth even when Emory herself could not. She refused to let it fail

her now, determined to push past the point of total depletion to do this one thing.

Emory was a Tidecaller, with power more unique than she could have ever dreamed. She'd pushed her magic to reaches yet unknown, had turned umbrae into newborn stars, made plants bloom to new life, walked into *dreams*, but she would give it all up in this moment for the tiniest drop of healing.

Please.

There—less than a drop, the tiniest speck of magic. It burned through her, and Emory slumped to the ground, exhaustion making her limbs so heavy she thought she might faint.

"Ro?"

The convulsions stopped. Color returned to Romie's face, and though her hands remained a mangled horror, tendons and tissue and bone stitched themselves together, enough that the burns weren't so life-threatening anymore, enough that she gave Emory a wan smile and said, "Finally got to use those healing skills on a live subject, did you?"

Emory laughed through tears, adding somberly, "It'll all be for nothing if we can't find a way out of here."

"I trust you, Em. If anyone can get us out of this mess, it's you."

Those words meant more to Emory than anything she'd ever heard. Tidecaller, Healer—she realized then that what she was never mattered to Romie, who loved her for *her*, not for the magic she wielded. Emory had been letting her Tidecaller magic determine her worth, seeing her significance through that and that alone as she lost herself in this power she so desperately wanted to make her special.

But maybe she'd always been exactly who she'd wanted to be. Not mediocre at all, not doomed to live in Romie's shadow, but her own person with her own worth.

How sad, she thought, that it took losing Romie to find herself.

Still, she was glad for it, even if it had brought them here, to this

place with no escape. The shrieks of distant umbrae were closer now than before.

"We need to find a way out of here."

Farther down the curved path, stars gathered and aligned, with voices rising between them.

Patience, they seemed to whisper. *Take heart.*

"Follow the song," Romie mumbled.

Sure enough, a melody took shape in the darkness, and it was a song Emory knew, having heard it before in a dream. An inexplicable sense of surety came over her. It started in her blood and seeped through to her bones. Calm and purpose in her heart. Direction in her soul.

The song was a compass guiding her on, the mournful chords of a lyre beckoning her down the starlit path, past the point where the path curved inward and disappeared into the dark.

And why should she be afraid of this darkness? She'd been born to it, after all. A new moon, a solar eclipse. She'd walked alongside it for as long as she could remember, and so had Romie. A Dreamer born on the very last sliver of a waning crescent.

She could have sworn she heard both their names woven within that melody, calling them forward like a lodestar.

Emory, Emory.

Romie, Romie.

Emory and Romie, their names practically an anagram.

Fate brought them together and ripped them apart and gave them a second chance here in this liminal space, in the seam between living and dead.

Emory threw one last glance at the silver door sealed shut. She thought of Baz and his stories, of Romie and her dreams, of the three of them running through fields of gold that bent toward the sea, their laughter making them soar like all the gulls flying in the cloudless skies above.

We are born of the moon and tides, and to them we return.

They would find their way back. One way or another, she would hear Baz laugh again, would see the three of them reunited, no matter the price. But for now, at least, they had to look onward.

Emory mustered whatever strength she had left to pull Romie up, shouldering her weight, and together they started stumbling toward the song.

Their feet sloshed in the water that traveled down the same direction, guiding them farther and farther. Emory's pulse beat quicker as she began to make out the shape of a door in the distance, a tear in the swirling stars, still out of reach yet growing closer with every step. The music grew louder as they neared. The door was dark marble, veins like the roots of a tree, with vines that twined in its middle to form a knotted knob. The cloying smell of earth and moss and wetness seeped from its seams, calling to mind the greenhouse that Romie had always felt so at home in.

And this might lead to the Deep or to another world entirely, but it did not matter because this was where they were meant to go— she was sure of it, felt it in her bones, a thrum of magic like none she'd ever known.

A bridge, a door, a song that beckoned to something more.

Emory's hand closed over the knotted vines, certainty sweeping in her soul in time to the music reaching its crescendo. She took a deep breath, pushed the door open.

Water spilled over the threshold. Only then did Emory hesitate, wondering what would happen to them.

"No turning back now," Romie said at her side, starlight dancing in her eyes.

The song of the stars followed them past the doorsill.

Wherever it led, whatever shores waited for them next, they would face them together.

BAZ

BAZ SLUMPED ON THE FLOOR. FROM KEIRAN'S LIFE-less hand a curious compass slipped, and Baz reached for it mindlessly, his gaze catching on the Hourglass—on the tear in the rock that nulled its magic, barred the door shut.

"Brysden," Kai said. "We have to go."

The others were huddled together near the time-still wave, a wary look in their eyes at the sound of the tide battering against Baz's magic on the other side.

More rocks and dust fell from the ceiling. The crack in the Hour-glass deepened.

Baz pocketed the compass and took a step toward the rock. He couldn't use his power to right every wrong, but he could use it to mend what was in front of him. If he could untangle the compli-cated threads that bound the door to time itself . . .

A dark, familiar thing brushed against his magic.

Dovermere, this presence that called to him and repulsed him

in equal measure. It whispered lovingly, urging him to wield its strange power.

Your magic is ours and our magic is yours and we are the same because time runs through our veins like rivers to the sea and blood through arteries.

Baz reached for it. He pulled on Dovermere's magic, no longer afraid of this place because he recognized its power, the same as his.

Time time time time time time time time time

Their heartbeats echoed in synch like the ticking of perfectly tuned clocks. Their magic combined, and Baz pulled back time, made it so that the Hourglass was never cracked. The crumbling cave mended itself, rock shooting back up to the ceiling it had rained down from, and the Hourglass stood tall and unmarred once more. A door repaired.

Baz didn't stop there. He pushed against the tide, reversed it so that it flowed back out into the sea until it was low tide again, and the way out was clear, giving them all a fighting chance to leave Dovermere unscathed.

When he finally let go of the magic, he felt Dovermere sigh around him, contented by its power being used to its full potential at last, perhaps for the very first time, by someone who understood time the same way it did.

Thank you, each of them said to the other.

Waves crashed loudly around Baz, the taste of salt bitter in his mouth as he sputtered, dragging himself out of the water.

Exhaustion made his muscles heavy. The others lay sprawled beside him, equally spent—but alive, all of them. Kai was closest, his chest rising and falling to the same rapid rhythm that pounded in Baz's ears.

They'd brought the two bodies back with them. Keiran and

Lizaveta. Virgil Dade watched over them, face grim, eyes hollow.

Baz crumbled on the sand and tilted his face up to the skies. The storm had passed, and the unveiled sun was just starting to dip toward the horizon. It was somewhat crescent-shaped, Baz noted–partly covered by the moon.

An eclipse.

He laughed. And then a shadow blocked out the entirety of the sky as Kai stood over him, offering him a hand.

Baz took it.

They stood panting at the water's edge, looking out at Dover-mere. The tide was low now, though it seemed to rebel against this reversal of fates that Baz had forced upon it, inching determinedly across the sand.

Emory might have gone where Baz could not follow, to answer a call that was beyond his hearing, but he still had a part to play. She was the sea, moving in and out of his life, between this world and the next. But what was the sea if it had no shore to return to?

The door to the Deep needed guarding. Dovermere needed a keeper. And if there was even the slightest chance that Emory might make it back, then Baz would ensure the door still stood. He would make sure it was safe for her and Romie to return.

He traced the upward slant of the stairs hidden in the cliffside. Light shone through the window at the top, and if he squinted hard enough, he thought he could make out Dusk's shadow, tail flicking as he waited for Baz to find him in the Eclipse commons. His heart yearned for that room, the illusioned field beyond. At his side, Kai looked up at the same spot, full of longing for the place they'd shared that had become theirs.

"Let's go home," Baz said.

To Aldryn, to Obscura Hall. To the world that still needed them, the truths that needed sharing to protect their own.

The school had always been Baz's world, more real to him than anything else. It was his home, and his to protect now.

He had glimpsed the stars to other worlds and the darkness that cradled them.

He was no longer scared of reaching for them.

EPILOGUE

IN THE MORNING, BAZ STOOD BENEATH THE ILLUSION OF a brilliant sunrise.

A gentle breeze made the tall grasses around him sing. Behind the swaying mane of a willow tree, in the Eclipse commons he called home, Kai slept. Dreamed. Soon they would have to head into town, where they were to meet with Jae, Theodore, Vera, Alya, and Professor Selandyn to make sense of this mess and figure out what to do next. They had evidence of what Keiran and Artem had done, how they'd been harnessing magic from Eclipse-born and meant to use Emory to destroy them, but exposing such injustice would require patience, a tactful approach. And then there was the matter of their Collapsing, this earth-shattering truth the world wasn't yet ready to hear.

The road ahead wouldn't be easy. But for now the world was quiet, and nothing could ruin it.

Baz didn't hear Kai until he was breathing at his side, his shoulder brushing his. He looked at Kai, and his heart soared to see the Nightmare Weaver back where he belonged.

"Did you get it?" Baz asked.

Kai handed him a single page that, if fitted into the spine of the manuscript it was once ripped out from, would change the story's outcome.

The epilogue, lost and found again.

Tell Kai I left it for him to find.

Baz had to wonder if this might all be a dream, if he was still asleep and Kai was playing tricks on him for old times' sake. But there was no deception in Kai's eyes, and the epilogue felt entirely real in his hands.

"I don't think Emory's the only one who can cross through worlds unscathed," Kai said at last.

Baz read the words once, twice, thrice, and when they finally sank in, he looked at Kai through tears, unburdened by fear as he thought, *The story has only just begun.*

SONG
OF THE
DROWNED
GODS

EPILOGUE:

THE SLEEPERS
AMONG THE STARS

There is a world between all worlds where dreams and nightmares slumber.

Stars wink in and out of being in the darkness that cradles them. They are tended to by their keepers, sometimes a girl who wears hopes and dreams like a glittering crown of stars, sometimes a boy who weaves fears and nightmares into a cloak he bears so she need not have to.

They, too, hear the song that soars through the skies.

The drowned gods knew of them, once. But they did not call on the girl of stars or the boy of darkness like the others they lured to their sea of ash; they did not need them, only the four. The scholar, the witch, the warrior, and the guardian. Four keys to open a door, four lives to serve as payment, four parts of a whole trapped in a world not their own.

The skies always remember the blood and bones and heart and soul—but never the fragments of dreaming in between, for those belong to no world, and so belong to all. The fifth key that slumbers unseen among the stars.

And so it is that when the skies grow quiet with the absence of song, the girl dons her crown, the boy his cloak, and together they sail through the dark toward the sea of ash, ready to join the others at last. To save them from their prison of dust and nothingness at the center of all things.

Tell me a story, the girl says dreamily as they sail through worlds and between them too.

The boy sets his eye on the distant horizon, his cloak of nightmares rippling in the wind.

There is a scholar on these shores who breathes stories, he begins.

It is a tale both of them know but have yet to make their own. And as they sail the skies and seas and everything in between, following the memory of a song like a map through the stars, the story becomes theirs, its ending yet unwritten.

ACKNOWLEDGMENTS

THIS BOOK WAS NOT MY FIRST LOVE.

There were two who came before it: the story that sparked my passion for writing, and the one that haunted me for a decade after. *Curious Tides* is the story I was always meant to find. The one that took time. It's got a lot of me in it: dreams, regrets, flaws, hopes. I wrote it looking back at my early twenties, a time that feels like a crossroads between who you are and who you want to be. I lost sight of who I was then, and writing this was a bit like finding my old self again. It feels right that it should be the book I debut with.

I couldn't have done this without all of those who took a chance on me. First and foremost, to my absolute rock star of an agent, Victoria Marini: grateful doesn't even begin to cover it. This industry can seem intimidating from the outside looking in, but having you in my corner makes it feel less so. Thank you for being the best, most trustworthy advocate I could have asked for—and for being Kai's number one fan.

To my editor, Sarah McCabe: there aren't enough words to

express how lucky I am to have found someone whose vision for *Curious Tides* so perfectly resonates with my own. Your edit letters always leave me brimming with excitement and ideas. Thank you for helping me bring this story to life. And to Anum Shafqat: I'm so happy you came onboard with Sarah. If two heads are better than one, then three's the winning number. Working with you both has been a dream—thanks for the brainstorming sessions, without which I would have been lost.

An immense thank-you to everyone at McElderry Books/Simon & Schuster who worked on this book in any capacity and helped make my wildest dreams possible: Justin Chanda, Karen Wojtyla, Anne Zafian, Bridget Madsen, Elizabeth Blake-Linn, Chrissy Noh, Caitlin Sweeny, Alissa Nigro, Bezi Yohannes, Perla Gil, Remi Moon, Amelia Johnson, Ashley Mitchell, Yasleen Trinidad, Saleena Nival, Emily Ritter, Amy Lavigne, Lisa Moraleda, Nicole Russo, Nicole Valdez, Christina Pecorale and her sales team, Michelle Leo and her education/library team, freelance copy editor Jen Strada, and of course Ali Dougal and the rest of the UK team.

A big thank-you also to designer Greg Stadnyk and artist Signum Noir for wrapping *Curious Tides* in such a beautiful jacket, and to Francesca Baerald for creating the most gorgeous maps. And to J. T. Sisounthone and Cam Montgomery, whose authenticity reads provided such valuable insight—thank you for the work you do.

This book would not be what it is today without the brilliant minds of Kat Dunn and Sarah Underwood, who helped me shape it into a story I'm proud of. Thank you for choosing me to be your Pitch Wars mentee. I love and admire you both. And to all my fellow PitchWars 2021 alums: what an honor it was to have been part of the last class with you. I cannot wait to see us all on shelves one day—and maybe go for some celebratory waffles.

I've always been a rather solitary person and thought writing

would be no different. I couldn't have been more wrong. To my very first writer friend, Kapri Psych, thank you for the hours of Face-Time chats and long voice notes about our stories and fur babies and hopes and dreams. One of these days we'll stop apologizing to each other when it takes us a while to reply.

To Adrian Graves, hype woman extraordinaire, thank you for coming into my life and letting me scream at you every step of the way. And for introducing me to *Ratatouille*.

To the beta readers who suffered through early drafts of *Curious Tides* and provided such thoughtful feedback; to those who read the first chapter so long ago and hyped it up when I needed it most; to everyone who let me pester them with questions about querying and other publishing matters; and to all the amazing, encouraging writer friends I've met along the way–thank you, *thank you*, THANK YOU. I could not have done this without all of you. To name but a few: Jen Carnelian, Kamilah Cole, Miriam Cortinovis, Lilian Lai, Chelsea Abdullah, Kiana Krystle, Bailey Knaub, Jenny Marie, Trang Thanh Tran, Emma Theriault for the coffee dates, SJ Donders and Suzey Ingold for that cozy writing retreat (I'm so glad Adrian brought us together).

And to the artists who helped me bring the characters in my mind to life when I was still struggling to visualize them: Amanda S. Dumky, Georgina Donnelly, @stellesappho, you are all so talented– and to Marcella (@mariamarcelw), who went above and beyond.

Thank you, of course, to the people in my life who have had to listen to me talk about this book for so long now and who have never doubted I could do this (as far as I know–otherwise thank you for pretending). To Crystal Lanois for the constant laughs over all our years of friendship (cue "Hold On" by Wilson Phillips). To Mylène Lavallée for your unwavering enthusiasm. Don't worry, you don't have to read this–your support is more than enough. To Valérie Patry for our many *connard-connasse-douchebag* outings

to Chapters, the movies, ComicCon, etcetera—our friendship has fueled my creativity and love of stories in more ways than you know. To Gabriel Landry for the late-night wine talks about all the books and shows we love, and for encouraging me every time I poked my head out of the office/writing cave.

And to Marie-Ève Landry: we've been called twins our whole lives, and while we may have never seen it ourselves, I've always thought there was some glimmer of truth there. You're my soul twin. Thanks for thirty years of friendship and counting—and for being a fan since *Les Dix Royaumes*.

Mom and Dad, you believed in me back when I was a teen with big dreams who could never put her books down, who monopolized the family computer to write, who printed out pages and pages of publishing info and said, "This is what I want to do." Thanks for still believing in me years later when I picked up the pieces of that discarded dream, and above all, for letting me crash at your place, feeding me, and keeping Roscoe entertained while I scrambled to meet deadlines; it made all the difference in the world. And Éric, thanks for cheering me on from across the country. Love you all.

A big thanks to all the teachers I've had who were so encouraging about my writing. Et surtout, à Noëlla Lacelle: J'ai écrit ce livre en anglais, mais sache que ce sont tes cours de français—et toi—qui ont inspiré en moi cette passion pour l'écriture, ce désir d'explorer des mondes nouveaux, ce rêve de devenir auteure. Merci.

And finally, to you, reader: thank you for picking this book up. I hope it can be for you its own kind of portal on a page.

PASCALE LACELLE is a French-Canadian author from Ottawa, Ontario. A longtime devourer of books, she started writing her own at the age of thirteen and quickly became enthralled by the magic of words. After earning her bachelor's degree in French literature, she realized the English language is where her literary heart lies (but don't tell any of her French professors that). When not lost in stories, she's most likely daydreaming about food and travel, playing with her dog, Roscoe, or trying to curate the perfect playlist for every mood. You can find her on Instagram and Twitter @PascaleLacelle.